WARRING STATES

SUSAN R. MATTHEWS

Meisha Merlin Publishing, Inc.
Atlanta, GA

Warring States

Published by Meisha Merlin Publishing, Inc.
PO Box 7
Decatur, GA   30031

Editing by Stephen Pagel
Copyediting and Proofreading by Easter Editing Service
Interior layout by Lynn Swetz
Cover art Christian McGrath
Cover design by Kevin Murphy

ISBN: Hard Cover 1-59222-093-2
ISBN: Soft Cover 1-59222-094-0
http://www.MeishaMerlin.com
First MM Publishing edition: January 2006

Printed in the United States of America
0 9 8 7 6 5 4 3 2 1

This book is dedicated to the memory of Jeff A. Elf. He was a charitable soul who truly left the world a better place than he found it, and we'll always be lucky to have known him. We miss you Jeff!

WARRING STATES

STATES

SUSAN R. MATTHEWS

PROLOGUE

WHEN THE SUN came up in Port Ghan the city started to stir; the hem-fringes of the docks first, where the poorest people lived. The warehouses were secure, but the loading equipment and the stacked pallets were not always watched as carefully, and there were almost always bargains to be had where produce was off-loaded. Fruit and vegetables would not survive the handling between the docks and the markets in the outreaches of the port, the green and gracious suburbs where the wealthier people lived beyond the towering sound walls that shut away most of the noise and stink of an active launch field. Ghan was in a desert. That was why the launch-fields were there, built in the early days where the ground was already flat and hard and packed down solid by the years of sun and heat so that the job of thermal hardening had been half-done already.

Out in ever widening circles from the launch fields, the residence areas and the business districts were more expensive in relation to how far they were from the launch field. There were good livings to be had in Ghan, though, even near the docks—the inverse relationship between proximity and price could work in a family's favor, and the important thing was to save enough money to be able to send the children into the mountains in the summer where they could play in the green woods and the clear water.

Little things like siphoning off excess fuel vapors that might otherwise be wasted helped to save money and the green woods at one and the same time, because excess fuel vapors were no better for the health of lakes and streams in the far hills than they were for the people who serviced the transport craft deep in the heart of the city.

It was not time to send the children into the mountains. It was still early in the spring, and it was cold at night. People turned on their heating when they got up to warm their houses while they roused the children and made mid-meals to be carried to the workplace to save the cost of buying expensive tidbits from the street carts. The municipal utilities were no less ready to take advantage of a savings than the people that they served, and there were places where fuel scrubbers had been tucked away, ready and waiting to take in heavier-than-air vapors from the launch-fields that could be denatured and rendered harmless for heating. Everybody knew that. Nobody cared. But everybody knew.

There was no way in which the introduction of the poison into the fuel mains could have been accidental.

When the sun came up in Port Ghan that morning, people rose and went to wash and cook their meals, turning on the fuel vents, opening up the feeder lines into their furnaces, starting up their stoves. Port Ghan ran on liligas because it was cheap and plentiful, environmentally friendly, easy to use and safe. The chemical marker that had been added to the fuel so that people would be able to smell a leak before it could get dangerous was more than enough to cover the subtle perfume of the poison in the lines.

It had been carefully planned, carefully done, and still luck played a part. It had been colder than usual; almost everybody turned on their heat when they got up. And it was a rest day, so the city's custodians weren't expecting a morning rush, and were inclined at first to chalk up the failure of the morning shift to come to duty as a worse-than-usual instance of excess celebrations the night before.

When supervisors tried to contact their crews, no one answered at their homes. When people went to look for their reliefs, they didn't return, but they didn't call in, either, so there was at first no panic—no understanding that an atrocity was in progress.

The civic shelters were warmed at night and in the morning as though they had been someone's home, and the floating indigent population of the city could be counted on to come out into the streets even on holidays to make their ways to the day-labor shops and the places where they could find a free meal. But the only people who were on the street that morning as the sun rose had been on the street all night.

Nobody came away from the municipal shelters. Nobody came away at all. Only the people who had already accepted that they were going to be cold, that they were not going to be able to warm themselves in any way, only those people survived the morning.

By the time enough of the poison had escaped to set off the alarms, more than three thousand people lay dead in the streets, and two thousand more died of poison, panic, or rioting in the horrible two days that followed.

No final tally was ever agreed upon. The rioting spread across the planet, and then across the system. Fleet did not have the resources to contain the panic because Fleet was already trying to contain civil unrest in too many other areas, and there was only so much the Jurisdiction Fleet could do in the absence of a strong central authority. The First Judge was dead. It had been a year, and there was no new First Judge. The Bench was rudderless.

Port Ghan, however, was at peace. It was the peace of the dead, but it was unquestionably the quietest place on the entire world. An open tomb, it was its own memorial. No single culprit was ever identified, and after so many dead it ceased to really matter. Whoever had done it gained no advantage from the crime, because the killing that erupted in reaction to the massacre harvested across all of Ghan's populations equally.

The true horror of what had happened at Port Ghan was not the thousands dead, or the thousands more who died in the months that followed.

The horror of Port Ghan was that it was just another incident, just another symptom of the uncertainty that plagued all of Jurisdiction Space in the absence of a First Judge to lay down the rule of Law and to enforce it.

CHAPTER ONE
FIELD EXPEDIENTS

ANDREJ KOSCUISKO, CHIEF medical officer on board of the Jurisdiction Fleet Ship *Ragnarok,* sat at his desk in his office doing his best to concentrate on the controversy over whether an increased incidence of a peculiar skin rash meant that there was a mutant fungus on board, or simply that they were brewing with mother-of-grain in Engineering, or both.

When the talk-alert sounded, he did not answer right away. He wasn't sure how to face what it might bring, and yet he had brought it on himself. Staff would expect him to answer promptly, however, unless he were in the washroom or passed out drunk, which had not happened on duty for simply months now.

"Koscuisko, here." In order to cover his tracks as completely as possible, it was necessary to respond. There were four procedures yet to accomplish, somehow. Would he be detected? If he could ward off accusation for long enough, it would not matter.

"Robert says Lek's up, sir." That was one of his surgical crew leaders. She didn't sound as though she were suspicious. Andrej took a deep breath, careful to exhale as quietly as possible. "'Respectfully requests an audience with the officer at his convenience,' I think it was. Are you available, your Excellency?"

Senior officers didn't usually come when they were called, especially not when called by bond-involuntaries, who had no rank to speak of and no status but as property.

"I am coming directly. Thank you, Jahan." At the same time he had performed the procedure himself, and people were accustomed to the display of a possessive instinct on his part where Security were concerned. The Bench had created them to serve a Ship's Inquisitor, after all. What was more reasonable than that he should think of them as his?

He tried not to hurry as he left his office for sterile quarantine, where patients were sent to recover from procedures that tapped a spine or crossed the blood-brain barrier. Telbut brain slug was something that could happen to anybody, especially among persons inhabiting worlds within the trading entity known as the Dolgorukij Combine. It was more likely to turn up in Sarvaw because of the poverty of the world and their general suspicion of authority, doctors, teachers, law enforcement officers. It kept them from seeking periodic care as freely as they should.

He could see Fantin coming from the other direction with her tray of doses in her hand, and he quickened his pace a bit as he approached the enclosed bay in which his patient lay waiting. He dared not risk Lek's self-control, not so soon.

"What is this?" he asked Fantin cordially, standing in front of the door. "Oh, good. I am just going in. Will you trust me to see the doses put through?"

She looked up at him, a little startled, and for one moment Andrej wondered whether he had gone too far. The moment passed, however. She smiled and surrendered the doses with a clear eye and a serene countenance. "Of course, sir," she said in that familiar "we-know-how-you-worry" tone of voice. "If you'd just post to the log, though, so we know how he's doing. Ugh."

"You are very kind," he assured her with genuine gratitude. "I will unfailingly perform this duty." Yes, brain slugs were moderately disgusting. That didn't matter. All that mattered was that in order to extract the sexually mature symbiot before it multiplied, a man had to lie on his belly and let the surgeon send a probe up through the place in his skull where his spine descended, and lure the greedy thing out of the brain in pursuit of a supposed mate.

Fantin went away about her business without any apparent second thoughts. Andrej collected himself then turned and opened the door. Robert was there. Robert did not look happy. Had something gone wrong? They would have called him. They couldn't *not* have called him. They weren't supposed to know what he had drawn out of Lek Kerenko's skull instead of a nonexistent brain-slug.

Lek pushed away from the cradle-chair in which he had been laid to rest six hours ago after the procedure; pushed himself up and away with such violence that Robert was hard pressed to restrain him, even though Robert had the advantage of leverage since he was already standing.

For a moment, Andrej was afraid that Lek would say something incautious. "This troop respectfully wishes the officer good-greeting,"

Lek said. He should have known better, Andrej told himself, than to fear that Lek would abandon his self-discipline. On the one hand, whether or not Lek knew what Andrej had done to him, he was still the product of careful training and years of experience living with a governor in his brain to see to it that he followed orders.

On the other hand, Lek also knew that to speak to his officer of assignment—which was to say, Andrej himself—with such elaborate formality carried an unspoken message that did not need to be translated. *With respect, your Excellency, I could perhaps be more angry with you than I am right now, but I'm not sure how.*

"Do not be annoyed with me, Lek." Andrej set a humorous and affectionate tone to his voice so that nobody who chanced to overhear would wonder if something were genuinely wrong. "I think no less of you for having one. Many decent people in this life have found themselves infected, and through no fault of their own."

It was too soon to be talking to Lek. He was overwhelmed by his realization, and still somewhat befuddled by the meds Andrej had used. "But it's been part of my life for so long." Lek was doing his best to keep his own tone of voice light, but Andrej could read his tension from a fair distance, and more clearly as he came nearer. "How am I ever going to learn to live without it? Always there. And it'll come back, sooner or later, I know it will."

Andrej had been unable to discuss any of this with Lek beforehand, and he dared not risk any very frank language. There was a good chance he could get away with Lek, at least for now. How he was going to take care of Godsalt, Pyotr, Garrity, and Hirsel, he did not know.

"Well, that's up to you," Andrej said sternly. "Stay out of insalubrious environments. Clean living, friend Lek. If you don't want to have a brain slug pulled out of your head again, all you really have to do is stay away from places where there are such things, and that can't be too difficult, can it?"

There were governors to be had in major administrative centers throughout Jurisdiction space. How was Lek to avoid them? By getting out of Jurisdiction space, of course. Simple.

Of course it wasn't all so easy as that. Lek knew it, Andrej could tell. He desperately needed to be able to talk to Lek some place where there would be no danger of being overheard, but there was only one such place on board the *Ragnarok,* and he was not about to take Lek to Secured Medical.

For one, he meant to never again enter the torturer's chamber in which he had exercised his Writ to Inquire. For another, the Captain could override even there, and people would be curious. The temptation to see what could bring Andrej Koscuisko to Secured Medical, especially with one of his bond-involuntaries, would be too much to expect anyone to withstand.

"Now. Robert will sit with you, and keep you company. It is a minor procedure, but there is no taking chances with brains, and I mean you to stay quiet and rest. My cousin Stanoczk will be joining the ship at any hour, and you must conserve your energies for the inevitable excitement."

Lek Kerenko was Sarvaw. He knew that Andrej's cousin was a Malcontent—an agent of the secret service of the Dolgorukij church, a slave of the Saint—and typically up to all sorts of mischief. Andrej had some very particular mischief in mind, and Stoshi was coming to tell him whether the freighter would be waiting at Emandis Station to take Lek, Robert, and the others far, far away from places where people could be placed under governor for crimes against the Judicial order.

What if Stoshi should fail him?

Stoshi would not fail. Andrej was the inheriting son of his father, the Koscuisko prince, the one man who could direct the resources of the entire Koscuisko familial corporation. More than that, Andrej was the father of an acknowledged inheriting son of his own. While a line of inheritance could be directed away from a man with no sons, it had almost never failed to accord with tradition in cases where there was already an heir's heir in training.

If he had been killed before he had made Marana his wife, and their son his heir, the position of inheriting son might have devolved upon Iosiv—the next oldest of their father's sons. Andrej wondered what Iosiv's son felt about that.

He was brooding, and he had no business doing so. With a cordial nod to Lek—who sat there watching as though to read his mind by main force of will—Andrej shifted his weight, ready to turn and go. The gesture seemed to provoke Lek beyond all hope of self-discipline; Lek was on his feet and face-to-face with him before Andrej had had time to realize that the sound of falling objects that he heard was Robert, knocked backwards by the impact of Lek's swift lunge.

Lek didn't speak. Instead he reached for Andrej's hand and grasped it in his two hands, trembling. "No, don't leave me here with Robert," Lek said with a tremor in his voice matching the shaking of his shoulders. "Please. Sir. He'll want to sing. I've done nothing to deserve it."

It was very forward of Lek to touch him, let alone restrain him in any manner. Lek's fingers moved against the backs of Andrej's own, but not because Lek was overcome with emotion. Fingercode. Andrej did not read finger-code very well, but Lek used small words, easy to understand. *All of us?*

"And yet that is my firm determination, Lek, and you may as well resign yourself to it." He meant to steal all of them. "Perhaps you will be the first to hear the saga with which he has so often threatened us. What is it, Robert? That of the exceptionally wayward flock, and the male animal of unusual endowment?"

But you're the first one. Andrej hoped Lek could find the meaning in his words, because he himself was not much good at finger-code.

"I'm insulted," Robert grumbled, picking himself up off the floor. "My tender feelings are cruelly bruised, your Excellency. Just for that, I'm going to wait. Some day. When we're all together. Then I'll have a tale to tell."

"Later, then, Robert," Andrej agreed.

This is too much, Lek said, finger to flesh, Andrej's hand held in his own. *Can't believe it. Why?*

"Perhaps once we have reached Emandis Station, and you are all to come with me to visit Joslire's grave-place." Where they would be, temporarily, not under threat of random surveillance, in a burial yard. A funeral orchard. Whatever. "Then we will all have cause to mourn together, and his spirit will be appeased."

Joslire had preferred to die and be free of his governor than live as a Security slave. Even when Andrej had told him that there was an official petition to free him and the others whose quick action had saved the *Scylla* from sabotage, even then Joslire had fixed his mind on freedom and had embraced his own death with joy.

Whether Joslire would have approved of what he was doing, Andrej was not sure. It was theft, in a way. But Joslire had been dead for more than six years, and was therefore unlikely to interfere in any material fashion.

Lek nodded. *We'll talk about it when we can. Very well, sir.* The fury had gone out of him. Face to face with the enormity of what Andrej had done to him, Lek staggered, and fell back against Robert who stood ready to steady him. "Holy Mother," Lek said, in a voice whose sincerity resounded clear and pure and true. "Begging the officer's pardon, your Excellency. My head. Herds of—Herds—trampling—"

It was not the surgery itself that was giving Lek a headache. It was the realization that the grim enforcer with which he had lived in intimate contact for years was gone. Robert passed him a dose over Lek's shoulder, and Andrej put it through.

"Rest and be still," Andrej ordered Lek. "I will be by to check on you again later."

Lek nodded, clearly beginning to feel the action of the drug. Robert took charge, herding Lek over to the cradle-chair to lie down as he had been ordered. Andrej left Lek in Robert's capable hands—hoping with great fervency that Robert would not attempt to sing—and let himself out of the room to go and see whether the *Ragnarok* had dropped vector at Connaught, where Stoshi was to meet them with letters from home and word on the progress of a plan to steal the Bench's property.

THE ROOM WAS dark, the air warm and still. When her talk-alert went off, Vaal woke with a start that shook her whole body, and she slapped at the respond with vehement force.

"What do you want?"

Her lights came up in response to her activity. Yes. Same room. Nothing had changed. She was still at the Connaught Vector Authority. None of the problems with which she had been wrestling had gone away, and an emergency call during her sleep shift could only mean more problems. A five-ship civil mercantile fleet outbound for Emandisan space, but Fleet wanted everybody stopped and searched and interrogated over any irregularities, and something horrible had happened in Port Ghan. She didn't have facilities for interrogation. She was going to have to call on Fleet.

Jalmers was on the duty boards. He sounded nervous, very nervous. "Sorry to intrude, ma'am. Ship off vector not responding to hail."

Ridiculous. "So web it out and wait, or what aren't you telling me?" Standard procedure. Ships came off vector without responding to hail, you locked their navs with a seizer. Few ships were willing to hit a vector with their navs offline, especially the Connaught vector, which was a little less tolerant than most.

"Um. Shielded navs, ma'am. Respectfully suggest the situation requires your presence."

Shielded navs? Well, there were other ways to stop a ship. Technically speaking, shielded navs were slightly illegal, though nobody worried too much about little things like that with all of Jurisdiction in an uproar over the still-undecided issue of who was to be the next First Judge. If she'd been a terrorist, though, fleeing from an attack on the great granaries in the Narim asteroid belt or the water treatment facilities at Lucis, she would certainly be tempted to shield her navs so that tracing her to the scene of the crime would be more difficult. That commercial fleet they'd stopped earlier today had had respectfully naked navs, but it would do them no good when the Fleet sent an Inquisitor to find out the truth about who they were and where they were going. Vaal sighed.

"Takame eight. Away, here." By the marks on the chrono, she'd barely gotten to sleep, too. She was having a bad day. A bad year. All of Jurisdiction was having a bad year. But she was the one who was going to have to place those people in the hands of professional torturers.

She pulled her boots back on—cold and clammy from the shift's sweat—and went out of her small room in quarters into the narrow hallways of the station. Vector Control was an administrative station, small, out of the way, of little interest to anybody. Vaal had enough armed escort craft to control five more ships, but that was about the limit of her power. Fleet had planned to expand the Connaught Vector Authority—there was a station under development near the vector, residential facilities, recreation, schools, a clinic—but plans for the future of the station were on hold. There was no First Judge. There was no unified central authority. People still paid their taxes and Fleet still regulated trade, but it was not the time to call for any special levies that might not be supported. That was just asking for trouble.

When she reached her command station she found her crew tense, white-faced, and unhappy, and as she moved toward her seat—looking to the main screens at a visual of the problem—she could understand why. "Give me hailing," she said, hoping that the hails were not already open. It was so embarrassing when that happened. "Unidentified ship. I can see that you're a cruiser-killer. Please respond."

It was huge onscreen. It was huge in actual fact. 'Vaal had toured a cruiser-killer class battlewagon as a part of her orientation only three years ago. Battlewagons were serious business. She hated the idea of getting in one's way, and yet she had no choice. If her duty required her to stop that mercantile fleet outbound for Emandis space, it certainly required her to confront any resource of this size trying to use the vector for which she was responsible without so much as logging its idents.

"Look—" somebody whispered, loudly enough for Vaal to overhear. The belly of the ship on screen was still hulled over from its vector transit. The panels that covered the maintenance atmosphere—the great glossy expanse of the carapace above— weren't really black, technically speaking, but it was black hull technology.

It had been all over the research braids when she'd been a child. Black hull technology, the enlightened investment of the First Judge at Fontailloe, the enormous outlay required to integrate a new pro- pulsion and navigation and communication paradigm onto the only test bed that could truly test its promise, a Jurisdiction Fleet Ship of the top class, deployed but never commissioned. Jurisdiction Fleet Ship *Ragnarok*.

There was a clear-tone and an answering feed came through. It was not reassuring. "You're mistaken," the comm said. It was a man's voice, calm, even soothing. "You don't see anything of the sort. Why? Because we're invisible. And everybody will be much better off if it's left that way."

The on-screen cleared. Vaal knew that the man was an Engi- neer, because he was on the Engineering bridge, which she recog- nized from her orientation. She knew he was Chigan by his height and the calm serenity of his expression. And she knew he was Serge of Wheatfields because that was the name of the *Ragnarok's* Ship's Engineer. Vaal fought the temptation to close her eyes in pain. She didn't want to be here. She didn't want to do this. She didn't want to try to tell a senior Fleet officer that he was blowing smoke, and she especially didn't want to have anything to do with the *Ragnarok*, because where the *Ragnarok* went, trouble followed.

"I have an assigned duty to see you." The on-screen Engineer relaxed back in his seat with an expression of amused pity on his face. She had to go on, regardless. "And to survey your whereabouts over the past eighty shifts, by executive order. You will unshield your navs, please, your Excellency."

Now her people were staring at her as though she had taken leave of her senses. It was a Fleet ship. She could see that it was a Fleet ship. She would never dare challenge a Fleet ship, but without verification and validation orders, did she know it was really what it appeared to be?

"Not likely," the *Ragnarok*'s engineer said. "I'd suggest you take our word for it. Or not. Since we're invisible. We'll be a few days to make a rendezvous at Connaught Yards and then we'll be out of your way. Nobody wants any trouble, needless to say."

She was supposed to stop ships that would not verify. She was supposed to close the vector and send an emergency call to Fleet. How could she send an emergency call to Fleet over a Fleet ship? She could close the vector by activating its defensive fortifications. Jurisdiction Fleet Audit Appeals Authority had tried to stop the *Ragnarok* with a minefield at Taisheki Station, a year ago. It hadn't worked. Taisheki had only lost its minefield, and those things were expensive.

"Reluctantly unable to authorize docking and use of facilities." What she could do? The *Ragnarok* could still get what it wanted at Connaught, though—whatever it wanted. If it couldn't dock, it could board. There was a Security force at Connaught Yards but it was not a big one.

If she went into lock-down, the *Ragnarok* would have to blow the yards to pieces to get at supply, and who was to say that the *Ragnarok* wouldn't do just that? Rumor had it that the *Ragnarok* had mutinied. Or not. Rumor failed to agree, and there was no official Bench position on the issue because, without a First Judge, the Bench was not in order.

The engineer on screen sighed, and shook his head. "I hoped it wouldn't come to this," he said, "but I'm going to have to tell my Captain on you. How long have you been at Connaught Station? Not counting tomorrow?"

There wasn't room for the *Ragnarok* at Connaught Station. She didn't have facilities. She had five merchant ships on impound there, harmless traders by every indication, waiting for Fleet to send an Inquisitor to find out who they were and where they were going. They said they'd come from Wahken, but that had to be by way of Ghan, and there had been murder done there, and atrocity. She could not release those ships without legal verification of their route and identities. She had an idea. "With respect, your Excellency."

He had been about to cut his transmission and stand up, by the looks of things. He let his weight back down with an expression of mild surprise on his face that he kept politely clear of any petty gratification. No. She couldn't let him go to his Captain. She didn't know what she would do if she was faced with the acting Captain of a possibly mutinous ship attempting to give her a legal order. She would have to call for Fleet convoy. That was expensive and would probably not arrive until after the *Ragnarok* had gone wherever it was going and would only annoy everybody.

"Let me explain."

The *Ragnarok* had more notoriety than just that gained by the rash actions of a brevet Captain. Before Jennet ap Rhiannon, the *Ragnarok* had been commanded by Griers Verigson Lowden, a thoroughly unpleasant man with thoroughly unpleasant manners. Lowden had in turn commanded the *Ragnarok's* Inquisitor, and the *Ragnarok's* Inquisitor was just the man she wanted for the job—if his services could be had.

"I'm holding ships in quarantine. I can't release them without official clearance. There's someone on board of your ship who could help."

Andrej Koscuisko, the *Ragnarok's* Chief Medical Officer—ship's surgeon, Ship's Inquisitor. There was not a more fearful name in the entire inventory, but there was something about Koscuisko, about his reputation. One of those ships had come from Rudistal. Koscuisko had history there. It could work.

Maybe she was going to be able to get those people away from here before Fleet sent Inquisitors, after all.

DIERRYK RUKOTA WAS an artilleryman, on board the *Ragnarok* by accident—more or less—but remaining of his own free will. They'd tried to get rid of him. They'd tried to get rid of Koscuisko, come to that, once Koscuisko had returned to his ship from home leave in a hurry with an explosive piece of evidence in his possession.

Koscuisko had stubbornly declined to go, even when the ship's status had trended slowly and almost irreversibly from unhappy to mutinous. He had more to lose than anyone on board, at least in material terms. As for Rukota, he had nothing to fear for his family, and little to lose that he had not already given away for the sake of his duty and his honor.

The First Secretary, with whom his spectacularly beautiful wife had so intimate an understanding, had not been Sindha Verlaine and was consequently not dead, but was still fully capable of protecting both dear friend and her children.

Rukota's career had been all but over when he'd arrived here, the victim of one too many self-inflicted wounds. What future he might have been able to salvage in Fleet had disappeared the moment he had decided not to accompany the rest of Admiral Settigan's corrupt audit team back to Taisheki Station.

There was therefore no reason why he should not remain on the *Ragnarok*, unlike Koscuisko who had property and position and who was worried about his new-made wife and his son. The real reason Rukota stayed, however, was simpler even than that: he was having more fun than he could remember having for a long, long time.

This ship had a humorless crèche-bred maniac for a Captain, a First Officer with no sense of political expediency, a chief medical officer widely understood to be a flaming psychotic, and an Engineer with a disconcerting but honestly earned reputation for making pretzels out of Fleet bureaucrats who looked cross-wise at him; the Intelligence officer was a bat. A girl bat.

An old bat, he had been given to understand, but one whose personality was so cheerfully idiosyncratic that, after these few months on board, Rukota was beginning to forget that he had always been uncomfortable around Desmodontae. It was nothing personal. Something to do with the gleaming canine teeth in the smiling black muzzle and the fact that Desmodontae in their native system farmed hominids for cattle.

He had no business being here. This was a Jurisdiction battlewagon, a cruiser-killer class warship. He was an artilleryman. His expertise was in artillery platforms and mine fields and even old-fashioned terrestrial field pieces, because sometimes there was just no substitute for a good old-fashioned siege piece. Or two. Or three. But the *Ragnarok* was short of Command Branch officers, and he was one. The ship had never been armed—it was an experimental test bed—so they needed him to talk about cannon. The main battle cannon. Was a ship of war all of that different from an artiplat? It moved a great deal more than an artiplat in geosync was supposed to do, but Rukota wasn't sure that really made much difference for his purposes.

He'd been ap Rhiannon's commanding officer once upon a time, and had been marked for life, not to say traumatized, accordingly. Now the most senior of the two Command Branch officers left assigned, she was the brevet Captain of the *Ragnarok* by default, and that made her the boss. That didn't bother Rukota. He could still pull rank if he had to—within the context of military courtesy, of course—but so long as she didn't try to take him to bed, he foresaw no problem.

He spent most of his time with Engineering and Security working on the ship's manifest. Infirmary—the generic term covered all of the *Ragnarok's* medical facilities—was less familiar to him, but he knew how to interpret the quickly smoothed-over frowns, the quick glimpses of boots and smocks' tails disappearing around corners. The staff was unhappy. They knew why he was coming, and they meant to be sure that Koscuisko was forewarned, or he missed his guess.

It cheered Rukota enormously to be conspired against in this manner. In the increasingly ugly, competitive, each-for-his-own world of Fleet, a unit that remembered how to come together was as good as a cold drink on a hot day: refreshing.

Turning a corner—he'd made sure to get a schematic from Intelligence so he knew where he was going—Rukota heard footsteps behind him, but declined to rise to the bait and turn around. Someone had been detailed to slow him down and divert him. Now, who would it be, and what kind of story would they try to sell him?

Whoever was behind him broke into a sort of a jog-trot to close the distance. Rukota knew that signal: Security. That was a Security pace, suitable for situations where one wished to move quickly but not so quickly that anyone got left behind an obstacle. His first real acquaintance on board the *Ragnarok*, if it could be so described, had been made with Koscuisko's bond-involuntary Security, the ones Koscuisko had meant to take home with him on leave and been obliged to leave behind at the last minute. That substitution had turned out to be fortunate, and the saving of several lives at least.

"Good greeting, General Rukota," the Security troop said, slowing to a respectfully matched pace half a step behind Rukota and to his left. He was right-hand dominant; most hominids were. Koscuisko was left-handed, and it was only one of the many perverse things about the man, but that was not the troop's fault. Robert St. Clare. Nurail. There'd been a problem with St. Clare's governor at Port Burkhayden, Rukota understood; his governor had died on him, and St. Clare had been lucky that he hadn't died with it.

"And you, Robert. Are you here on fifthweek?"

Everybody on the *Ragnarok* did fifthweek, a periodic rotation from a normal assigned duty station to somewhere different. Bond-involuntaries could only do their fifthweek in Infirmary, though, because they needed specific medical skills to support their officer, and to keep them close to their officer for their mutual protection.

St. Clare was not wearing Infirmary whites, however, but his Security colors. St. Clare didn't blush. He answered Rukota candid and open-faced as any man, and Rukota's sense of respect—and amusement—only grew.

"Sent to fetch his Excellency for laps, if the General please." It was an inside joke, Rukota had gathered: Security Chief Stildyne, and Koscuisko, and laps. "The officer saw Ship's Engineer on the tracks the other day and has refused to return. This troop is to tell the officer that a Security detachment will be standing by to prevent any accidental mechanical, ah, accidents."

There was no real need for St. Clare to choose his words carefully so as to avoid falling into error. There was no governor there to punish him, but bond-involuntaries were thoroughly conditioned. Maybe it didn't really even matter that the governor was gone. After all, it took months of adjustment to prepare the occasional man who survived his sentence to be returned to normal life.

Rukota stopped, and held up his hand. "Let's just pause for a moment," he suggested, "and I'll predict the future. We'll get around the corner, but at some point between the next turning and the one after that, you'll lose your footing and knock into me. It'll be an accident, of course, and you'll be horrified, and I'll quite naturally take appropriate pains to assure you that there has been no violation."

Operant conditioning didn't require unfailing negative reinforcement. So long as the negative reinforcement was negative
enough, it didn't really matter whether it was there every time.
The strength and persistence of the conditioned behavior depended on the intensity of the stimulus that either rewarded or
punished it, and if there was anything that could do a better job
of negative reinforcement than an artificial intelligence with direct linkages into pain receptors in a man's brain, Rukota didn't
know what it was.

"If I don't take long enough to do that, you'll suddenly realize
that you've wrenched your ankle, but very oddly there won't be a
soul in corridors, not even though we're between Pharmacy Restock
and Issues, which by the breadth of these corridors is generally well-
traveled. And it's all so unnecessary. I don't want to ambush your
officer. I do have to pass on a message to him."

If he was wrong, he might have just done an unkind thing, the
sort of thing he himself had never tolerated—bullying a bond-involuntary troop, pressuring them until the stress convinced the governor that something was wrong and punishment was in order. He
waited, then he turned his head. St. Clare was looking straight ahead,
and the only part of his face that was smiling was such a minute
number of muscles in his eyelids that he couldn't be accused of
smiling at all by any reasonable soul. But he was smiling. For a bond-
involuntary, it was as good as a broad grin.

"With respect, General. This troop regrets having no idea what
the officer means to imply, due to this troop's limited understanding
and inability to grasp advanced concepts of cause and effect. Had
considered attempting to lock the officer in a stores-room, but not
the officer's suggestion. Request permission to offer thanks. This
troop appreciates the opportunity to benefit from superior wisdom
and understanding of tactics and strategy. Sir."

Oh, very good. "What's the plan, then? Do I hunt him through
Infirmary, or lay in wait outside of quarters?" Rukota started moving again, confident that he and St. Clare understood each other. He
might still get knocked to the floor or locked in a stores-room, but
at least he and St. Clare were clear on whether or not it would be an
accident. It was a pity, in a sense. It might have been worth being
locked in stores to hear what story St. Clare could possibly have
come up with to cover.

"His Excellency is usually in his office at this point in shift, if the officer please," St. Clare said blandly, as coolly as could be imagined. "Which is why this troop was sent to fetch him from there for laps. If the officer will follow me"

It was with a sinking feeling in his gut for having been played a fool—and richly deserving it—that Rukota followed St. Clare the rest of the way through Infirmary to an office in which Koscuisko sat, apparently hard at work on clinic reports, but in Infirmary whites rather than his duty blacks. Medical officers didn't wear Infirmary whites unless they were actually in Infirmary. For a moment, Rukota thought he remembered a whisper of a recent rumor about Koscuisko and bond-involuntaries, but it was gone before he could grasp it.

One way or another, he'd been out-maneuvered, for whatever reason. There was no shame in that. It was just too bad that such successful strategic misdirection could be done by bond-involuntary troops and not fifteen out of sixteen of the junior officers that Rukota had been privileged to know—though perhaps ap Rhiannon herself might be admitted as belonging to the one out of sixteen category.

"Your Excellency," Rukota said. He was senior in rank on the face of it, but he was not the senior Command Branch officer on board. That was ap Rhiannon, by default. Therefore, in the hierarchy of military courtesy, he was to address Koscuisko respectfully by title, whereas Koscuisko was free to address him by rank. Which was respectful enough. "The Captain expects you on the courier launch apron in order to brief you prior to your immediate departure for Connaught Station. There is a call on your professional services."

Of which fact Koscuisko had clearly already been apprised, even if the Captain wished to respect his dignity—and ensure that her instructions were perfectly clear—by sending Rukota to communicate the information to him personally, face-to-face. Koscuisko stood up. "Has Stildyne been told?" he asked, but Rukota was certain that it was just for form's sake. "I shall need my kit."

Koscuisko knew that someone wanted information, but he was annoyed, not worried. Ap Rhiannon had been very clear on what she expected from him as far as Inquiry was concerned, and Secured Medical had been converted into storage space for some time.

"I've no doubt that Chief Stildyne will be meeting you on the docks, your Excellency. Perhaps you should take Robert with you, as well." An Inquisitor was accompanied by bond-involuntaries any time he left the ship—both for his own protection and because the only reason an Inquisitor left his ship, unless he was on leave, was in order to execute the Protocols against an accused, and the Bench had made bond-involuntaries specifically to give Inquisitors captive hands with which to do the dirty work.

Rukota wondered suddenly whether Koscuisko's man Pyotr would be allowed to travel. He remembered the whisper, now. There had been a rumor about bond-involuntaries. One of them had been suddenly diagnosed with a brain slug, and another almost as suddenly came down with a moderately rare case of crystallization of matter in the limbic system or something of the sort. It was none of his business, however.

"We'd best not keep the Captain waiting, Robert," Koscuisko said, sorting his documents-cubes into a tidy array and standing up. "Let us be going directly. Thank you, General."

Speculation and rumor were just that. Where there was a dust cloud, there was a dust cloud; no more, no less. Surrendering any residual curiosity to the basic good sense of minding his own business, Rukota went whistling down the narrow corridors of the *Ragnarok* to go see the Ship's Engineer and review the requirements for the *Ragnarok's* battle cannon.

"THIS THEN IS the officer in charge at the Connaught vector control," Andrej Koscuisko said, with his arms folded across his chest and one hand wrapped around his elbow to keep a firm grip on his upper arm. To prevent himself from hitting her absentmindedly, Vaal thought, but did her best to keep her military bearing. Of course she was afraid of him. That was Andrej Koscuisko, and everybody knew that he was either completely out of his mind or ought to be. "Tell to me again what service you mean me to perform for you."

Her people had gotten her up altogether too early into her rest-period, and after that things had gone very quickly. She was supposed to be asleep, not standing in her office face-to-face with a notorious painmaster. A professional torturer. And still the opportunity that Koscuisko's presence suggested could not be wasted, no matter how much it upset her to be talking to a man with his history.

"Thank you for coming, your Excellency." It hadn't been his sleep shift. No, he looked fresh and rested, and the beautifully tailored curve of the black fabric of his over-blouse seemed to breathe a clean bright fragrance of citrus and snow. That was nonsense. Snow didn't have any fragrance. It was just fluffy ice. "We have orders pertinent to the terrorist attack at Ghan that require us to stop any specified traffic through the vector that doesn't have a valid audit stamp."

Ghan was different from other recent mass casualties. Someone had gone to great lengths to maximize murder, and there seemed to be no sense to it, but was there ever any sense to terrorist activity? The fuel pipes could have been poisoned at any time over a period of days, with the right time-release; up until the morning on which the port had died, traffic had been leaving Ghan on the usual closely timed schedule of a busy mercantile port. There had been a lot of traffic, but the records were for the most part unrecoverable, destroyed in the fires that panicked rioters had set.

"And you have to feed them until Fleet can spare an Inquisitor," Koscuisko added. His tone was not very cordial. Officers at his level of rank didn't have to be cordial, unless it was to their own senior officers. Few people under Jurisdiction outranked a Ship's Inquisitor.

Andrej Koscuisko was more than just a Ship's Inquisitor. He was widely reputed to have the truth-sense on him. Whether there were such a thing as truth-sense or not, Vaal neither knew nor cared. He was a professional uncoverer of secrets. He would know if she was keeping any.

"When you're a maintenance technician, everything looks like a salvage job, your Excellency." When you were an officer who dealt with sabotage and treason, everything looked like the one thing or the other. Inquisitors saw everybody as guilty, in part because once an Inquisitor was called in everybody either confessed or died. Usually one, and then the other. By a quick flash in Koscuisko's very pale eyes, Vaal deduced that he had taken her meaning. She hurried on while she still had the nerve.

"Five of the ships we're holding are from Port Rudistal, outbound for Emandis space, your Excellency. The story is that they are to establish a mining colony on one of the slow moons in system." The truth was that they meant to take the vector through Emandis to Gonebeyond space, and escape from Jurisdiction entirely. That had been her conclusion, at any rate. "If you could just verify their story, sir, we could let them go on about their business."

She had to feed them, yes. That was so. She had a legitimate reason for wanting them out of here as soon as possible. Technically speaking Nurail were classed as displaced persons confined to a limited number of systems where labor was in short supply; they could not be expectedto be able to reimburse the Bench for room and board.

The Domitt Prison was closed—Andrej Koscuisko had closed it, years ago, and exposed a catalog of horrors that remained one of the blackest blights on Jurisdiction in recent history. Hadn't the Nurail earned the right to flee the Bench for Gonebeyond if they could? The Domitt Prison was drenched in the blood of Nurail men and women who had, in the end, been guilty of no crime but that of wanting to be free.

"Take me to your facilities, then," Koscuisko said, unfolding his arms. His voice was no longer quite so glacially superior. "Have you a manifest of the cargo?"

She had. "There are one or two anomalies," she admitted. "Some of the equipment appears to be make-shift. Ore-crushers are expensive. I expect a good mechanic could make do with a lighter, more portable vehicle." Agricultural equip ment ran significantly smaller and lighter than mining equipment. Nurail had limited funds. It only made sense that they'd had to pool their resources and buy what they could, knowing they'd have to retool it when they got to the mines. And if they never got to the mines, but ended up somewhere else—oh, well. There were no economic enterprises without risk.

"No matter," Koscuisko said, and waited while his silent standing Security opened the door to Vaal's office to let them all out. "I will take the manifests as audited. Send me your persons of interest. Have you holding facilities?"

It was with difficulty that Vaal mastered the warm rush of gratitude that she felt. It would not do to show any unexpected emotion. People might think. Koscuisko was going to play along—he'd said so. Well, he'd said *send me your persons of interest*, but it amounted to the same thing.

"No cells at the hospital, your Excellency, but we can hold people in a clinic wing. Since there's nothing there. You will wish to use—ah—"

There was no Secured Medical, no dedicated torture room. Not in a small hospital at an administrative station. Koscuisko smiled—yes, actually smiled—and preceded her out of the room, according to the protocols of military courtesy.

"I will want bedding enough to keep my people," Koscuisko said. "Also open for me a field kitchen so that people may eat. I do not need Secured Medical, Vaalkarinnen. I am accustomed to working with minimal infrastructural support. That is why the Bench has granted to me Security."

Bond-involuntary security, yes, of course. Green-sleeves marked as Security slaves by the thin edge of poison-green piping that trimmed the cuffs and collars of their uniforms. She wished he hadn't said that, about infrastructure; some of the most famous horror stories about Andrej Koscuisko had to do with his genius for improvisation.

"As you say, your Excellency." It was too late now, one way or the other. She had called for Andrej Koscuisko. She would simply have to trust that nothing would go awry. If it did, it would be her fault.

If it all worked out, though, she need have nothing in her memory to accuse her. She would put her trust in Koscuisko's reputation for anarchy—and for having a weak spot for Nurail after so many of them had been cruelly murdered, a significant number by Koscuisko himself, at the Domitt Prison in Port Rudistal, so many years ago.

CHAPTER TWO
REMINISCENCES

HOW OFTEN HAD he found himself here? Andrej Koscuisko asked himself, with an emotion that he could not quite identify or bear to examine too closely. Some makeshift torture cell in some station with a problem and no solution in view. Prisoners. Security. Drugs. All of his favorite whips.

"Just like old times," he said to Stildyne, who was hovering—just a bit. He was wrong about the whips. He hadn't brought them. There was no sense in testing one's resolution; and a whip was traditional, but unnecessary. Andrej was Dolgorukij born and bred. Dolgorukij had respect for tradition, and his family was among the more traditional of the great Houses of the Dolgorukij Combine in these latter days. If he'd brought a whip, he would have had all that much more difficulty refraining from using it.

"Don't get started in on that," Stildyne replied, setting an array of doses down on the shining surface of the sterile table in front of them. "You'll only work yourself into a mood. And you've been in a mood ever since you got here."

Just now? Or five—nearly six—years ago, when he had joined the crew of the *Ragnarok*, and met his new Chief of Security? It was perhaps better not to ask, Andrej decided. Brachi Stildyne had taken good care of him and good care of his people as well. There was nothing to be done about the fact that Andrej could return Stildyne's awkwardly expressed if deeply felt regard with gratitude and respect, and nothing more.

The best way he could communicate the gratitude that he owed was to do as he was told and not argue. Yes, he was the superior officer. Yes, technically speaking, it was Stildyne who had to shut up and get on with his work. It was also true that Stildyne had spent more time holding Andrej's head over the basin of the toilet than could reasonably be expected of anybody save a wife or a servant, and Stildyne was neither.

There was a subtle sound behind Andrej's back. Stildyne looked over his shoulder and called, "Step through."

Robert St. Clare, with lab results in cube. "The officer's documentation," he said, passing the cube to Stildyne. "And the officer's rhyti coming directly."

Rhyti now, liquor later, perhaps. It wasn't that Andrej didn't know how to be humiliated at being so drunk that he had to be washed and changed like an infant, wrestled into bed, forcibly restrained from taking unsafe actions with sharp objects. He knew perfectly well how contemptible a drunk he was. The humiliation of his drunkenness was a species of self-inflicted punishment that kept him returning to drink when he could no longer bear the fear of his own dreams.

Had it not been for Stildyne's nursing and the support of his people, his own medical staff would have had to confine him on ward as self-destructive, and then he would have been publicly humiliated every time. For all he knew, his medical staff would like to have done just that, though not out of any particular desire to humiliate him. Captain Lowden had seen to it that they left him alone—and placed the entire burden of his care in the hands of bond-involuntaries, like Robert.

Now Captain Lowden was dead, but Andrej's medical staff was apparently willing to trust Security with the care of drunken officers. If he'd known that his staff was going to take that approach, Andrej told himself, he might have murdered Lowden much sooner than he had.

And it was better not to think of it, because although Bench Intelligence Specialist Karol Vogel had claimed responsibility for the assassination—Lowden had needed killing, and Vogel had the authority—it would still be Tenth Level command termination for Andrej if the truth ever came out. He was living on borrowed time.

"Clean scans." He would keep his mind on his own business. That was the best bet for staying out of trouble—and for keeping his people clear of trouble, besides. "Robert, ask for Navigator Dawson, please." The reports told him the bloodlines and blood chemistry, and that information in turn told him what he could use on whom to what effect. Dawson was Nurail without detectible admixture. The Bench had dispersed the Nurail in order to destroy their identity as a people; it was not likely that Dawson's children would be purebred.

But it was likely that they would be handsome, Andrej decided, watching as Godsalt and Kerenko brought in Dawson. He was a tall young man with a figure rather like Robert's own, but something had gone wrong with the side of Dawson's face so that it was pulled to the left around the mouth ever so slightly, and the color of his eyes—Andrej noted, as his security sat Dawson down— was unusual.

"Dawson, that's your name?" Andrej asked. "My name is Andrej Koscuisko, and I hold the Writ to which you must answer. I have some questions for you."

There was nothing on the table between them but doses. The table itself was in the pharmacy prep room—spacious, airy, well stocked with everything a man might want for healing—but there was no staff to make that healing happen. Depressing.

"I'm called Chonnie Dawson, yes," Dawson replied. "Your Excellency." The rank address came at the last minute, almost as an afterthought. There was no disrespect in Dawson's tone, but no particular fear, either. Wariness. Anxiety. No terror. Andrej was glad that Dawson wasn't afraid of him. It was going to make talking to him much easier.

"Have we met?" At the same time, there was no sense in letting familiarity pass unnoted. Too comfortable a relationship created its own difficulties.

Dawson raised his eyebrows. "Twice, as his Excellency please." He put out his hand to the tray of doses as he spoke, moving slowly and carefully, leaving plenty of time for Andrej to tell him to keep his hands to himself. "You murdered my father."

This convoy claimed to be from Rudistal, so that would logically have been in the Domitt Prison. What was Dawson's point, reaching for the doses?

"Hardly a distinguishing characteristic." Andrej watched Dawson's hand. Dawson was doing his best to make a deliberate gesture. There was something Andrej was supposed to see. "You're curious about these doses, I see?"

"You're right, I'm sure, your Excellency. About distinguishing characteristics, I mean. It's only the fact of it being my father makes the connection personally significant to me." Dawson had reached for one of the doses, apparently at random, and picked it up. "Which of these did you use on him?"

Distinguishing characteristics, Dawson had repeated. As Dawson raised the dose to eye level, the oily frayed cuff of Dawson's jacket sleeve fell away from his wrist, the fabric pulling against the flexed elbow. Dawson had worn manacles for long enough to scar him. They were old scars, though. He must have been quite young when he had got them.

For no particular reason Andrej caught the joke now. He remembered a boy in transit, on their way to Port Rudistal—a young man, fifteen years Standard, perhaps. That young man had green-gold eyes with a ring of yellow like a sunburst around the aperture of the pupil. It wasn't a common eye color for Nurail, who ran to the black in that area.

"Well, you must understand that, in those days, my sense of humor was imperfectly formed."

He ignored the ghost of a snort from Stildyne, who had posted himself behind Andrej's chair. There were men on either side of Dawson already, and Stildyne knew that they were good because Stildyne had trained them. On one memorable occasion more than a year ago, Andrej had been forced to defend himself in a knife fight. Stildyne hadn't recovered. Andrej had—from his wounds—but Stildyne brooded bitterly over how easily it could all have ended badly.

"Somebody had said that your father was an important man. I wanted to see what there was to him."

Not just an important man. The war-leader of Darmon. Had Andrej realized at the time that he had accidentally abetted the successful escape of the last member of that family who remained at large? How could he have known? He hadn't met the war-leader until weeks after he'd arrived at the prison. By that time, a young man whose wounds Andrej had treated, whose manacles Andrej had absentmindedly removed and set aside, would surely have been long gone.

"Different from here and now in what way?" Dawson asked politely. Dawson wasn't Dawson. Dawson was Chonnie, the son of the war-leader of Darmon. Chonniskot Sillerbanes—*"Chonnie's got silver bones"*— he was that precious to his people, at least as an idea.

Andrej's sense of humor was different now in a number of interesting ways. "For one, this person at my shoulder was a woman of striking physical beauty. For another, we had a great many questions to ask, while here and now there are only two or three questions that interest me at all."

Twice, Dawson had said. He was eyeing Stildyne with an expression of awed horror on his face, but Dawson had companions as beautiful. Didn't he? There'd been a man with a great long livid gash across his face. Andrej had seen the two of them, Dawson and Beauty, in a dream in Port Burkhayden on the night that he'd killed Captain Lowden. Maybe it hadn't been a dream.

"Questions," Stildyne snarled at Dawson, who fell back, dropping the dose to the tray with a clatter. "Pay attention."

Andrej stood up. It was going to be harder than he had realized, this sitting and asking questions. Of course it almost always started with asking questions. But then it had almost always gotten a little bit extreme from there, and there was a blood-eyed beast in him that wanted to hear this perfectly harmless—or relatively innocent, anyway—young man speak to him in tones of anguished fear.

"Window," he said, gesturing to explain himself in case anybody was wondering. "Wouldn't normally have one for this business. People don't like to have to see. Unless they're the kind who likes to watch, of course."

Captain Lowden had liked to watch. Lowden had done more; he'd violated the trust and confidence of Fleet by trading on markets that Andrej didn't even want to think about, using illegal copies of interrogation records—torture—as currency. And the Malcontent, the secret service of the Dolgorukij church, had told him that the market was too vigorous to be shut down. Andrej would not put it past the Malcontent to be actually trafficking in the name of the Saint himself.

What would happen if his son should chance on such a record, and see with his own eyes the things of which Andrej was capable?

"Questions, your Excellency?" The tone in which the young man asked was interesting. It was cautious and wary, but there was the smallest hint of forbearance—even encouragement. *You can do this.* Of course, it was in Dawson's best interest to get questions out and over with. He would be eager to be getting away.

"It has not been eleven days since horror was visited upon Port Ghan and those who live there by some enemy of order and civil law. The Connaught vector is only two or three days off from

Ghan. And your party cleared the entry vector from Port Ghan to Connaught nine days ago."

It was quiet in the room behind him. Andrej could almost hear people breathing. The Security troops he had with him were bond-involuntaries. They knew how to be as silent as the dead, or more so, since the dead were frequently surprisingly loud—in the first few hours post mortem, at any rate.

"We heard," Dawson said. There was an echo in his voice of a man much older, and accustomed to duty. A war-leader. The son of his father. "And we were there. But we were on vector before the news started to come out."

Which meant nothing, of course, since any reasonable maniac would take care to arrange things just so as to be well clear before the city started to die. "Come here to me," Andrej said. He had to know, and he didn't want to sit down. He knew how to get answers. He knew all too well. "And tell me that you had no hand in vengeance upon Pyana."

Most of the dead had been from that genetic group, the ancestral enemy of Nurail everywhere, and the party that had convinced Chilleau Judiciary that the Nurail were dangerous and had to be put down. It might have been a coincidence, all the same.

There was the sound of the chair's brace sliding over the floor, and Dawson came up behind him. "All right, we'd nothing to do with it. There. I'll be going now, it's been very interesting, but there are people waiting for supplies at Bell."

"You're not going to Bell," Andrej said firmly. "Or at least you're not stopping there." No, a small commercial fleet of Nurail headed into Emandis space was more likely to be seeking the vector for Gonebeyond. What was it? Dar-Nevan? "Mister Kerenko. If I might have those doses, please."

He was going to have to step away from the window, and that was too bad. But whether or not something horrible was going to befall to Dawson, anybody outside the window who saw anybody at the window would be likely to conclude that something very unfortunate was happening to somebody, and Andrej didn't wish that experience on anyone.

"Your scans indicate a subcategory six hominid of very strong definition." Nurail, and Pyana. When it came down to it, Nurail were Pyana, and vice versa, but there was no sense in being insulting.

"Here are three doses for Nurail, designed to disable your internal editors and deprive you of your natural ability to dissemble."

He knew these drugs. He'd purchased the life of Robert St. Clare from the Bench with one of them, years and years ago. "Naturally there are ways to conquer it, but it doesn't have to overwhelm you to be effective. It only needs to make it difficult enough for you to dissemble that I will know you are in fact dissembling. You will sit down."

Dawson was a brave young man, but not stupid. Only a stupid man would feel no fear in the presence of a torturer with drugs. There were drugs that did much more than loosen tongues. Dawson sat, but could not quite keep still. His eyes when he met Andrej's gaze were defiant and still hopeful, as though he were doing his best to believe that nothing was going to happen to him. When Andrej approached him with the doses in hand, Dawson struggled, but not for long; as soon as the first dose went through, he froze, and suddenly started to grin, going rather limp and boneless against the restraining hands of Security as he did so.

"Damn," Dawson said. "This is good stuff, Uncle. Mixmox, isn't it? I had some once. Only once. Can't afford it. There was a woman—"

Uncle. A Nurail authority figure; Andrej had been called that by Nurail before. Standing at the table in front of the seated and now intoxicated man, Andrej put his head back, staring at the ceiling, taking deep and calming breaths. He was not going to hurt Dawson. He didn't have to, and nobody could make him. He wanted to hurt Dawson. He wanted very much to make Dawson suffer, but he was not going to. And Stildyne, standing at his back, Stildyne would not let him hurt Dawson, either.

"I'm happy for you," Andrej said at last, and sat down with the chair pulled away from the table. "What were you doing in Port Ghan? Tell me."

"Port Ghan," Dawson said, and seemed to stop and think.

Although Dawson all but crossed his eyes in concentration, Andrej could sense no cues that would tell him that there were hidden secrets here. He had already said that he knew Dawson was not taking a convoy to Bell, not exactly, so it was not as though that could be said to be a secret.

"Solar cells. It took months to collect the load, couldn't buy too many at once, people might remember you and get suspicious."

One set of cells might be needed by any prudent person as a backup, but not twenty. Unless a person had twenty buildings to power, or a person was taking them out beyond the reach of Jurisdiction into an environment in which there were no solar cells to be had unless one had brought one's own.

"Did you get them?"

Dawson was very drunk on the drug now, and snorted with unfeigned derision. "Did we? Who do you think you're talking to? We got them. And then we left."

No, not entirely unfeigned. There was the very small shade of a wrong note in Dawson's voice. Dawson would like him to believe that Dawson was drunker than he actually was. Andrej could increase the dose, but why? It worked just as well for him if Dawson thought he didn't know.

"It would be difficult to blame a man for seeking to be revenged on an enemy who had served his entire people so villainously," Andrej said, to be saying something. "Especially if a man felt more responsible, perhaps, because of a traditional family position, for instance."

Dawson had started to shake his head before Andrej had finished speaking, but was yet polite enough to wait to raise his voice. When he did, it was a denial as emphatic as that which Andrej had expected, but the direction in which Dawson took the denial was surprising.

"Yes, and then their people must take revenge for their hurt, and your people for the hurt that their people will do if they can in response to the hurt that you have done them for the hurt that they did you. Let me tell you a thing or two about the law, Uncle."

Very strange. Andrej could sense the amusement and confusion with which his Security heard this outburst, but only because of long acquaintance. The self-discipline of a bond-involuntary was terrible to contemplate. Andrej was counting on that self-discipline to see them all safely through, but he couldn't afford to think about it. Stildyne might hear him, and he hadn't had a chance to talk to Stildyne about what he had planned, not yet.

"Tell me," he agreed, encouragingly. "I would have thought that you would have no interest in speaking of the rule of law."

Dawson hadn't said "the rule of law." He apparently decided that no correction was needed, however. "It's there to stand

between us and our own annihilation. Not here, maybe, no."
Here, under Jurisdiction, the law had been used by Pyana against
the Nurail to obtain the annihilation of Dawson's folk. So Dawson
wasn't speaking of the rule of law under Jurisdiction.

"There has to be an agreement," Dawson said. "Or there's no
community. There must be an end to vengeance, once and for all.
We got together and talked about it, and we decided. Unless we
share our hearths, we'll all die, and the weaves with us."

At this particular moment, Dawson did not sound drunk at all.
Andrej frowned. "Brachi," he said; then remembered that he did
not call Stildyne by his name in public, but could not call it back.
"Remind me to check the pull dates on these doses. Something is
not right. A Nurail speaks to me of abandoning feud."

And yet he knew one particular Nurail whose capacity to return
resignation for great wrong permitted him to live a happy life, if any
bond-involuntary could be said to have a happy life. Robert was
considerably happier than Andrej himself in some respects, but Andrej
felt it was almost insulting to Robert to even think such a thing in
light of what Robert had suffered, and put the thought away.

It was just that Robert had no particular rank, that was all—under
most circumstances, bond-involuntaries could lead even the smallest
work units only when the group was entirely comprised of other
bond-involuntaries,. It meant that there were many more women on
board the *Ragnarok* with whom Robert could hide in a storeroom
for a few moments than were available to senior officers. Yes. That
was the way to approach it. Robert had lost his family and his freedom, but at least Robert could go fishing, every day if he liked.

"Is it only fear of consequence that has kept your life so long,
Uncle?" Dawson asked. "Do you believe that? I held your life in my
hand not two years gone, in Burkhayden."

It was not something Andrej had ever felt comfortable thinking about. No, there had been few assassination attempts against
him; yes, he was visible and notorious. Stildyne was growling in a
sort of sub-vocal way, however, so Andrej moved to forestall loss
of control over the situation.

"You mustn't ask such questions in front of Security," he said,
so that Stildyne would know that he had noticed. "I always thought
it only reasonable that you should hate me, though. All of you. There
are so many of you." In the general sense, at least.

"We may hate you yet." From the tone of Dawson's voice, his personal feelings were far from dispassionate. "Don't mean to kill you for it, that's all. Because if Nurail continue to kill other Nurail they have good reason to hate, there won't be any Nurail left for our children to hate. No children."

Andrej had to stand up again. Something was profoundly disturbing him here, and he could not afford to stop and think it through. He nodded to Security to have Dawson stand up. Dawson kept his balance very well for a man on drugs. Maybe there *was* something wrong with the dose-lot.

"Now you are making me nervous," Andrej said. It was only the truth, however mocking it might sound. "But I almost believe you. About Port Ghan, if nothing else. Give me your hand and swear to me on your father's death and the manner of his dying that you and your people are not to blame for it, and I will be satisfied."

Dawson had gone white in the face. Was the drug catching up with him? He seemed to be feeling some sharp discomfort beneath his skin. As Andrej watched, Dawson's face cleared of hatred and contempt, and the ferocious anger in his eyes was replaced with something much more disturbing. Hope. Hope, and distance, of a sort.

"I so swear," Dawson said, and put out his hand. Left-hand dominant, Andrej noted. That was almost funny. He was left-hand dominant as well, but if Dawson's father had been left-handed, Andrej did not remember even noticing. "On my father's death, and the burning of his corpse in the furnaces. And on the manner in which you killed him, torturer. There is no one among these people who has had any part in horror at Port Ghan. Not even if they were Pyana. There."

Curious to see how far Dawson would go, Andrej put out his own hand in turn. Dawson took it. There was no sudden shock of antipathy so strong that it repelled the threat of physical contact with a father's murderer. Dawson frightened Andrej, now. How could such strength be natural?

Dropping Dawson's hand, Andrej stepped back half a pace. "Very well." Dawson was watching him with what seemed to be almost equal parts uneasiness and fear—that Andrej would go back on the promise he had made, perhaps? "I will have to interview each ship's commander, and perhaps three or five others, in order that the record be complete, and no question remain. You may have your representative at the interviews. It may be reassuring to them."

"And I've got just the man for the job," Dawson replied. "Thank you, your Excellency, and I don't suppose there's an extra one of those doses about that wouldn't be missed? No? Oh, well."

It was perfectly true that Andrej needed to talk to enough people to reassure the vector control officer that Dawson's party could be released. But it was also true that this unexpected assignment offered opportunity, as well as challenge. There was a surgery here.

The operation was actually a rather simple one. Only the fact that the slightest perturbation in the process would mean an agonizing death complicated matters. That, and the fact that it was illegal, but he had not been notified that his Writ to Inquire had been rescinded; and, until it was, he remained immune from prosecution for any crime he might wish to commit short of mutiny, as represented by the wanton murder of a superior commanding officer. What was a little misappropriation here and there in the face of such immunity?

"Send that person to me this evening." It was mid-afternoon already. "By which I mean, halfway through third-shift. I will have a list."

Between now and then, he would go and check the surgery, and undoubtedly discover that the surgical machines were in need of calibration. It would be several days before he could be finished with his investigation and leave; and the *Ragnarok* was still several days away from finalizing its supply manifest with Emandis Station. Andrej was expecting to rendezvous with his cousin Stanoczk, whose aid he had enlisted in his purpose. Several days, six bond-involuntaries, three of whom required no surgery—he did not have very much time.

Security took Dawson away. Andrej was alone in the room with Stildyne. After a moment, Andrej spoke. "Send someone to inventory stores," Andrej said. "Physical inventory. Controlled List. I'm concerned about the quality of stores."

No, he was not. He simply wanted a decent excuse for pulling excess medication from the *Ragnarok's* ship's stores without being too obvious about it. Would the ruse fool anybody?

It didn't matter. "I'll set Robert right on it," Stildyne said, and left Andrej alone to brood about justice and retribution and mortality.

THE ANGRY GRIEF that the Second Judge held so fiercely within her heart seemed almost to shimmer visibly in the brutal heat radiating off the baked flat clay walls of what had been the Chively Dam. Jils Ivers waited silently at a respectful distance. She'd seen the horrific aftermath of natural disasters before. This one had not been natural.

The Second Judge Presiding at Chilleau Judiciary was a tall hawk-boned woman with pale hair and brown eyes who picked her way through the rubble at the base of the breach in the dam with grace and assurance. As she turned her head down to mind the shifting of the wall's wreckage, she happened to glance behind her, and caught Jils' eye. Jils knew how to read the subtle gesture of that minute nod, and came forward to accompany the judge on the way across the broken threshold of the dam.

Chively had been holding the spring run-off from the Ato watershed for generations. The city had grown up on either side of the spillway's watercourse to nestle in the shadows of the beneficent protector of them all. There might never be a true tally of the lives that had been lost when somebody had blown the base wall and loosed the accumulated weight of Chively Lake, as old and venerable as an inland sea, over the roofs and highways all from the way from Chively to the ocean.

"Only a year," the Second Judge said. "In the name of the Law, Ivers, if you had told me that people could do such a thing to one another. Under my own presidence."

It wasn't the sort of thing that really called for an answer, or to which there was an answer. *Only a year.* Jils stood with the judge on the sloping slab of a piece of dam-wall, sheared away from the breach with explosive force under the pressure of an almost unimaginable weight of rushing water. The broad scar of the watercourse was as smooth as the back of her hand. It was an effort to look down and away toward the remains of the city and realize that the bits and fragments of rubble and rock were each of them the size of a small school, in which all of the children had been killed.

"There's no underestimating the corrosion of anarchy." She was sorry that she hadn't found Verlaine's killer. She was almost sorry she wasn't Verlaine's killer. It would have been easy to lay the blame on the person who had discovered the body in Chambers, but the only reason the Second Judge hadn't—so far as Jils could guess—was that it wouldn't have done the slightest good. The problem wasn't so much that Verlaine's murder was as yet unidentified, unfound. The larger problem lay in the fact that nothing could bring him back.

"Go to Brisinje for me, Ivers." The courier ship was waiting for her there, a short distance removed, resting on the scoured surface of the flood-bed. It was dry now. It would be months before the water level in the holding basin behind the ruined dam wall was high enough to wet the base of the rocks there. "Tell them it was all a subtle ruse. Tell them that Sindha isn't dead, and that his dying wish was to see his life's work come to fruition. Maybe not at the same time, no, but tell them. And then get back here. When you have a suspect, I want you to fetch Koscuisko for me."

A *viable* suspect, of course. That was what the judge meant. There were no lack of suspects—political enemies, agents of other Judiciaries angling for advantage, Free Government terrorists aiming to destabilize the Bench by throwing it into disarray, even Fleet assassins bent on countering a challenge to Fleet's autonomy and privileges. Plenty of suspects.

Plenty of dead ones, particularly, but the Second Judge had passed the point of being angry enough to authorize extreme measures on speculative grounds. Plenty of suspects, plenty of confessions, a useful opportunity to purge the body politic of undesirable elements, and yet they were no closer to a lead than they had been a year ago.

It went without saying that the Second Judge would much rather have sent Karol Vogel to Brisinje to represent Chilleau Judiciary. But Karol Vogel was not here. Nobody that Jils had spoken to or with seemed to know where he was or what he was doing, unless there had been information in the odd little quirk that the Malcontent "Cousin" Stanoczk had gotten to the corner of his mouth when Jils had raised the question with him. And there was never any telling with Malcontents.

"As you say, your Honor." The Second Judge didn't want Koscuisko to solve the mystery for her—it was Jils' job to discover who was responsible for the killing. That hadn't been her point. No. The Second Judge wanted Andrej Koscuisko to execute her vengeance with the demonic flair characteristic of his notorious genius. "Your front office said there was material to take with me." Andrej Koscuisko would execute no Tenth Level ever again, not even if his life depended on it. He had successfully convinced her of that.

All of Jurisdiction space needed the Selection resolved and a new First Judge named to the supreme authority so that peace and order could be restored, and so Andrej Koscuisko could surrender his Writ to Inquire and go home. His was a very small part of the greater problem, but it was a part.

The judge turned to look back over her shoulder. There were several clerks of Court in her party, as well as Security. "These are the completed traffic assessments," she said, nodding for one of the clerks to pick her way awkwardly through the debris. "Thirty-two days before and after, all vectors. The last pieces just came back from analysis yesterday."

There was something wrong with what the judge was saying, but Jils couldn't afford time to think about it now. Holding out her left hand to the clerk, the judge passed a flat-panel data display to Jils, who accepted it with a respectful bow. Data could contain evidence, and evidence could cost lives. It was worthy of the respect due any potentially dangerous weapon.

"Very good, your Honor." Jils could see from the activity of the groundcrew down range of the courier that it was ready to launch. "I'll give you regular reports, and hope to return to my primary task as soon as possible."

The murder investigation was her primary task. She remained the single strongest default suspect; she knew that to be true. She couldn't afford to let it interfere with her reason or her judgment. She knew perfectly well that she had not stabbed Sindha Verlaine, even if she still had very little idea who actually might have done.

Would the judge give Jils over to Koscuisko, to try to settle her own mind once and for all? She'd think about it later.

The courier was waiting for her, the roaring of its jet propulsion escape engines sounding curiously hushed within the great bowl of the destroyed dam. It was a tidy little beast with modestly raked canards, a standard model of vector courier wearing the marks of the Emandisan Home Defense Fleet. Boarding, Jils secured her kit before joining the pilot in the wheel-house.

Through the courier's forward viewports she could see the judge walking away back into the wrecked breach in the dam-wall as the flight techs deployed the field blast-barriers so that the courier could lift. She wondered suddenly whether the judge had wanted to be personally assured that Jils was safely loaded and would not take advantage of an opportunity to disappear.

It was an unsettling thought, but the joke was on the judge. If Jils had murdered Verlaine—if she'd had the skills to bypass all of the security that surrounded the office and the person of the second most important soul, the most important man, in all of Chilleau Judiciary— a few of the judge's Security would not stop her from disappearing.

The pilot was a man of moderate height whose amber skin and black eyes were as Emandisan as the fleet-marks on the courier. He greeted her with a polite nod, neither smiling nor frowning. Emandisan characteristically presented a stoic and serene front to the world and to each other.

"Let's get out of here," Jils suggested. Had an Emandisan killed Verlaine? Emandis exported security operatives, sharpshooters, military snipers. There had been a political upheaval in the government at Emandis perhaps five years ago. Chilleau Judiciary had been identified with the ousted government's disgraced officials. Were the Emandisan holding a grudge?

"Very good, Bench Specialist," the pilot said, locking into the comm braid. "Courier Gamesil, prepare to launch, secure for lift. Launch control. Request permission to escape atmosphere outbound for Brisinje Judiciary via Anglerhaz."

Traffic at Chively was very heavy these days as the local government struggled to get disaster aid to the area and to the people who, having survived the terrorists' breach of the dam, had been displaced by the horrific if inevitable result of emptying the great lake in a fraction of the time that it had taken to grow the lake to its former extent. Jils, however, was traveling for the Second Judge, and the Second Judge was anxious for Jils to be off and away to represent her interest in the convocation of Bench Specialists at Brisinje, where the Ninth Judge presided.

"Launch control here," the control station said. "Cleared to exit, courier. Going home, I take it, good space to you."

"And to all those who have to travel through the dark." The pilot returned polite phrase for polite phrase, but Jils thought that he sounded distracted by more than just his pre-flights.

She waited until the courier was on trajectory and headed out of atmosphere before she asked her question. "Have you been traveling long?"

The look he gave her was surprised but only mildly. Perhaps he was too absorbed in his task to notice being surprised, and of course it didn't take a Bench Intelligence Specialist to put "going home" together with a tired pilot and derive a long mission.

"Seems like much longer than just four months, Dame Ivers. Yes, ma'am. Anglerhaz vector in twenty-four, and expected drop in Brisinje by four days."

"Thank you, pilot." She'd just be getting aft to brood, then, or maybe get started on the data that the judge had given her as she left. Unlike Karol Vogel, this pilot was apparently perfectly confident of his vector spin calculations. No crosscheck would be solicited or required.

Karol Vogel and Jils had partnered at Chilleau Judiciary for years, and partnered well, too. The sexual tension between them had been the comfortable background pulse of a heartbeat, something that made it pleasant to be in each other's company—bearable to be sequestered together, sometimes in impossibly small places—without losing perspective.

He'd been moody the last time she'd seen him. She'd thought she understood—he'd been carrying a Warrant, an execution or assassination order, and Karol had always found killing mildly distasteful—but it had run deeper than that. Karol had dropped out of sight on his way out of Burkhayden, and had not been seen since.

It hadn't made sense, though. Forensics had shown that Captain Lowden, the *Ragnarok's* notoriously corrupt commanding officer, had been dead before the fire had started in the service house that night. It wasn't like Karol to set buildings on fire. He had always been careful in the past about endangering uninvolved bystanders, and a fire in a service house was a recipe for disaster. All of those patrons in all of those rooms, and the power had been off in Burkhayden that night. It was only a lucky accident that there had been so few injuries—and no fatalities—in the evacuation.

In the secure privacy of her small passenger bed-cabin, Jils laid the flat-panel down on the table and addressed its secures, verifying her identity with the chop she wore around her neck. It was a very full collection; she could tell that as the initiating diagnostics ran. She'd been waiting for the traffic reports from the very start—from the moment it had been reported that something had gone wrong at Upos and destroyed the gate records covering eight days' worth of data from the stores. From the backup. From the virtuals. From the disasters. Physically destroyed.

The records hadn't been physically destroyed at Wellocks—no, only part of the damage had been fire and corrosion there—but what they had recovered had been irretrievably over-written by a very sophisticated blanking protocol that Jils wanted for her own. And Burig as well, not only the two vectors out of Chilleau itself but two of the vectors from which one could gain access to the Wellocks vector and thus to Chilleau—oh, it had been thoroughly done.

Panthis and Ygau had been unharmed, except for some minor damage all too clearly designed to dilute the focus of an investigation by widening the field of avenues that had to be investigated. There wasn't much doubt in Jils' mind about that. The key to the problem was to be sought first where the unknown quarry had tried to hide it most completely. There'd been Fleet at Burig, Fleet at Ktank, Fleet at Upos and Wellocks and Panthis as well; so if it was a Fleet initiative, Fleet had certainly had the resources in place to cover its tracks. Yes, if it had been Fleet.

Months to restore the traffic reports by tracking every ship that had arrived at any vector it could have reached from any of the vandalized vectors. Months to collect and rationalize and sort the data, to try to make information out of it. It was up to her, now. There were still connections and clues that could not be elicited from any of the non-sentient analysis tools at the Bench's disposal.

Report of traffic, Bury Vector, inbound and outbound, minus sixteen to plus eight. Analysis record. Do you wish to proceed? And yet something made Jils pause, and secure the log, and stare down at the flat-panel on the table for a long moment, thinking.

It was an analysis record, and an analysis record by definition was an extract. The judge had publicly entrusted her with sensitive documentation, but it was derivative. Second-hand. Nothing that couldn't be easily replaced, re-run, and—perhaps crucially—compared against a master record to check for errors and omissions.

The Second Judge probably had her own people working on it already. It was just a piece of window dressing, even if it was also something Jils had been waiting for. And any of the other Bench Specialists she was traveling to meet at Brisinje would reach the same conclusion as Jils had: if something compromised this data, there was no harm done. The judge didn't expect Jils to get anything out of it anyway.

This was not encouraging. It didn't always take a warrant to authorize a Bench Specialist to carry out an execution or Judicial assassination. Warrants were required to communicate the Court's decision that someone had to die for the good of the Judicial order; Bench Specialists were empowered to make their own decisions about whether someone needed termination.

Jils was going to Convocation, to represent the Second Judge's interest. There would be a Bench Specialist from each of the eight other Judiciaries, even Fontailloe, which by long-standing custom could not compete for the position vacated by the death of the previous incumbent. Eight Bench Specialists, each of whom had the legal right to kill when it seemed necessary, so long as they felt they could justify their decision before a panel of their peers after the fact.

A target didn't even have to be guilty to need killing. If failure to demonstrate some sort of sanctions would encourage defiance of the Bench, if it was taking too long to find the guilty parties and the public had begun to wonder, if the greater good of the Judicial order demanded a quick close to a problem so that that everybody could just move on, then sometimes it was enough that a public perception of guilt existed. Any one of those people could take her life if they decided she was or might as well be guilty. She would do the same.

They'd have to take her by surprise, if they took her at all. Had the judge's choice of data been a subtle warning, then, a reminder that a dead Bench Specialist could not speak for the rights of Chilleau Judiciary?

It was four days Standard between here and Brisinje, even by elite courier. Computer analysis and statistics could only go so far. It could take months for even the most sophisticated computer analysis protocol to surface a connection that a human with the right background could make in a single flash of insight. Whether or not somebody else was already working on this information, it was her business to see how far she could get with it.

Whether nor not somebody was going to try to kill her at Brisinje Jils had no intention of losing sight of her goal: to discover who had caused the turmoil that was costing lives and resources from one end of Jurisdiction Space to the other, who had thrown Chilleau Judiciary into such disarray, who had cast Jils Ivers herself under suspicion of murder. And kill them.

OUT OF MONOGRAPHS. Sick of the Keldar mysteries. Out of patience with even Dasidar and Dyraine, and he had never been a man capable of gaining a meditative trance through prayer. Four days of questioning had left Andrej bored to a perceptible degree, but at least it was almost over. Just one or two more interviews. That was all he needed. He had finished in the surgery; now all five of his bond-involuntaries had headaches and wore their Safes for show and necessary camouflage. He had six bond-involuntaries, but Robert's governor had been legally and lawfully pulled, in Port Burkhayden. The thing was done. Stildyne was suspicious. Andrej hadn't decided how much he dared tell Stildyne, but he was going to have to tell him something.

It was the middle of the morning, but his interviewee was only just now arriving, and that was annoying. Andrej couldn't blame the wench for being nervous, not really, but he was bored and irritable accordingly. "Your Excellency—"

He turned from brooding out of the window with a touch too much anticipatory greed so that his interviewee, the ship's stores inventory officer, shrank back visibly, backing into her escort. If he were to get as drunk as he thought he might like to be, it would be a week before he could promise the vector control officer that she could release her detainees, and if that happened, Fleet's interrogation group might catch up with them and decide to do just a little spot-checking in light of Andrej's status as a might-be mutineer. That wouldn't do.

The stores inventory officer was a redhead who reminded him vaguely of somebody. Maybe she was one of those women who flirted when she was terrified? He could hope. But not much.

"Come on, Hatt," her escort said. "You know we've got to get it over with. Have any of the others been so much as touched? Come on."

Birrin Banch was the mess officer, the man Dawson had sent to represent the interests of the detainees and observe the proceedings to be sure that Andrej did not lapse into any old, bad habits. Dawson need not have worried, Andrej told himself bitterly. Stildyne was not about to let him lapse into any old bad habits either, and it was very tedious of Stildyne to be that way, too. They were none of them any fun at all.

Did they have the first idea of how much it tormented him to be here in this place, to be constantly in the company of people who were frightened of him—with good reason—but who could not be touched, not in any interesting manner?

The woman, Hatt, seemed to collect herself. She squared her shoulders and marched in through the door from the corridor to step right up to the table in the middle of the room, seating herself with a species of nervous bravado that Andrej could recognize and empathize with. Yes, she was frightened—and disgusted—by him. There was to be no flirting, clearly. That was too bad. He liked redheads. Women, for that matter.

"Has Birrin here told you what will happen?" Andrej asked politely, keeping his distance. "There are doses there, on the table, whose effect is to relax you and make it easier for me to tell that you are truthful. Or not."

Not all of the people to whom he had spoken since he'd started here had told him the truth, but it hadn't mattered. It was only one sort of truth he needed, that which pertained to complicity in the disaster at Port Ghan. The confidence that came from believing that one had put one over on Andrej Koscuisko was as effective as any drug in the Controlled List, and considerably cheaper. Not that the cost concerned Andrej personally, no, but this station had not been re-supplied for some time, and there was no telling when they would be able to refresh their stores of high-grade pharmaceuticals.

"I've nothing to lie to you about." She had a thin tight voice full of resentment. She was angry because she was afraid. "Dose or no dose. Ask."

Fair enough. "I ask you to accept these doses, then. I will not force them on you." He hadn't asked Dawson. But the deeper he got into this, the clearer it was to him that things were clean, and people had a right to be terrified and overstressed if they liked. It was all the same to him.

If it had been the way it used to be, Security would have held the prisoner for the dose, and then he would have done anything he liked to, anything at all. Captain Lowden had been good to him. Captain Lowden had seen to it that he had as much recreation as he could stand, and then some.

Hatt turned her head to look at Birrin, who nodded reassuringly. *Go ahead. It's all right.* Taking a visibly deep breath, Hatt nodded and turned back to Andrej. "Do as you like."

How could she know? It wasn't what he liked that troubled him. It was the fact of liking it. He had had such freedom, and been its prisoner. Now he was free of the freedom to commit atrocity, prisoner of his own determination, and subject to the penalty of death by his own free will.

He put the dose through at the back of her shoulder, through her garment, then sat down. It would be a moment before the dose began to take effect. Andrej looked around for whomever was handy, catching Godsalt's eye. *A flask of rhyti.* By the time Godsalt had brought the beverage, Hatt was very relaxed indeed. Taking a deep breath and closing her eyes, she smiled with evident appreciation.

"Do you take rhyti, Miss Hatt?" Andrej asked, surprised. Dawson's observer shifted where he sat, just a bit, but Andrej already knew that Birrin didn't take rhyti.

"Yes, please, if there's to be had." The eagerness of her response was unfeigned. "Beautiful stuff, that. At least by the perfume of it."

Godsalt hadn't needed Andrej's implied instruction to bring a second flask, one as milky as the first. Less sweet, Andrej hoped. Dolgorukij liked sweet things to be sweeter than the general taste of many other sorts of hominids. It was because the Dolgorukij base metabolism ran high to the Jurisdiction standard.

"One is a little puzzled," Andrej said politely, watching her take a clearly appreciative sip of the hot infusion. "One has rarely met persons not from Combine worlds who care for rhyti."

There was a limited luxury market for good quality rhyti, true enough, and naturally it was a staple of ethnic restaurants. There was not much demand for Dolgorukij cuisine outside markets with displaced Dolgorukij populations, though. Where would Hatt have had occasion to acquire a taste for it?

"In Port Rudistal, I had an information service," Hatt said. She was sensitive to his confusion, Andrej guessed. "One of my clients was a guest of a religious establishment. They always offered rhyti. Cakes. Pastries. You didn't dare eat for a day you went to see the cousins at the sister's house."

No, wait. A feeling of unrest had started to build in Andrej's mind as Hatt explained, and it grew worse as she got further. A religious establishment in Port Rudistal, and they served rhyti, so it was a Dolgorukij religious establishment. There was only one Dolgorukij religious establishment in Port Rudistal that Andrej knew anything about—the one that he had himself had established so that the Nurail service bond-involuntary who had shared his bed while he was at the Domitt Prison need not go back to enforced prostitution once he was gone. It couldn't be Ailynn that Hatt was talking about. Cousins, she'd said. Cousins. Well, that could be anybody, but cousins at the sister's house—Ailynn.

"I think I know of that establishment," Andrej said. He didn't have any brief to talk about it; he was here to ask about Ghan, and for no other reason. He had to finish his inquiries and let these people go so that he could have a word with Stildyne about bond-involuntaries. "If I do, it is a woman named Ailynn."

Hatt nodded. "It's well his Excellency should know. It's your own house, after all. That man of yours. The one who died there." Joslire, she meant, Joslire dead in the street. "I met Birrin there, did you know?"

Was that why Birrin had seemed so uncomfortable? He'd been steady enough over the past days, acting his role of advocate-observer with quiet competence, but now he gave unmistakable evidence of nerves. Andrej could smell it in his sweat.

"That's none of my business, Miss Hatt." He wanted to ask how things were. The Bench had called him back to Rudistal to execute judgment against Administrator Geltoi, tenth-level command termination. He'd made a good demonstration of it. It had been a public execution, it had been important that it be as horrifically impressive as possible. Kaydence had been there with Ailynn at that time. And a party had come from Emandis space demanding the return of Joslire's knives, but they were his knives now. Joslire had given them to him.

He was letting himself become distracted. Emandis and Joslire's knives were very much on his mind; he'd asked Two for research on any family Joslire might have left, and hoped to visit the place where Joslire's ashes had been buried. They did it in orchards on Emandis, he understood. "I've no interest in extraneous matters. I only need to know about Port Ghan."

She shuddered and put her hand to her mouth as if her stomach hurt her suddenly and very badly indeed. "Horrible," she said. "Children. Animals. I thought the furnaces at the Domitt were the worst thing I could ever see, your Excellency. I was wrong."

Andrej thought he knew what she was saying, but he had a duty to be sure. "You saw the children dead at Port Ghan?" he asked carefully. Just because he wanted her to be innocent so that he could let them all go did not mean he could take any short cuts. It was horrible, at Port Ghan: children, yes, and their parents and teachers and friends, every living thing within the entire zone serviced from that one fuel distribution station, all dead.

"No," Hatt said, too clear and honest and mildly confused for there to be any ambiguity in her meaning. "I saw the furnaces. And the pit. But I've seen pictures from Port Ghan. Terrible."

Birrin was more uncomfortable moment by moment. It piqued Andrej's curiosity; nothing to do with Ghan, surely, but something to do with the Domitt Prison. "Tell me, Miss Hatt," Andrej said. "Do you know anything about who was responsible for that? Anything at all?"

What she said next caught him by surprise, again. This interview was full of perplexities. "He was a guard, that's true. But the days of blood for blood are over. Birrin's a good man. It doesn't matter what he might have done, before, and it's yourself that shares the shame of what happened there, but do we count it against you? No. We're mindful of your word that stopped the burning. It more than counts. With both of you."

Andrej understood. "And we are both rightfully humbled," he assured her, not looking at Dawson's observer. "But as to what has happened at Port Ghan. I ask if you have any knowledge of who is responsible for that. You were there. Did any among you put the plot forward, in any way?"

Opening her mouth to answer him with strong words, she seemed to collect herself, to remind herself that after all the whole point of the thing lay in that question. She shut her mouth and swallowed once, and then spoke.

"I had no knowledge of it," she said. "And have gained no knowledge since. No, your Excellency. We took on goods at Port Ghan, but brought none, nor did anybody but a few even go out of ship. For fear of arousing suspicions. You can guess."

True enough. They would have minimized their contacts in the port, and he could indeed guess why. "Thank you, Miss Hatt. Gentlemen, if you would see Miss Hatt safely back to her place, please." He did not offer to excuse Birrin. Birrin did not attempt to leave.

When the security were gone and Hatt with them, Andrej leaned back in his chair and looked at Birrin, curious. "You're Pyana. Not Nurail at all."

"You pretend you can't tell?" Birrin demanded, but it was in a tone of voice that was defeated, almost helpless. "Yes. I was a guard at the Domitt Prison. His Excellency would not remember ever seeing me."

Well, Birrin hadn't been a work crew boss or among the unauthorized and unofficial torturers from that one long ugly barrack, or he would not be here. It didn't mean he hadn't committed abuses. It was merely that so many crimes had been committed there that bringing the worst of the criminals to account had exhausted the resources of the Judicial system. After a point, there was no point in criminalizing bullying, distasteful as it was.

"But you saw me? We were there together?"

Birrin nodded, his face full of shame. "I was in the guard mount on the morning that you turned off the furnaces. There was something that was beyond natural about the fog that morning, and I was afraid."

Andrej wasn't sure he quite followed Birrin's line of thought, but he wasn't trying very hard. If he wanted to remember, he'd have to think about it. He didn't want to think about it. He relived it all frequently enough, in his dreams—

"We are both well quit of it. That's all that matters." And yes, he understood very well why a Pyana with blood-guilt to atone for might be here among these Nurail. "It can never be made right, but we have finished with it, you and I."

There was no making amends—at least not for Andrej. His crimes had been too great. For Birrin, Andrej had no doubt that his atonement overbalanced whatever fault he had committed, but the important thing was only—first—to stop. To quit. It didn't matter in the least how sorry you were about what you had done if you were at the same time still doing it.

"Done," Birrin agreed with a nod. There was a peculiar catch in his voice; what was on his mind? "I've watched you, and I can't tell. Am I the only one who—sometimes—is sorry that it's over?"

For all the hesitation in Birrin's voice, there was no mistaking his meaning. Andrej stared, and Birrin stumbled on, clearly feeling more miserable by the moment.

"And it's not that I would ever do it again. When I think about the things I did, I can't believe it was me. I know I did them. I can't imagine doing anything like that. But I can't stop wishing. I remember things when I'm not thinking about it. It was so easy. It felt so good to have so much power."

Certainly Andrej knew what Birrin meant. "You can't help it." Neither could Andrej himself. "Of course you remember. It's your mind trying to make sense of it all. 'How could I have abused those people,' you ask yourself."

"What do you do?"

Birrin had been a prison guard. His crimes, whatever they had been, could hardly be comparable to those that Andrej had committed in the name of the Judicial order. But Birrin was in pain, and this was no time for perverse pride. "I stay out of situations that remind me, as much as I can," Andrej said. "And if the truth be told, I drink a great deal, friend Birrin, though I cannot recommend that as a strategy."

"You miss it also?"

Andrej could hardly bear to answer for a moment. Yes. He missed it. He wanted—"Fiercely, but it is only right, that I should be in pain." He didn't want to talk about it. Had Birrin heard what he needed to hear, to know that there was nothing uniquely monstrous about longing for days of power and lordship that were over, when they had been enjoyed at the expense of other feeling creatures? "Let us go to the vector officer. I have all the information that I need to release the convoy with full confidence."

All of this time, Birrin had stood at his post, leaning against the wall just to one side of the doorway. He turned without another word, and waited. Andrej stood up and followed him, resigned, depressed, but glad at least that he could help Dawson's convoy on its way.

CHAPTER THREE
MANIFEST IRREGULARITIES

JILS IVERS STOOD up from the small table of the passenger cabin and stretched with her hands at the back of her waist, her fingers not quite touching the track of her spine. She was getting nowhere.

Her mind kept wandering; she couldn't concentrate. She found herself scanning the scrolled sections on her viewer, awakening to the fact that she couldn't remember a thing about the last sub-segment or the section prior to the one on which she'd just stopped, going back to find the last place she could remember and discovering that she didn't recognize a single data-point between where she'd left off last and where she was now.

She could almost have believed that someone had laid down a hypnotic subliminal in the text except that she didn't believe in subliminals. She'd never validated a single instance where they'd worked with any degree of consistency at all. She'd known that she was stressed. She hadn't realized that it was as bad as it was. She knew what to do about stress, though.

Closing up the data reader, Jils tucked it away in the secured locker with her kit and then started to clear the room. The hollow globe was really the best solution. She had stowed the table and was latching the bed into its wall-mount when the talk-alert sounded. It was the courier's pilot.

"Twenty hours clear of Chilleau, Dame," he said. "There's news from Brisinje. We won't be coming in to the launch fields near the city. They're burning. Trade protests of some sort, they say."

The Bench was all about regulation of trade, at its heart. Its form was that of a Jurisdiction—nine judges on the Bench, each responsible for lower courts and circuits and the entire range of governance—but when it came down to it, all the Bench was really interested in was protecting and perpetuating itself for the greater good of the Judicial order and the maintenance and regulation of trade.

Jils sighed in frustrated resignation. "All right. Has anybody put their name to it?" Twenty hours clear already? She hadn't really noticed the passage of time. She was sure she'd learned the first few sections of that data by heart, but that was a poor return on a Bench Specialist's time.

"There's a preliminary report on it, Dame, but nothing official. I'll let you know if anything comes in."

Right. "Thanks, pilot, Ivers away." She'd spoken to him four or five times on her way to or from the galley; personable sort with an unusual name. Weren't they all unusual names? The pilot was Emandisan. She'd track down her nagging sense of recognition later, when she had time. Jils reached for the pull-strap above the lintel of the door that separated cabin from corridor, and pulled.

The ceiling panels moved apart to either side of the cabin, and there was the exercise apparatus, stowed and waiting. Its own pull-strap fell free of the ceiling panels, and Jils put her weight to it to deploy the device, an exercise globe, flattened for storage but unfolding into the metal skeleton of a sphere as it descended.

Each of the cabins contained a piece of stowed equipment in its ceiling compartment. She had made sure that she got the cabin with the globe. There were times when the only thing to do was to step into the cage and strap in and work it into a free spinning inertial resistance-training machine.

The straps of the man-mount in the middle unfolded and fell straight from their anchors as the globe completed its descent, and something fell to the floor. A piece of paper. Caught up in the apparatus from the last time it had been deployed, perhaps?

She didn't care. This was a well-maintained little courier, but things could be overlooked, and a stray bit of paper in an overhead storage bin was no big deal. Opening the door of the spherical cage, Jils stepped inside and started to strap herself in, thinking. How far had she gotten in the data?

She'd gotten through most of the Terek vector's records, only partially distracted by its casualty list. Terek was powerful—giving access to more than five exit vectors—but loose; it was easy to end up where you didn't expect to be, if you didn't pay attention.

Some of the Terek's multiple exit vectors were in undeveloped territory. There were supposed to be emergency depots at even those, in theory, but Fleet was stretched thin and complaining about re-source starvation. If the re-supply and maintenance crews hadn't been by, and the last ship had taken atmosphere, you could find yourself without enough good air to last until next planetfall if you had to turn around and take the vector right away. Setting the wheel in motion was a gradual process, and she had to exert herself to get the wheel started. That was the whole point, after all. There'd been a lot of traffic through Terek lately, at least during the audit period. Never any shortage of people willing to risk their lives to save time and resources. A really good pilot had nothing to fear from the Terek vector, true enough.

The wheel was beginning to warm up and start spinning, slowly. The piece of paper in the floor was like a visual brake that interrupted Jils' train of thought every time the rotation of the wheel carried her past. That wasn't just an ordinary piece of maintenance log sheet. There was something disturbing about the way in which it was folded.

Terek vector, Jils told herself firmly. Ships could occasionally slip through Terek during a solar disturbance that reduced the capacity of the vector control's recording devices. Might a ship have come in the wrong direction—from Gonebeyond—carrying an assassin?

Why wasn't that piece of paper resting on the floor moving in the air currents that the movement of the exercise sphere created as it spun faster and faster? Just how heavy was it? She'd seen heavier paper and thinner paper, and even metal foils could be used for hand-writes from time to time. Metal foils could be quite heavy. But if it was a metal foil would it have fallen the way it had?

She braked the machine with the weight of her body, going limp, leaning back against the harness. This was no good. She wasn't getting anywhere. The wheel spun to a stop. Jils unstrapped herself. Reaching through the metal frame of the sphere, she picked the damned thing up and unfolded it. Heavy paper—sketch paper—and a simple cartoon in which Jils recognized a message.

It was a hanged man. A stick figure on an old-fashioned tee-frame, the noose—a specific noose, a technically correct detail—clearly indicated. And across the stick figure a scrawled strike-out, heavy and black as if the person who had done the cartoon had wished to call the image back. Jils knew better than to imagine that to have been the case, however, because she recognized the style.

She always sought the cabin with the globe. She frequently diverted herself with exercise when she was thinking hard about something, and she had been thinking hard ever since she'd found Verlaine's body.

The doodle would mean nothing to anybody else. It had been left there for her, only her, in the hopes that chance would bring her to this cabin. The news of a Convocation had been leaked months ago; that it was to happen at Brisinje was common diplomatic knowledge. Chilleau Judiciary had no Bench Specialist to send but her. The odds of Jils traveling to Brisinje on this one courier were by no means as long as they might at first seem, and who knew how many doodles had been planted in how many cabins, and by whom?

Karol Vogel wanted her to know that Simms "the Hangman" Balkney had not done the murder of First Secretary Verlaine.

Ever since she had realized that Karol had gone missing, she had sought for—clues to his whereabouts and what he was doing—any scrap of information that might explain why he had disappeared so disgustingly completely on his way out of Burkhayden space nearly a year ago. She had found nothing. She knew what the doodle meant in the immediate sense, at least on the surface, but what its meaning might carry as a deeper message—and how long it had been here, waiting for her—she did not know.

Would Karol be in convocation? Surely not. But Balkney might well be. At least Karol wasn't dead, or hadn't been, recently enough to have left her a message.

She left her cabin as it was and took the piece of paper to the wheelhouse where the pilot sat at his station. He looked over his shoulder as she came in and started to rise, but she waved off the courtesy gesture and sat down in the second seat at the pilot's right. What was she going to ask him? What was she going to ask first?

"Feed from Brisinje space," the pilot said, and cued a visual. "It's shameful."

She could see the pearl-gray globe of Brisinje, its great oceans, the brilliant white sands of its countless beaches outlining the landmasses clearly even hours and hours away. She could see the dark smudge in the atmosphere at Brisinje's equator feathering like a plume from Brisinje Judiciary's seat on the famous Reggidout River. It was the gem of the Judiciary, so pure and clear a river that it was celebrated throughout the Judiciary and even beyond; and the black smoke lay across that beautiful blue thread for what had to be octaves and octaves.

She didn't have to wait for the reports to be written to know the cost in human suffering. The river had no defense against the outrage that was done to it, and on behalf of the white sand beaches and the clear blue river Reggidout, Jils knew a special kind of anger in her heart.

"We're scheduled in at Imennou," the pilot said. "Priority override, we're the last party to arrive. You'll be met."

She'd just bet. Met by a guard of honor, yes, but one that was a guard detail beneath it all. They needed her for Convocation, though; Karol wasn't here to speak for Chilleau, and there was nobody else who'd been associated with Chilleau at any recent time who wasn't already absorbed in the affairs of other Judiciaries. That gave her a reprieve of sorts. Perhaps.

She opened her mouth to ask a question but closed it again when she realized how little good it would do her. She could ask the courier's pilot where he'd been, and he would tell her. She could check its records, for that matter.

She could ask the pilot if he knew where Karol Vogel was, but Bench Specialists could travel unregistered; it was part of their privilege package. They were not obliged to tell anyone where they'd been or were going. If Karol had been here, the pilot might well have been instructed not to mention it, and pilots were by definition conscientious and careful people. If Karol had not identified himself, he was traveling as someone else, in which case a passenger list in and of itself would do her little good.

What did it matter? Karol had been here, and left her a message. "Imennou." She wasn't sure she even knew where that was. "How long to Brisinje from there?"

"Six hours by ground-car, they tell me, Dame. I've never ridden in a top-of-the-line ground-car. Is it true that they stock the refreshments bar with all of your favorite snacks?"

"Bench Specialists don't have favorite snacks." It was the response he would expect; she'd play along. "And we live on plain water and survival rations. It's to avoid establishing a pattern that could be used to locate and identify us when we're under cover. And when you've been living on survival rations, almost anything else counts as a favorite snack, believe me."

The pilot grinned. "I'll send ahead, Dame," he promised. "Refreshments bar to be stocked with plain water and survival rations. Supplement tabs."

She almost had to laugh, and missed laughing so much that she did. "Very good," she said with an assumed frostiness of dignity. "Carry on. I'll just be going back to quarters."

She didn't want to watch the world come closer. She didn't need a clearer hint of how Brisinje was suffering from fire and sabotage. The fuel tanks on the launch field had been breached. The toxins in the atmosphere would be damaging the river's flora and fauna for years. It was criminal. But that was stating the obvious.

If she survived the Convocation, she would ask to be allowed to stay on at Brisinje and see the villains punished herself, if possible. If she didn't get through to the truth about Verlaine's death, her own execution was all but inevitable.

"TRUE ENOUGH," KOSCUISKO said to the convoy commander Dawson, standing on the platform before the last of the mercantile ships to be unshackled. The unchaining was figurative, of course. It seemed to Stildyne that what Koscuisko had just offered to tell Dawson about Dawson's father was likely to be distressingly concrete. "He might have liked you to know, all the same. Shall I tell you?"

Dawson looked at the vector officer, who seemed to shrug her shoulders as well as anybody could while she was standing on her dignity. She was operating at a significant handicap in the dignity department because she was on Koscuisko's right, and Koscuisko could project ferocious self-possession in his bare feet and a soiled nightshirt. Stildyne had seen him do it.

Looking back over his shoulder, checking the progress of the preparations for departure, Dawson took a deep breath and thinned his lips with an expression of resignation. "I repeat, that I can't imagine what a man might want to hear about his father's death by torture," Dawson said. If there was hatred in his voice, Stildyne couldn't place it. "Speak as you like, Uncle."

The familiar tone Dawson took had surprised the vector officer, obviously. She knew how to take her cue from Koscuisko, though; that was obvious as well. And Koscuisko didn't seem to be bothered by the imputation of kinship.

"I paid little attention to it at the time," Koscuisko said. "And only now realize what it meant. Your father knew that you were not taken. I showed him the list of friends and family known to be dead and in custody; you were not on it."

A strange light leapt into Dawson's coppery eyes as Koscuisko spoke, but it seemed to die away as quickly as it had kindled. "It's a small matter," Dawson said. "Thank you, but I—"

Koscuisko shook his head emphatically. "Excuse me that I insist, Dawson. It is no small thing. I meant to dishearten him by showing him that all was lost, and he knew by my showing that hope remained. Had that changed during the course of our acquaintance, I would have told him, he would have known to be sure of that, and it had been some weeks. Months. That you had not been taken or identified among existing prisoners meant good hope. I left him little enough to take with him as he died."

The whole Domitt Prison thing had been before Stildyne's time, though it had been at Rudistal that he had first met Andrej Koscuisko. Fleet had elected to effect Koscuisko's formal transfer from *Scylla* to the *Ragnarok* while Koscuisko was back in Port Rudistal to execute the sentence of the Court against the Domitt Prison's administration. He'd met Koscuisko's former chief of Security and made some assumptions about their relationship that had created problems for him later. He was glad he hadn't been there the night Koscuisko had taken Joslire Curran's life, though.

"And he left you with the weave." Dawson went pale. "I never learned my mother's weave, Uncle, nor my father's either. And you. You wrote them down. You said so."

Had Koscuisko had a conversation with Dawson that Stildyne hadn't known about? It was possible, if difficult to imagine. Stildyne liked to know where Koscuisko was, and with whom. It was his job. Koscuisko only nodded, though, so it had clearly happened, somehow.

"Eight and eighty of them," Koscuisko agreed. "And have given the text to the Church to be protected, since there is no security on board the *Ragnarok* for any of her crew." He added for Stildyne's benefit, "No personal criticism is meant by this, Brachi."

Of course not. It was the security of the *Ragnarok* as an entity that Koscuisko meant, not the quality of protection provide by any of its Security teams.

"Does the Dolgorukij church speak scream?" Dawson asked with an almost completely suppressed tremor in his voice. Koscuisko shook his head.

"Not so much in these latter days, but my cousin Stoshi can read my handscript better than most. We have a similar handscript, or at least we have had in the past."

That was true. There was a family resemblance. Stildyne was in a position to know, having seen one or two examples of the writing of Koscuisko's cousin Stanoczk. It had been a shame that he hadn't been able to keep them, but the content of the notes that Stanoczk sent to Stildyne was not such that Stildyne could take the risk of accidental disclosure.

"What must we do to get the weaves back, then?" Dawson demanded. The maintenance crew was coming off the last of the convoy ships, and the members of Dawson's crew who had been detailed to accompany them looked satisfied and eager. They would be leaving soon.

"It is your property, or rather the property in common of any Nurail. The Saint holds the manuscript in trust, and will transcribe it. I meant in this way to be sure the books were safe." It was technically illegal to transcribe Nurail weaves, and had been for years—part of the Bench sanctions—but Koscuisko could do so with impunity. The Law did not apply to Inquisitors, or applied only in a limited sense.

The vector officer's maintenance chief had waited politely for Koscuisko to stop talking. Koscuisko could see her waiting as clearly as Stildyne could, of course, and raised his eyebrows at the woman, inviting her to speak.

Which she did, to her vector officer, as was appropriate. "Cleared and registered, vector officer," the maintenance chief said. "Buy-off on all stats. Ready for immediate departure."

Vector Officer Vaalkarinnen nodded. "Get out of here, Dawson," she said. "I wouldn't waste any time. Go. Move. Shift."

"And take your surgical kit with you," Koscuisko added. The vector officer looked up sharply at Koscuisko as he spoke but Garrity and Hirsel, taking their cue, were already moving the two solid crates forward at as brisk a pace as the assists would tolerate.

Dawson offered the vector officer his hand. She seemed to think about whether she would protest, but apparently made up her mind to let it go. She shook Dawson's hand, and he turned away to hurry into the open passenger loading ramp of the nearest ship with Garrity and Hirsel following close after.

"I looked at their manifest," Vaalkarinnen said to Koscuisko. "They're not carrying surgical kit. Just standard medical maintenance and emergency."

"And I have done an inventory of your medical facility, Vaalkarinnen. Do you know how outdated a significant portion of your stores have become? I have been forced to destroy *materia medica* that might otherwise fall into the wrong hands. You will have to make due with a single inventory set until your replacement stock arrives from Emandis Station. It may be ten days, but I have placed the requisition on urgent status."

Was that what Koscuisko had been spending all that time in the station's surgery doing? Building a colonization medical kit for Dawson's fleet? Stildyne wouldn't put it past him. And it would explain. When Koscuisko got off on a medical tangent, Stildyne tried to stay out of his way. Koscuisko had threatened him with reconstructive surgery more than once, and Stildyne was not taking any chances.

"Thank you, your Excellency." Koscuisko had left Vaalkarinnen with nothing else to say. She sounded sincere enough all the same. Stildyne could empathize with the dilemma that she'd been in, and with Koscuisko here she had been able to release the entire convoy without so much as a bruise or a yelp or a drop of blood. "I understand that I am responsible for imposing on you. I'm very grateful to you for your assistance."

Well, it wasn't as though it had been Koscuisko's idea, precisely. He said as much. "Your sense of conservation is to be heartily applauded, Vaalkarinnen." Koscuisko's sincerity startled a blush out of her. Stildyne wondered if she minded. Blushing was a much under-rated ability, so far as Stildyne was concerned. He didn't think he'd ever been able to do it. "I commend your dutiful care of souls under Jurisdiction. I have said as much when I made my report."

"His Excellency is very kind." Her blush had deepened, but she gave no sign of being aware of it. "If you'll excuse me, sir, I'll return to my duties, now. Please clear the docks for release of convoy."

Koscuisko returned her salute with a cheerful, almost casual nod. He watched her back in silence for a moment before he looked around him, carefully, and spoke again. "I wish to speak to you about a matter of some delicacy, Brachi."

That could mean almost anything. Anything which might be interpreted—from Koscuisko's parochial Dolgorukij point of view—
as potentially representing a remark about deficiencies in a person's
performance of their duty was a matter of the utmost delicacy, and
the Dolgorukij interpretation of "duty" extended all the way from
what a man had for fast-meal to the manner in which he shat the
following morning.

It was with somewhat mixed feelings that Stildyne, taking a survey himself before responding, saw someone who was probably
Dierryk Rukota by his size and shape and the color of his uniform
pausing at several mark's remove to receive the salute of the vector
officer and exchange a few words with her.

"Have to wait," Stildyne said. "Artillery officer abaft the labboard
beam."

He had no idea what it meant to be abaft the labboard beam,
except in the general sense of approaching. The phrase came out of
his mouth from the antiquated retrieval systems of his childhood
memories, which was a surprise in itself, as he hadn't remembered
ever having had a childhood.

"The bonds," Koscuisko said. "I have stolen them. I need to
talk to you about what happens next."

Stildyne had suspected as much, but Koscuisko had handled
things carefully, and the fact that he had had serendipitous access to
a surgery where nobody was watching him come and go down here
on Connaught Station meant that nobody else would have thought
twice. General Rukota was moving toward them again, however, so
Stildyne had to put away his feelings about Koscuisko's confession
and his apparent desire to make Stildyne his co-conspirator for later
examination.

"I'll look out for them," Stildyne said. "We can talk later, when
we get to Emandis, or is there something I need to know sooner?"

Koscuisko had turned around to watch Rukota's approach. "I
would want you to know before I tell them," Koscuisko said unhappily. "Out of respect, if nothing else." What did that mean, when
"respect" was all he was ever going to get from Andrej Koscuisko?
"But you are right. It will be safest."

Koscuisko had a privacy field available to him in his office, where
it was understood that sensitive formal discussions on medical issues
might take place. Koscuisko couldn't have him in to the office for a

private tête-à-tête without somebody in communications getting too curious about it, though, not unless Stildyne was under medical care for one reason or another.

The temptation for someone to do a periodic maintenance override when the standard "privacy field invoked" notification came up in the communications center might be too much to expect a bored technician to resist, and the Ship's Intelligence Officer herself was one of the most bored people on board the *JFS Ragnarok*, from what Stildyne knew of her history. Either bored, or unnaturally curious—the effect was the same, and he had been grateful enough for Two's prying in the past when he had needed to know where Koscuisko was. One way or another, Koscuisko's feeling that he didn't want to talk about next steps on board of the *Ragnarok* made perfect sense to Stildyne.

"Later, then, your Excellency, and I'll look out for it." Stildyne didn't know how good Rukota's hearing was, and did not want to risk calling Koscuisko "Andrej." Stildyne wasn't sure he'd ever heard anybody use Koscuisko's name in all of the years that Koscuisko had been assigned. Except for Captain Lowden, come to think of it—Lowden had enjoyed flaunting his superior rank—but Lowden was dead, and Rukota hadn't been with the *Ragnarok* then anyway. "General Rukota, sir."

Rukota didn't need to tell Stildyne to stand at ease; Koscuisko was the superior officer, so it went without saying that Stildyne was doing as Koscuisko had instructed him. Rukota gave Koscuisko his salute accordingly. "Thanks, Chief. Your Excellency. Captain sends me to retrieve you as soon as possible. Wants your report on our current virus situation, sir."

Garrity and Hirsel had come back out of the ship and were waiting at a polite distance. Koscuisko nodded. "Very well, General, let us go to the transport ship. Mister Stildyne. Have the gentlemen pack."

Not if there was much to pack, although Koscuisko would be anxious about the rhyti-brewer. He was running low. His cousin Stanoczk would be bringing a fresh supply of leaf, Stildyne guessed. "Very good, your Excellency. Right away."

And he'd find out all about whatever else was going on when Koscuisko got to Emandis proper. The sooner they got there, then, the sooner Stildyne would know, so there was no time to be wasted.

He went off to quarters with Hirsel and Garrity to get packed and report to transport for return to the *Ragnarok*.

THE APPROACH TO Imennou launch field was grimmer and more depressing moment by moment as the courier flew through great greasy clots of black soot even in the upper atmosphere. It was more similar to flying through the ash-cloud days after a volcano had blown out its side than anything Jils could think of, except of course that volcanic ash would settle and work its way back into the soil and improve the drainage of the fields and generally display its positive side in time.

There was no excuse for the roiling gouts of ash from Brisinje's launch field. It would take a much longer time for each particle to settle out of atmosphere, longer still to sink into the background and degenerate and yield what nutrients or supplements the Brisinje florae and faunae could take for their use from burned fuel and vaporized metal.

By the time the courier touched down at Imennou launch field, Jils was even more depressed about the whole thing than she'd already been from her first glimpse of the cloud over the Reggidout River. Her feeling was out of proportion, she knew that, but all of the tension she had been unable to banish or redirect over the months of the murder investigation seemed to have surfaced strictly in order to attach itself to the first good external cause she could find.

Imennou was a pretty launch field, with white walls for blast containment and cheerful green vines of crimson-and-gold trumpet-shaped flowers draped over almost every vertical surface. The architecture ran to flat roofs and low buildings—nothing more than four levels above ground—so that as the courier ran its excess momentum out on the launch field, one saw nothing more than the flower-covered vines, the brilliant white of the blast walls, and the deep blue sky beyond.

It was a restful sight, presenting the illusion that one was almost alone, but there were of course people waiting for them behind the window of a thermal barrier—Security by the color of the uniform—and a ground-car on the track at the back wall by the sliding gate.

The courier slowed as it neared the waiting party. She could count the Security from her place in the wheelhouse; Security she understood, but there was someone there who was not Security, and something inside her chest believed she recognized him.

"Flown into Imennou before?" she asked the pilot, whose handling of the landing had been expert. It didn't have to mean that the approach had been as smooth as it had been because the pilot was already familiar with the air currents and the prevailing weather conditions, but the skill displayed in the landing had been a potential hint. If the pilot was familiar with the area, maybe he'd know who those people were.

"Not really, Dame. Through Brisinje, mostly. Ferried your counterpart there, from time to time, if it's not a breach of confidence to say so."

No, of course it wasn't. Not unless the pilot had been instructed to say nothing. If he'd been told to keep shut, he'd never have mentioned it. "If I didn't know better, I'd be tempted to guess that I know him," Jils said carefully, soliciting the name without coming right out and asking for it. The closer the courier got, the more familiar that one man looked. Above average height for a Jetorix hominid, his arms crossed over his broad chest with his hands wrapped around his elbows in a very familiar fashion, an easy smile, hair that curled and waved around his temples and fell to his strong shoulders like the decoration of a ritual mask—

"Specialist Delleroy," the pilot said, as if he hadn't noticed being pumped for information. "I don't have much experience with people at your level, Dame, if you don't mind my saying so. He's got the common touch, though, doesn't he?"

And surely there was not another Bench Specialist in known Space who stood quite so confidently and self-contained as that, perfectly calm, perfectly ready for any event, perfectly in command of the very ground on which he stood. Delleroy. Padrake Delleroy.

She wasn't going to think about his common touch, or his uncommon touch, or any of the different sorts of touches at which Padrake excelled. It hadn't been five years; she'd thought it was hard enough five years ago, but seeing him there, now, as if he was waiting for her, was almost more than she could bear.

There was refuge and sanctuary to be had in Padrake's embrace. No one had ever made her feel so cherished, so vulnerable, so taken care of—all things to be avoided like a death sentence, by a Bench Specialist, because any sort of loss of objectivity could be just that, and when a Bench Specialist failed and died, there was too good a chance that innocent civilians would suffer for the error. It was just the nature of the profession.

Padrake had understood that as well as she had. They had parted by mutual agreement, severing their swiftly-becoming-too-close relationship while it could still be done without hurt and recrimination. She hadn't seen him since because she couldn't help remembering how good it had been with him, how it had just kept on getting better, how she could have given up her career and her duty and her mission and lived happily as Padrake's partner if only she had not been Bench Specialist Jils Tarocca Ivers. If only.

That wasn't the point, she admonished herself. The point was that it hadn't been feelings of hostility that had kept them apart, but rather too strong an echo of the reasons why the connection had had to be severed in the first place.

"I do know him, then." She'd been silent for almost too long; the pilot would be wondering. "I hadn't realized he was at Brisinje, though. I hope he's not driving. He's a demon in a land transport."

"Been here about five years that I know of, Dame." The courier was stopped. The pre-disembarking checks were running with the efficiency that characterized everything on this ship, including its pilot and crew. "There's the all-clear. Free to disembark, Bench Specialist, and it's been the honor of the Emandis Home Defense Fleet to have provided you with transport, on behalf of the rule of Law and the Judicial order."

Formal and polite, as well as efficient, but there was nothing obsequious about the reading the pilot gave the standard formula. "Thank you, pilot, it's been a very enjoyable trip." Maybe that was the wrong word. But it was said. All she could do was move on.

Her kit was already packed and waiting; Karol's note was tucked into her blouse. Down the ramp and out into the painfully clear sunlight. Suddenly the white of the blast walls was almost glaring, too intense to be looked at directly. Was that the reason why so much of the surface was covered with flowering vines? To cut down on the dazzlement?

Padrake had started toward her as she cleared the ramp from the courier's loader. Now he broke into a lazy sort of a jog, something she remembered as hellishly ground-eating even while it looked almost effortless. For a big man, he was very light on his feet, as befit a specialist renowned for his subterfuges and stratagems.

"Jils Ivers! Really you!" he crowed, and took her into his arms for a warm embrace. Which he loosed before she had a chance to decide exactly how she felt about it but not before she noted that he was using the same scent in his toiletries as he had before, something with crisp notes and elements reminiscent of roots and fragrant bark and sharp spices all at once.

"So good to see you, Jils. I hoped it would be you, how many Bench Specialists named Jils Ivers could there be? But still it could have been a ruse on the part of the Second Judge to keep you for herself, at work on a criminal case when the fate of the Jurisdiction is to be determined. Glad it wasn't a ruse. How are you, how have you been?"

How did he think she'd been, living under suspicion, the constant possibility of being assassinated lurking just out of sight behind her chair every waking hour? "Well, all the better for the seeing of you," she mocked him gently with one of his own catchphrases. "Padrake. How have you been keeping yourself?"

"Busy." Of course. He seemed to remember himself only barely in time to refrain from attempting to carry her kit bag, something a man with Padrake's background did almost by reflex in the company of women but which she had suffered only as a special favor during the days of their intimacy. One did not presume to fetch and carry for Bench Specialists—not even, or especially, if one was a Bench Specialist. "This way."

The ground-car that was waiting for them could well be the First Secretary's official vehicle; it almost had to be, unless Brisinje was in the habit of provoking its subordinate Courts by flaunting its wealth. Not a good idea, in Jils' estimation, but some administrations did take the stance that a convincing display of power and luxury could contribute to the public wealth and welfare—so long as it was perceived to be attainable. So long as people believed that anybody could grow up to be First Judge—or at least First Secretary, if they were men.

"Nice transport, Padrake. Have you been prospecting in ice fields in your spare time?"

He snorted. "You know better than that." Bench Specialists didn't have any spare time. "It's a long ride overland to Brisinje, six hours, maybe longer. No-fly zone in effect because of the unpredictable thermals and the smoke, and nobody was using this, so why not? Hop in."

The driver would be in the front compartment of the ground-car, shielded, isolated in the cabin. The ground-car opened its doors politely as she approached, the near recliner offering itself to her. As she sat down and let the recliner carry her into the interior of the car, she felt the padding adjust itself around her body, a little more support here, a little lower for the neck-roll there. It was a very nice ground-car indeed.

She lay back and gazed up into the star field displayed against the inside of the roof while Padrake's recliner moved around into its position. The doors closed themselves, the security bands crept slowly and meekly across her belly, across her thighs, to meet and mesh and welcome her in so that she would be protected from translation injury in the unlikely event of an accident. Or at least prevented from becoming a translation injury herself. Security webbing could do little to stop objects from coming toward her at a high rate of speed; the ground-car had other defenses, for that.

Suddenly she wished that Padrake had taken a much less comfortable car. She was so tired. She could hear the subtle crackling sounds in her spine and in her neck as long-tense muscles relaxed. If she wasn't careful, she was going to fall asleep. Maybe there were stimulants on board?

Reaching for the slider that secured the refreshments bar, Jils opened it to have a look at what was available to her. Luxury goods: expensive sweets, premium savories, small containers with some of the most intriguing names in mood-altering potables in known Space. All strictly legal, of course, that went without saying; conspicuous consumption. Jils frowned. She wasn't sure she felt quite comfortable indulging herself in Neris extract or banner-honey or nectar of obaya while Brisinje's launch fields were burning.

"Something the matter?" Padrake asked. "There's kilpers, if you want some. Jade-pressed and shell-filtered, the best stuff, or so people who drink kilpers have told me."

Shaking her head, Jils reached for a retort flask of rhyti. It was the least expensive drink in the cabinet, and it was expensive enough from the label—she'd learned a bit about rhyti and where it grew and what made its grades, keeping up on Koscuisko at Verlaine's instruction.

Most commercial rhyti was a sweet mild pale beverage, but what Koscuisko drank was brewed from the leaf from one series of hill-stations that caught the rain and the wind in the right way or had a unique blend of minerals in its soil or some such combination of factors that yielded an herb that steeped as red as fury and as sharp as iron. It was no wonder he put all that milk and sugar in it. Koscuisko's favorite would take a person's stomach lining right up, surely, if drunk incautiously.

"I was expecting survival rations and water," she lied, to cover her discomfort. "My pilot promised me."

Padrake seemed to consider this claim for a moment, his head half-inclined toward her in the soft soothing yellow cabin light. The ground-car had started moving; she could see its route-reports update, alongside the front console. She scarcely felt it. "I think I've seen that make of courier before. Only one in active service, if I'm not mistaken—Fleet size restrictions, of course. If it's the ship I think it is, I might have met the pilot. Interesting fellow. Who'd you have?"

There was something about the rhyti that was peculiarly delicious. What was it? Surely she was not to be doomed to develop a taste for expensive leaf? Had her issue with rhyti been the result of foolishly restricting herself to what a reasonable person could afford?

"I didn't spend more than a few hours in the wheelhouse. I had work." Which she hadn't done, looking for clues about Karol's note, but Padrake didn't need to know that. "Seemed a competent sort. Emandisan. Ees-ihlet, I think he said."

"Ise-I'let." Padrake's accent made sense of something Jils' ear had almost, but not quite, grasped. She'd heard the name before. She'd thought so at the time, and not wanted to make an issue of it. Now—unwilling to open herself up to teasing from Padrake about losing her powers of recall—Jils shrugged, and put the information aside.

"Yes, something like that. He and I were talking about ground-cars."

"Well, if anyone could have gotten you in to Brisinje under these conditions, it would've been him. Work, you said. The murder? My money's on a jealous subordinate, if you ask me."

"Of course. I can tell you," Jils said confidentially. "For your ears only, needless to say. Not to breathe a hint to another living soul, and so forth. The Clerk of Court did it."

The Clerk of Court had always done it. It was rule number one of popular entertainment. Sometimes she was a Free Government agent in deep cover trying to destabilize a struggling community by cruelly murdering a popular and hard-working Judge and blaming it on the devoted and dedicated First Secretary. Sometimes she had been misled by the First Secretary in his youth, and her child was dead, probably through the long-term effects of something the First Secretary had done to worm his way into the Judge's trust and confidence by making things other than they actually were.

Sometimes she had actually aimed for the position of First Secretary herself, which was widely understood to be a bit unfair since, after all, the most gifted legal scholar under Jurisdiction couldn't hope to be First Judge, not ever, if he was the wrong sex. Administrative posts were a masculine reserve, almost by way of a consolation prize.

People had been arguing the issue of men and the Law for as long as there had been a Bench. The one thing that could always be relied upon was that, in the ultimate analysis, nobody could bring themselves to entrust the highest posts to creatures as ruled by passion and the short-term imperatives of a male's biological role in reproduction as men were. And it was always the clerk of Court who had done murder in Chambers.

It was perfectly true that Undersecretary Tallies—one of Verlaine's protégées—would have had to wait for years and years to be First Secretary himself under any usual circumstances. And there were unquestionably plenty of places where the sudden vacancy at the top had resulted in windfall promotions for numerous intelligent and ambitious people.

None who, unfortunately, had enough of a motive to murder the man who had made their places for them, and all of whom had either good record of where they'd been or other valid and convincing evidence to disqualify them from the list of possible assassins.

There was a Clerk of Court who would have been first on Jils' personal suspect list: psychologically unbalanced, a woman of great cunning but little long-term planning ability, someone who had undergone a fearful ordeal at Verlaine's direction to further Verlaine's agenda, and had seen it come to nothing; who had found herself ignored, back-officed, deprived of Verlaine's confidence and access and finally even any particular regard. It was just too bad that Mergau Noycannir had been dead well before Verlaine was killed.

Jils hadn't been able to puzzle out how Noycannir might have gotten around Verlaine's security, but it was an attractive fantasy to entertain because it was satisfying, comprehensible, made a great deal of intuitive sense, and was also strictly hypothetical, so that a woman could dream all she liked about how Noycannir could have done it.

How could Noycannir have done it?

The ground-car traveled; the cabin was pleasantly cool and quiet and dim. She'd had a flask of rhyti, but rhyti contained a range of chemical compounds that could relax the stressed as easily as they could raise the alertness level of the relaxed or fatigued. There were hours between here and Brisinje, and she was so tired. She closed her eyes.

Forensics was still trying to work out exactly how it had been done, how someone had gotten the monitors to watch their own records and take them for live action. Passive sensors, active surveillance, motion detectors, samplers and scanners and sniffers—and all of the resources compromised, gotten around, fooled into looking the other way while convinced that they were keeping an active guard. Someone had known a great deal about the most sophisticated security the Bench had available; it limited the pool of available players. But not enough.

The recliner adjusted itself to the progressive relaxation of her body, offering warmth where its pinpoint sensors detected muscle stress, firm cushiony support beneath her knees and thighs and ankles that had started to just lie there. She stretched, sighing, and turned her head away, finding just the right angle for her head against the high back of the recliner. It was a good angle. She decided to stay there for a while.

There were private enterprises whose security systems were as complex—or more—so there were people in private enterprise who knew how to get around them. And the issue of whom, exactly, was only part of the interest of the question. Why had Verlaine been murdered? If they knew that, they would know where to look for the whom, and until they could determine the answer to that question, it was a long slow search for evidence and the identity of the perpetuators.

Something shifted near her side. She heard Padrake move—to catch something, she thought—and opened her eyes, blinking at the schematic that displayed their route, trying to focus. Had she fallen asleep?

Something had slid over to one side on the luggage-stow overhead. That was what it was. Padrake was just setting things to rights. Her kit. His reader-panel. Whatever else was up there. He could be a bit compulsive about neatness, but there were circumstances in which his personal dedication to symmetry and balance and not leaving things undone—or worse half-done—could yield very enjoyable results, which she was not going to contemplate because she didn't need the distraction.

Once upon a time, she and Padrake had known how to take advantage of a ground-car and a few stray hours. That was over, but it was a useful reminder—she still knew how to take appropriate advantage of opportunities such as this when they were offered. Why shouldn't she? This was Padrake. She knew him. She was as safe with Padrake as she would have been alone.

Stretching and settling herself with a clear intent she closed her eyes again. "Wake me when we get there," she suggested, and quieted her mind to sleep.

CHAPTER FOUR
NEWS FROM FAR PLACES

SECURITY CHIEF STILDYNE signaled at Koscuisko's office door with a fair degree of intrigued anticipation in his heart. It was a very unusual feeling, because for years he'd forgotten what it was like to have any feeling in his heart at all. "Due on dock in sixteen, your Excellency. Shall we go?"

The door slid open without a return signal, and Stildyne stepped through with a small, secret grin. Koscuisko had mixed feelings about the Malcontent "Cousin" Stanoczk, a man who in this instance was actually Koscuisko's blood relation as well as "Cousin" by religious title.

Stildyne had some feelings about Cousin Stanoczk himself, mostly having to do with the fact that Stoshi was very like Andrej Koscuisko in some ways and completely unlike Koscuisko in other rather interesting ones. Cousin Stanoczk was coming aboard just before the *Ragnarok* started the preliminary approach to its vector spin, so he'd be staying for several days, until the *Ragnarok* came off vector in Emandis space. Stildyne had an issue or two to present to Cousin Stanoczk for reconciliation.

"I am directly going," Koscuisko said, standing up from behind his work table. "For a moment I was concerned, Brachi, that you meant to scold me for laps."

Oh, better and better. "Yes, if you're going to bring it up. But we can discuss that later."

Giving Stildyne a disgusted look, Koscuisko set the jumble of data cubes on his desk-surface into array. "Of bullying, you will please restrict yourself to a single item at a time. And if I hear any words from Stoshi, I will know that you have been telling tales, so comport yourself accordingly."

So much unsaid, and that was better than an hour-long monologue. Stildyne's smile broadened almost despite himself. Koscuisko shuddered theatrically, and left the room, shielding his eyes with one hand as he passed the clearly horrifying sight. Stildyne didn't mind.

He knew perfectly well that he was ugly. He'd been born ugly, raised ugly by ugly in the middle of ugly's eldest brother, and improved on ugly by acquiring appropriate decorations over time: a permanently deformed nose, the scar tissue that had made it possible for him to raise a single eyebrow because the other wasn't working any more, and similar beauty marks too numerous to mention.

Until Dierryk Rukota had come on board, he'd been the ugliest man assigned to the *Ragnarok*, and even now the question was undecided. They met for regular competitions on the killshot court. Stildyne was confident that, in time, his native ugly and accumulated enhancements would prove more than even "Sharksmile" Rukota's charms could match, superior rank or no.

By the time Stildyne and his officer reached the docks in the *Ragnarok's* maintenance atmosphere, the courier was already clearing the hull, which had been opened only as far as necessary to let a ship pass into atmosphere. It wasn't prudent to make a vector transit with an unprotected atmosphere. Even if the hull could be replaced, there was drag to be considered, and the risk of a rogue particle— even on vector, the emptiest space in known Space.

"He has brought the thula," Koscuisko said. "I hope this does not also mean his pilot." There was an unusual tone in Koscuisko's voice, one of hunger and resentment. Stildyne knew that Koscuisko was still struggling with things he had learned—and people he had found—when he'd gone home to marry his wife and make an heir of his son; but he didn't think Koscuisko had anything to worry about. The Malcontent Cousin Ferinc was unlikely to have come.

Regardless of what Koscuisko felt about it, Ferinc had impressed Stildyne as being genuinely—and passionately—invested in the welfare of Koscuisko's child. Also Koscuisko's wife, but Cousin Stanoczk had explained that men were expected to turn a blind eye to Malcontents in their households, or suffer the displeasure of the Saint.

"Surely not, sir," Stildyne said soothingly. "Ferinc's probably too busy." Perhaps that wasn't so very helpful, after all. Fortunately the courier had docked and the ramp had descended, so Koscuisko didn't have time to consider how deeply he would elect to be offended at the reminder.

"You are as helpful and supportive as ever," Koscuisko noted sourly. "I should complain to Stoshi about you." Rather than the other way around. "See if I do not. It is not enough that a man is to be hounded for his laps. There is no justice in the world, no charitable forbearance, no—"

Koscuisko's Cousin Stanoczk came down the ramp, and Koscuisko shut up. There were ways in which Koscuisko might be said to be afraid of his Malcontent cousin; Stildyne had often considered attempting to discover what the trick was, but there were more interesting questions to be asked.

Behind Cousin Stanoczk followed not another Malcontent—certainly not the Cousin Ferinc about whom Koscuisko was so exercised in spirit—but someone Stildyne recognized as being potentially even more controversial.

"Derush!" Cousin Stanoczk called happily, and quickened his pace down the ramp to embrace Koscuisko with an enthusiasm that was not notably reciprocated. "It is good to see you. And Chief Brachi Stildyne, yes, you are looking well." Cousin Stanoczk didn't offer to kiss him, at least not in public. Probably just as well. "You remember the Bench Specialist, I expect?"

Following Cousin Stanoczk down the ramp and toward Koscuisko at a much more moderate pace, keeping his distance, came a man of middling height—taller than Koscuisko, but that wasn't difficult—with an iron-gray moustache and clear blue eyes whose weariness was general to all life: Bench Intelligence Specialist Karol Aphon Vogel. Stildyne recognized him if Koscuisko did not, but Koscuisko apparently did.

"Specialist Vogel, yes." Koscuisko seemed at least as wary as he was surprised. "To what do we owe the honor? There are people who have been looking for you."

Vogel nodded very politely, all but bowed. Bench Specialists were under no obligation to salute anybody, let alone mere Ship's Inquisitors. Vogel was a polite man, however, and the less he reminded people that he was a Bench Specialist the more likely they might be to forget that he was uniquely dangerous, Stildyne supposed.

"You're holding evidence that I'd like to have a look at, your Excellency. Cousin Stanoczk was kind enough to offer me a lift."

Now Cousin Stanoczk took Koscuisko by the arm and turned him toward the airlock that gave access to the interior of the ship. The multi-chambered airlock was open; it was only ever closed when the maintenance atmosphere had to be purged for periodic refresh.

Cousin Stanoczk seemed very sure of where he was going, but why not? He was a Malcontent.

In light of the Malcontent's access to things, Stildyne wouldn't be surprised, he reminded himself, if it turned out that the Saint had a cruiser-killer class warship just like the *Ragnarok* of his very own. People who could afford a Kospodar thula—so expensive a piece of machinery that even the Bench had been unable or unwilling to afford more than a few of them—were clearly capable of presenting all sorts of similar surprises.

"You would do well to secure your craft before you leave the area," Koscuisko grumbled. "I will not be held responsible. Wheatfields desires the thula. I hope you have brought war-hounds."

"Only the crew," Cousin Stanoczk assured Koscuisko in reply. "Nobody you know. Trust me on this."

He was lying. Stildyne was sure of it. Why didn't Koscuisko detect the smell of it immediately? Maybe he just declined to notice, because Stanoczk was Malcontent and Koscuisko's socialization would not allow him to challenge the Malcontent on much of anything. Or maybe, just maybe, Koscuisko didn't see that. Hard to believe. But Koscuisko hadn't spent as much time watching people who looked a great deal like Cousin Stanoczk in terms of their size and build and habit of speech as Stildyne had in the years since Koscuisko had been assigned to the *Ragnarok*.

He'd have to ask Cousin Stanoczk about it. Unlike Koscuisko, he had no problem challenging Malcontents on things. There were ways in which challenging specific Malcontents could be a lot of fun, in fact, though Stildyne didn't really think he should be thinking about that with Koscuisko and Cousin Stanoczk alike right in front of him. He waited respectfully until Vogel had followed the two of them before falling into place behind Vogel, instead.

There was only one piece of evidence in Koscuisko's custody that a Bench Specialist was likely to be interested in. There was only one piece of evidence in Koscuisko's custody at all, just at present. A clerk of Court from Chilleau Judiciary had come to Chelatring Side—the ancestral fortress of Koscuisko's family—to draw Koscuisko into some sort of a trap, and had used a forged record as bait.

The clerk was dead.

Koscuisko had returned to the *Ragnarok*—after putting the longed-for freedom that First Secretary Verlaine had offered him on hold—because so long as the forged record existed, the false evidence it contained had to be handled carefully, and the lawful custodian of any given record was an officer in possession of a Writ to Inquire.

Cousin Stanoczk would have been interested in how the forgery had been done as a matter of abstract principle. At the time, Bench Specialist Ivers, who had been present at the exposure of the record's evidence as false, had been too deeply shocked at the implications of its very existence to have expressed much interest in the mechanics.

Vogel had gone missing out of Burkhayden months before all of that had happened, however. So what Vogel had to do with the evidence in Secured Medical was beyond Stildyne.

"For that you must to the captain speak," Koscuisko said over his shoulder to Vogel, as Cousin Stanoczk drew Koscuisko on.

When Vogel began to produce the appropriate rote response—something along the lines of "naturally nothing will be done without Brevet Captain ap Rhiannon's knowledge and consent," Stildyne expected—Koscuisko shook his head and cut him off.

"No, I mean that you must speak to her. The Engineer has crates of disposable vent solvents stacked five tiers deep in Secured Medical, and I do not have the authority to order them moved."

True enough. When Koscuisko had returned to the *Ragnarok,* his presence had been accepted only upon understanding of some rules and guidelines—some Koscuisko's, some ap Rhiannon's. Among those rules and guidelines had been Koscuisko's warning that he would execute the Protocols only on a strictly limited footing; and ap Rhiannon's answering requirement that Koscuisko would do nothing whatever in Secured Medical, which would be made over to the Ship's Engineer for a closet. There were things in Secured Medical to which Koscuisko alone had access, but first he had to get past Wheatfields' crates.

"We are going to staff meeting, even now," Cousin Stanoczk assured Vogel. "My cousin would know, but he is not good about staff meetings. No doubt his captain will be speaking to him on a not very distant occasion about that fact—" perfectly fair, Stildyne knew, Koscuisko was a very unsatisfactory attender of staff meetings, but he always had been, so it was nothing specific to Jennet ap Rhiannon "—but for now he evades censure because he is prompt to the mark, and with company. He is grateful to me for this. Is he not? Look you, Chief Stildyne, have you seen such a sincerely grateful scowl in all of your years?"

He wasn't seeing any such scowl right now, because Koscuisko had turned around. "Never," he admitted truthfully, wondering if it had been strictly necessary for Cousin Stanoczk to remark on "all" his years.

Cousin Stanoczk shook Koscuisko by the shoulder enthusiastically. "See? See? We are all in agreement, Derush. No, don't thank me." A request more likely to be honored than many of Cousin Stanoczk's, Stildyne expected. "Chief. I will come and see you later, if I may. I will tell you about staff meetings, and many other interesting things."

Yes, he'd just bet Cousin Stanoczk would. He'd been hoping for it. "I'll be waiting," he promised. "Your cousin owes me laps, though."

"Then I shall see to it that he is safely out of the way, and will not interrupt. I have letters for you, Derush. Also for your good Kerenko."

They were at the lift-nexus that would carry Koscuisko, his cousin and Vogel deep into the heart of the *Ragnarok*, to the officer's mess. To staff meeting.

The frown Koscuisko gave Stildyne as he turned around in the lift to face front was worth three month's pay for its combination of betrayal, resentment, and underlying amusement. Stildyne bowed to that frown, feeling very cheerful, and went away to his office to wait for Cousin Stanoczk to come and fill him in on all the gossip from Chelatring Side.

THE OFFICER'S MESS on the *Ragnarok* was actually a common room of sorts. The chief warrant officers and shift supervisors took their meals here, and Ship's Primes and Command Branch; Andrej's department chiefs ate here as well—but below the Bar, which had always seemed unreasonable to Andrej. They were older than he was—or had been, in the earlier years of his Fleet duty—considerably more qualified for leadership by virtue of actual experience, and everybody knew that the only reason an edge-new surgeon from Mayon's colleges took pride of place was because Fleet granted special privileges to Inquisitors, one of which was rank.

Ship's Inquisitors with a decent sense of their own shortcomings sat quietly back and let senior officers run the section. Most of the people who elected to enter Fleet Orientation Station Medical to qualify for a Writ to Inquire were decidedly under-qualified, after all. Medical students who could find anything else to do with their certifications, anything else at all, generally took other routes in preference to accepting rank in Fleet when rank came with particular responsibilities.

Andrej knew that—as an honor graduate, a man with the generously bestowed praise of his teachers and the administration of the Mayon Medical Center—he was an exception to the rule of mediocrity in ship's surgeons. The fact had never afforded him much satisfaction. A patient had nothing less than an absolute right to expect the very best a surgeon could possibly manage to provide. No healing Andrej was fortunate enough to effect through skill and education and the grace of the Holy Mother of all Aznir could balance out a single blow struck in cruelty, to punish or deter, in Secured Medical.

"No, we ask for all nine battle cannon," the artilleryman, Dierryk Rukota, was insisting as Andrej reached the open doorway to the officer's mess. "All right, so we already have one in reserve. If we only ask for eight, we only remind people that we've got one. That gun is contraband. We shouldn't be counting it."

One wall of the officer's mess could be covered with a plot-scan for schematics or strategic planning. Rukota stood there now, one hand to the wall, arguing with the captain—brevet or acting Captain ap Rhiannon—a short woman with her hair done up with the pins that bore the rank-markers peculiar to crèche-bred, her shoulders squared, her arms akimbo, all points skeptical in her body language and her expression alike.

"Two says Emandis Station only has nine battle cannon. One full issue, so they can respond to replacement requests. If we ask for all nine, they can decline to issue any. It would leave them without a cannon in reserve until they can get a new issue from Central Stores, and that could take months in this environment."

"Which is Emandis' problem and not yours, your Excellency. You are looking for your base load. Any depot rated for full replenishment has a charter to be able to respond at any time, and if they only give us eight—if we asked for eight, we'd get seven. Maximum. We put in for nine battle cannon, your Excellency."

Rukota had the rank-tags right in his speech, but there was not much to doubt in Andrej's mind that Rukota actually saw a junior officer in front of him. He had that issue himself, to a lesser extent. She had warned him—Stildyne as well—if he wanted back on board the *Ragnarok* on anything like a permanent basis, he was going to have to accept her as his captain, not because she had earned it, but because that was the way it was. He was rather proud of the progress he'd made, but it was also true that she was not over-punctilious about her perquisites, sensitive to the limitations inherent in the situation.

Had it been as difficult for his clinic chiefs to call him "sir"? It could only have been more distasteful yet; ap Rhiannon was very young, but she was not a professional torturer.

Neither was he any longer. He and ap Rhiannon had agreed: he would use a speak-serum if information was truly required, and she would not direct him to return to Secured Medical, not ever. How was she going to react to this?

Stoshi coughed politely, apparently unhappy with the rate at which Andrej was proceeding to the introductions. The captain glanced over to where Andrej stood in the doorway, looked away again to the schematic on the wall—the *Ragnarok*'s armaments plan, how many of how heavy of what to be put where. She had no more turned back to the schematic than her head jerked back to stare at Andrej again. Andrej dared not smile.

"Please excuse my tardiness, your Excellency," Andrej said, and bowed to his superior officer. "I was meeting this disgusting person on the docks. He is called Cousin Stanoczk, a religious professional, a Malcontent. And yes. We are also in fact related in the same degree."

When they'd been children, it had been a joke to play on people who didn't know them very well: from a suitable distance, the fact that Stoshi's eyes were dark and Andrej's pale did not distinguish them immediately. There had been pranks. But Stoshi's voice had gotten deep and resonant, and Andrej was still tenor. There were other differences between them, but Andrej was not going to speculate on how well his good Chief of Security might have studied on what they were.

"Doctor." She sounded surprised; he almost always found a good reason why he was not needed at staff meetings. "Cousin

Stanoczk, Two warned us that you were coming. We're pleased to
grant you the freedom of the ship. We're indebted to you for the
previous use of your thula."

"Yours" in the general sense, of course; it wasn't Stoshi's thula, it
was the Malcontent's thula. "You are very kind, your Excellency. The
Saint is pleased to have been of service. I impose upon you now for
a different purpose, however: to request a favor, which Specialist
Vogel will explain."

Whether Vogel would remember ap Rhiannon was not something Andrej felt inclined to guess. It seemed clear that ap Rhiannon
remembered Vogel.

"This person was not on your passenger manifest," Two said
accusingly, rustling her wings. She was standing in a chair at the table
above the Captain's Bar—on the raised platform where only Ship's
Primes and Command Branch were supposed to sit—bored, surely,
Andrej imagined, because she couldn't see the schematic that the
captain and Rukota were arguing over. Perhaps there was a tone-
map of some sort there for the benefit of bats.

Andrej stepped into the room and to one side, to make way for
Vogel. Vogel stopped on the threshold and bowed, very properly
indeed, first to the captain and then to the other officers—Ship's
First, the Engineer, Ship's Intelligence—gathered around the table
on the platform. First Officer had stood up, Andrej noted.

"I'm very gratified to hear it, your Excellency," Vogel said to
Two. "A person's got to have some secrets, after all." And Bench
Specialists didn't necessarily show up on anybody's manifest. "Captain ap Rhiannon. I've come to request access to a piece of evidence
that your Ship's Inquisitor is holding in Secured Medical. In order to
pursue an investigation, I'd like to examine the forged record that
Koscuisko brought back here from Azanry when he returned from
leave."

When he'd cut his home leave short and come back to the
Ragnarok, Vogel meant. Or maybe not. Maybe Vogel didn't know
the details. Why would he care that Andrej had left his wife and child
without even a good-bye in order to bring evidence back to a ship
which had somehow transformed itself into a dangerous mutineer
in his absence?

Ap Rhiannon sat down at one of the tables that had been
pushed back toward the front wall of the room to clear a space

for close-up study of the schematic on the wall. "Interesting," she said. "Who says we have any such item on board? A forged record, you say. I'd expect a Bench Specialist to be much more careful with his language."

Specialist Ivers had been anxious to keep its very existence as quiet as possible. It had been Mergau Noycannir, an old enemy and quite mad, who had brought it to Azanry—to Chelatring Side; Mergau Noycannir had been a clerk of Court at Chilleau Judiciary. The incident could have been used to discredit the Second Judge just when the Selection was due to be made. It was still a potential weapon, Andrej supposed, but more than that, it was their best evidence that the alleged conspiracy to murder the previous captain of the *Ragnarok* was a frame of particularly shocking illegality.

The Record in concept was still the cornerstone of the Law, the impartial keeper of legally admissible, lawfully obtained evidence. If evidence that was not legally admissible or lawfully obtained could be put on record, then the entire system that relied on evidence would lose its credibility.

"I understand your concern, your Excellency, and speak as bluntly as I do only because I believe myself to be in the company of people who are perfectly well aware that a Record has been compromised. Now I will share another piece of dangerous information with you, so you'll understand why I'm here. I have evidence that the forged record that your chief medical officer brought here from Azanry is not the first such forged Judicial instrument. I believe, in fact, that at least one judicial warrant has been similarly improperly released."

A warrant? Or could it be *the* warrant, the one Vogel had given to him at Burkhayden before he'd left, the one with his name on it—an execution order that Vogel had claimed to have exercised against Fleet Captain Lowden of unlamented memory?

Not possible. Vogel couldn't be talking about that warrant. If he'd believed that warrant was forged, he wouldn't have exercised it. If he hadn't exercised it, then Lowden had not been executed by Judicial decree. If Vogel hadn't killed Lowden, someone else had. If Vogel hadn't been the person that the harried housemaster at the service house had shown up to the suite that Lowden was occupying shortly before the murder had taken place, then it might even have been Andrej himself after all.

And he'd given that warrant to Stoshi, besides. But he'd asked Stoshi to investigate, and what would be more natural than for Stoshi to have called in a Bench Specialist? Stoshi wouldn't have known the background. Andrej hadn't told him. How could he have told the Malcontent, "Stoshik, I have murdered my commanding officer because he sent an innocent man to torture. Vogel came to Burkhayden to kill me, but he pretended it had been Lowden all along, because Vogel didn't like Lowden even more than Vogel doesn't care for me." No, impossible, clearly impossible.

Ap Rhiannon had no such insight to paralyze her. "If you say so, Specialist Vogel. What do you hope to gain by examination of the record?"

"It's taken time to analyze the warrant, your Excellency, but I believe I've isolated the forgery's fingerprints. There's a genuine authorization imbedded there, but in such a way that there had to have been collusion. I suspect that there's genuine evidence similarly imbedded in the forged record, and you may recall that all such authorization codes are specific to an individual or judicial center."

That was true. A Record was legal evidence in part because its contents were placed on record by a legal officer. Ship's Inquisitors served a dual function for that purpose.

Ap Rhiannon frowned. "Locate the code, find the origin? If I was forging a record, I'd see to it that you couldn't track me, Bench Specialist."

"Indications are that the forgery might not have been that carefully done, your Excellency. There are signs of an unskilled user. The Bench warrant would never have been examined after its exercise, had it not been for specific, suspicious circumstances. The record might have been built to accomplish only a specific, time-limited purpose, to be safely destroyed as soon as possible by the woman in whose possession it was at the time that the forgery was discovered. There's a risk. You'd like to know, though, as much as anybody, I'm certain of it."

The captain shook her head. "Not really. Koscuisko says the record is forged and I believe him, but that doesn't mean I want anything to do with it. Serge, can you get a path cleared through to Koscuisko's evidence locker?"

"I'll have to send my crew through decontamination afterward," Wheatfields said. "Give me three eights, your Excellency."

Ap Rhiannon nodded. "Done. General Rukota, please accompany the Bench Specialist to Secured Medical to represent the interests of this Command. Doctor, every professional courtesy, and so on." She was speaking to him now, so Andrej had to do his imitation of a man who had been paying close attention. "Specialist Vogel, it will be a few eights, and I don't care to have Bench Specialists wandering around my ship without more of an idea about why they're here and what they're looking for. How does a ready-room in Security sound to you?"

Well, that was moderately rude. Vogel had told her why he was here and what he was looking for, but Andrej couldn't fault her for not being too ready to take Vogel's statements at face value.

Vogel bowed his head. "I'll be very comfortable, I'm sure, your Excellency. I'm told that the bean tea is much improved lately since the *Ragnarok* restocked at Silboomie Station. Thank you."

"Right. Very well, then." Ap Rhiannon shifted her gaze back to Dierryk Rukota, who had been standing quietly with his back to the schematic on the wall, his arms folded—perhaps coincidentally—directly in front of some details on the *Ragnarok's* combat readiness assessment. "We'll continue this later. First Officer. Let's review the munitions stores, shall we?"

Rukota bowed to ap Rhiannon and came forward for Vogel, not quite putting arm around Vogel's shoulders but something close to it. "Ready room, it is," Rukota said cheerfully. "Do you play cards?"

Stoshi tapped Andrej on the shoulder and jerked his head toward the corridor behind them. Oh, Andrej supposed Stoshi was right; they were dismissed. Wheatfields would be looking for him at his duty station. It was mid-shift. He had documentation to review, always documentation to review, and he wanted to make an appointment to consult with his Chief of Psychiatric, Doctor Farilk, on a personal issue.

Andrej made his salute to his captain, who nodded crisply in return. Stoshi had him by the arm. Wheatfields was staring. No. He was not even going to begin to travel in that field.

Still and all, and quite apart from the aggravation that Stoshi could represent, they were related and had been much together as children, and he was fond of his cousin. When they reached his office—Andrej willfully ignoring the stares they got as they went

past; what, had these people never seen a Malcontent before?—
Andrej went to the rhyti-brewer to draw the both of them a flask.

"You travel with Bench Specialists in these days?" he asked, just
to open the conversation. "The Saint keeps strange bedfellows."

Stoshi accepted the flask that Andrej offered him with a cheerful grin. "Else would not be the Saint, Derush, may he wander in
bliss. The first thing that a person discovers in search of the truth
behind an article is that there was an unhappy man who had left
himself in Gonebeyond to research a similar problem. It is always
good to use someone else's resources, Drushik. The Saint approves.
It leaves much more money to buy drink."

It did make sense. Vogel had been unhappy about the Warrant;
that was why Vogel had not exercised it against its named intended,
Andrej Ulexeievitch Koscuisko. If he thought about it, he wouldn't
expect a Bench Specialist to simply let such a question drop, and it
had been Vogel, after all, who had suggested that Andrej enlist the
assistance of the Malcontent.

The record had come from Mergau Noycannir, Chilleau Judiciary. Vogel wouldn't have known exactly where the Warrant had
come from—that was held in confidence to minimize reprisals after
the fact—but the simplest explanation for its existence led back to
Noycannir. How had she obtained it? How had she forged the record?
Andrej had not attempted to examine the record himself; he was
not a forensic specialist.

"How are things at home, then, if you have brought me news?"

He didn't want to go to his desk. There was documentation
there. Work that he had to do, and meant to be neglecting, in the
next several days—once they arrived at Emandis Station. Instead, he
led the way to the two-chair conference area at the back of his
office, invoking the privacy field on his way. No one would think
twice about it, and they were more than welcome to sneak by his
open door and stare. A man couldn't conspire with his door open,
could he? They didn't see many Dolgorukij in Fleet. At least not on
the *Ragnarok*, whose population had been more stable in recent years
than was the Fleet norm because people posted to the *Ragnarok* very
frequently had absolutely nowhere else to go.

"I have brought letters, Derush," Stoshi said. In his courier pouch
that he was wearing over his shoulder, and which he unlimbered as
he spoke before he sat down. "And words about the melon harvest,

but that will wait. You are stuck with me for several days, after all. What does one do for a party on board a warship?"

"One assigns oneself extra laps, Stoshik, and takes a cold shower." Parties. On the *Ragnarok*. The very idea. Yes, he'd had a going-away party as he was leaving for his visit home—ultimately cut short; the visit, not the party, which had been going strong when he'd left it. "We are all sober and hard-working and abstemious here and have no recreation to offer Malcontents."

Oh, as soon as Andrej said it, he wished that he had not. Hastening to continue before Stoshi could make an impertinent remark about one's Chief of Security, Andrej grasped at the thought uppermost in his mind and voiced it with a sort of desperation. "What is it that you have been doing, to find the Bench Specialist? Dame Ivers would very much like news of her companion."

Stoshi shook his head. "I am prevented by my promise to Karol Aphon, Derush, who feels that it is up to him decide when he is ready to return from Gonebeyond space. Where he's been courting the Flag Captain, the Walton Agenis, and I'm fond of the man who married her niece, even if he is a Sarvaw born and bred. No. I've been to Rudistal, and borrowed some resources from the Church there. You might remember if I asked you for a pocket handkerchief that had no hole in it."

As references went, this was one of Stoshi's more obscure, but whether by premeditation or accident, it hit on things that had been very much on Andrej's mind recently since his work with Dawson's people down on Connaught Station. Handkerchief. Kaydence, one of the bond-involuntaries who had been with Andrej at Rudistal, a man granted revocation of Bond for his role in saving the *Scylla* during the battle over Eild. The nun at Rudistal that Andrej had hired out of the service house and installed to pray for Joslire's spirit; Kaydence had taken up with her, with Ailynn, Kaydence who had so frequently been on Chief Warrant Officer Calleigh Samon's disgraced list for a worn spot in his boot-stocking or failure to produce a clean, mended white-square. So that was it.

"Dangerous avenue for investigation, surely." Kaydence had been Bonded for incautious play in security systems. It was something he apparently found very difficult to control, his passion for getting into computing systems that were none of his business just to see what might be there. Andrej had invoked those skills at the Domitt

Prison to discover the horrifying truth about how Administrator
Geltoi had been stoking his furnaces all of that time to save on fuel.

Now Kaydence was a man reborn, a privileged citizen of the
Bench exempted by the Bench instruction from most taxes and legally immune to many forms of punishment for petty civil trans-
gressions; but warrants were Bench instruments, and if Kaydence
was investigating, that meant that he would necessarily be at play in
Bench judicial systems, and how could he risk it? How could Stoshi
permit such reckless behavior?

"I have my own resources dedicated to special areas of the
hunt, Derush, do not become concerned. We would not endanger
either the person at Rudistal or the one with whom he consorts. No,
we rely on that person for advice and strategy. Technique. In order
to ensure that the Saint may not be associated with the smuggling of
Nurail, which is none of the Saint's business."

Andrej closed his eyes with a grimace of pain. Oh, Kaydence. A
grown man, and one who had survived horrors that Andrej could
not even imagine—though he had been responsible for several—
and involved with the smuggling of persons out of Bench control?
Nurail refugees, escaping to Gonebeyond.

Joslire would be proud to have his name associated with
such an enterprise. And that of course led Andrej back very naturally to his concern, the reason Stoshi had come. "That cannot be
condoned. To attempt to cheat the Bench of the lawfully adjudi-
cated punishment that a man has earned by his own crimes? It
cannot be tolerated."

Stoshi nodded enthusiastically. "Indeed not, Drushik. But it can
be arranged," Andrej was counting on Stoshi to have done just that.
"And desperate men are no respecters of property, either, not chattel or goods or transport, whether in Chambers or the city or in
Church." Or somewhere close to the memorial barrow where Joslire's
ashes had been laid to rest, where his tablet was to be found. Andrej
meant to visit Joslire's tablet, if there was one.

"You know how it is sometimes, Derush," Stoshi continued. "A
man knows that he should not say thus and such a word, because it
will inspire an idea that might not have occurred otherwise to a
person of weak character. It would be best if you held this carefully
in mind, because it may be that there is a Khabardi small freighter
that must stop over near the city of Jeltaria, and you would not be

the man to introduce the concept of wrongdoing to one who is only his assigned duty currently performing."

So Stoshi had done as Andrej had asked him. There would be a ship, loaded, fueled, waiting, with a pre-approved exit trajectory through the dar-Nevan vector for a perfectly innocuous destination that it would never reach. All that was left now for Andrej to do was to explain to his gentlemen and wave good-bye as they left, because it was not to be imagined that a man once freed of his governor would wait meekly for the day when he would be enslaved again in so horrible a fashion.

"You have not answered my question." He couldn't keep the gratitude out of his voice, but he would wait to weep until his gentles were gone from him. "At home. My son. Marana. Tell me how it goes."

Leaning forward, Stoshi reached for his courier pack and opened it. "Letters, Derush. Your parents. Housemasters' reports. Here is the one that you want, though, I think."

Yes. A heavy square of thick white paper folded very carefully by a young person, its face inscribed with a deliberate hand whose hesitation of line, and the thickness of it, spoke of a young lord with a large stylus being as careful as he could manage with the dangerously wet ink. *To my lord father, Andrej Ulexeievitch Koscuisko, of our family prince and heir.*

He'd had letters from Anton from time to time in the past, but seeing this one had quite a different impact on Andrej than they had before. It was so formal. And now that he had met the child, his longing to have him in his arms right here, right now, was almost too heart-piercing to be borne.

"Also, these." Stoshi had not ceased to draw letters out of his bag. "The lady sends to you, Derush. I do not know if she speaks here of Ferinc, but he has never in all of the years that I have known him been so close to happy. I am grateful to you for this, because I have become very fond of him, though he is not of the Blood."

No, Cousin Ferinc was not of the Blood. Cousin Ferinc was Stoshi's pet animal, and pets were not evaluated according to their pedigree. The issue was a sore one with Andrej; he had known Cousin Ferinc by another name before the man had fled to the protection of the Malcontent, the only off-worlder—in Andrej's knowledge—to have been granted the protection of the Saint. It was because of his own fault, his crime against the man. And yet to return home and find a criminal—one whose crimes were so sordid, whose punishment had been more sordid still—so closely associated with his own now-wife Marana, and loved so tenderly by his own son—

"In all of that time believing that I had duty, Stoshik," Andrej said, "I was losing something that I did not even understand. Day by day. It is not only my honor and my sleep that Fleet has cost me. My son's life, Stoshik, my son. Thy Ferinc has been a better father to him than I will ever be, forever after."

"And yet what do you imagine would have been different if you had been at home, Derush? Thickheaded. Your father would have married you to that Ichogatra princess, and the respected lady Marana would have been separate from you until you'd bred a boy to your princess wife regardless. And also there would not have been Ferinc, for whom you have finally done what I have sought to do and failed all of these years, Andrej, and freed him from himself at last."

Tapping Anton's letter against the fingertips of his right hand with an abstracted sort of confusion, Andrej tested Stoshi's claim against his own knowledge of his birth-culture for some flaw, and was unable to find one. The failure gave him no comfort. He looked down at Anton's letter, seeking understanding, but just looking at it made Andrej want to weep for all the time he could have had, had he but realized much sooner that he had no one to blame for the stubbornness that had kept him at his post except himself. Oh, and perhaps the fact that it was treason in the first degree for a man who held the Writ to Inquire to quit his post—but even that perhaps could have been gotten 'round.

"'Yes, good, thank you, Andrej, my special charge in the name of the Saint is now much happier keeping warm the bed of your wife, and loving your son.'" Andrej couldn't keep a species of savagery out of his voice, though he could see the humor. And Stanoczk, shameless and heartless alike, actually laughed, and leaned back in his chair to sup his rhyti.

"Yes, and shows that there is a wolf I had not suspected after all who bares his teeth at your family and sets them all at bay. It is impressive. He could not fight for Marana and your child any more ferociously if they were his, Drushik, and not on loan."

Oh, this was intolerable. "And this is comforting to me?" Andrej demanded. "What sort of new challenge do I face when I can go home, Stanoczk, a duel for the affections of my own Marana? There is strange comfort in this missionary work."

Closing one eye to obtain a better focus, Stoshi peered into the depths of his rhyti-flask, and clearly found it wanting in its emptiness. But Stoshi was clever, and accustomed to doing for himself; and rose to his feet and started across the room toward the rhyti-brewer.

"I can't speak for your lady-wife, Derush," he said with his back turned to Andrej, drawing a fresh flask. "But you need have no fear for the place you have in Anton's heart. He adores you like a saint under Canopy. Surely it is just as well, if you can't say when you will go home. You know that your family has much of an adjustment to accomplish. Marana needs a wolf."

He didn't want the place of a saint under Canopy in Anton's heart. He wanted Ferinc's place. It should be his, to be the wolf to protect his wife and child. How could he call himself a man, and let another do it?

"What else have you for me?" Andrej asked, putting away his morose self-pity for the time being. Malcontents had no patience with self-pity. If there was anybody in this room with genuine cause to feel sorry for himself, surely it was his cousin Stanoczk, condemned to choose between a life of fear and lies on the one hand and the total loss of family, property, rights as a citizen, even title to his own person on the other, and all because he had been born both Dolgorukij and a man who desired the caresses of other men.

For that, Stoshi had elected the Malcontent and a life as a slave, albeit a peculiarly privileged one, rather than attempt to deny his own nature which the Holy Mother herself had decreed for him at the moment of his soul's rebirth; and there were so many other places where he could have been born instead, in which a man's choice of a partner to love and cherish was not restricted to the opposite sex.

"Oh, this? This is for your Kerenko, Derush. Anton has written to him about the sparrows. Something about the sparrows in the gutter outside of his bedroom. I will go and find him and deliver it myself, I have promised very solemnly."

A much thinner letter, to be sure—and the same thick childish hand—but with much more assurance in the lettering. *Right trusty and well beloved.* It was a formula that had been ancient when the Blood had come to Azanry from wherever it was that they had come. Andrej didn't know which of the theories about that he preferred, but he didn't mean to be distracted from the point that this raised.

"He is a dutiful child." The highest praise a parent could bestow: dutiful. Filial. But Anton was so much more, and duty was so trivial a thing beside loyalty and love. "Also very charitable, to remember Lek. It gives me hope for the day when he comes to understand exactly what I am. My family—they mustn't be allowed to spoil that."

It hadn't mattered to him so much before he'd met his child. So long as his son was an abstraction in his mind, a stranger with a limited vocabulary and no learning to speak of, the knowledge that some day his child would understand the shameful truth behind the spectacular acts of cruelty attributed to Andrej's name had been one that had troubled him only on an abstract level.

He had lost perspective. He had met Anton. If he were a lucky man, he would be dead before he had to face the horror in his child's face, and try to condense an answer to the inevitable "How?" out of the fog of blood that filled his brain.

"You will go home, Andrej, and protect him yourself. What does it matter, in the end, whom is to be First Judge? There will be famine in Supicor if we cannot reach them with grain, but they are not Dolgorukij in Supicor, so do we honestly so much care?" Yes, he did, but Andrej knew what point Stanoczk was making. "What may happen on Sarvaw should the selection pend for very much longer, though, I cannot say. And that reminds me."

Stoshi bowed over the table to pass the flask of rhyti to Andrej, as if it was the most gracious gesture under Canopy to give a man a flask of his own rhyti—in a glass to which some forward Malcontent had already pressed his notoriously filthy mouth, and where that had been recently, Andrej did not wish to so much as speculate—when he had not finished his own entirely adequate flask.

"I will carry this away to your Kerenko, and see how you have exercised your good lordship since you have returned. And then I shall have a word to say to thy Stildyne. You will find me on the thula when you want me, Derush, so long as you do not finish your letters within the next six to eight hours."

Your Kerenko, but *thy* Stildyne. The variance in intimacy was all too telling. "I wish you good hunting," Andrej said, a little sourly. Surely it was in poor taste for Stoshi to flaunt his religious duty in Andrej's face in this manner, but that was part of the privilege of the Malcontent, after all. No one expected any good of such depraved souls—which only made Anton's fondness for Ferinc all the more galling. Andrej knew how depraved a soul Ferinc had been, once upon a time. And for any crime Ferinc had done, there were worse crimes to be laid against Andrej's own account, and so many of them.

"Stoshik, I—"

He didn't want to go back out to Secured Medical. They would expect him to wish to avoid it; all except Wheatfields, perhaps. Of all the people on board, it was the Ship's Engineer who was most likely to guess at Andrej's secret. It would not surprise Wheatfields if he guessed. It would not surprise Andrej either.

"It is only Stanoczk, Derush, not Stoshik-eye." But Stoshi had stopped, halfway across the room, and very conveniently still within the privacy barrier, too. A Malcontent was shameless, but discreet. "What is it that you say to me? Bearing in mind that you and I can talk, but later, because I have my rounds to do."

Andrej would not go to Secured Medical alone. He was not even permitted to do that; so he was proof against the trouble of his own spirit. If he attempted to creep back into that place at some odd moment, he would be discovered. And then he would be expected to explain.

"It does not import. Go on about your disgusting Saint's disgusting business, Stoshi." He tried to lighten his tone. Stoshi would not be fooled, but he would respect Andrej's desire to talk about it later. Stoshi waved and was gone, trotting briskly out into the corridor with the letter Anton had written to Kerenko in his hand. One of the Security that had accompanied them from the docking bay to the staff meeting and thence back to this office would be jogging after Stoshi, trying to keep up. Should Andrej check in with Engineering, and see how things went? Should he perhaps seek out Brachi Stildyne?

No. Stildyne would have other things on his mind. And perhaps he didn't even really want someone who knew him as well as Stildyne did to be there when he went back to Secured Medical for the first time since he'd placed that record into evidence.

The first time while he was awake, at any rate. He had been to Secured Medical in his dreams, and that was no particular innovation; it was the emotion that accompanied the visits that had changed. Regret, not for what he had done but for the fact that it was over. He missed it. He knew exactly what had been on that man Birrin's mind. He missed the overwhelming passion and the savage joy, transcendent pleasure that was so much more than merely sexual.

It was humorous. It was a good joke. He had taken secondary honors in psychopharmacology. He was supposed to understand the mechanics of addiction, physical and psychological. Why hadn't he, of all people, realized that a man could not take in so powerful a drug as mastery for all those years, and not feel its lack keenly when it was no longer available to him?

There would be good to come of this, surely. Some year, perhaps Farilk or some other qualified psychiatric doctor would write about the combination of hormones or the brain chemistry that made torture so irresistible a drug for flawed souls like his. It would assist in the diagnosis and treatment of sociopathology and the criminally insane, perhaps.

Only just for now, and even in the midst of so many so much more important things, Andrej was suffering withdrawal from the habit of the past eight years, and did not know how he was to live through it without bringing shame on himself and everyone around him.

CHAPTER FIVE
BRISINJE

THE GROUND-CAR and its escort had loaded, left. Shona Ise-
I'let sat at his station in the wheelhouse of his courier, waiting. Where
was his refuel, where was his atmosphere refresh, his ground crew?

The landing management people had completed their check-
list and gone. Yes, the courier had landed. Yes, the engines were
safe to hot-fire. Yes, he had sustained no thermal damage, at least
none that mattered to any of the standard diagnostics. He'd be
happy when he got home and had Emandisan diagnostics; they
were much more thorough. Fleet said unnecessarily so, but it wasn't
Fleet's courier. Fleet just borrowed it from time to time. He'd been
at Chilleau. He'd wanted to get back to his home Judiciary. It didn't
bother him to ferry a Bench Specialist on his way. He'd ferried
Bench Specialists before. Interesting people.

The ship grew quiet, though he knew that the three other crew
the courier carried were busy at their own preflight tasks. He
couldn't start his pre-flights until the additions-and-amendments
had been run. He could make it to Emandis Station with the atmosphere he was carrying—he'd taken on atmosphere fresh at Chilleau
and he had oxygen generators on board—but it was imprudent to
make a practice of it, and the port authority wouldn't clear him
for departure until he could certify that life support had been independently audited and passed, since he was using a civilian launch
field. It was a very pretty little launch field. There were red flowers.
He wanted out.

He toggled into braid and waited for the port authority to notice that they had a courier to clear for immediate departure. "Launch
control, may I have a ground crew, please? Need to be getting on."

"Be right with you, courier, on pending."

Leaning back in his clamshell, Shona stretched his legs and looked
up through the wheelhouse's view-ports at the sky. Beautiful evening.
All of the smoke and haze in the upper atmosphere caught and
refracted the sunlight.

Shadows lengthened. Sighing, Shona keyed his transmit. "Need a ground crew, please, launch control. Required to return to my station upon completion of courier duty."

Things had quieted down in launch control, to judge by the swiftness with which the response came. "Sorry, courier, didn't mean to make you wait. Just finding the overnights. We've got you nice billets, though, to make up for the delay."

Worried, Shona took a moment to phrase his next words carefully. "Not a problem, launch control, but we're not billeting. If I could just get a ground crew, please. I'm due at Emandis Station in two days."

It was two days between Brisinje proper and Emandis Station. The *Ragnarok* was there. The last he'd heard from friends in Stores and Issues had been that the re-supply was being pulled for 7.7.1 by the Standard calendar, and that was today. Load out would take seven days at the absolute most; the *Ragnarok* would be leaving Emandis Station in seven days. He had to be there before that happened. He had promised himself. He had promised his brother, on the hillside.

"I'm sorry, courier. Unable to oblige at this time. We're down to three ground crews and they're all working priority. Is there someone at Home Defense that we need to clear you with?"

No. His superiors knew that a courier's schedule was irregular, that Shona couldn't always say exactly where they'd been or how long they'd been there or what they'd been doing. The Bench Specialist at Brisinje preferred to use Home Defense Fleet couriers for exactly that reason, because they were more independent—had more autonomy, offered more flexibility, than the Jurisdiction Fleet. His need to get back to Emandis Station was strictly personal. The crew was overdue for stand-down, yes, but they could do that here just as well as anywhere else.

The one thing they could not do at Imennou or Brisinje was watch the great curved hull of the *Ragnarok* maneuver into close orbit and hold for re-supply, and watch its personnel come off for personal time, and wait and wait and wait until they saw the one man Shona had to see: Andrej Koscuisko. Ship's surgeon, Ship's Inquisitor, the man who had taken Joslire's life. To do that. Shona had to be at Emandis Station.

"Thank you, launch control, not necessary." If there were only three ground crews available, and they were on priority already— "Do you have a projected for us? Really very anxious to get back."

"Sorry again, courier, could be a week. There are cargoes pending with pharmaceuticals and no place big enough to handle the booster but one at a time, unless you haul all the way to Pilos. Which we're doing."

A week. Two days from here to Emandis Station. If he didn't get away from here inside of four days, he might never see the *Ragnarok* again, and what would his brother's spirit have to say to him then—to have had the chance to put out his hand to Joslire's killer, and failed to meet Koscuisko face to face?

"Understood, launch control." None of it mattered to anybody else, except perhaps his crew. And they could no more create a ground crew out of dust and twigs than he could. Joslire had been his brother and Koscuisko carried five-knives, but pharmaceutical shipments had to be given the priority, because honor and obligation could only ever be placed ahead of one's own life, not that of uninvolved and unknowing parties. "Will go on whatever you can get us. Thanks for your help. Maybe we can lend a hand with scheduling."

They'd cross-trained in dispatch and maintenance, of course—it was the logical extension of the tradition of their cultural heritage. No one was privileged to enjoy glamour and glory who did not also put in his time on supply and transport. There were no elites among Emandisan: except for knife-fighters, and they were different.

"We could really use some extra bodies if you can manage. Thanks. We'll get you off as quickly as we can."

Keeping busy might not get them off any more quickly, but at least they'd be doing something positive to contribute to recovery from the problems created by whoever had vandalized the launch fields at Brisinje proper. Shona didn't know who, if anyone, had taken credit, and he didn't care; he didn't know anybody who did. Vandalism never made a point, unless it was about the cowardice and stupidity of the sort of people who engaged in it.

"We'll report soonest, launch control. Courier out."

All right. He was stuck here. As were the rest of his crew, but none of them had a dead brother on the hillside or things to say to the man who was carrying his knives. He'd keep busy, he wouldn't brood about it, and he'd just have to trust in his luck and his brother's honor to see him through to the day when he could stand face to face with the killer and restore honor to his family.

BY THE TIME Jils shook herself awake, the ground car was tracking through the traffic of an obviously prosperous business district. The deep public walkways with their generous plantings and welcoming benches were only sparsely populated, however, and there seemed to be more rubbish in the street than could be indicative of a well-ordered city in control of its own destiny. A subtle black smut hung over it all, the soot collecting from the air to smear the sides of the white buildings like a sort of a nightmare ivy.

"Arik hates to come through the city any more," Padrake said, looking past her through the window on her side of the car. "He's taking it personally. I have to admit I hate to see it myself."

He couldn't be talking only about the burning launch fields, clearly, but Jils had seen similar signs of civil unrest at Chilleau Judiciary: people not quite comfortable in public; evidence of increasing carelessness, apathy, on the part of a city's custodians.

"Who's Arik?" she asked, curious, because the sound in Padrake's warm clear voice was one of confidence and sympathy. A friend? A lover?

Padrake smiled a little and settled his shoulders against the padded back of his shell, staring straight ahead now at the schematic display that told them where the ground car was relative to his goal. "Oh. Tirom. Arik Tirom, Jils, the First Secretary. A man of intense conviction. You'll meet him soon."

And Padrake was on a first-name basis with him? Interesting. "How long have you been at Brisinje, then, Padrake?"

Tilting his head to one side, Padrake half-turned to face her again with a quirky expression on his face that sank straight into her stomach, and warmed her there. "Oh, don't worry, Jils. You'll meet him." This was repetitive, but Padrake seemed convinced that it answered all questions. "No harm to it, he's just a personable sort. And there's no reason to be rude. Two years."

Two years what? Oh. Two years at Brisinje. She wondered what he'd been doing before then, but it wasn't the sort of question Bench Specialists asked each other—or answered.

The car turned away from the business area of the city, through long empty stretches of ground transport lanes toward a cluster of buildings whose white brilliance—besmirched with soot and ash—made them look unutterably tawdry in the setting sun. The smoke of the Brisinje launch fields was behind them; so the river was on the other side. Chambers, Jils supposed. The car cleared security and slowed to trundle through the beautiful well-kept grounds of Brisinje's administrative center; here was no sign of unrest or violence, but Jils knew that it took security to keep it that way.

She walked side by side with Padrake from the motor stables up through floors of office space into the upper levels of the administrative center. Padrake was different, and Jils couldn't quite put her finger on it. Yes, it had been years since she'd seen him, but there was something odd in his manner itself: he was cheerful, pleasant, engaging, pointing out things and people, beguiling her with conversation.

As they neared what had to be the First Secretary's office complex, Jils finally realized what was wrong with Padrake. He seemed to be at peace with himself and the world. That wasn't like Padrake. What had happened to him?

She'd seen enough of Chambers to be able to tell what was what; they were in the heart of the administration. People knew Padrake, and looked at her with calm polite interest. What had Padrake told them about her? Nobody seemed to have a question of murder at the back of their mind, and after weeks of living with the unexpressed suspicion at Chilleau, the relief was as significant as it was unexpected.

"Here we are," Padrake said, and leaned into a door to push it to one side. His office was in the middle of Brisinje's administrative complex, in the heart of Chambers. This was interesting. Emphatically unusual. Was he so comfortable here that he no longer cared what it looked like to be so close to the judicial offices, to occupy space like a member of the administration?

It was a nice office. Jils set her kit bag down beside a gracefully curved and elegantly padded Kartmanns chair, looking around. A large window with a restful view of an apparently extensive botanical gardens; a beautiful desk, clear, glossy, all but entirely innocent of anything that looked like it might represent actual work. Still Padrake had said that they were to go into isolation together. That might explain it. He'd cleared off his desk, and what he hadn't cleared off he'd secured appropriately. Padrake had always been a meticulous man, careful, precise. Tidy.

She sat down. "You have a briefing for me?"

Circling around to behind his desk, he drew a flat-file docket out of one of its slots and held it out to her, keying a toggle switch at the same time.

"Delleroy here, Specialist Ivers just arrived. Can I get in?" The transmitter was on directional; Jils didn't hear the response, but Padrake nodded. "Thanks, we'll be right there. Jils. Let's go meet the First Secretary. He's been anxious for your arrival, as have I."

All right. Jils closed the docket with a shrug. Padrake clearly had things on his mind, and he could be difficult to stop or stay when he had his Jetorix up. A man of immense and persuasive determination, Padrake Delleroy, and the years that had silvered those several strands in his beautiful mane of black hair had not apparently made any appreciable dent in his momentum.

Just five doors down to the inner office. Padrake was expected, the doors stood open for them, the Security post bowing them through past the clerks' stations into the First Secretary's office. It was bigger than Padrake's, and the view was of the river. Jils saw the First Secretary at Brisinje Judiciary—Arik Tirom—look up from the view-screen on his desk as Padrake opened the door into the office and invited Jils to precede him into the room with a sweeping gesture of his free hand.

The First Secretary was a man of medium height but significant shoulder whose broad high forehead and long heavy braid of stunningly black hair indicated that the brown-ivory color of his skin was that of a Manicha hominid, class one. Meeting Jils' eyes, Tirom stood up quickly and nodded his head in a polite greeting. "Specialist Ivers, I've heard so much about you."

And that could go in several different directions, too, Jils thought. She stopped two paces shy of Tirom's beautifully polished sandgrass veneer desk, and bowed. "I'll admit to any good things, but for most of what you'll have heard I'll plead duty to the rule of Law, First Secretary. Pleased to make your acquaintance."

Padrake had closed the door behind them, and now he came to join Jils at the desk. Tirom had not sat back down. "Specialist Ivers is just now in, First Secretary, redirected through Imennou. I've taken the liberty of having a beverage service sent up."

She hadn't planned on sitting down and having a talk just this minute. She'd had a long transit, she'd gotten an unexpected and ambiguous message from Karol Vogel, and the First Secretary was saying something so she had better pay attention.

"Thanks, Padrake, I could use a break. If you'd care to sit down, Specialist Ivers?"

It was her practice to be polite to senior administrative officials, unless they had given her specific reason not to be. It only surprised them more when one had to pull rank on them—rank that technically did not exist, but rank that was hers as a representative of the entire Bench and which therefore overruled that of any one single Jurisdiction's administration. The moment of surprise between realization that someone had just said "no" and the reaction was frequently the moment on which the entire carriage of an investigation depended, and Jils had been glad of it on more than one occasion.

"Very kind, First Secretary. Thank you." Right now she was the one who was a little stupefied with a combination of stress and fatigue. The arrival of the beverage service saved her from the immediate embarrassment of having to say anything intelligent right then, so that by the time kilpers had been handed all around and the trays of crisp snack cakes and fruit had been passed, and everybody had settled back in the cushiony embrace of the very comfortable chairs in Tirom's conversation area, she was ready to engage.

"Padrake hasn't briefed me yet on the status of the convocation," Jils noted, politely. That was a little unfair, perhaps—she'd been asleep, after all—but true. "Am I the last to arrive, First Secretary?"

Tirom nodded with an air of understanding more than had been said. "Old friends with a lot of catching up to do," he said, and finished off a slice of fragrant golden-fleshed melon with evident relish. "I quite understand. And you'll have plenty of time to get your feet under you, Specialist Ivers. You're not in one of the chairs until the preliminaries have been completed."

Preliminaries. Bench against Bench against Bench, one-on-one, and then winner against winner, Supicor against Dasidar and Dasidar against Haspirzak and Supicor against Haspirzak and so forth—and at the end of it all, only then, Chilleau against Fontailloe against the strongest other candidate on the Bench, for one final contest to decide the Selection based on the finest macro-analyses the Bench could offer.

"I've been following a little of the developments. But not very clearly." Much of what was going on was behind the scenes and not accessible even at Bench offices to people without a specific need to know. There was probably more that the Second Judge had simply not bothered to share with her. Jils knew that the judge had been hoping that Karol Vogel would turn up and spare her the necessity of sending Jils to Convocation. And Karol should have turned up. It was hard for Jils to understand what could have been important enough to keep Karol away from Chilleau at this crisis point in the Bench's history.

Unless it was Karol who had assassinated the First Secretary. If he had, it was not with the Second Judge's knowledge or consent—that went without saying. And her mind was wandering again. This was not good. She needed some time to stand down, to clear her mind and concentrate on what she was going to do. She had to forget all about Verlaine's murder just for now. She would have enough on her task list without worrying at old problems, except to rest her mind from Convocation issues.

"You're to become more familiar than you'd really care to be with the arguments, I'm afraid, Specialist Ivers."

She was glad that he didn't try to call her Jils. "Yes, First Secretary, quite so. Do you have a personal opinion you would care to share, though?"

Padrake set his flask down on the table with a decided gesture, pinching his upper lip with his thumb and forefinger as though to clean some moisture from his mouth. "I certainly do," he said. "My personal opinion is that Brisinje should take it."

Tirom just grinned at her, rolling his eyes at Jils as if to say that this was an old quarrel that she was not to take seriously. Of course Padrake would speak for Brisinje. That would be his exact role, but Padrake had to know that Brisinje was not in serious contention, though it would be as carefully represented as any of the others. Brisinje was the newest Judiciary, with the least powerful and influential set of historically developed alliances and relationships with other Benches.

That was precisely why Brisinje had been selected as the best place to hold the convocation: it was as close to neutral territory as any place under Jurisdiction. For a more unaligned location, they would have to go out into Gonebeyond space, which was clearly impossible.

Tirom opened his mouth to joke back at Padrake, but before he could speak there was a sound at the alert on his desk.

"Fleet Captain Irshah Parmin, Jurisdiction Fleet Ship *Scylla*. Ready to proceed with detachment to Emandis Station for resupply, First Secretary."

It was a woman's voice, and Jils knew that Irshah Parmin wasn't a woman, though she'd never met the man in person. But it wouldn't actually be the Fleet Captain calling, but the First Officer on his behalf. *Scylla* did in fact have a female First Officer—Saligrep Linelly, a woman due for her first command, but who had made no move to demand one, apparently comfortable where she was and willing to lay low until the environment had become more settled once again.

There were plenty of excellent First Officers in Fleet who didn't want to transition to Command. They tended to be the best, as a matter of fact—people who knew that they would never do another job better than the one they were doing right now, or people whose political intransigence, whose personal integrity, had marked them as people who would decline to execute orders to which they took exception.

There were captains like that, too, and the Bench had sought to address the problem of Command Branch officers who insisted on thinking for themselves by raising up its own: crèche-bred Command Branch, children culled from the ranks of orphans to be brought up with the most thorough indoctrination the Bench could design, who would do as they were told to preserve the rule of Law and the Judicial order.

It was a good theory. But in practice it had been too successful, producing either mindless martinets or signal failures like Jennet ap Rhiannon, the acting brevet captain of the Jurisdiction Fleet Ship *Ragnarok*.

Tirom frowned as if he was trying to remember something, and started to shift to stand up and go to the desk—to look for a reference, perhaps—but apparently thought better of it, and relaxed back into his chair again.

"Thank you, *Scylla*," Tirom said. "Have a good transit. See you when you get back, Tirom away."

That was the communication center's cue to cut the transmission and return the First Secretary's office to private status, off monitor. "*Scylla* away," the *Scylla's* First Officer said, and the clear-tone clicked through. Still Tirom frowned.

"There was something about that," he said, mostly to Padrake. "I can't bring it to mind right now. Can't have been very important. I hope."

"Not as if you've got any worries about those people," Padrake agreed. "Not like the other places."

Tirom nodded, and spoke to Jils. "They've been our Fleet assigned resources for three years now, Specialist Ivers. Sixth Fleet detached at Brisinje. Very formal relationship, but no inappropriate pressure. Not like what's going on at some of the other Judiciaries right now."

"You'd like a little more cooperation on access to their Inquisitor, of course," Padrake said, as if reminding Tirom of the fact. "The man himself is willing to do his duty, from what I understand. But Captain Irshah Parmin balks."

Tirom nodded. "Well, that's a chronic issue, isn't it? I don't like to think what we'd have had to put up with if Verlaine's reforms had gone through. No offense, Specialist Ivers."

Tirom apparently made the assumption that Jils had been personally—as well as professionally—committed to Verlaine's announced agenda: an immediate halt on the issue of any new Writs to Inquire, no new orientation classes once the current cycle had been completed, and an in-depth examination of the cost and benefit of the entire system of Inquiry and the Protocols.

Its monopoly on the exercise of legal, Judicial torture was one of Fleet's most jealously cherished prerogatives. Jils wondered if Tirom was one of those who believed that Fleet had been behind Verlaine's assassination.

"That's right," Padrake said suddenly. "The *Ragnarok's* going to Emandis station. You wanted to speak to *Scylla* about that. Warn them, no untoward incidents, delicate situation with Convocation, and so forth."

The two ideas—Verlaine's reforms, and the *Ragnarok*—connected through Inquisition, clearly enough. Whether or not Padrake and Tirom were aware of the fact that *Scylla* had been Andrej Koscuisko's first ship of assignment, Andrej Koscuisko was the first person anyone would think of when the general idea of Inquisitors came up, and right now the entire Bench was acutely aware that Koscuisko was on board the *Ragnarok*.

What it meant. she was sure nobody could figure out. Dolgorukij were in general ferociously conservative people. What the *Ragnarok* was doing was reactionary at best, and yet Koscuisko had returned to the ship voluntarily and was apparently intent on staying there, thus reducing the range of punitive actions that the Bench could take against the *Ragnarok* without offending the powerful Dolgorukij

Combine to a very narrow range of highly unsatisfactory and mostly symbolic gestures of disdain.

Jils, however, knew precisely why Andrej Koscuisko had returned to his ship. Furthermore, she knew that Koscuisko had asked her to put the recording of the relief of Writ that Verlaine had offered him on hold until the *Ragnarok's* appeal had been decided: an act of significant personal courage on his part, in her estimation.

Both she and Koscuisko knew that, pending his relief of Writ, he could be called to duty at any time as a professional torturer, as well as the *Ragnarok's* chief medical officer and ship's surgeon. Both she and Koscuisko knew that he would refuse to execute the Protocols unless he could do it according to a strict standard of his own, and that nothing above the third level would fit that definition. Also that refusal to implement the Protocols at an adjudged and authorized level was an act of mutiny, one of the very few crimes for which even an Inquisitor could and would be prosecuted at the Tenth Level.

Tirom was rolling a cookie on edge on his snack plate as though the gradual erosion of the crumb held a message for him. "Yes," he said. "Quite right. I wanted to discourage *Scylla* from having any contact with that outfit. I particularly wanted to ensure that any ship-to-ship communications were on record and between officers only."

Tirom was afraid that something on the *Ragnarok* was catching, or could spread from crew to crew like an infection. The real problem with the *Ragnarok* wasn't its crew. Jils had been there; she knew. The problem with the *Ragnarok* was that its officers were noncompliant, and its commander Jennet ap Rhiannon had been so thoroughly indoctrinated by her Bench crèche teachers that she did not doubt for one instant that her duty to protect her crew from illegal imposition was self-evident to any right-thinking person.

"But you know Irshah Parmin. You can be confident of his discretion." Padrake spoke as if of a pre-decided solution, reaching for a fresh flask of kilpers. "None of the pressure Fleet's putting on Haspirzak, for instance."

Jils stirred her now-lukewarm kilpers and listened. She hadn't kept up on everything that was going on.

Tirom made a face, and shook his head. "I'd like to see anybody attempt to suggest that the Emandisan Home Defense Fleet wasn't up to any incidental increase in civil unrest. Fleet has no basis for trying to squeeze more tax revenues out of Brisinje for more ships and crew. You don't see them kicking up at Sant-Dasidar either."

The Emandisan Home Defense Fleet, the Dolgorukij Combine's Home Defense Fleet. The Bench had been quietly waiving one restriction on the Combine fleet after another, over the years. What harm did it do to let the Combine maintain more ships, heavier armament, more crew than the original accords had permitted? There was only one Combine, and nine Judiciaries. The more money the Combine wanted to put into its Home Defense Fleet, the more available resources there were for Fleet to borrow for one reason or another when they wanted a little extra muscle that they didn't have to pay for.

"That's right," Padrake agreed cheerfully. "So long as they don't go Langsarik on us. I'll show Specialist Ivers to her quarters, Arik, see you tomorrow?"

As a subtle way of taking control of the conversation and ending it, this was nothing of the sort. Jils covered her surprise. It was difficult not to pass judgment on both of them, but she clearly didn't understand the nature of their relationship so it was best to avoid disapproving of it until she had better information.

"Opening ceremonies," Tirom confirmed with a sigh. "Make sure that Padrake gives you a good dinner, Dame, because you're going to be eating pre-packs for the rest of the convocation."

Lovely. But reasonable. Convocation would be conducted under quarantine, Bench Specialists weren't generally known for their culinary skills, and it wouldn't be appropriate to ask them to cook for one another if they were, what with all of their energies needed for the work of the convocation itself. Prepacks were the obvious, if unpalatable, solution.

"I'll do so without fail, First Secretary," Padrake answered for Jils, with a polite bow. "Jils. Shall we?"

There were worse offers. She was tired; she'd had enough of duty, responsibility, the rule of Law and the Judicial order—at least for one night.

Just for tonight she was simply going to go along with Padrake, have a good dinner, find out what had been going on in Padrake's life. And let the rest of it go until tomorrow.

THE ARCHIVED IMAGE on the screen was identified by its margin-codings, generated off parallax from Taisheki Station on the occasion—nearly a year gone by, now—of the *Ragnarok's* declining to stop in and stay for a while.

Information and data received from the ships and monitoring stations in the immediate area had been used to build a picture that could be viewed from any angle. To Calleigh, it seemed as though she were in a neutral observer station standing well off of Taisheki, watching the *Ragnarok* heading for the entry vector and the artillery platforms that were there waiting for it.

But there was more than that—there was a thula. A Kospodar thula, weaving its way among the artillery platforms, blowing them up, one by one by one, and even with the data-refs that the footing line was displaying on the screen it was hard to believe that the picture had not been doctored to increase the relative speed of the little ship.

"I want it," Ship's Engineer said. "It's my natal day, Captain. Have I ever asked you for anything? I want that thula. I've never seen anything move like that in my life."

Chief Warrant Officer Calleigh Samons had been assigned to the Jurisdiction Fleet Ship *Scylla* for eleven years, most of which had been about as good as anybody would expect. She'd handled Security teams for the chief medical officer, which meant of course that she also managed bond-involuntaries for the CMO's use in his or her role as Inquisitor.

Up until the time Koscuisko had been assigned, she had touched those teams as lightly as possible, not wanting to know what use their officer of assignment made of them, perfectly content to restrict herself to training and physical conditioning. They were condemned criminals, after all, but they were there because they could be forced to do things that few people would do of their own free will, and nobody liked to think about that.

After Koscuisko, it had been different. Koscuisko had been young, naïve, inexperienced, at ease in surgery and nowhere else, conscious of his general lack of experience in every aspect of Infirmary that mattered; but he had insisted on engaging with his personal discomfort, pressing forward to learn and gain in understanding even at the cost of being made to look foolish, and he had not been content to turn his back on bond-involuntaries. They were not objects. They were not beyond help or hope. All Koscuisko had done was to look into their faces in the same way he would look at any soul, and it had changed things forever.

The captain had seen enough of Koscuisko's relationships with his Security to respect his junior officer more deeply than he'd ever cared to admit. A man like Irshah Parmin was accustomed to taking an officer's measure by the way he treated his subordinates when nobody was there to see, and it had become clear that whatever Koscuisko was doing with his people, it was powerful enough to transform them from men who lived in fear—condemned never to act but always only react—into people who had realized that there was a way after all for them to reclaim a portion of their freedom in their own minds, in their lives.

It was only because of Koscuisko's relationship with his Security in general, and the bond-involuntaries in particular, that Fleet Captain Irshah Parmin had not enforced the letter of the laws of military courtesy and discipline against Koscuisko on a daily basis.

And ever since Koscuisko had cried failure of Writ at the Domitt Prison, the captain had blamed himself for failing to put the fear of Hell into his young officer, convinced that if Koscuisko would not learn that discretion was the better part of valor he would never survive his time in Fleet. She knew.

The captain had discussed the issue with her on more than one occasion, using her as a sounding-board to work out the itch of his personal aggravation so that he could evaluate and judge some stunt that Koscuisko had pulled on its own merits rather than its potentially implied disrespect of, and consequent insult to, Koscuisko's chain of command.

She hadn't heard too much about it in the five or six years since Koscuisko had been transferred away to the *Ragnarok*, except when the captain chanced to express his frustration with his CMO's performance by comparing it to the ship's surgeon he'd had in Andrej Koscuisko. At such times, it was clearly not helpful to remind the captain that, while Koscuisko's technical competence in surgery could not be faulted, Irshah Parmin had found fault with almost everything else about the man.

The captain pushed the toggle feed on the bar in front of his chair to its neutral position, and the image on the far wall of the officer's mess froze on a slice of the archival record. She'd heard about it, but this was the first chance she'd had to see it— that was why the captain had sent for her especially. Shared experience of aggravation.

"So long as I'm not needed here, your Excellency, I'd be more than happy to take a temporary posting to help handle the processing, when they run the *Ragnarok* to ground. Imagine. Interrogating Andrej Koscuisko. What a privilege that would be."

That was Doctor Weasel-Boy. Doctor Lazarbee, but it was almost impossible to think of him by that name. Sooner or later she was going to slip and call him Weasel-Boy, she knew it. It was just as well that she had bond-involuntaries to learn from: there would be less danger of making a slip if she took care to address him as "your Excellency."

Captain Irshah Parmin didn't seem to have heard Weasel-Boy speak. "Look at that son of a bitch," he said. "I heard that he was on that monster. Him. A surgeon. I knew he was a problem, but I never dreamed it was catching."

From Koscuisko to the entire ship's crew of the *Ragnarok*, he meant—Calleigh thought. "That's not fair," First Officer said. "He never bit anybody the entire time he was here. And that Lieutenant ap Rhiannon had a reputation of her own, don't forget, capable of anything."

Irshah Parmin smiled, but shook his head. "It's him, I tell you. Four years under Lowden would make a rabid dog out of anybody."

There'd been betting, though Calleigh wasn't supposed to have known about it. It was nothing personal. They'd all heard about the *Ragnarok*: four Ship's Inquisitors in five years. An accident in a service house, an accidental overdose, something very regrettable in Secured Medical that not even the gossips would talk about; what had happened to the other one?

"He seems to have done almost everything except his plain duty." That was Weasel-Boy again. For a disagreeable man he had an unusually sonorous voice; she was still getting used to it. Cognitive dissonance, she thought it was called. "Did this joker ever actually do any work? Any work at all?"

The question was in poor taste on more than one level, one of which was the fact that it implied criticism of Irshah Parmin, Koscuisko's former commander. And everybody on the captain's staff in this room, with the possible exception of Weasel-Boy himself, had seen evidence of Koscuisko's surgical skills for themselves, never mind his other duties.

Sighing, the captain keyed the toggle back a few instants and then forward again. The Kospodar thula moved like a much smaller ship, lithe and agile. Even at extreme magnification, the speed with which it moved was remarkable to see.

"One of his Bonds flying that thing," Calleigh said, proudly. "That's the rumor I heard, anyway, Captain."

"Well, of course the man was on Safe at the time—" Weasel-Boy started to protest.

The captain raised a hand. "Let's just avoid spreading any wild irresponsible rumors," he said. "It clearly couldn't have been a bond-involuntary, that would have violated restrictions and requirements. So the question of Safes is immaterial, and I don't want to hear anything more about it."

Calleigh bowed, solemnly, well and truly reprimanded. Or something. Irshah Parmin winked—but so quickly she couldn't be sure she'd seen it—and continued.

"The point, gentles, is that the *Ragnarok* is clearly capable of anything." Shooting its way out of Taisheki Station to avoid being forced to surrender any crew to Inquiry, knowing full well that a Fleet Interrogations Group had been seconded. Well, shooting out an artillery net that was being fielded to prevent the *Ragnarok's* access to the exit vector, at least—with a battle cannon on a private courier, and where had the *Ragnarok* come up with one of those, unless it was true about the case of deck wipes and Admiral Settigan's arrangements with reasonable people?

"And as we are en route to Emandis Station, we may be unfortunate enough to encounter this dangerous renegade. Emandis Station is administratively assigned to the Emandisan Home Defense Fleet, which has jurisdiction, and it would be prudent of us all to remember that everybody is very sensitive about their prerogatives these days. No trouble."

Doctor Weasel-Boy snorted contemptuously. A relative newcomer, he hadn't encountered the rough side of the captain's temper yet. It'd only been a few months since he'd been transferred from the Galven at Ygau. Koscuisko's successor hadn't been half the surgeon Koscuisko had been, but she hadn't needed a fraction of the management, either, and the ship had gotten along very well with her.

If she used bond-involuntaries to execute the Protocols, that was what bond-involuntaries were for, and Parmin had never liked sharing his medical officer with the Bench and did so as sparingly as possible. It had been a good few years. What Doctor Weasel-Boy's regime would be like was anybody's guess, but he hadn't made a promising start by going through channels suspected of being reasonable in order to arrange a mid-assignment transfer. They'd been sorry to see Doctor Aldrai go.

"No down-leave?" First Officer asked.

The captain shook his head. "I see no reason why my crew should suffer because there are questionable influences at large. Downtime will be duly authorized, just exercise your discretion, that's all. As a matter of fact, I'd like to have a word with you and Chief Samons, First Officer. Has anybody got anything else? Thank you, next time."

The Ship's Engineer and the Intelligence officer had both been with *Scylla* for as long or longer than Captain Irshah Parmin himself. They knew, if Doctor Weasel-Boy didn't, they'd been asked to clear the room. The officer's mess was emptied within moments, despite the doctor's evident desire to stay behind and keep up on the events, whether or not they were any of his business. Especially if they were none of his business.

Once the door had closed behind the Intelligence officer and the clear-signal had sounded, Irshah Parmin stood up. "Will there be trouble, Salli? Strong feelings on board, I gather."

First Officer thought for a moment, and shook her head. Her expression was one of grudging satisfaction, as though she had decided what was going to happen, and had determined that it was what she would have done in the same place, but couldn't bring herself to go so far as to admit it, possibly even to herself. "We don't know what ap Rhiannon is going to do. But if I were her I'd be making liberty as available as possible."

Irshah Parmin frowned. "She'll lose half the crew. And be unable to shift hull."

First Officer nodded. "Exactly so. People have had several months to think about what happened at Taisheki Station. What options did the crew have there? But at Emandis Station they can quietly turn themselves back over to Fleet and plead clear and present danger to life and limb."

"And she'll let them." Irshah Parmin made a face Calleigh recognized, something with a thrust-forward under-jaw and a pursed mouth. "It's the only way to be sure of their support. And no one who has the chance and doesn't take it will have much credibility later if they try to convince the authorities that they'd been prevented."

He sat back down again and put his head into his hands in a rare gesture of perplexity. "I can think of one hopeless case who won't be leaving. I failed that young officer, Salli. I never got through to him."

There was more to it than that, Calleigh knew. Whatever residual sense of personal responsibility the captain might elect to cherish for his once-officer, there were reasons to be concerned about Koscuisko's fate if the *Ragnarok* were left undefended by mass defection; and even more reason for concern should the *Ragnarok's* crew not take their first opportunity to extricate themselves from a very awkward situation that could turn lethal at any moment.

Koscuisko had enemies in Fleet. It went far beyond inter-system rivalry; he had made more enemies than he had inherited, earned them fairly through his own effort and by his own volition. The Intelligence officer had heard a rumor about a Bench warrant out on Koscuisko's life, but nothing seemed to have come of it. Calleigh would have been surprised if anything had, with a Selection pending.

"You want to talk to him," Calleigh said slowly, forgetting in her awe to add "your Excellency" or "Captain" or even "sir." "All of these years, and you haven't had enough."

Koscuisko was ap Rhiannon's problem. But Irshah Parmin didn't trust Koscuisko's captain to be sensitive to some of the specific threats that had accumulated around Koscuisko like the scent of blood and steel and the cold pavement of an alleyway where a man lay dying under a mercilessly clear night sky. Koscuisko had a perfectly good captain of his own, but Irshah Parmin was Calleigh's captain and First Officer's as well.

"Ap Rhiannon will send him down," he said, straightening up. "She's sure to. She can't take the risk of keeping a man like that on board unless she's sure of him. At least I wouldn't risk it, and has anybody ever been sure of Koscuisko?"

Yes, Calleigh thought. Koscuisko's bond-involuntaries had been sure of him. There was a limit to how well they could protect him, however; against one man in particular, even their powers had been limited. That one man had been Andrej Koscuisko, of course, and Calleigh didn't think anybody could have done a better job of protecting Koscuisko from himself, howsoever incompletely.

"So when we get to Emandis Station, find out where he is, that's all. I just want to talk to him."

He didn't sound convincing. He didn't sound convinced. When Verlaine had gotten Koscuisko assigned to the *Ragnarok*—in a move that had been widely perceived as an act of petty vengeance on his part for Koscuisko's role in embarrassing the Second Judge and Chilleau Judiciary over the Domitt Prison—Irshah Parmin had taken it almost personally. *If I'd only taught him better he might have handled it differently.*

"Are we arresting him?" First Officer asked quietly.

Irshah Parmin grimaced, as if in pain, and shook his head. "No. No. Protective custody, maybe. Maybe he doesn't understand the trouble he's gotten himself in to this time. Just talk. You'll have to collect whoever he's got with him, though, so plan accordingly. All right?"

From the look the First Officer gave Calleigh, it was clear that they both agreed on how uncomfortable Irshah Parmin was with this entire conversation. "Very good, sir," First Officer said. Maybe Koscuisko wouldn't mind, Calleigh decided. Maybe he'd be pleased to come and visit with a former commander, and his Security with him. Maybe it wouldn't even have to be at gunpoint.

What lawful pretext Irshah Parmin imagined he could possibly find for poaching another ship captain's senior officers, Calleigh couldn't guess, and believed that she knew better than to expect that there was one. "Quiet and discreet. Wouldn't do to insult the Emandisan Home Defense Fleet, of course, your Excellency."

"It's an internal Fleet matter." Irshah Parmin sounded genuinely surprised, as though the potential for conflicts in jurisdiction had not occurred to him. "No concern for Emandis either way, surely, Salli. I've asked Bassin to run a whisper on it so we'll know if Koscuisko comes down and where he goes if he does. Thanks, both."

Bassin Emer was the ship's Intelligence officer. So the captain had had this on his mind for some time now. Jurisdiction space was vast; Fleet small by comparison. It was by no means astonishing to contemplate encountering a former officer of assignment at one point or another so long as she, and they, remained in Fleet.

But she had never imagined herself in a position to detain Andrej Koscuisko. She wasn't sure how she was going to do it. She could only hope that Ship's Intelligence would have good information—or, failing that, no information at all.

CHAPTER SIX
CONVOCATION

CHILLEAU JUDICIARY HAD had no shortage of potable water, but Chilleau had been on an ancient delta through which a river had not flowed for octaves, the Sannandor having long since disappeared into a desert that had once been a vast inland lake. People didn't sit in tubs of water, at Chilleau Judiciary: they showered, or they bathed in public bathhouses, and never minded the amount of filtration and purification required to make it cost-effective to run such an enterprise.

It was an interesting change to be at Brisinje on the river in a world that had been colonized for a mere sixty generations. Jurisdiction had come late to Brisinje and brought wisdom, knowledge, prudence with it. There was no danger that the Reggidout River would suffer the fate of the Sannandor—at least not through the intervention of demands for irrigation or generation of hydroelectric power.

It was good, yes, but it made Jils a little bit uncomfortable. Padrake had shown her to this luxury suite on an upper floor of one of the beautiful buildings in Brisinje's judicial center, and left her to rest and change. She'd been somewhat taken aback by the palatial dimensions of the place—a library, a lounge area, a dining room, a bedroom, a washroom the size of her whole apartment at Chilleau—and all with a panoramic view of the river and the mountains beyond. Except for the washroom, of course, where a person could feel a bit exposed no matter how familiar she was with unidirectional polarization of view-pane materials.

There wasn't much by way of a view just now: the smoke from the launch fields filled the atmosphere and soiled the beaches, though no hint of any unpleasant odors made it past the filters into her suite. This was an apartment fit for a Secretary, for a First Secretary, for a District Judge, and not for one hard-working supposed-to-be-functionally-anonymous Bench Specialist. She'd have to ask Padrake about it.

After her bath.

The tub was something to see, round, with benches and steps up, and its water temperature was zone-controlled, and its pulse jets felt almost as good against her tired muscles as the touch of a professional masseur might have. The fragrance of the water-lotion she'd selected was clean and crisp and very relaxing, and there was a stack of warmed toweling waiting for her when she got out.

She lay her head back against one of the contoured scallops in the tub's lip and let her body float on the powerful current of the water jets, counting the stars that twinkled in the ceiling—cleverly painted so as to appear domed—and traveled across the ceiling in a slow progression possibly designed to follow that of the actual night sky above Brisinje, since she didn't recognize anything obviously familiar about it. The white noise generator with its transmit in the walls surrounded her with a soothing sound of surf against a shore.

She could easily fall asleep again, cradled in this huge tub of hot water. But Padrake had said that he'd come back to take her to dinner. She couldn't risk being caught naked in the tub; she might not get her dinner until breakfast time, if that happened.

Reluctantly, Jils pulled herself out of the bath, dried herself on warmed towels as soft as a midsummer breeze, wrapped herself in a cool silk robe with full sleeves and long skirts, and went out into the bedroom with its plush white carpet and its very large bed to see about getting dressed.

The bed was the only thing with reduced power to impress her. She had been Andrej Koscuisko's guest at the Matredonat, she had been the guest of the Autocrat's Court, she had been welcomed at Chelatring Side in the Chetalra Mountains where the Koscuisko familial corporation had its ancestral seat; she had slept in beds large enough for an entire family.

The traditional master's bed in an aristocrat's household was big enough for the master, his sacred wife, the nurse, and an infant child. The guest bed she'd been provided had been large enough to require a map to get in to and out of. She couldn't think about the linen bills without shuddering. It was no wonder Dolgorukij households were so large. Keeping up with the sheets would be a full-time job for a crew of six, and she didn't even want to contemplate how much power it required to dry all of that linen in the wintertime when it could not be hung out to take advantage of the sun.

She hoped Padrake wasn't hoping she'd need company to keep her from getting disoriented and lost here. As lovers, they had been rather spectacularly successful, and she still thought of his embrace from time to time, dozing, when she had nothing better to do. But intimacy couldn't be just picked up where it had been set down, not after the passage of years. Could it? Would she mind very much if he tried? What harm could it do to put everything aside for a few hours and live in the moment, when that moment could have Padrake's caress in it?

There was no guessing whether Padrake's interest remained, she reminded herself, pinning up her hair in front of the huge mirror. She didn't see much change in the image that was reflected there—she was still short, still square-shouldered; her eyes were still blacker even than her hair, which was still thick and glossy and needed a trim because it was getting to be too heavy to wear comfortably in a tuckaway.

She'd never had much of a figure. Keeping in combat trim tended to harden and realign any curves, but she had the appropriate feminine secondary sex characteristics in the appropriate locations. So did any other woman in known Space, too—well, by and large. No reason to believe there was anything of peculiar interest to anybody about her body.

Thinking to invoke the latest news on the reader in the library, she went out into the lounge area to get to the other side. Padrake was sitting in one of the great cushioned chairs, watching the colors change as the sun went down and its declining rays caught the ash particles in the smoke of the launch fields in new and ever-shifting patterns. Confused—she hadn't expected to see him there, and she felt at a bit of a disadvantage, being only half-dressed—she stopped abruptly. Padrake heard something, or perhaps sensed something, and turned his head to look at her over his shoulder.

"Ready for dinner?" he asked, cheerfully. "I thought you might be tired, so I had something sent up. That way you don't have to face your footgear."

Boots were regulation, but a person got tired of them after five or six days. It was a thoughtful gesture on his part. And why should it bother her to think that she had nothing on under her robe? Padrake didn't seem to think it was the least bit out of the ordinary.

"All right." It would give them a chance to talk. And Padrake hadn't changed his clothing, so it wasn't as though he was likely to have courting on his mind. "What's on the menu?"

"Cold supper, merely." He waved her ahead of him into the dining room. "But a very nice view. A little obscured tonight, but it's an interesting effect when the moon comes up."

Fruit. Several beautifully tall flagons of iced beverages, lightly sweetened red citrus, black thick Gremner berry juice, rhyti from fragrant green leaf, more. An immense tray of varietal cheeses, dishes of seven different kinds of pre-cracked but unshelled nuts, several platters of cold sliced meat of one sort or another. A cold cream-cake with ruby-red berry syrup dripping almost obscenely down its snowy flanks.

Padrake pulled a chair away from the table, politely, and pushed it back in once she'd seated herself. "No waiters," he said. "I thought you'd rather do without. And I don't dare risk anyone here hearing one of your better stories, Jils, I'd never live it down. Crackers?"

Yes, he was. Utterly crackers, but in another sense perhaps than he had meant. "I could get used to this rich living," she warned, reaching for a bowl of grapes. Huge, purple, seedless, and chilled. Heaven. There was wafer-melon there besides, its layers of succulent orange flesh lifting in tiers from its core as it reacted with the air. "A few days of this and I'll never go back to Chilleau."

"Promise?" he asked eagerly, but then slapped his thigh with one hand in a manner that told her he meant her to take it for a joke. "Well, bring on the milk baths, then. Why would you want to go back to Chilleau anyway? From what I hear, they haven't been treating you very well. As if anybody seriously thought."

Yes, as if anybody seriously thought. But it was kind of him to let her know that he, at least, didn't believe that she had done it. She wondered if Balkney thought she had. Then she wondered whether Widowmaker was at Convocation as well, because she and the Hangman had married, and the Widowmaker had retired her uniform to bear children—three, maybe four by now. Bloodthirsty babies, if they were anything like either parent, but she'd better not think of babies and baby-making just at this moment with Padrake in the room. His physical presence was so very there. It was distracting.

"Seriously," she said, trying to discipline her thoughts. "Is this how Bench Specialists live at Brisinje? Not that I'm complaining, and I know

I'll be paying for it. Still. This is the sort of treatment I'd expect out of, say, Aznir Dolgorukij." Just to pick a benchmark of flamboyant and conspicuous consumption. "What would people say?"

"Nothing at all, if they have a decent amount of respect for the Law." Padrake crushed a cracked nutshell between the heels of his palms and let the fragments drop to the table's gleaming surface as though he were a shaman, casting bones. "Think of what the life of a Bench Specialist is, Jils. We spend years in the worst possible environments, we're barred by the nature of our duty from having friends or families, at least for the most part. All we have is each other, and we're not very good company as a rule, are we? We might as well be Dolgorukij Malcontents, but they live better. We deserve a little taste of the good life for ourselves."

He popped the nutmeat into his mouth as if to illustrate his point. "We're the people who make the good life possible. You can't hire people like us, we're not for sale. We do our duty because it's our duty. And for what? So some Judge who wouldn't last six eighths on the streets of her own capital can suspect us of murder the moment things go wrong with her plans?"

Padrake had a persuasive rant to him. He was one of those men who didn't mind in the least listening to himself talk, and it was all right because nobody else minded either. There was a sort of music to his cadence, when Padrake was on a rant. The closest thing she'd ever heard to it was one altogether too-late evening when she'd been in deep cover in some desperately poor hovel of a public house and a skinny, unwashed Nurail in the corner had started to sing.

He hadn't had a good voice. It hadn't been a pretty tune. It had raised the hair at the back of her neck straight up into the air and sent an electric jolt down her spine to her toes and back up to tingle in the crown of her head, and she'd realized—with the one small portion of her mind that didn't belong to that dirty, smelly, unkempt Nurail completely and entirely, at that moment—that she was sitting in the presence of a weaver.

Padrake had a touch of that power in him. She'd wondered, from time to time, whether he was hiding any Nurail at the back of the closet of his genetic profile. "If any of us wanted wealth and power, we'd not have passed the basic psychologicals," she reminded him. "And you used to be savage enough about Fleet personnel who enjoyed their perks a little too well. Changed your mind?"

"Now you're trying to talk sense." He threw a bit of nut-meat at her. She rolled it up in a slice of filleted cold roast, dipped the roll in mustard-and-vinegar relish, and took an emphatic bite by way of showing how little threatened she was by his behavior. "Stop it. I just don't see why we shouldn't enjoy some of the respect that we've earned. And we're going into isolation, don't forget. Preheats. Ugh."

There were arguments to be made on both sides of that issue—the enjoyment of luxuries issue, not the preheats one. She'd argued it with Karol often enough, but on the Padrake side of the question. She wasn't going to indulge that line of thought. "Tell me about the isolation. Who's come? You're speaking for Brisinje, I know that, but who's at Supicor these days?"

A man with a persuasive rant, and a terrible gossip. It was one of the most enjoyable things about him: he always knew things, and he would tell you what was being said about you behind your back as well, so it wasn't as though he was deceitful in any sense. Not really.

"Nion is here for the Seventh Judge at Supicor. New kid. I don't know too much about her, except that she came out of Core. Tough. She'll be good if she lives long enough. The really interesting thing, though, is the Bench Specialist out of the Sixth Judiciary. Guess."

The Sixth Judge sat at Sant-Dasidar, and that Judiciary included all of the Dolgorukij Combine. "Don't tell me. Not Sarvaw."

"Better than Sarvaw. Female. A female Bench Specialist from the Dolgorukij Combine, she's Kizakh, I believe. There are rumors about her, Jils, indicating that the string she wears her chop on isn't just any old bit of red cord. If you get my meaning."

Malcontent. That was what Padrake was implying; that the Bench Specialist at Sant-Dasidar was a Malcontent, and wore the Saint's halter, the symbol of her slavery.

Stubbing her rolled up slice of meat in the relish dish in much the same way as she had seen people stub out the lefrols they'd been smoking, Jils considered the implications.

"Well. It'd make sense, I suppose, but I didn't think the Bench ever commissioned talent out of system government." That wasn't exactly true, but close enough. "I guess it would fit, in a perverse way. It'd take a really unusual personality to make a Bench Specialist out of a female Dolgorukij, what with the cultural biases. So she might as well be Malcontent. She's not likely to have had any chance of fitting in on her own. Who is this woman?"

"Name of Rafenkel. Blonde hair, brown eyes, soft voice, impressive vocabulary. Oh. Capercoy's here for Cintaro."

She hadn't seen Capercoy for years, either. Under the influence of her hot bath and the delicacies on the table, Jils decided to risk a blunt question. "Any of them likely to be carrying a Bench warrant with my name on it?"

No, she hadn't surprised him. She would have been surprised if she had. He just took a moment to think, pouring her a glass from one of the flacons. Thick peary juice, by the perfume of it. Peary juice with a slice of citrus to keep the sweet sharp and focused on the edge of the senses.

"I don't think so, Jils. Despite what any given Judge might think, people who actually know are not going to take the idea that you killed him and then tried to discover the body seriously. Too many problems. And there's the other thing."

What other thing was that? It certainly was good juice. She held out her flask for a refill, listening.

"You're here from Chilleau, to observe and then defend. We need to get this done. We all know that. You're as safe as any of us until the Selection is decided, Jils, you can have my life on it."

Oddly enough, that was comforting. It wasn't the same as claiming that nobody with the lawful authority to murder her for cause believed that cause existed. Pointing out that it would not be expedient to murder her until an answer had been agreed to in the matter of the Selection was much more limited an assurance, but much more solid regardless.

"Well, it's my life, not yours." But she appreciated his candor. "I'll have that tray of the semi-soft, please."

She couldn't quite eat, drink, and be merry. She'd always preferred moderation in most things anyway, but she'd been warned: preheats for the next while and, whether or not she was comfortable with what seemed to be an assumption of earned privilege, there was no sense in letting this feast go to waste.

THE LIGHT ACCESS ports in the cave roof high above shone against the darkness like stars from the surface of a low-atmosphere moon, brilliant, steady, dangerous to gaze upon too directly for too long. Even though the ventilation shafts were sunk through level upon level of igneous rock to provide air to the cavern complex, the solar reflectors and refractors that carried ambient light down through the earth were efficient enough to transmit intensities of light that were not safe to be long gazed upon with an unshielded eye.

Erenja Rafenkel sighed, and dropped her head to focus once more on her target. She liked deep places as well as she liked high places, which was not particularly. Yes, she was actually Kizakh Dolgorukij by birth, but her people had been city people. Tradesmen and mercantile women. Skilled piecework in fabric, wood, and ceramics, born and bred to an urban environment for generations, and as attached to the famous high aeries of the Chetalra Mountains of Azanry as she was to any other abstract and otherwise meaningless concept.

Rivers she understood; rivers had featured in some of the happiest memories of her childhood—walking in a public park on her saint's-day, hand in hand with her mother or her father or an aunt or uncle down a gentle path along the riverside. Feeding the ducks on bread crusts.

There was a perfectly beautiful river in Brisinje, but it might as well have been in Tuberchiss for all the pleasure she could take in it. It was well north of the ancient and blind shore on which she stood. Some octave, it would wear its way finally down past its bed into this cavern, perhaps, and then there would be a cataract of spectacular beauty to enjoy but nobody to enjoy it with the cavern flooded out.

She was being watched. The skin at the place where the fur over her shoulder would lie if she were dire-wolf instead of Dolgorukij was prickling as though it remembered what it had been like to raise its hackles. She welcomed the knowledge; there was always the danger, in throwing a knife, that concentration would blinker the senses and shut away peripheral information that could be crucial. It made her aim much less reliable. But keeping her senses open to all the input around her would keep her alive, in the long term, much longer than simply superlative aim with a throwing-knife.

The range was a stretch of the midnight beach that ran between the cavern walls and the black lake, almost unimaginably old, lit with all-spectrums to supplement the channeled light of Brisinje's sun and moons. There was no sense in speaking to Bench Specialists about "alien environments." Few environments were totally alien to a Bench

Specialist with anything more than a handful of missions in memory, and yet this one was as fantastic as any Rafenkel had seen yet.

This facility had been a research station, a place to study rock formations and analyze the chemical composition of the cold but living water and catalog the life that had adapted to this bleak and nearly eventless ecological niche. Once its presence had contaminated the environment past hope of remediation, the station had been abandoned. Functionally forgotten, it made a good site for a convocation the likes of which the Bench had never seen—a gathering of Bench Specialists to decide the fate of the Jurisdiction.

Steadying her arm, she took aim. The air was pleasantly cool, and the flavor of the moisture in the air was sharp and clean like that of an autumn wind. Whoever was watching had stilled their breath, but was shifting position so that fabric caught against fabric. The vestigial scales of one of the black lake's blind eel-like fish caught the sun and reflected it, a gleaming silver serpent in the obsidian waters. She threw. The knife flew clean and true to target, and sang as it struck home.

She straightened up. "Capercoy," she said. "Maybe Balkney. But I'd be surprised if you were Rinpen. What's on your mind?"

"Time," her watcher replied, and stepped away from the shadows at the rock wall to show himself. Balkney. The Hangman. A Bench executioner, and welcome to the job, but he was no more personally unpleasant about it than the next man, so long as the next man was understood to be a Bench Specialist. There were much worse ways to die than by Balkney's agency, and she had implemented some of them from time to time herself. Time. That was what Balkney had just said. There was more to it than that, though, she was sure. She moved downrange to her targets to retrieve her knives without reply, to leave him plenty of space in which to speak.

"Specifically, the time that has elapsed between the death of the First Secretary at Chilleau and now. What can we do to speed the resolution of the issue?"

He'd tell her. This wasn't any sort of a casual conversation. Examining one blade, holding it up to the sun-stars in the sky—there was a minute nick in the edge, wasn't there?—Rafenkel wondered what was on Balkney's mind. "Go on."

Now he was beside her, and reached out for the knife she had been frowning at. Holding it up to the light himself. "Yes. It's sharp.

It's a knife." He could be very unpleasant when he meant to be; now he was just being moody. He handed the knife back to her. "We have two problems with our instructions as they stand, as I see it. One, they call for revisitation of issues that do not need to be discussed. Haspirzak is willing to freely admit that it should not be the next First Judge. It therefore makes no sense to take the time to challenge Haspirzak against all comers."

He could say that. He was here for Haspirzak, to represent the Third Judge's interest and put forth the Third Judge's platform. He was right, too: Haspirzak was not in serious contention for the Selection. Was it really necessary to go through a formal disqualification of a Judiciary that had never entered itself into competition in the first place?

"We've never done this before," she reminded him. "It's best to be careful, accordingly. History will judge. It's up to us to ensure that we find the best solution to a situation that is already deeply to be regretted without creating any unnecessary turmoil to sap our resources and trouble our citizenry."

"Which is exactly why I think we should reconsider," he said, agreeably enough, taking her arm to walk her to a stone bench beside the door of the air-lock that would lead them back into the research station, embedded in the living rock. He was not a tall man, and she was tall for a Dolgorukij; but "tall for a Dolgorukij female" meant about the same thing as "medium height, Standard," when applied to city people, and so he had to lower his head to maintain eye contact.

"I'm not in the least interested in proving to history that Haspirzak was really and truly not an option. I do want to be sure that some alternatives are at least addressed. It's not just Chilleau, one question. It's at least three."

And he had a point, there.

She could hear the soft plashing of oars. Someone was out there in the darkness beyond the full-spectrums, lit only by the piped light from the surface. Zeman would be having a scull. There were no breezes here to disturb the surface of the water. She saw Zeman now, and that scull seemed to glide upon glass.

"Chilleau at Chilleau now, Chilleau at Fontailloe, Chilleau at Chilleau later." Yes, she had heard the issues identified. "And, of course, Fontailloe at Fontailloe. Or nothing."

Balkney snorted. The sound carried over the still water to echo vaguely in the dark. The acoustics of this place were strange. Zeman would be able to hear the entire conversation. That was one of the reasons it was safe to be having it: a third party could witness to the exact nature of the conversation, and testify as to whether was evidence of collusion or undue influence.

"The confederacy model. Yes. If you ask me that shouldn't be so much as discussed. But it's as you said. The verdict of history."

"So what do the others think?" Rafenkel asked casually, fitting her knife into its soft wrap alongside its fellows. They were beautiful knives. She was fond of them. Far from Emandisan steel, of course, but there was very little that could really compare.

"Tanifer spoke to me about it." The question clearly did not embarrass Balkney in the slightest. "Said that he'd discussed it with Nion and Rinpen. I talked to Capercoy. No one's spoken to Delleroy or Ivers, of course."

Because they weren't here. Well. It was hardly a conspiracy, then, if everybody was in on it. "Zeman?"

"I thought I'd stick around and wait for him. I like the idea of cutting out some iterations to save time, Rafe. I don't like the thought of not working out every real alternative, and that means time, and I can only stand the idea of taking more time if I can make it up somewhere."

If things went on much longer, Fleet would have to cede much more responsibility to the Home Defense Fleets for police duty than Fleet wanted to, because Fleet simply didn't have the resources to do all that needed to be done by way of patrol and containment, and even if Fleet managed to wrest the additional taxation privileges that it sought from the Bench it wouldn't solve the problem. Money couldn't create a disciplined recruit class overnight.

But Fleet was holding out against ceding any of its authority to the Home Defense Fleets for reasons that Rafenkel knew to be excellent. Once give people the idea that they could patrol their own spheres of influence and keep their own peace, and they would be very reluctant to give that power up, and even more reluctant to continue to remit tax money to fund an external Fleet to do a job that they could do themselves.

There was the other consideration, as well; the Combine had never quite adjusted to Bench-dictated equal rights for Sarvaw, and what was to stop the Combine's Home Defense Fleet from finishing the job that Chuvishka Kospodar had so notoriously started, generations ago? The Bench meant one law for all people, at least where trade was concerned. Home Defense Fleets had their own stores to house. What was the phrase? Their own oxen to gore?

"No harm in at least speaking to Tirom about it." Brisinje's First Secretary was their official point of contact with the Bench for the purposes of this exercise; he would be coming down with Delleroy and Ivers, when she got here, and they could be started.

They could have been started already, but Ivers was for the Second Judge, who had been cruelly robbed of the Selection and there was nothing anybody could do about it. There was no honorable way in which they could decide issues between themselves, without the wronged judge's representative on hand to follow the events and agreements, and speak for Chilleau's interest. "We could meet after third-meal. Clarify parameters. Be ready to go."

Balkney was gazing out over the black lake now, at the bioluminescence in the water stirred and roiled by the oars of Zeman's scull. "Do you think she did it?"

Knives stowed, Rafenkel rolled the bundle and tied it closed with one hand. Practice. "Ivers?" Could have. We all know that Verlaine's agenda would have been difficult to implement, especially where Fleet's concerned. But unless she had reason to believe that the penance was genuinely worse than the peccadillo, assassination seems too extreme. Fleet wouldn't have allowed any drastic measures. He'd have had to take it slowly."

"Interesting analysis," Balkney said, waving for Zeman to come to shore. People like Balkney were employed against sensitive targets—and dangerous ones. Like other Bench Specialists. Like senior administrative officials? "Thank you. See you in common after third-meal, Rafe."

There hadn't been a Bench warrant on the First Secretary. How could there have been? And yet Chilleau's security system had been gotten past. That took a very sophisticated understanding of Security codes. Whether or not Jils Ivers had that level of in-depth knowledge Rafenkel didn't know, but she would have been surprised if Balkney didn't have what it would take. Balkney and Tanifer, to name the two most obvious.

Preconceptions and assumptions were the enemy: they would put out your eyes and blind you to the army that stood gathering in the young wheat until it was too late and the raiders were upon you. Rafenkel put hers away in the locked place in her mind that she kept for such enemies of analysis, and went to wash and change before she took third-meal.

"REALLY?" RUKOTA SAID, impressed, and set a *yaohat* token down in Sperantz. The card array was almost complete. Had Vogel noticed that, with the placement of yaohat in the Sperantz slot, the way was clear for Rukota to put Caliform in Jabe, and take the hand with *forests?* "That was you, at Ankhor? I'm impressed."

He meant it, too. The Ankhor campaigns had been among the ugliest and unhappiest with which he had ever been associated. He'd been a much more junior officer then.

Vogel nodded. He was a man of more or less usual height, with a grizzled iron-gray moustache and a battered campaign hat pushed well back on his head, whose relatively broad high forehead coupled with the deep set of his pale blue eyes pointed at a lineage somewhere down along the Glenglies group, class six hominid.

"Fleet had ten cruisers in reserve," Vogel said. "Port Carue had stealth atomics. We'd never have been able to stop it if both sides hadn't been equally convinced that the balance of power was in their hands."

"How d'you mean?" This was intriguing. Rukota knew what Fleet had been holding, standing off on vector transit, due to arrive within hours if the cease-fire hadn't been declared. He hadn't heard about any stealth atomics, but neither had he ever noticed Fleet's cruiser array in any of the official narratives.

"Game theory." Vogel plucked a card out of his hand and put it down in Magenir.

Wait a minute, Rukota thought, alarmed. There were three, five, seven tokens containing water all around Magenir. If Vogel played anything with an earthquake in it he could sweep the board on a lahar.

"Each party believed they were negotiating from a position of strength. Neither party felt that they'd been forced to it by circumstances, because both had secret weapons that they could easily have deployed. At the same time, each side believed that the other really had no choice whether they knew it or not. Stable outcome."

He was in trouble. He was in serious trouble. He didn't have a single card that had containment anywhere in it. Could he get away with *delta* in Gamie? That would channel all the water away safely. He wasn't sure what else he could try. He set it down.

"Well, we were all just as glad to see it over." Many of the people Rukota been with, at any rate, though some among them had resented being deprived of a chance to work off a little steam. The only trouble with a successful Jurisdiction, Rukota decided, was that there was too much law and order in the world for people to have a good appreciation for how horrible chaos and conflict could be. They'd been lucky at Ankhor. There'd been a large civilian population in Port Carue, non-combatants, citizens and the trading community.

Even people who had held the civilian population responsible for the extremism of its government had found no way to blame the merchant community. For himself, Rukota hadn't been able to ever quite figure out how some domestic laborer in a public school could be held responsible enough for the political intransigence of an oligarchy to deserve to die for being there.

Vogel frowned at his hand suddenly, but it wasn't a worried frown. It was one of concentration. Rukota felt a sinking sensation in the pit of his stomach. No, it would be too unfair. But nobody had played nibs, not yet, Vogel could have it in his hand, and if he did—and if he put it in Sacroe—there would be almost no way to avoid a cataclysmic *worldfire,* if that happened, and Vogel would win the game as well as the hand.

"It was a close one," Vogel admitted. There was a note of decision and determination in his voice. "But we pulled it off, because both sides were willing to avoid slaughtering the other if it could be done. Best basis for an entente, really, positive desire to not inflict tremendous losses on the other side. I think maybe I'll try playing—"

The talk-alert sounded at the door to the ready room just in time. Vogel looked up toward the door with an expression of mild annoyance on his face, and played *belange* in Sacroe. Belange, and not nibs. Belange had gale force in it—why, if Rukota played his last remaining *severanc* in Hellox he would have a near-nova, and he'd never even seen one played before, the odds against the combination were—The odds were—

They were more than he could calculate. "Step through," Rukota called, and put down his hand. "Are they ready for us in Secured Medical?"

The door opened; one of Koscuisko's people entered. Micmac Pyotr. Maybe Pyotr Micmac, Rukota decided, since he'd heard Koscuisko call the big black-skinned Skaltsparmal bond-involuntary "Pyotr" but never "Mister Pyotr," and Koscuisko called his bond-involuntaries by their names. Something to do with delicacy in the issue of reminding them of the detention facility in which they had been Bonded, Rukota understood, since a bond-involuntary took his formal name from the establishment at which he had been placed under governor for the thirty-year term of his sentence. Unless he was Nurail. Rukota didn't think there were any Pyotr Detention Facilities, but he couldn't recall having heard of a Micmac Detention Facility, either.

"Yes, General Rukota, thank you. Ship's chief medical officer to be waiting for General Rukota and Bench Intelligence Specialist Vogel in Secured Medical, sir, if the officer will follow me."

Well, he could finish the hand, or he could just go. Vogel might believe he was taking an easy escape from a losing position if he did that, but it didn't matter. He had seen the potential for a genuine near nova. It was enough. He could die without regret, even if not happily.

"Shall we?" he asked.

Vogel pushed back from the table, set his cap on straight, and almost saluted. Almost. Vogel knew. "After you."

Resisting the temptation to see what Vogel had been holding in his hand in reserve, Rukota led the way out of the room, following Pyotr and the two Security with him down the corridors. One bond-involuntary, Godsalt; one not, a woman, Smath, he thought.

Koscuisko was waiting for them when they got there. Secured Medical was in one of the most remote areas of the entire ship—not that a ship of even the *Ragnarok's* significant size could have any remote places on it, especially when you'd been living there for as many years as some of the *Ragnarok's* crew had been. Koscuisko didn't look happy. Why should he? Rukota couldn't imagine anybody being happy about going into a torture chamber, and Koscuisko was the one who knew exactly what had gone on in there.

It was widely understood that Koscuisko's peculiar advantage in Inquisition lay in the combination of empathy and exquisite sadism—a culturally inculcated passion to be the master of all that he surveyed, coupled with the unpredictable psychological quirk that afflicted a small but select group of unfortunate souls. Koscuisko was

a decent enough sort in other areas of his life for all that, and nobody had sent him down to Secured Medical since Rukota had come
on board, so he had no particular problem with Koscuisko.

In fact, Rukota almost liked Koscuisko, if only by association.
Koscuisko's troops were as solid as any Rukota had ever had the
pleasure to associate with. Koscuisko didn't get the credit for that,
of course, but he did get credit for being an officer that honest
troops respected and were fond of even when they couldn't exactly
bring themselves to admire him.

"Specialist," Koscuisko said, and bowed. "General. We may
go in now." But he made no move to key the admit until Pyotr,
standing behind Rukota in the corridor, coughed gently. The sound
seemed to wake Koscuisko up in some sense, and he turned to the
panel beside the door with no visible sign of reluctance save for
the white lines of his tensely compressed lips. Rukota didn't usually
notice much about men's lips, but there was so little color in
Koscuisko's face to begin with that the additional paleness of
Koscuisko's mouth was hard to miss. This was harder for the doctor than he'd anticipated, perhaps.

The door slid open on its diagonal track. Koscuisko stepped
through and waited—facing the far wall, which wasn't all that very
far—until the female troop Pyotr had brought with them had closed
the outer door and given the all-clear. "Secured, your Excellency."

He could see the rise and fall of Koscuisko's shoulders as the
man took a deep breath then eyed the admit. The inner door slid
open, and there it was: Secured Medical. Rukota had seen one of
these places once before in his life—it was an orientation item—but
this was different. This had been one of the most frequently used
such rooms in Fleet until Captain Lowden's death, and a person
generally didn't expect to see the Ship's Engineer in the Inquisitor's
seat, either.

Koscuisko had certainly not expected that. Rukota could tell by
the half-a-step backward that Koscuisko took, raising one hand halfway in the classic gesture of suspicion and reproach and defensive-
ness. Wheatfields stood up and stepped off the little platform, a
gently malicious smile not so much on his face as expressed in his
entire body. "Nice to see you, Andrej," Wheatfields said. "I just
thought I'd be present for your return to your old environs. You
must have so many happy memories of this place."

But there was something else going on here as well. Rukota could almost smell it. He couldn't figure it out, but he could sense it. "Memories, at least," Koscuisko said, with no particular emotion that Rukota could identify in his voice. "You've re-arranged, I see."

The wall in front of the Inquisitor's chair had been completely covered, floor to ceiling, by stacked crates, perhaps two crates deep. The wall panels behind which the instruments of torture were stored, the door at the far end of the room that led to the small cell where a prisoner under interrogation would be kept—all completely blocked off. Rukota didn't know what was in the crates, but he knew he wouldn't be surprised if they were the heaviest things the Engineer could come up with.

Even the ceiling had an anomalous look, paneled with flatform storage in netting; no sign of the grid or any of the suspension points. Thorough. A person wouldn't know that this had ever been anything but a storeroom except for the chair in the middle of it— a perfectly innocuous seat with padded arm-rests, comfortable, provided for the Inquisitor's use—and the aisle that had been cleared through to the right of the doorway to give access to the evidence locker. Just another anonymous panel in the wall, but one of the most secure places on board the *Ragnarok*.

"Do you like it?" Wheatfields asked, standing very close to Koscuisko in a casually threatening manner. "I'm sure we could arrange to forget you're down here, Andrej. Except that your damned Security would probably come looking for you," he added, looking at Pyotr over Koscuisko's head. Wheatfields was an extraordinarily tall man, fully an eight taller than Rukota himself. Rukota glanced back over his own shoulder, just in time to catch Pyotr's polite bow of acknowledgment. Wheatfields didn't like Koscuisko, but he was apparently unwilling to make Koscuisko's Security uncomfortable just to make the point.

"I could watch tapes to pass the time," Koscuisko said. His voice had turned chillingly cold. "I understand you have some. Thank you, Serge, it is kind of you to be here for me."

The attack seemed to be as effective as it was apparently unexpected. Wheatfields stepped back a pace, but it was almost as if he'd actually staggered. From what Rukota had gathered of the tribal knowledge of the *Ragnarok*, this was a rare moment of ascendancy for Koscuisko, but he didn't seem to have noticed.

Koscuisko turned to his right instead, stepping through the shallow aisle between boxes to the wall to code his secured-access admits. Rukota hesitated for a moment before deciding that noticing the possibility that Koscuisko had floored Wheatfields would only contribute to the awkwardness, and followed Koscuisko to watch over his shoulder.

The locker opened. There were two records inside that Rukota could see. Koscuisko lifted one out—top shelf, a small box, no larger than a modestlysized meal-tray—and held it out for Rukota to take, not looking at him, before taking the second record out.

"Access modification," Koscuisko said. "On authority Andrej Ulexeievitch Koscuisko, Ship's Inquisitor, assigned to the Jurisdiction Fleet Ship *Ragnarok*. Confirm."

The record seemed to think about it for a moment. Rukota knew that what the record was doing was confirming Koscuisko's voice, the genetic information in the sweat of Koscuisko's hands, and scanning the central Judicial files for any hint that Andrej Ulexeievitch Koscuisko was no longer the appropriate authority. Finding none—obviously enough—the record said, "Confirmed" in its calm clear voice, and Koscuisko seemed to relax by some unquantifiable fraction.

"Access is granted for purpose of lawful investigation to the following named individuals. Please state your name and your rank. Karol Aphon Vogel." Koscuisko passed the record in his hands to Vogel, who took it.

"Bench Intelligence Specialist," Vogel confirmed. "Karol Aphon Vogel. Judicial ad-hoc investigation in process. File in record." Or, in other words, the record could check and make sure that Vogel was Vogel, but would not be expecting to find any other information; nor would the record release any to inquiries from its controller in Judicial systems. As far as anybody would be able to find out, Vogel would still be exactly as disappeared as Rukota understood he'd been before he'd arrived on the *Ragnarok*, no more, no less.

And now it was his turn. He passed the record that Koscuisko had handed to him off to the nearest person—Smath, as it happened—took the genuine record from Vogel, and spoke.

"General Dierryk Rukota, Second Fleet, Ibliss Judiciary. On detail, assigned." Well, that was what his last status had been, at least—detailed on behalf of Pesadie Training Command to oversee a preliminary audit investigation. He couldn't help but wonder what the record would make of his claim, though.

"Identity confirmed. Status is not confirmed."

So he wouldn't find out. Oh, well. Maybe he didn't want to know.

"These two named and registered individuals are to have access to Secured Medical, by order and direction of Captain Jennet ap Rhiannon, Jurisdiction Fleet Ship *Ragnarok*, commanding. They are to have joint access only. No unaccompanied access is authorized."

Another intriguing question, there, but the record didn't seem to notice it. Koscuisko would have invoked ap Rhiannon's name and status as captain when he'd secured the forged record in the first place, however, so maybe that hurdle wasn't so very high, because the record only said, "Confirmed."

Koscuisko put the record back in its locker where it lived. The entire room was on record. It did not need to be anyplace in particular to talk to Ship's Security. "Give the Bench Specialist the evidence," Koscuisko said. "Specialist Vogel. This piece of evidence is that which you wish to examine." It was marked, as well: Koscuisko's secure-code, evidence, bright and clear as its status panel. "Serge, I need you to move some more of these boxes. Two can tell you where. Because Specialist Vogel will not begin his analysis until we are on record. Also, I expect another chair will be required, and a table, and lights."

Rukota hadn't really thought about it, but Koscuisko was right. Vogel clearly couldn't be allowed to take the forged record out of this room. Koscuisko would lose control of his evidence; and this evidence was the foundation of the *Ragnarok's* defense.

Without proof that the accusations against the *Ragnarok's* Security were false—as demonstrated by the torture and confession and death, on record, of four people who were undeniably alive—it was back to an internal squabble about protocol and insubordination. An internal squabble that would require investigation, which meant Inquiry, which meant torture and killing of at least some of the *Ragnarok's* crew; and the execution of its acting captain as well, if Fleet upheld a finding of mutinous intent.

"And I expect to see you damned in Hell forever, Andrej." But the tone of Wheatfields' voice didn't match the venom of his words; it was almost cheerful.

"You'll have plenty of company there, Serge. The Balancers will have to build a special arena, I expect. One can hear the news report already: Andrej Koscuisko has died, demand for visitor's passes to Hell swamps administration."

Wheatfields snorted and moved as if to go past Koscuisko and away, but did the most peculiar thing. He stopped on his way past, and put one hand to Koscuisko's shoulder.

"Adding arrant egomania to your already impressive list of personal shortcomings," Wheatfields said. "I'll send some people."

Koscuisko merely nodded, as if he was accepting a rebuke. Or expressing appreciation. For what? He hadn't taken Wheatfields' hand off at the wrist for touching him, either. Once Wheatfields had left, Koscuisko spoke to Vogel. "I will ask Cousin Stanoczk to send people to attend you," Koscuisko said. "You will have no difficulty understanding why I do not wish to ask any of the ship's security to be here. If there is anything that you need, please let me know."

"Very kind, your Excellency. I'm sure we'll be very well taken care of. No need to keep you."

Go away. Koscuisko was clearly just as happy to do just that. It was only the stray glance that Rukota chanced to intercept that clarified things in Rukota's mind; the expression on Koscuisko's face, turning his head to look around him as he walked away, was one of a truly indescribable longing.

Koscuisko was suffering from being here, yes, but it was worse than that; because Koscuisko all too clearly almost wished that he was staying to ask somebody questions.

But Wheatfields already knew that, didn't he? That was why he'd been here, and that was why Koscuisko had made so brutal a reference to the murder of Wheatfields' beloved, so many years ago. Wheels within wheels within wheels. It was dangerous to let people stay on one ship with one another for so long. When a Command had time to forge bonds of such intimacy between its crew, there was no force in known Space that could tear it apart.

Now more than ever Rukota understood that the captain and crew of the *Ragnarok* were capable of anything, absolutely anything, and nothing that Fleet could do would stop them. It was a profoundly depressing thought.

Vogel pulled a packet of playing cards out of the chest-plaquet of his uniform. "While we're waiting?" Vogel asked, and handed the forged record to Rukota. "We can use the chair."

The arms for a surface, the seat for the playing field. The floor had not been covered over. It was still the grim gray lattice of a torture cell, through which blood could drip and be washed away when it was all over and the body had been fed to the conversion furnaces. That the room was clean, Rukota had no doubt. He still couldn't quite envision playing a game of cards on such a surface as that.

"You're on," he said. "Your deal or mine?"

CHAPTER SEVEN
UNEXPECTED DEVELOPMENTS

EARLY IN BRISINJE'S morning, the talk-alert sounded. Jils Ivers woke from a deep sleep and blinked twice at the darkness above her. "Yes."

Brisinje. A bed in a luxury guest suite. A very plush and ostentatious luxury guest suite, and one she would have enjoyed much more if it hadn't been for the hints she'd gotten that she was expected to require such expensive perquisites as due her, at least at Brisinje Judiciary.

There was nothing to stop a Bench Specialist from enjoying luxury, of course, because a Bench Specialist was as likely to be found in a crib that rented by the hour, or a tiny sleeping-hex in a port, or in a slum in a shack roofed over with waste packaging material, as lolling around in a tubful of heated scented water in a suite the size of a city block with a view of the river worth millions. If she wanted to sample the life of an autocrat, however, she could always just visit Azanry, and see if she could wrangle an invitation to attend on Andrej Koscuisko's parents at Chelatring Side, in the mountains.

"Warning order," the talk-alert said. Padrake, Jils realized. "There's fast-meal on the table, Jils, get yourself dressed. We've got to move out before sunrise."

Traveling at night didn't present any real barriers to a determined observer; it simply reduced the odds of being accidentally observed by some casual passerby. "With you shortly," she replied, and then waited for the clear-tone on the talk-alert to sound before she got out of bed.

She hadn't bothered to unpack most of her kit last night, so it didn't take much time to pack up and get dressed. Fast-meal was on the table as Padrake had promised; the kilpers was hot and the cream was buttery, just as she liked it.

When she'd retrieved her data-reader from its safe and opened up the outermost door of the suite to step out into the very early morning, Padrake was there, sitting on a low stone bench in the atrium, waiting for her.

"Slept well, I hope?" he asked with a wink, which she filed away for future reference. "Arik's waiting for us, let's go."

Was he really? She wasn't sure she liked the sound of that. There was a thin line between a First Secretary waiting because a meeting had been scheduled or a late development had to be pursued and reported on, and a First Secretary waiting because a Bench Specialist felt she outranked him and he could very well just wait.

There were two ground cars waiting at the gate to the guest compound, and Arik Tirom was in the first one waiting—hands folded in his lap, evidently meditating with his eyes closed. Someone got out of the second car, saluted, got right back in; Security. Padrake pointed; Jils went to join Arik Tirom in the first car, murmuring a polite "Good-greeting, First Secretary," as she ducked her head to climb in and sit down on the padded bench facing the rear of the vehicle.

Tirom opened one eye and grinned at her. "If you say so, Specialist Ivers. I call it altogether too early in the morning for any greeting to be good. Nothing personal." It was a common complaint for the First Secretary, apparently, because all Padrake said—respectfully enough, Jils supposed—was "You've got just enough time for a short nap, Arik," as he joined her on the bench in the ground-car.

By the tell-tales in the framework all around her, Jils could see that it was a high-security model of ground-car with the full range of detection avoidance technologies on board, but perhaps the single most important of those was the fact that it looked like a perfectly innocuous, not too new, not too expensive, general-purpose ground-car, from the outside at least.

That made things a little cramped on the inside of the car, but Jils couldn't make up her mind to be very much bothered by the heat and the pressure of Padrake's body so close to hers. Her body knew his body, and remembered it fondly for its strength and grace and the abstract beauty of the masculine frame when it was unclothed.

She could feel her own flesh relaxing against his as against a familiar and comfortable support, a safe place, and had just gotten to the point of deciding whether or not she was going to start thinking about sleeping arrangements wherever they were going when the ground-car pulled to a stop and the doors slid open.

"Site secured," the ground-car's systems said. "Shuttle is on stand-by. Confirm departure in twelve."

The second ground-car was stopped as well, but she couldn't see any of the Security: quite possibly they were already emplaced. There were no hints of sunrise on the horizon, any horizon—the sky was a faintly glowing deep-napped charcoal gray, the smoke and ash in the upper atmosphere catching the lights from the burning launch fields and diffusing it through the sky until it wasn't even possible to tell which direction the launch fields were.

When a fire of that sort got large enough, it was frequently all that could be done to contain it. There was no way to actually extinguish an entire field of burning fuel tanks without more resources than the Bench apparently had here at Brisinje—not with a city so close by. All they could do was to keep the surrounding areas from harm as well as they could, and let the fire burn out.

Most of the fuel stores would have been safely bunkered in hardened compartments with significant thermal buffering, but thermal buffering was only good for a range of temperatures over a period of time, and if the fire burned too hot—or went on for too long—even thermal buffers could fail. It was unnecessary for her to remind herself that a sabotaged thermal buffer would fail much more quickly and efficiently.

The uniform glow in the sky and its unnaturally gray-black color gave the scene a very surreal cast. They had stopped on an old concrete apron at the riverside, in front of a seemingly dilapidated one-story building—quite small, one or two rooms if that, surely. There were weeds growing up between the cracks in the concrete and the apron.

But the bracket lock on the door only looked old; that would never yield to a key code sequence, Jils thought, watching Padrake invoke the secures with his identity-chop. That bracket lock was a fully functioning security spider, suspicious and conservative, that kept them waiting for several long moments before it grudgingly agreed that Padrake's chop was exactly what it claimed to be, and let its bolt slip.

That meant the defensive traps and alarms set around and within were temporarily deactivated, Jils knew. Or else the spider had decided that there was something just a whisper web-filament thin the wrong side of "all correct" about Padrake's chop and wanted them all inside where it could keep them until Port security could arrive.

Inside there had once been an office, with a squared-off inner office in the middle of the otherwise unpartitioned building. It looked a little bit like a public ground transportation station to Jils, and then she realized that that was not too far from its actual purpose. Padrake led the two of them, Jils and the First Secretary, around to the rear wall of the inner office, where the controls were. The shaft car was waiting for them. Self-braking linear descent module.

A mine elevator, in principle, but a very well appointed one with built-in seating and pleasant surfaces, freshly oxygenated air in circulation, all of the amenities. She checked the ceiling by force of habit as she stepped in: yes, there was the emergency escape hatch, right where it was supposed to be.

Padrake locked off the doors and keyed the program, and the elevator started to move. There was nowhere to go but down from their current level, though, so—Jils asked herself—was "elevator" really the right word? It would be when they were ready to come up again, yes, but who knew when that would be?

"It'll be fifteen or twenty," Padrake said to her, seating himself near the control panel. "Make yourself comfortable." Tirom had already done so, Jils noted; he'd made this trip before, obviously enough.

"Where are we going?" She knew the answer. Padrake would know she knew. She trusted him to answer the right question.

"Chambers here are built on an old flood plain, Jils, a gigantic lahar runoff zone. But underneath the layer of mud deposit that went down when the Broken Crown Mountains blew there are caverns in the rock that were there even before that happened. There's an abandoned research station."

How far down were they going? She didn't want to ask. If she stopped to think about it, she'd get claustrophobic, but that explained the constant air circulation, right there. Claustrophobia. People could frequently succeed in ignoring the fact that they were encased in a tiny box descending at an unknown rate of speed for an unknown distance through layers of what had once been mud and rock and boiling water to spend an indeterminate period of time in an undisclosed location if they could feel what their most primitive brain would interpret as a breeze in their faces.

A research station buried deep would have had limited contact with the surface; limited accessibility, and probably in-depth life science monitoring, so that there could be no off-the-record collusion between Bench Specialists. As if there would be—but then such collusion would be all the more dangerous if it did happen, Jils reminded herself, because of just that presumption, that of course there would not be.

"And your role in this visit, First Secretary?" she asked.

Tirom had been listening quietly, with one hand resting on his knee and the other arm flung over the back of the empty seat next to him, across from where Jils sat on the corner angle adjacent to Padrake's left. He looked very comfortable. No issues with very deep places, or if there were any he was good enough at hiding them to fool Jils.

"Official Bench sponsorship, Dame Ivers, formal approval of predetermined scheme of procedure. I get to make a speech. Then I get out, and leave you and Padrake to do the job we need for you to do."

There were no view-ports in this car and she was glad of it. She couldn't see depth, speed of descent, time remaining, on the controls; Padrake's body was in the way. How long had they been traveling?

"You'll be getting regular reports, then, I expect?" Her normally precise time-sense did not feel quite trustworthy to her; she decided against trying to second-guess herself. Maybe there was something about traveling down rather than up or across that had a disorienting effect on her internal chronometer—at least where the gravity was not artificially generated. She hadn't been deep in a long time, not deep in the earth rather than deep in deep space.

And the deep she'd been hadn't been so deep as this. Surely, it had taken her three hours to descend the cable-line into Cabinap, but that had been on her own power with a simple gravity-assist. More controlled. Safer. She and Karol—she cut off that line of thought and frowned, trying to concentrate on what Tirom was saying. She'd asked the question. The least she could do was pay attention to the answer.

"There's a central comm console, secured transmit, needless to say." Prudent and proper, just and judicious, Jils thought, irreverently. "The Bench needs you to concentrate all of your special skills and qualifications on the one issue. Forget all about the rest of known Space just for now, Dame."

She'd gone into isolation to brainstorm solutions and model approaches before. She had to admit that this sounded like the most complete isolation she'd ever done. Even on vector in the middle of nowhere, you could get a conversation of sorts going with someone, if you had the power and there was someone scanning frequency or waiting for a predetermined contact.

She couldn't think of anything intelligent to say. Lapsing into silence after a polite "Thank you, sir," she brooded. If they killed her, they would leave her here. They might even simply leave her here, and let the "killing" part take care of itself.

The announcement of the Selection would be a wonderful time to release intelligence about the execution of Bench Intelligence Specialist Jils Ivers in connection with the investigation into the death of First Secretary Verlaine. It would be the truth, too, just not enough of it, but the investigation could be declared officially closed.

They would need to minimize the uncertainty in the environment, regardless of the final determination on a new First Judge. She would be a very tidy surrogate solution. She had until the Selection was decided, though.

She couldn't let her mind whirl like this. She had to put it away. She had a task facing her that she knew to be of more importance than her own life. Now was not the time to deny the Bench the best she had to offer just because it might include her own execution, for the good of the Judicial order.

"And we're here," Padrake said, reaching out to touch one of the controls. "It'll just be a moment for the doors. They'll be waiting for us in the theater, Arik, Jils, right, here we are, let's go."

The face of the car opened on a horizontal track to reveal a narrow, dimly lit corridor of dressed rock, and an airlock at the end of it. Contamination measures, Jils decided. There were three airlocks in all, each combining a number of different techniques to keep the interior as free of pollutants as possible—light, subsonics, positive air pressure.

Three airlocks, and on the far end of them when the door opened to let them pass Jils saw a welcoming committee waiting for them, more Bench Specialists than she had ever seen in one place before in her life. Not that that was so difficult a benchmark to exceed.

There were five of them waiting, Balkney in the lead. For a moment, Jils was convinced that she had traveled through three airlocks for nothing—that she would be shot down here and now, and what a mess that would make—before reason reasserted itself. They'd not shoot her in front of Brisinje's First Secretary. They'd wait.

"Gentles," the First Secretary said, and it occurred to Jils that apart from answering her question it was almost the first thing he'd said all trip. It was early. Maybe he was asleep. "You honor us. Is there a particular reason for this greeting party?"

There was a woman there with them, middling tall, dark blonde hair done up in a thick glossy braid, a face like a stereotypical pastoral worker of some sort—ruddy mouth, beautiful skin, dark arched eyebrows over dark brown eyes. Milkmaid, maybe. When she spoke, Jils knew in an instant that she was Combine, from the accent, and realized who the woman had to be. Rafenkel. Sant-Dasidar Judiciary. Was it her imagination, or did she see a hint of a bright red something hanging around the woman's neck beneath her duty-dress, something like the red halter of the Malcontent?

"It's an historic occasion," the woman said. "We don't initiate a convocation every day. We felt a little formality might be in order. The others are waiting for us in the theater."

In fact they'd never come together in Convocation before—or, if they had, it had never been recorded.

"Thank you, Dame Rafenkel," Tirom said, confirming Jils' assumption about the woman's identity. "After you."

Yes, the corridors were narrow and low-ceilinged, but they had room to walk two abreast. They'd have had to get heavy equipment into and out of the research station, Jils reminded herself. It wasn't far to another airlock, but one that opened onto a paved floor rather than one lined with sanitation fabric this time, and there was significantly more light.

"This way," Rafenkel said politely. The double doors of the theater were propped open to welcome them. As theaters went it was very small indeed, with seats in three tiers to accommodate a total of perhaps eighteen people all told. There was a table at the base of the theater, its lowest level, seven or eight steps down from the entry doors. Some chairs.

Capercoy, from the Fifth Judiciary at Cintaro, was seated at the table along with a sleepy-eyed man with glossy black hair whom she know by reputation as Rinpen from Ibliss. Capercoy stood up, Rinpen

went up the middle of the room to close the doors, Balkney ush-
ered the First Secretary to a seat and sat down himself next to Tirom.
Jils found a spot for herself, and Padrake seemed to waver between
several choices before he elected to place himself just in front of
her, in the lowest tier of seats.

Once the doors were closed, Capercoy spoke. "Thank you for
coming, First Secretary. Welcome back, Delleroy; welcome, Ivers."
Why did they bother to secure the doors? Jils wondered. Everybody
was here. Nine Bench Specialists; one First Secretary. "You know the
main purpose of our gathering, First Secretary, to present the Bench
instruction to proceed and to establish the ground-rules. We've been
talking about it and we think we want to change some of the ground-
rules, so we want to place a revised agenda in front of you before
we go on record."

She could see a subtle twitch in the uniform fabric across Padrake's
shoulders. Surprise. Wariness. Nothing too obvious, but it was there
for people who knew how to look at Padrake, and she did.

"Indeed," Tirom said, with commendable aplomb. "Do your
fellows know about this?"

Capercoy glanced over in her direction, his golden-brown
eyes touching first on Padrake's face and then on hers. Calm.
Sure. Confident. "No, First Secretary, neither Delleroy nor Ivers
have participated in this discussion. You'll remember, sir, that
when the Bench decided on convocation it was with full knowledge that there was not much by way of an idea on how to
proceed. But we had a plan."

"Which you wish to emend," Tirom agreed, perhaps to show
that he had been listening. "What do you propose?"

"We take it as given that the most obvious solution is to find a
way to select Chilleau Judiciary. If your counterpart at Chilleau had
not been murdered, it is almost certain that Chilleau would have
taken the selection"—with a Bench Specialist's characteristic care,
Capercoy had elected to characterize the selection as "almost" certain, Jils noticed—"and in fact it's widely believed in some areas that
Verlaine was killed in order to prevent that from happening."

Yes. Old news. "And if that's why Verlaine was killed, it's a bad
idea in principle to let anyone get the idea that it works." Rafenkel
had seated herself opposite Padrake, on the other side of the room.
She spoke calmly, reasonably, and she made a lot of sense. "Our

first priority should be to see whether there's any way in which Chilleau could still be selected."

"We do the Bench a disservice if we artificially restrict our selection set," Capercoy continued, building on Rafenkel's point as smoothly as though they'd scripted it. "After discussion we've decided that we'd like to propose consideration of Chilleau's selection standing without challenge as our first step. Because; if there is a way, we don't need to spend weeks working to the least worst alternative. The best solution remains Chilleau, if it can be done. We are all agreed on it."

That would gratify the Second Judge to a significant extent if she could hear it, Jils knew, but she was unlikely to. If she ever did, it would be only well after the convocation had concluded, announced its findings, and dissolved. Too bad.

"Does the Fifth Judge know about this?" Padrake demanded. "She can't have intended you to propose any such thing, Capercoy."

The Fifth Judge stood to gain the most from a consideration that excluded Chilleau Judiciary, and Capercoy was her representative.

Capercoy shook his head. "Of course not, Delleroy, we have communication security in effect. No, it wasn't in her instructions, anywhere. But she knows as well as anybody that we're here to make the best choice. If we can find a way, we can all go home early. Your endorsement, First Secretary."

This was a waste of time. Wasn't it? Hadn't they come here exactly because Chilleau Judiciary could not be selected so soon after losing its senior administrative officer? Well, no, they hadn't. They were here because it was assumed that Verlaine's death put Chilleau out of the competition. Bench Specialists didn't like to assume.

Padrake didn't like this proposal either, she could hear it in his voice. "Wait one moment, Capercoy, we can't stop there. It's not enough to ask if Chilleau can be selected. Why not ask whether a Judge should be promoted at Fontailloe, instead? Their administrative apparatus is intact. Or why not select the Second Judge, but send her to Fontailloe while Chilleau recovers?"

Ridiculous. Fontailloe was out of consideration. It was an old, tried, venerated practice to exclude the previous incumbent's Judiciary from the selection for the new First Judge, and the very few times when an exception had been made—always for only the very best, the very most pressing reasons—the Bench had invariably learned to regret it all over again. It was a solid curb on the natural tendency of power centers to pull more and more and more into their gravitational fields. Corruption was all but inevitable. Abuse went without saying.

And yet Capercoy merely nodded. "All reasonably possible alternatives will be considered, Delleroy. I ask again for your endorsement, First Secretary, we need to be sure we know what we can't do before we turn to the question of what is not impossible, and seven out of nine of us are agreed. Ivers and Delleroy have not yet been polled."

"I'm surprised," Tirom said. "But I can see your point. There is an additional issue, however. We have already suffered serious losses to the infrastructure of the Bench while we have been trying to figure out how to handle the situation. What if you derive no different result from such preliminary arguments from those already argued and discarded?"

That had been the first line of scrimmage, after all: the Second Judge insisting that the selection go forward, and the balance of the Bench declining to make any quick decisions. Well, most of the balance of the Bench, anyway—all of the Judiciaries that had been prepared to back Cintaro among them—and without a First Judge there was no tie-breaking vote to overbalance an even four-four split against Chilleau. Fontailloe didn't count. The First Judge was dead. And this was all the First Judge's fault, Jils thought resentfully, for dying so inconsiderately of a stroke in the first place.

"We've done an informal survey, First Secretary, and we believe that there are enough stipulations in place to address that issue. Ibliss will waive its place in the match. Supicor is willing to cede if it can't beat Cintaro. It was anticipated that Brisinje might be willing to cede as well. We can make up the time. And since those of us who've had a chance to discuss it are determined on seeing the test through, we will be testing those arguments along with the previously decided procedures if we have to. Your endorsement, First Secretary."

Tirom was backed into a corner, and he obviously knew it. "Very well, Capercoy. All present in favor of modifying the agreed-upon procedure along the lines proposed by Capercoy here in your presence and on your behalf will so signify by saying 'Yes.'"

Seven voices, all more or less determined, but all seven. Jils wasn't sure what she thought about it. She knew she wanted time to think before she would be ready to cast her vote, but her vote was not needed. The majority opinion was clear.

"So be it." Tirom stood up, with a grim expression on his face. "As it has been spoken, so it shall be done. Now. I should be getting back. Padrake, if you'll take me back to the elevator."

"We'll go with you," Capercoy said. Jils hardly heard him. They were going to start by arguing for Chilleau Judiciary. She'd thought she'd have days ahead of her, days to sit and observe the debate and not think about much of anything except whether the debate was fully and freely executed without intimidation, duress, improper influence, or evidence of collusion. That was out the airlock now as surely as Tirom would soon be.

Jils stood up and fetched her kit from under the seat as Padrake and Capercoy went away with Tirom. There was a woman she didn't think she'd met—young woman. It was hard to remember how young Jils had been when she'd sworn her duty: young, ambitious, and almost too sure that there were answers and she would find them. She'd found them. But they'd been to the wrong questions.

"Dame Ivers?" the young woman said, offering her hand. "We haven't met. Ghel Nion. For the Seventh Judge at Supicor."

Ah. Yes. "Good to make your acquaintance, Dame," Jils said, returning the offered handclasp with a cordiality that she did not really feel. "Could I ask you to show me to quarters? I've got all of this unpacking to do." She hefted her kit, and Nion grinned.

"It's a convocation, Ivers, not a beach party. How did you get a cabaña into that little package? Delighted. This way."

The Seventh Judge, at Supicor. Supicor had been the first of all the Judiciaries, the original—a long, long time ago. Supicor that had given birth to Jurisdiction, nourished it, promulgated it across known Space as the Bench expanded and encountered other hominid cultures as it came. All hominid cultures could be traced on genetic markers back to Supicor, so either the Bench represented Supicor's second wave of expansion or they'd come to Supicor from somewhere and rebounded.

Genetic evidence suggested support for the "second wave" theory but, as far as Jils knew, nobody except for the occasional zealot really cared. It had been a very long time ago. What mattered was where they were now, not where they had come from. Supicor was old and frayed and dingy, desperately poor, with only its story of cradling all hominids to sustain its pride. No more than that.

Just outside the door to the theater, Jils had to stop herself abruptly to avoid knocking in to Rafenkel, who was just straightening up from leaning against the far wall of the corridor with her arms folded across her breast. Watching. The doors had been open; what had she been watching for?

"Tirom's got an escort," Rafenkel said to Nion, who was behind Jils. Jils couldn't see her face, but could guess that Nion was a little surprised to be confronted. "Only polite to give a fellow Bench Specialist at least as much honor. Lead on, Nion, I'll bring up the rear and provide the travelogue."

Jils shrugged. "Just so long as I get to quarters," she agreed, hoping she didn't sound churlish. She was just tired. "Need to rinse my mouth." No, she needed a year off, and to discover who had killed First Secretary Verlaine and why, and where Karol Vogel was, and what it had been about Padrake's exact tone of voice that was bothering her ever so slightly at the back of her brain.

As if he'd been surprised, but not enough. As if he'd seen it coming. Could he have been in illicit communication with the Bench Specialists here, before he had come down himself? He'd probably escorted them all down. That was true. He had been back and forth. He could have seen it coming. That was true. There was no need to invent complications where none existed.

"We'll get you taken care of," Nion said cheerfully. There was a note of annoyance at the back of her voice, but a very subtle one. Too early for Jils to begin to think about what it was or why it was there. "It'll be this way."

It was clearly between Nion and Rafenkel, one way or the other. "Combine?" Jils asked Rafenkel, following Nion down the corridor. "I understand that the Koscuisko familial corporation is particularly rich, this time of year."

Rafenkel grinned. Jils hadn't had time to form much of an opinion apart from a baseline assessment: Bench Intelligence Specialist—good at her job or she'd be dead—with a good smile, cheerful and open and attractive. Something in the water in the Combine, maybe. Every Combine national Jils had ever met had an engaging smile.

"This or any other time, Dame Ivers. Is it true that you were a guest at Chelatring Side? The stories that they tell about the place. I don't know how you survived it."

Neither did Jils. The Dolgorukij notion of festive dining at the top echelons of the Koscuisko familial corporation had been almost more than she'd been able to take; and then to be expected to dance, within an hour of rising from the table—

"'Tongue cannot speak nor mind conceive the words to contain the horror,'" Jils quoted at Rafenkel, and smiled back. One of Padrake's sayings. Rafenkel didn't seem to recognize it.

"We'll get you settled," Nion said. "And go find the others. You can tell us all about it."

Of course. How had she missed it? She was not to be allowed to speak privately with anybody. Not to wander in the corridors by herself. But was this to protect her against someone—or themselves against her?

Her temporarily cheerful mood destroyed, Jils nodded silently and followed Nion through the halls to quarters.

CHAPTER EIGHT
EXPLOSIVE EVENTS

SHE DIDN'T TRY much by way of small talk as Rafenkel and Nion escorted her through the narrow corridors to her billet. Looking for ambush at every turn—it was second nature—Jils admired the straightness of the hallway and the relative scarcity of either turnings or doors. There were relatively few places where one could lay in wait. Unless people were on fairly intimate terms with one another, it would be difficult to actually pass, in these confined conduits, without going over or under each other. Somebody had taken all of the fire safety and evacuation management officers away and gotten them good and drunk during the planning phases of this station.

Around one corner the corridor suddenly widened to more than twice its previous allowance; living quarters, Jils guessed. There were doors. Rafenkel stopped in front of one about halfway down the corridor and keyed the admit. "Home," Rafenkel said with a flourishing gesture of one hand.

Jils went through and put her kit bag down on the little table, thinking. If they took her, they'd probably do for her, but then both women would have to be in on it, and the odds that one of them would change her mind about the propriety of the action at some later date would be high enough that Jils herself would not care for them.

Therefore neither Nion nor Rafenkel was likely to try to kill her right now. Was that why Rafenkel had waited—to protect Jils from Nion? Or had that been why Nion had offered to escort her, to give Jils a little security in Rafenkel's company? Rafenkel had not seemed surprised to see Nion, but Nion had seemed a little startled to see Rafenkel. Tentative score: Rafenkel positive, Nion neutral, Ivers on the edge.

"What happens next?" Jils asked, looking around her. It was a small room with its own shower and toilet. The station had converters on its water supply, clearly enough, or else she was just mis-remembering about the generally unhealthy properties of centuries-old water in caves. Standard ventilation—she could put an alarm on that—a security locker, and someone had made the bed up for her, narrow though it was. That had been a charitable impulse. Was she going to have to tear the bed apart to check for silent assassins?

No. If someone were going to hide a bomb in her bed, they would not have made up the bed. They would have let her do that, to lull her into a false sense of security. Someone had made up the bed. That was saying that there was no need to tear it apart. Maybe it was a complicated double-braid. Maybe there was a bomb. Maybe there was to be poison in her food, gas from the ventilator, a quick silent assault in a dark corridor.

Maybe she was surrendering to fear and paranoia. If someone was going to kill her, they would, but they needed her right now for the convocation. She had to concentrate. She had a duty to perform.

"There's a schematic on the wall, there, but I wouldn't trust it," Rafenkel said. "Maybe it'll be different for you, but I can't seem to keep my directions straight down here. We've started to make signs." Some of which, Jils realized, they had passed on their way here, though she wouldn't have realized they were guideposts per se. "And the way the station is laid out, one wrong turn and you could be in for a long walk once you finally realize you're going in the wrong direction."

Rafenkel was fiddling with the schematic as she spoke, standing just to the inside of the door. When she had successfully invoked a route on the interactive map, she stepped back and away, out of the room again. She had her back to Nion. But she kept between Nion and Jils, Jils noticed.

"So get yourself situated, and call in to the commons. There's rhyti. Cavene. Kilpers, someone said you drank kilpers—Delleroy, I think. We'll come and fetch you. Better to get an escort until you've had a chance to familiarize, and if you want a laugh, ask Zeman how far it is from the airlock to the laundry. Be ready to duck."

Waving cheerfully, Rafenkel turned and—taking Nion by the arm—headed back up the corridor in the direction from which they'd just come. Jils shut the door and secured it thoughtfully. She didn't have any unpacking to speak of; she almost didn't bother securing the data she'd been carrying with her since she left Chilleau—there was nobody here but Bench Specialists.

On the other hand, not even a Bench Specialist necessarily had a good reason to know what was in that data, and failing to secure data was a bad habit to cultivate. She locked it up and had a wash, changed her boots out for padding-socks, and sat down on the bed to stare at the closed door for a while. Rafenkel had suggested she call for an escort. Jils wasn't sure she was interested. It was good to be alone, even if not very alone, even if only for a little while.

It wasn't to be left to her to decide. The crisp chime of the talk-alert startled her. It was an old style of signal, more confrontational in a sense than the newer generation whose parametrics adjusted for the number of people in the room and whether their rate of respiration indicated that they were sleeping or otherwise engaged, and adjusted frequency and volume accordingly. Sighing, Jils stood up to go to the door. The station's talk-alert was not so primitive as to wait for a manual toggle, however, although Jils could have wished it were. The signal came through once the talk-alert knew that it had gotten her attention.

"Jils." It was Balkney, Jils thought; she didn't know him very well, but she had worked with him before. "Got a flask of kilpers with your name on it, but the management doesn't want me carrying flasks through the corridors. They're afraid I'll spill things and spoil the rugs." Of which there were none, but that wouldn't stop Balkney. The man was ingenious. He could manage all sorts of impossible things; Jils had seen him do it. "Rinpen and Nion are coming out to collect you. Don't want you to get lost. See you soon."

Out. And all without waiting for a response. Don't want you to get lost, Balkney had said, but wasn't that exactly what she had at the back of her mind like an unclean dish-rag? Someone wanting her to get lost?

One way or the other, she didn't feel like waiting passively for an escort. There was a perfectly good schematic on the wall. She studied it for a moment or two and opened the door just in time to not see anybody.

Somebody had been there. She could smell it. Her mind was convinced that she had seen something out of the corner of her eye but it couldn't make up her mind which corner had processed the fleeting image. This was one of the shorter corridors; a person could disappear around a corner. Unless she selected one or the other end and sprinted, the odds of actually catching sight of anyone's back were too uncertain to make the trial worth the tariff.

Shutting her eyes, she stilled her mind to let the fugitive impression process into retrievable memory in her brain. Scent. Something almost not heard, a footfall or the sound of fabric against fabric. She would find out who it was. There were voices coming down the corridor. It took stern self-discipline to keep that fact apart from what her mind almost remembered about which direction someone might have gone. She could afford no assumptions that, if people were coming from one direction, any observer who might have been in the corridor had gone away in the other. She could afford to make no assumptions at all.

"—said to clear out. So she did, that's all. Then the judge got angry about it, but it was the judge who'd told her, so I'm not sure what the point was."

Not a voice Jils recognized, and so there were good odds it was Rinpen and not Nion. When the second person replied, Jils felt the satisfaction of a hypothesis confirmed.

"You see? There. That's just what's wrong with the Courts these days. A judge, of all people, and if a judge is surprised at what people make of her words—these people need keepers—"

It sounded like a complaint that was both traditional and familiar among Bench Specialists, the incompetence of the supreme power under Law—the Judges who codified and interpreted the Law—to think their way out of a puzzle grid. Familiar but disquieting. Surely this was not the time or place to be mocking the judges on whom the stability of the Bench relied, but on the other hand where better than here? There was no one around but Bench Specialists. She was being too sensitive. Pressure valves were critical to their psychological health.

"You called for a transport?" the one who wasn't Nion called, pitching his voice to carry. Young to not-exactly-young man, brown hair, a face and features that called no attention to themselves whatever: now this, Jils thought with satisfaction, was a Bench Specialist. Not one of those flashy models like Padrake Delleroy or Capercoy or Balkney.

"Moments ago. Your gratuity is in question. Rinpen, I expect?"

Nion made a quiet little face that gave her expression a very fleeting charm, apparently chagrinned. "Sorry, Ivers, it's either introduce you to people you've known for years or forget to introduce you. I once tried to introduce a judge to her own First Secretary. True story. But I'll deny it."

As a line of banter, it was successful, as far as it went. There didn't seem to be much genuine camaraderie in it, though. It should have carried an "and wasn't I embarrassed, too" scent to it rather than the faint whiff of "yes, and any really good Bench Specialist would have done exactly the same in my place".

"How did you manage that?" Rinpen asked, apparently interested. Jils went along between the two of them, listening to Nion talk.

"Cintaro," Nion said, as if that explained everything. Rinpen laughed as though it did. Jils kept shut, concentrating on the route, waiting for it to deviate from the direction in which she expected it to be going.

"What a flopper," Rinpen said, after a moment in which it apparently became clear that Jils did not mean to react. "Did you ever hear about that one case in Circuit, Ivers? The one with the three stud bulls and the—"

Yes, she had. It sounded absurd enough on the surface, and the judge's approach to a solution had certainly been unique and original. It had been unique enough to stop the situation from escalating. The judge had won that case, in Jils' estimation, and had never minded that she looked a little silly all the while.

"Yeah, I heard." Jils laid an extra layer of respectful appreciation on top of her meaning, just for the sake of being difficult. "Brilliant jurisprudence. Brilliant."

Nion looked at Jils a little sideways now, and Jils noted her expression approvingly. *You do know when you're being laughed at.*

"No need to tile that hearth, Ivers," Nion said. "You're here for Chilleau. But Capercoy likes you. It won't be as if it was your own Judge who won, but he'll share the wealth. He's decent. Reasonable."

For a moment, Jils didn't know what to think. For one, the Second Judge at Chilleau Judiciary was no more "her" judge in any sense than she was Chilleau's assigned Bench Specialist—Bench Specialists were based, but not assigned, precisely in order to avoid the development of particular interests. That was one of the things that made Padrake's level of intimacy with Secretary Tirom a little unusual.

But more than that, Nion's choice of adjectives could hardly be a coincidence. Reasonable people were corrupt. Unless Nion was trying to imply something about Capercoy, it was in very poor taste to say any such thing, and if Nion was trying to do just that, she'd better have evidence to back up her insinuations.

While Jils was trying to decide how to react, Nion caught her eye and winked. Jils relaxed, only slightly mortified. What was meat for one Bench Specialist was grain for another. Payback, that was all, no more and no less, and here they were at the end of the communal kitchen area where three Bench Specialists were sitting on stools around the high sleek metal surface of the worktable, waiting for them.

Simms Balkney was there with Rafenkel, looking very owlish— he had larger eyes than most people she knew, and very deep-set they were. Cadaverous skeletal structure, so far as his head went in any case, and the effect only got more pronounced as he grew older and the flesh slowly thinned across his face.

He had a cup of kilpers ready, and pushed it across the high broad chromed-steel tabletop toward her. "Nice to see you, Jils," he said. "Things have been interesting at Second, I guess. Tell me about it. We're starving for gossip here, starving."

Now that Padrake was here, that would change. Jils could be confident of that. Karol's note had indicated that Balkney hadn't done the murder. That didn't mean he wouldn't murder her. The thought gave her a place to start as Nion and Rinpen joined them at the table with their own beverages of choice. Zeman was here, too, but he was snacking on a cracker of some sort with nothing to drink at all.

"Not interesting enough, Balkney. For interesting, we'd have to have developments, and this is going on slimmer than anything I've ever seen. It's ugly. I'm glad to be here—on vacation. I still haven't heard from Vogel, though."

Rafenkel drank her rhyti, looking at the blurry reflection of her face in the tabletop.

Zeman looked at Balkney, who shrugged. "So far as I know, nobody else has, either," Balkney said. "I heard he'd left for Gonebeyond, though. To take up with a woman he used to know."

A woman? That was absurd. Karol didn't know any women. Not in anything like a going-off-to-Gonebeyond sense of the term. She'd never even heard gossip about—oh. The Langsariks' Flag Captain. Walton Agenis.

It could be. Karol had cherished—or at least harbored—feelings for that woman, feelings that had been complicated by his sense of frustration over the failure of the amnesty he'd arranged. Jils wasn't sure Verlaine had ever forgiven Karol for his creative solution to that particular problem, but the issue was academic now.

"Mixed up with Malcontents, is what I heard," Rinpen admitted. Jils glanced over at Rafenkel quickly, curious to see if she would react to the suggestion, but Rafenkel gave no sign of finding it of any more than merely passing interest. "At least there were indications that some Malcontents were looking for him. I didn't think he even liked Dolgorukij. Maybe that was why they were looking for him."

She could explain that she had asked the Malcontent for help in finding out what had happened to Karol, whether he was living or dead. That would entail a moderate amount of embarrassment, though, and maybe it was just as well to let people speculate on why the Malcontent might be interested in Karol's whereabouts. Karol needed more dark hints in his dossier to keep it interesting.

"Tell me what's been going on around here," she suggested, instead of bothering to explain. "What's our plan?"

"Well, we had one," Balkney said. "We even got started a little early. We weren't sure when you'd make it through, and we all need to be back on the job. The other job, I mean." Keeping the peace. Assisting the judges. Carrying out the Bench's instructions. "But we weren't entirely satisfied. If we can rule out Fontailloe and Chilleau at the beginning, some of us can leave right away. Or not, of course." And if they couldn't rule out either or both Judiciaries at the onset, they'd be no further behind because of it.

"Tanifer is all for a break in tradition." It was a bit of a surprise to hear Rafenkel speak; she'd been quiet throughout, nursing her rhyti. "Nion is pretty adamant about Chilleau's unfitness, aren't you, Nion? Maybe you should refocus your investigation, Jils."

In other words, maybe Nion had done it. That wasn't even funny. It was particularly unfunny because she'd thought along the same lines, and made sure that no Bench Specialist had been anywhere near Chilleau at the time—no Bench Specialist but her, that was—and maybe Karol, since nobody knew where he was, and therefore could not say where he hadn't been.

"Oh, yes," Nion said, as if playing along. "I killed Verlaine because Chilleau was the only thing standing between Supicor and the

Selection. Yes. Right." Was it her imagination—Jils asked herself—or was there a note of genuine resentment, there? "But we all know it wasn't you, Ivers. You'd have been set for life. Bench Specialist presiding at Chilleau Judiciary with a First Judge in residence—you're the last person who could have wanted Verlaine dead."

No, the Second Judge was the last person. Second to the last person. Surely the last person who could have wanted Verlaine dead had been Verlaine himself. "I expect to reap my reward when the time comes," Jils retorted frostily. "But only if Supicor takes it. As we planned, Nion."

Still there was that odd undernote, an assumption that a Bench Specialist had a personal stake in the Selection and could expect to reap a personal profit.

Balkney snorted into his flask of water, or water-like whatever. He certainly seemed relaxed and comfortable enough, though Jils didn't smell alcohol or any other fragrant intoxicant. "Sorry you lost your post, in that case, Ivers," Balkney said. "When everybody knows it's Cintaro."

About whose Judge Nion and Rinpen had just been joking in less than complimentary terms. "I can neither affirm nor deny your assertion," Jils said. She needed to shut herself up and sleep. Fatigue and stress were eroding her faculties. There were no hidden motives to be adduced from two Bench Specialists mocking a Judge. It was in poor taste, but that was all. "It'll be interesting to see what history makes of it, after the fact, when the First Judge is presiding at Chilleau Judiciary."

Bench Specialists suggesting that their peers were reasonable. But there was a point to be made there. Sooner or later, reason would prevail. She had no cause to assassinate Verlaine, and—if base motives were to be appealed to—every reason not to. She could only be guilty if there were undisclosed motives or a sincere conviction that Chilleau's proposed reform program would do more harm than good, and she trusted in the intelligence and common sense of her peers to conclude that such was not the case. All she had to do was wait.

It would help if she could find the way through to the identity of the murderer while she was waiting. For that she had to get through Convocation, and back to Chilleau.

A warning tone sounded across the station's internal comm. Nion looked up at the speaker in the ceiling. "They're back," she said. That would be Padrake and Capercoy, Jils assumed, back from escorting Secretary Tirom back to the surface. "Let's go. The sooner we can settle this whole problem the sooner we can all get back to the real world."

Jils' sentiments, almost exactly. Carrying her flask of kilpers, Jils went with Balkney and Rafenkel, Nion and Zeman and Rinpen, to sit down and discuss where they would start to argue for the least worst solution to the chaos into which Verlaine's murder threatened to plunge all of Jurisdiction space.

BOND-INVOLUNTARIES WERE criminals. So much was clearly understood by everybody in Fleet, with the possible exception of Andrej Koscuisko. They were no ordinary class of criminals, however. The Bond could only be imposed in cases of crimes against the Judicial order, which was generally held to apply to sabotage, persons vandalizing or otherwise damaging Bench property, some minor political dissidents, and—in recent years—Nurail.

It was a privilege extended only to people whose psychological profiles gave a reasonably good assurance that they could survive the ferocious stress that life under governance meant for a Security slave, or a service slave—there were people under Bond in the service houses, but they never earned back the cost of their indoctrination and benefits package so there were fewer of them. They didn't last. Someone was always taking a bribe on the sly to let a patron alone with a service Bond for a few hours, and then professing shock and outrage when something happened.

It had happened to a service bond-involuntary in Port Burkhayden not very long ago, Robert knew. He knew because the service bond-involuntary had been his sister, and the officer had been sent ahead to make good the property damage before the officer's cousin Paval I'shenko Danzilar could file a grievance for delivery of damaged goods.

Fleet hadn't been making Bonds for very long—the technology had been slow to perfect, and there were the cost-benefit problems, of course. It was expensive to put a man under Bond because the governor itself was a sophisticated piece of deviltry, training and indoctrination took time and effort, men had to be taught to fight and fear and there were still altogether too many unfortunate accidents.

A man under Bond could kill himself if he could face the consequences both of making a sloppy job of it, and of succeeding in
ending his life but not in concealing the self-willed nature of his death.
Failed suicide attempts were interpreted by governors as willful damage to valuable Fleet property and were punished accordingly. Robert
couldn't remember what it had been like when his governor had
started to cook off on him in port Burkhayden, but he knew it must
have been impressively terrible because Chief Stildyne had been much
kinder to him since, even when he wasn't thinking about it.

Success in killing oneself but failure to disguise the intention of
the act meant that the Bench would cancel the waiver it held as a
guarantee of good behavior against prosecution of your family and
friends and their families and families' friends and their kye and their
domestic poultry and the rodents behind the stove in the cook-
house for crimes against the rule of Law and the Judicial order, and
all of your suffering on their behalf to try to protect them would be
for naught.

If you were Nurail, that didn't so much matter because the
Bench already had your goods and chattel, but they would still try to
find somebody who could be made to repay the cost of your training, maintenance, and upkeep.

Not more than forty years, Standard. The Bench had not been
making bond-involuntaries for longer than that. It had been only
forty years ago since the Bench had begun to authorize some people,
and not others, to inflict torture, as an attempt to control the use of
torture as an instrument of State and bring the abuse of sentient
creatures under the control of the rule of Law. It had been well
intentioned, perhaps. The people who had built up the system of
Inquiry had felt that it was humane and pitiful of them to do so. If
they'd only been able to see where they'd been going—

There had been forty years for bond-involuntaries to learn how
to manage with a governor, how to live to claim the prize that waited
for them on the Day their sentence was completed. On that day, a
bond-involuntary became a reborn soul with accumulated pay and
benefits, a full pension with honors, exemption from all local taxes
and tariffs wherever he wished to go and from most of the Bench
assessments as well, free passage on Fleet transport on demand—so
many perquisites and privileges that it hardly seemed possible to
grasp. But Robert had seen it happen.

When he'd been on *Scylla*, one of Koscuisko's teams had pulled a narrow one through a narrower cleft, preventing some saboteurs from gaining control of one of her main battle cannon, saving the ship. Captain Irshah Parmin had petitioned for revocation of Bond in light of this signal service. Joslire had been dead by the time the petition had been approved, but three others of Robert's fellows had gone free.

Over forty years, a culture of self-defense had developed from nothing. It was a culture of finger-code, and groupings, the unwritten but strictly observed convention that a bond-involuntary could not be teased or tormented with questions or demands that could place any man in conflict with himself and engage his governor—and one of those conventions was that bond-involuntaries were never to be quartered but with other bond-involuntaries, and their quarters were not to be under surveillance.

They were under thirty-two-hour surveillance by definition. Ship's Security declined to intrude on what limited privacy they had, and there were penalties assessed any unbonded troops caught in bond-involuntary quarters unless as a party of three or more with at least one officer of the rank of Chief Warrant or higher—another provision intended to protect bond-involuntaries from more abuse or punishment than their lives were to them already, though it didn't always work out quite as well as that.

There were only six of them assigned to the *Ragnarok*. There were, technically speaking, quarters for twenty-five, but nobody knew of any ship with a full complement of bond-involuntaries, and the fact that they were six gave them two que-bays, enough space for ten. The common areas could be connected. They were connected now. Everybody was here except for Pyotr, and there was suspicion and confusion in the air.

"He wouldn't," Godsalt said flatly. "Makes no sense, to take us out from underneath that thing and then just have to put the screws down again. I don't care. I haven't got family."

Bonds didn't talk about their families. Not about their crimes, not about their experiences with the dancing-masters, not about where they'd come from or hoped to return to. Bond-involuntaries especially never talked about the future. It was too painful to fantasize about that out loud.

"So he knows," Hirsel argued back. Godsalt was tall and lean and limber in the conventional sense, but Hirsel was as curly-headed as a yearling. "Robert?"

He was responsible for finding things out, just because he liked people, and they generally seemed to like him back, for whatever reasons of their own. Especially female people. He was the intelligence officer of the group, he supposed, but shouldn't that mean that he got custard for bribes?

Two liked custard, and when you wanted a favor you could generally obtain at least a hearing with the promise of a dish of custard to be delivered well out of Koscuisko's ken. Desmodontae did not digest milk sugars very effectively. She liked custards, but they gave her a bellyache, and she and the officer had been squabbling over the issue almost since he had come to the *Ragnarok*, and Robert with him.

"Just after he came back," Robert confirmed. "Trips down to Intelligence, and couriers. Also no questions asked about stomach-powders. And she said something to me about my mother's brother's wife's family, so I think he was doing his research."

They generally gave him more credit than he thought he actually deserved as a Koscuisko expert, just because he had known the officer for longer than any bond-involuntary still living in Fleet. The only bond-involuntary that Koscuisko had known longer had been Joslire, who was dead.

Kerenko was Sarvaw, and Sarvaw was a kind of Dolgorukij. Kerenko should know if anybody did; but Kerenko was chewing his under-lip thoughtfully. "And there's a Malcontent involved. You never know what Malcontents are about. They're capable of anything."

This was something esoteric and private to the shared experience of Sarvaw and Aznir Dolgorukij that Robert did not understand at all. However, he had no difficulty understanding why Chief Stildyne was in so cheerful a mood since Cousin Stanoczk's courier had come on board two days ago. The officer's cousin had had a letter that Kerenko had received with astonished pleasure, read to himself and without his lips moving, and carried around in his bosom ever since.

"So this is the situation." It was Garrity's turn to speak. "He's been checking up on our families. He plans a leave on Emandis.

Nobody understands what good he might think it will do to give us a taste of freedom if we were just going to have to go back, and we know he doesn't expect to be here for very much longer."

That was true. Koscuisko was here because he had evidence that would protect the *Ragnarok* against its enemies in Fleet, but once the Ragnarok had been exonerated by an inquiry Koscuisko could go home. Verlaine had freed Koscuisko, given him relief of Writ to be executed at Koscuisko's good pleasure, so Koscuisko was in the same situation as he had put them in, except backwards: he had come back from his home to rejoin his Command, and would be leaving Fleet to go back home, but not before he took care of business.

"So he's made a plan to steal us from the Bench. That cousin of his."

Robert could tell from the tone of Hirsel's voice that he was having a hard time getting used to a man who looked a lot like the officer but behaved so differently. He knew he was. Koscuisko's cousin was due to leave as soon as the *Ragnarok* dropped vector, though, so that was something.

"Are we going?" The Bench could not do more to his Megh than it had already; and she belonged to the Danzilar prince now, at any rate, who had decided to make of her a token of the contract he wanted between him and the people of Burkhayden, and would defend her accordingly. There were Nurail in Gonebeyond and rumors that the son of the war-leader of Darmon had escaped and was growing to manhood there, with all of the rest of his family dead. Maybe somewhere in Gonebeyond there was someone who remembered that Robert had had family. Megh would expect him to go. He would never see her again.

"That's to decide," Godsalt admitted. "Pyotr's twenty-four and some, less than five years short of reborn. I don't know what I would do in his place. But none of us really knows what's going on in the officer's mind, do we? And I'm not asking Chief."

There was nothing in Godsalt's brain to reinforce the respect due to rank, no reason they need call Koscuisko "the officer" and Stildyne "Chief" in quarters. But habit was a powerful force. And Koscuisko had warned them about giving themselves away; it would be too ungrateful to let all of that good work come to nothing. It was important to maintain appearances.

"I would." For what it was worth. "Whether it was six years or six weeks. I knew a man who embraced his death to be free." He hadn't actually been there when Joslire died, though. Koscuisko had one of the others kiss Joslire on Robert's behalf. He'd heard about it from Code, who had come back to *Scylla* without the rest of his team. "I never doubted his decision."

Garrity stood up. It was almost time for him to report to Infirmary. Garrity was on sprains-and-strains in orthopedic this fifth-week. Robert had never cared for that particular assignment. He had emotional associations with particular sorts of disjoints that were not to be quieted when there were too many near reminders.

"We'll hear about it before the end of his leave comes up," Garrity said. "So we've got a few days. But I'm glad we had a chance to synchronize. I couldn't believe what I thought he was thinking of. I should have just remembered that he's mad."

Robert nodded, and thumped Garrity in the shoulder in a friendly fashion as Garrity passed, to comfort him. Yes. Koscuisko was mad. Koscuisko was mad in this instance like a war-leader, who could imagine indescribable retreats when it came to saving the lives of those who had accepted his direction.

They hadn't been given any choice; a bond-involuntary had to accept direction, that was the whole point. That, and punishment. And still Koscuisko was quite correct to take them for people who had put their trust in him to direct and to guide them. There were contracts in a man's life that not even the Bench could break or regulate, unspoken and intangible; which reminded him for no particular reason that he owed Engineering an extra half-a-day's maintenance on the Wolnadi fighter for which his team was responsible.

The basic truth of the whole thing was simply that the Bench was about pain and fear and force, and there was no force in all of Jurisdiction that could stand against trust and faith and charity. That was the real reason that Koscuisko was so dangerous. All of this time the Bench had believed it was because the man had the truth-sense in him and could hear a person think, and the Bench had been wrong.

Robert took that simple truth down with him to the maintenance atmosphere and set it on a shelf while he changed into a coverall, then carried it with him out to where the Wolnadi fighter stood in wait for the cleaning of some of its intake vents. It was a plain fact, no more and no less, but it was worthy of admiration still: breathtakingly seditious, categorically revolutionary, absolutely conservative, all at the same time, and he was proud of himself for having welcomed it.

"OF COURSE IT'S not impregnable," Vogel said. Rukota couldn't see Vogel's exact expression, because of the goggles Vogel was wearing. They'd borrowed some of the equipment from Koscuisko's surgery, though Rukota didn't think anybody had gotten around to telling Koscuisko that yet. With luck, the equipment would all be back in place, safe and sound and never the worse for wear, before Koscuisko noticed it was missing; and taking it to Secured Medical was simply moving it from one medical area to another, really, wasn't it?

"But there are good reasons to pretend it is. For one, the Bench expects every citizen to hold the Judicial process in the very highest respect. It certainly couldn't suggest that there could be any question at all about the integrity of its own employees. Particularly its elite."

Rukota could see the point, but it was a weak one, in his opinion. Leaning back in Koscuisko's chair, he stared up at the ceiling. It had been two, nearly three days, and he was almost beside himself with boredom. Yes, Vogel was an interesting man. But Vogel was busy. Concentrating. And a Bench Specialist, so he wasn't comfortable talking very much in the first place.

"For another—" Making a final adjustment, Vogel grunted in apparent satisfaction. The record lay on a portable table under a bright light. It bristled with wires and probes from Koscuisko's surgical set, and Vogel was using a scaling glove to move about within the record's interior, watching his progress on one of Koscuisko's monitors. All Rukota could see from where he sat was the plain box that housed the record.

"For another, the moment you mention any such thing, people will start looking for it. It's human nature. Not their fault. And then if they get past one level of security they'll realize that there's another. And then another. It's just asking for trouble."

Not that anybody would believe that a record wasn't protected, not if they stopped to think about it. Rukota guessed that Vogel's point was along the lines of discouraging people from stopping to think about it. Records couldn't be had by just anybody, anyway.

Yes, there were powers of eights of them, but they were still a controlled-access commodity.

"Any hints yet on how this one was compromised?" Hour after hour watching Vogel sit perfectly still, moving his probes so carefully that Rukota couldn't see that he was even moving them at all. He'd watched over Vogel's shoulder for a good while, but that hadn't been able to hold his interest forever. The fact that he hadn't any idea what he was looking at—apart from the obvious circuits, access nodes, input-output channels—hadn't helped him concentrate, either.

"Well." For a moment, Rukota thought Vogel was trying to decide which version of "mind your own business" would best suit this particular circumstance. Vogel surprised him; completing an adjustment that had apparently distracted his attention, he began to talk.

"It's Pesadie's on-base record. There's not much question of that. Noycannir had access codes. They were inactive but not revoked, which would make it easier to sneak one past the record. But these pieces of evidence had to be formally logged by someone with an active Writ, or else she had to have talked someone out of surrendering an open code. She had the open and close marker with her when she got there, I suspect, just a question of deciding what to fit in the space between them. I need to find where that code's hiding out. Once we find it, it can be analyzed, but until we do—no telling."

And it took as long as it did because records had complex and interrelated anti-tampering protocols, self-defense mechanisms in place. Also because Vogel wanted to avoid accidentally damaging any of the false evidence that had been read into this record, to preserve the best picture of how it had been done.

"Now, the warrant that was issued to me to execute wasn't anything like a record in terms of its sophistication. But once I got suspicious and began to look at it, I decided that the wear around the edges of the authorization chops wasn't quite normal. Looked as though they were perfectly ordinary Judicial chops, at first analysis, very well done. But by the third run-through, there were some interesting anomalies in the layering. It's a signature of sorts. I'm wondering if the signature we find here will be the same."

"Any idea how much longer it's going to take?" This was a rude question, but Rukota was an artilleryman, and it was armed transport that was supposed to be genteel if anybody was. No, it was the Combine Home Defense Fleet that was supposed to be genteel. Beautiful manners, Dolgorukij, and such beautiful cheerful smiles that you almost had to smile back even as they rolled right over you—a Sarvaw had told him that. But she'd been an artilleryman herself, so a little attitude was to be expected.

Vogel shook his head. "I'm picking off the layers from the back to front till I can get at the internal auditor. Once I get through to that, I can see whether or not it recognizes some elements in common with the forgery on that warrant. One way or the other, I should be able to talk it into disclosing the pedigree of the Writ that logged the core details of that false evidence, as well as the Writ that applied the shell. Reports say that the evidence was presented in good form, so there has to be a valid interrogation record buried in here someplace, and I want to know—where—it—came from."

Fair enough. Maybe he shouldn't be talking; it could distract Vogel. Vogel kept talking, though; talking to himself, maybe. "Forging a Judicial chop takes considerable technical sophistication. I couldn't do it. It was hard enough to catch the little nick in the edge that tipped me off. In a manner of speaking."

Soft, low-voiced, and apparently talking to the record as much as to Rukota. "There's this, and we were lucky, there's no other word for it. Sheer luck. If ap Rhiannon hadn't sent those troops home with Koscuisko, he might have gone off with Noycannir. We'd never have seen that record again. Maybe not Koscuisko, either. I heard that they found some ugly things in her baggage."

Somebody could have taken a shortcut of some sort, in other words, not expecting the forged record to ever have to stand up under any kind of scrutiny. Rukota stifled a yawn. Watching Vogel work was about as exciting as testing a maintenance atmosphere for leaks in its plasma field.

"But that Clerk was from Chilleau Judiciary. And just very shortly after someone tried to get Koscuisko off on an unauthorized transit of some sort, Verlaine is killed. The security systems expertly compromised. Chilleau. Could be a coincidence."

If he stared too long at the ceiling, Rukota decided, he could begin to make out the shadows of equipment panels behind the false-netted surface that the Engineer had in place. He didn't care to do so. It was hard enough to get clean when they left this place. He'd scrubbed the palms of his hands all but raw after their first session. He didn't know how Vogel was taking it, but for himself his strategy was to avoid noticing anything that might remind him of where he was. He decided to study his thumbnail for a while. He didn't have to worry about falling asleep by accident.

"Don't believe in coincidence, do we, sweetie? No. No, we don't."

Vogel's voice had changed. Rukota straightened up, intrigued. Not only had Vogel's voice changed, but something was different about the relationship of Vogel's body to the probe array—focus, perhaps. He had been sitting there delicately playing a probe and talking about things just a moment ago. Now Vogel wasn't there at all—he was somewhere deep in that record box, all of his attention directed at some single point with an unnerving concentration that seemed to intensify by the moment.

"Yes, that's right. We don't believe in coincidence. We're suspicious. We're paranoid. We're hostile and unpleasant, aren't we, girl? Yes. You're such a clever record. Show me what you've got. You can tell—"

Vogel stopped. His voice cut off abruptly in mid-phrase. The track of the probe on the screen that Rukota could just see from one side didn't waver. Vogel had frozen in place. As near as Rukota could tell, he wasn't even breathing. When Vogel spoke again, it was in a perfectly normal tone of voice, but the word he said explained it all to Rukota, a little too well.

"Destructor."

It was a bomb.

The record wasn't a bomb, but it had been provided with a little cyborg intelligence that would put a bomb together from the materials provided in a record, if anything happened to set off its sequence. Two layers of normally inert microfoam here. A minute chip of an ordinarily harmless spacer-card there. A safely isolated impulse-generator way over there, where it could not possibly interfere with anything going on with the mechanical workings of the record, until some tiny crazed guardian rushed from pillar to post collecting bits and chips and rerouting circuitry—

Rukota dove for the open door between the chamber and the ready room to close it down, to contain the damage as much as possible. He and Vogel were on the wrong side of that door, but he wasn't going through by himself. He'd been given an assignment: to observe. He couldn't observe from the wrong side of a closed door. He had only Vogel's word that the record was going to explode—Vogel's word and his body language, and the tension that communicated between souls on a subconscious level and said get out get out, get out, get out now, get out—

"After you," Rukota said. The door was closing. He wasn't going to stand here and let it just close. Was he?

Vogel sprang like a tension-wire slipped out of true, up and away and through the closing door to crumple in a heap against the far wall of the small ready-room, the other side of the outside corridor. Rukota swung himself through the fast-narrowing aperture after Vogel, wheeling to one side, snatching his arm away just in time to prevent his hand from getting caught in the door and confusing it into opening wide all over again. Vogel was clawing his way to one side of the wall opposite Rukota—away from directly across from the door, well, that made sense—

It was quiet. Very quiet. Blissfully, peacefully quiet. He didn't want to distract it. It was wonderful. Quiet. No sound. No noise. Nothing. Tranquil.

Something jingled at him. He tried to scowl at it. Nothing happened. Scowling was noise. He could hear the creaking sound of his numb muscles. He didn't want any disturbance. No. It was too nice just the way it was. Quiet. Quiet was the good way to be.

Where was he? He opened his eyes, but he couldn't see anything. Had he opened his eyes? Sometimes a person just thought he'd sat up, and gotten up, and gotten dressed and started to put his boots on, and then the alert would go off again and a person would realize that he'd been dreaming. This was like no dreamscape Rukota had ever seen. It was a soft pearly white, absolutely uniform in tint and hue. When the atmosphere did that, a man couldn't tell eight from an eighth for visibility. No clue. But he'd heard his eyes open, the scrape of the inside of the lid against the surface, the clanging sound his eyelashes made knocking against each other as he dragged the upper past and away from the lower. Terrible racket. He'd never realized that his body was as loud as it was.

Something big and black suddenly swooped down upon him from somewhere in that pearly mist. It startled him. He couldn't move. What? What? He smelled—

He smelled the snow-edged tang of bottled atmosphere, and realized that he couldn't move because he'd not been breathing. It wasn't mist. It was fire suppressant foam. Someone was here with a mask. He still couldn't move. Protective gear, that was the answer, people in full environmental suits lifting him onto a litter. Air. He needed air. He wasn't getting enough air.

He could feel his muscles tense to take a breath, and something told him that it was a mistake, but his body wasn't listening, and then it hit him in the left side like a reverberation round and he recognized the sensation. Ribcage again, damn it. He hated cracked ribs. Single most aggravating injury a man could sustain, in Rukota's opinion. It had happened to him twice or three times before in his life, and he was heartily sick of the experience. Muscles didn't seem to learn, though. They were still working, gasping for air.

Down the corridor—he presumed—then stop and wait for the corridor to clear. Airlock, obviously. He could see walls again. Here were his good friends in Security, at least he thought that was one of Koscuisko's people—Garrity? Into a mover and hurrying through the corridors, hell-bent for Infirmary. It was still eerily quiet. He could hear the blood pulse in his jaw beneath his ear, a rushing sound like white noise, but it wasn't constant. Volume up; volume down. Volume up; volume down.

Then, while they carried him down the corridor, just as they angled past a turning with impressive precision and commendable urgency, sound and sensation returned with equivalent suddenness and brutal force, taking his breath away all over again. Damn. That hurt. What had happened? He couldn't remember.

The litter-bearers slid the litter expertly onto the therapeutic bed in Infirmary's emergency room, and here was the scowling face of Koscuisko himself. Hospital whites, so that was good. Even in his duty whites, Koscuisko's rank was lined through with crimson, however. There was no forgetting that this man was an Inquisitor, which made things just the littlest bit awkward for a man in Rukota's position, not knowing what position exactly he was in.

Koscuisko was an Inquisitor. Part of his reputation was that of knowing what you were thinking. Rukota had no idea what expression might be found on his face, but Koscuisko apparently read enough of the question in Rukota's eyes to answer it.

"An explosion in Secured Medical has destroyed a small area of Ship's Stores with unusual efficiency for so contained a blast. One assumes that there has been a problem with the forged record that you and Vogel were examining. Doctor Narion will attend to you. You are not bleeding, and nothing appears to be broken, but we will assume the worst until we can complete a scan. I must go and pick some pieces of the wall out of Vogel's cerebral cortex. More later."

Rukota listened very carefully, trying to be sure he could commit the speech to memory. There were large parts of it that made no sense to him. He needed to be able to retrieve those later, at which time he could examine them more carefully with better hope of determining the actual meaning of the words.

It sounded like Koscuisko had things under control. Rukota closed his eyes. When he opened them again, there was another officer there, one he recognized as Doctor Narion—Koscuisko's soft-tissue specialist. "We're ready to go for scan," she said, "so we'll be able to tell you what your status is within an eight or so. All right? Yes. Good."

If she said so. He could hear, but things were a little fuzzy around their edges, as though everybody in the room was drunk but him. There were good odds that, in that case, he was the one who was drunk, or drugged.

Fair enough, he told himself, and closed his eyes again.

CHAPTER NINE
UNTHINKABLE ALTERNATIVES

FARILK'S OFFICE WAS much smaller than Andrej's own, but there was no sense of confinement—merely the security of a quiet, comfortable room. The chairs were set up carefully so that the one in which he had been invited to sit faced the entrance, enabling the occupant to see the door was closed. Andrej had never been seated in Farilk's chair before. It was very comfortable.

"As it happens, Vogel had a pad of scar tissue on his scalp already," Andrej said, looking at the milky surface of the flask of rhyti in his hand. "And it was a small sort of a bomb. Damaged tissue, yes, but it's all insult and no bleeding. I put in a temporary plate. It'll metabolize itself away inside of two or three months."

He'd feared the damage to be much worse when they'd brought Vogel in, just yesterday. Farilk hadn't given him the least indication of needing an explanation for why Andrej had rescheduled his appointment; it was only Andrej's own discomfort that made him chatter on about it.

But he had noticed that he was chattering on about it. And that was not acceptable. It betrayed an acute case of nerves, and Farilk would simply sit quietly until he was ready to talk, and then he would have to make another appointment. He felt uncomfortable enough as it was, despite the chair. He didn't want to have to make another appointment.

"Scar tissue can come in very handy sometimes," Farilk said. "And there's definite value to not having to feel anything at the site of injury. Not feeling can also become an issue, of course. It's hard to know when to let scar tissue alone, isn't it?"

All right, Farilk wouldn't sit quietly and let Andrej talk. Maybe he wasn't interested in another appointment either. He had a fairly full caseload, between stress and sleep disturbances associated with the *Ragnarok's* current status and recent adventures. With more than seven hundred souls on board the *Ragnarok*, there were always issues arising. What would Farilk do if Two needed the assistance of a psychiatrist?

No, Farilk was just trying to help Andrej get over a difficult spot. That was all. He should accept the help when it was offered. Farilk was the professional here.

"I have a survey of the literature conducted." He was going to lose track of that flask of rhyti, and drop it. Better to set it aside. "The experiences and police records of Fleet inquisitors returning to civilian life. Many of them I find form a relationship with the local civil authorities. In one instance on record, there was a problem with the abuse of patients, but other indications in the personal history perhaps concealed the truth. You will laugh at me. I laugh at myself. I never imagined that I would have this difficulty."

Farilk dropped his gaze to his lap, considering, giving Andrej a moment to struggle with himself. "The first thing that must be done is to name the problem, your Excellency. This is helpful on many levels. On the most obvious, it helps to reduce the possibility of a mistaken diagnosis, and consequent inappropriate treatment recommendations on my part. On a less obvious but more meaningful level, there is in many cultures the feeling that to name the thing gives us power over it."

Or gave the monster life. Names were difficult to predict that way. "It is the absence in my life of torture." He could name it, if Farilk needed to hear that. He had spent enough time wrestling with it in his own mind before now. "I yearn for it. The pleasure that I had. The fact of taking pleasure was a horror to me. Now I thirst."

Farilk was not surprised; or, if he was, he hid it exceptionally well. Andrej had known Farilk for years. Although the talent was a product of habit and attention and learning how to read—and not the occult curse of some demon bestial or angelic—it was true more often than not that Andrej did know when a man was dissembling with him.

"You still experience distress in the consideration of the requirements of Secured Medical, your Excellency?"

Farilk was just checking. Andrej stifled his temptation to leap to his feet and kiss Farilk on both cheeks, declare himself cured by virtue of overcoming his dread at last, and rushing out of the room to hang himself. Farilk was just establishing the clinical baseline. That was all.

"When Captain Lowden was alive, and I was to go to seek confession on his direction, I felt always the conflict between

knowing what I was about to do and knowing that I was going
to enjoy it. The passion that I feel in my heart when I remember
frightens me. How long can I endure this before what is left to
me of common decency is worn away at last?"

How long would it be before the savage hunger in his heart to
hear the helpless cries of pain overpowered him, and betrayed a
patient to the Inquisitor? Was Lowden to conquer him, was Lowden
to continue to rule him, from beyond the borderlands of Death?
Was it Lowden's vengeance against Andrej for his murder?

"Let's explore this, your Excellency."

*No. Let us not. Let me go find a gun and shoot myself. Or—better—
yes. Let us go down to Secured Medical, you and I, and I will provide you
with all of the practical demonstration you can bear.* "Yes?"

"You're accustomed to this stimulus, a very powerful one. Many
others have failed to sustain the degree of stress you have been
under. Your accommodation was extreme, but survival-oriented."

It was no such thing. It was the beast in the blood, the tyranny
of his ancestors and the shame of his pretenses to decency. It had
been no accommodation strategy. It had been the unfettering of an
appetite so huge and powerful that he had had to struggle to restrain
it, every time, every day, every hour. He had not always won. But if
Farilk needed to believe that his delight in torture had been a psychological quirk evolved under pressure, if that was what Farilk
needed to believe in order to continue to speak to him as though he
was a human being—"I do not feel that I am not surviving with any
notable degree of success at this time, Doctor."

Farilk smiled, a bit painfully, at the formality of that title. "You
are our staff expert on the mechanics of addiction, your Excellency.
A thought experiment, and I only propose it to you now for you to
conduct later at your leisure. Sometimes an addiction can be managed with smaller doses of a pharmacologically similar drug whose
effect need not be as damaging."

Yes, and sometimes a very small amount of a related substance
was enough to bring an addict's craving to the fore with redoubled
savagery and force. "A thought experiment, you say."

Farilk nodded. "I mention this to you strictly in my capacity as
your mental health partner, your Excellency. I don't know whether
your personal experimentation has ever led you to take advantage
of the services of a pain-worker. But the therapeutic value of a

professional pain-worker's services is unquestioned," Farilk said, very firmly, as though to get it all said before Andrej could strike him across the face and stalk out of the office. "A wide range of both physiological and psychological deficits can be very adequately addressed in selected individuals with the carefully controlled provision of extreme stimulus. The thought experiment that I propose to you is this, your Excellency, if you will entertain it."

He did feel like striking Farilk and stalking out. He wasn't sure what Farilk was getting at, not exactly, but whatever it was, it was deeply offensive. He was certain of that much.

Or it could be his emotional reaction to a threat, to a suggestion that terrified him. Either way, Farilk was not going to continue unless Andrej agreed to hear him. Tiresome. As strict as any Protocol, but for much the same reasons, Andrej realized. Cooperation could not be forced. Temporary compliance could be obtained with fear and pain and the fear of pain, but people had to be tricked into cooperation, especially if it was to be in the service of their own torment. "I am listening."

Having said so, he was honor-bound to do so. No matter how violently his heart rejected what he thought Farilk was about to tell him.

"Imagine, if you will, your Excellency, that there is a person whose body will not respond to normal pleasurable sensation until it has been sensitized by the application of controlled stimulus. A person is suffering, your Excellency, and you are in a position to provide healing in a form that is unusual for you. You are going to treat this person who is in need of healing, but you are not going to harm her."

Farilk meant to make a sex professional of him. That was all this was about. Farilk meant to prostitute him to some silly girl who thought she wanted to be hit. No, of course Farilk meant to do no such thing; Andrej struggled to sit and listen while his mind and heart raged against the shocking suggestions that Farilk continued to propose, calmly, carefully, quietly.

"They are very glad to surrender their suffering to you because they are in need, so that you may take pleasure in it with their consent and their entire goodwill, which is given to you freely and without coercion or duress. There are people who will intervene if the situation warrants it, and if at any time distress overpowers her, she will stop the exercise."

Farilk stood up. "Would such a situation be the drug that helps manage the addiction? Or the irritation that makes withdrawal all the more difficult to bear? Which?"

Andrej admired his timing in more than one way: yes, the period for the interview was over—neither of them could bear too long spent in so intense a conversation—and also, yes, he had had all that he could bear to hear for the present, and he had to get away from here now. Right now. He couldn't even think of what Farilk had proposed to him. His mind was full of turmoil; he could not stop thinking—remembering—wishing. He had to get away.

"Think on it, please, your Excellency," Farilk said. Andrej stood up, dizzy. "And come back to see me in a few days. If I don't hear from you by next five, I'll see about getting a place on your scheduler."

Because Andrej was not to be permitted to let this lapse, now that he had raised the issue. That was only fair. That was only to be expected. He would himself find fault with Farilk if Farilk let any other soul come to him for assistance and then never come again, unless the problem solved itself, and this one was not going to solve itself—unless someone should chance to honor him when he went to Emandis to visit Joslire's tablet by setting the memorial hill slope on fire, and ending his life.

Therefore Andrej nodded, and choked out the appropriate response. "Yes, of course, Doctor. In a few days. Till then."

The door to Farilk's office opened as Andrej drew near, and he fled through it, so caught up in his own distress of spirit that he could not more than nod in response to the salute of the Intelligence technician that he passed in the corridor on his way out of Infirmary.

THERE WERE A limited number of places on this station that could reasonably be used for formal argument. It required a room large enough for one observer to sit far enough away from the two disputants to be effectively ignored while still being close enough to hear and see. It had to have privacy—for concentration—and have observation capacity in place, for the historical record.

At the same time, there were only nine of them, which meant that the most sessions that could possibly run concurrently were three. Three sites had been agreed upon: one in the pantry, one in the main theater, and here. This was the one that Rafenkel liked best.

"Specialist Ivers, the Second Judge should be selected at Chilleau Judiciary; Specialist Delleroy, there should be no selection. Initial discussions. Specialist Rafenkel observing."

Her voice sounded oddly flattened to her in this little room, in some sense. It wasn't a room, exactly; it was a floating observation station, eight-sided, tethered to the station on shore by a narrow causeway on pontoons. It hadn't been out on the lake earlier. They'd only gotten it set up over the past day, since Delleroy had arrived with Ivers.

Who were both waiting for her. "Call it," she said to Ivers. Ivers represented the status quo. The status quo, to the extent that it could reasonably be supported, was the default solution for the conservation of peace and order—if the mare hadn't foaled, there was no need to milk her.

"Even," Ivers said. Square-shouldered and cautious, she sat there at the worktable opposite Delleroy, one hand loosely clenched on the table's surface. "Chilleau should be selected even though the First Secretary is dead."

All right. Rafenkel smiled—she'd have said odd, because of how odd the entire situation was. She toggled the random repeater and waited for a binary hit. Even. So Ivers got the first argument. There were advantages to going first; but there were advantages to hearing the other person's opening arguments first, too.

"You're open, Ivers," Rafenkel announced, just for formality's sake. Delleroy—slumped slantwise at his ease in his chair with his feet stretched well out—nodded his maned head in acknowledgement. Delleroy was all willow and brick where Ivers was an octave's growth of nut-bearing blackwood; a different sort of a tree entirely, but each with their own strength. Delleroy was prettier, but Ivers—she wasn't taller, darker, fairer, balder, anything that Rafenkel could think of just now.

All in all, Ivers really hadn't made much of an impression on a person at first meeting, no more than any other regiment of tactical cavalry might. No flash, no noise, no light reflecting off polished surfaces, just a quiet self-assured block of mortuary stone communicating a serene understanding of the fact that she would roll over you as though you weren't there, if need should be.

"Short meeting," Ivers said to Delleroy. Once the discussion started, it was Rafenkel's business to become invisible unless something came up. "No contest that I can see, no contest at all. The Second Judge had already been identified as the dominant choice across all Judiciaries. We know what the citizenry want. We know who is preferred. Confederacy wasn't on the options list, and there is no reason to introduce it now. I'll take your tiles and we can all go take naps, Padrake."

Ivers held out her hand flat-palmed and precisely centered on the broad white line that divided the worktable into two symbolic spaces. There was a small stack of ceramic tiles in front of Delleroy, another at Ivers' elbow. Each of them represented one of the time-honored measures of the public welfare and prosperity of the common weal: incidence of violent crime, public compliance as measured by tax receipts and off-the-market economies, durable and perishable goods in pipeline. All of them issues that Bench Specialists were accustomed to examine to make a determination on the health of any given system or situation; all of them measures of the effective rule of Law and the regulation of trade.

"Not so fast." Delleroy's tone of voice made it clear that he was no more serious about his theatrically exaggerated resentment than Ivers had been about her demand. Rafenkel didn't envy Delleroy the battle. She didn't know of anybody who would have chosen to defend the confederacy model, not with any other alternative available. "Let's just start at the beginning, here, Jils. Specialist Ivers. Sorry."

"All right, Delleroy," Ivers agreed. Reaching across the table, she muddled about with her fingers in his tile array, and turned one up at random. "What have we got, here? Taxation base. How is the total tax burden of an enterprise in Haspirzak improved by not selecting the Second Judge? Instead of one central authority there will be nine, and each of them will inevitably develop its own procedures and requirements."

Ivers sat back, playing with the tile, turning it over and over again in her fingers. "Which means nine times as many people to go between and implement, lawyers and law courts and port authorities and the explosion of existing administrative structures into a whole new entrenched hierarchy more concerned with perpetuating its own survival and development than encouraging the free and fair exchange of goods and services."

Rafenkel let her breath out in a rush, almost staggered, leaning against the padded curve of the low-backed chair. Delleroy straightened up in his seat for his own part, and if Rafenkel wasn't mistaken

Delleroy winked at her. *Yes. It was an impressive rant, wasn't it? But that's our job, ranting impressively.*

"You are so cynical," Delleroy said, a note of humor in his voice that just barely escaped being blatantly affectionate. "But that's good. Cynical is good. We need cynical to examine all angles with open eyes. Chilleau doesn't have a chance of keeping the lid on inconsistent taxation. We select Chilleau, and what happens?"

Ivers raised an eyebrow and waited.

"I'll tell you what happens." Of course Delleroy would. The question had been rhetorical. "People see a First Judge selected at a Judiciary in which a senior officer was murdered, and no culprit brought to justice. They conclude that the law can be gotten 'round, and if murder won't be pursued and prosecuted, who's going to seriously bother with a little spot of fraud here and there?"

There was the most peculiar sound in the air on the Ivers side of the table, Rafenkel thought. A little bit like the nap on a velvet wall-hanging spontaneously surging from one side to the other with a low-voiced sound that communicated only menace, just out of the reach of Rafenkel's ears. The sound of Ivers' hackles rising, and snarling as they came.

"Assuming, of course," Ivers said cheerfully, giving Delleroy no satisfaction of a perceptible reaction, "that it is known to have been a murder. And that a culprit is not apprehended, guilty or not. While the unwholesome effect on taxation and trade obtains with the confederation model whether the murder of Chilleau's First Secretary is ever solved or not, as it will be, without fail."

Delleroy raised one hand where it lay on the table and showed Ivers the palm of his hand: peace. "Of course," he said. "But we don't know when that'll happen, do we, with Chilleau's only Bench Specialist available pulled off on to other assignments like this one? And, if the murder is solved, the public perception remains of an administrative apparatus without an experienced head. Advantage will be taken."

Delleroy could rant with the best; Rafenkel considered it a privilege to be witness. He was only getting started, too, so much was evident as he continued. "Percentages skimmed off tax collections, ad-hoc and off-the-record taxes assessed or disguised as fees, proceeds to pay for Bench offices reduced because collections are being harvested and the Bench forced to raise taxes to pay for the agents to investigate what's gone wrong with tax collections."

It all sounded so reasonable when Delleroy said it. He had the rhetorical flourishes down in his body language as well, leaning into his argument, leaning back to let his final bolt home. "If the Judge gets to keep all of her own taxes, it's in her best interest to maximize the efficiency of collections and minimize fraud—a much more manageable task at the individual Bench level. Enlightened self-interest."

Ivers, however, had known Delleroy—Rafenkel reminded herself—and was apparently at least partially immune to his persuasiveness. "Inequitable taxation," Ivers retorted. "Every Judge for herself and the devil take the hindmost. Influence brokering. Arms races. There must be a clearly identified and perceived central authority. Chilleau Judiciary, in fact."

One tax collector was better than nine, in other words. Rafenkel could see both sides of the argument, which surprised her a little bit.

"Selecting Chilleau means funding Fleet for civil order operations on a greatly expanded level," Delleroy warned. Not giving up. Ivers grinned. What, had Ivers been afraid that Delleroy was going to roll over?

"Not selecting Chilleau means funding Fleet for the same purpose, and for the formation of dedicated Bench detachments besides. More tax revenue requirements. It won't wash, Padrake. Delleroy."

He started to lift his hand to make a point, shut his mouth and closed his hand, glanced over to one side; then his face cleared and he leaned forward, both forearms on the table.

"Fleet detachments which can be funded out of revenues no longer required to support a central administration, sufficient to pay for Fleet agency enforcement of collection of existing taxes in a manner uniform Bench-wide. Confederation won't increase citizens' taxes. Confederation will be tax-neutral."

"While selecting Chilleau guarantees that existing Fleet resources, requiring no additional tax revenues, enforce the tax codes across all of Jurisdiction space, uniformly. You know it perfectly well. You son of a bitch."

The almost-too-apparent affection that Rafenkel had heard from Delleroy was there in equal measure in Ivers' voice. Ivers was pleased with Delleroy's stubbornness, Rafenkel decided. She had been afraid he'd fail to prosecute his case as vigorously as possible, in light of the previous association—and out of consideration for the challenges of her current position as well.

"So's your old man," Delleroy said. "I know nothing of the sort. So maybe confederation would increase administration costs of shipping. Benches responsible only for themselves will see their own best interest served in efficient and cost-effective management. They'll be working for themselves, not the First Judge."

Ivers' present situation was not enviable, Rafenkel knew. The easiest and most obvious solution to the problem of Verlaine's unsolved murder was to assassinate Ivers for the good of the Judicial order and declare her guilty after the fact. Specialist Nion had been talking a little too openly about related subjects; that was part of the reason that Rafenkel had decided to make it her business to see that Ivers and Nion weren't alone together.

"At the expense of the common weal, Delleroy, Bench against Bench, and the citizens paying the price for power struggles at the upper echelons."

They were clearly only getting started on taxes, and before any tiles could pass they had to agree, Delleroy and Ivers, that the advantage lay with one argument or the other. If they could not agree she, Rafenkel, would rule that there was no advantage to either for that element, and take the tile out of play. Taxes clearly had a great deal of play left in it.

"Bench against Bench gives us unprecedented opportunities to test alternate strategies on a local level. The one that is most efficient will prevail, and other Benches will adopt it out of their own self-interest. Confederation will improve the common weal by driving out the best tax model for adoption."

Rafenkel settled her back against the padded seat of her chair and folded her arms across her chest.

It was going to be a long session.

HOURS LATER, AND Ivers had taken the victory so far—one tile. Delleroy had finally conceded that it was entirely possible that confederation would result in a short-term increase in the tax burdens and potentially middle-term tax increases as well. He'd surrendered the tile only with a reconsideration marker on it, though. They were both stubborn. Rafenkel was impressed by the strength of the defense Delleroy was putting up for the choice of last resort, but she wasn't unhappy about it when the time came to take a break.

"No, with increased administrative infrastructure it becomes more—and not less—difficult for people to obtain medical care," Ivers was insisting, calmly. "Especially specialized medical care. How many Mayon surgical colleges are there, under Jurisdiction? Not more than fourteen—if you don't count Mayon."

That was a bit of a stretch, maybe. There were plenty of surgical colleges, just few with the range and depth and breadth of Mayon's resources. Since that was Ivers' point, Rafenkel decided to let it go, on her own personal private score-board—and was just shifting in her seat to listen to Delleroy's rebuttal when something caught her eye, from outside the room. At the end of the floating path, on the ancient shore on which the station had been built—Capercoy. Capercoy with one arm raised high overhead, waving—what? Oh. A preheat package.

"Yeah," Ivers said, before Rafenkel or Delleroy had a chance to react. "And I'm on kitchen with Capercoy today. He probably just wants to make sure he doesn't hog all of the fun for himself. Rafenkel, we'll pick up after mid-meal, all right?"

Rafenkel nodded. Breaks were part of their schedule. An element in the common knowledge of Bench Specialists was the maximization of intellectual analysis by careful management, periods of focus and concentration balanced by periods of rest during which apparently random thoughts could be safely entertained. In which case they frequently turned out not to be random thoughts at all.

"Agreed," Rafenkel answered, and closed the record she was making of proceedings.

Ivers started out the door and down the floating path, across the still black waters. There was no light except for that marking the way or reflecting from the station. In the blackness of the cave, Ivers seemed to be walking through the void of Space. Rafenkel frowned, and then reminded herself that Capercoy was waiting for Ivers. There was no need for her to hurry after Ivers and come up with some excuse to go with her to the kitchen. Capercoy would look after her.

Alone in the small glassed-in room with Delleroy, Rafenkel set her things in order while he stretched from toe to fingertip and back again before he relaxed abruptly against the back of his chair once more, as though the sinews stringing his limbs together had suddenly been cut. "Long session," Delleroy said. "Tough argument."

He was right on both counts, so Rafenkel nodded. "You're really pushing it, aren't you?" It wasn't easy to remember that Delleroy was just the debtor's advocate here, and charged with putting his assigned solution forward as vigorously as possible. He argued with such conviction. If she hadn't known better, she would have concluded that he'd been thinking hard about it for a very long time.

"She'd respect nothing less," Delleroy said, with a decided nod. "I couldn't do any less. She'd know."

Yes, Delleroy and Ivers had history. But also yes, if Ivers suspected Delleroy of softening his attack for whatever reason, she would lose respect for him. So would Rafenkel herself.

"Gotta respect your professionalism." She could give him that ungrudgingly. "I wouldn't want to be defending confederation."

Raising his head, Delleroy gazed thoughtfully into the middle distance at the opposite side of the floating room. "That's what I thought at first," he said, in a tone of voice that Rafenkel could only characterize in her mind as one of reluctant confession. "But the more I think about it, the more sense it makes. Will Cintaro accept the Second Judge? No. Cintaro wants it for herself. We can't go any of the Fontailloe routes, not if we pay the least bit of attention to the past. None of the other Judiciaries have the support to take over the role, especially if Cintaro is not selected and must be dealt with. Confederation works for me, Rafenkel. It does."

He should save the persuasive speeches for people who could be moved by them, Rafenkel told herself. Still, he sounded sincere. "Confederation is anarchy." The Sixth Judge, Rafenkel's Judge, was willing to accept even Supicor in the role of First Judge rather than have no First Judge at all.

The Sixth Judge and her advisors foresaw no difficulties in resisting any undue demands on Supicor's part if it came to that, and Sant-Dasidar could afford to spend a little extra by way of common benefit tax money to Supicor for infrastructure restoration and management. "My Judge will demand she be Selected, before it comes to that."

Delleroy shrugged. "An interesting point, Rafenkel, because in the final analysis, what can the Sixth Judge actually do? Call out the Fleet? No, Fleet is more than happy for any excuse it gets to preserve its autonomy by coming up with reasons why it oughtn't do as the Judge tells it. At least not right away. Not without careful consideration."

She had to laugh, because he was right. That was one reason why the Sixth Judge liked it at Sant-Dasidar: the Jurisdiction Fleet might withhold resources, but so long as she had the cooperation of the Dolgorukij Combine—a solid five-in-eight of the population, a good seven-in-eight of the Bench resources—she had a perfectly good fleet of her very own to direct at will.

It didn't seem quite right to let his claim go by without a challenge, though, no matter how true she thought it might be. "The Judge is the voice of the Law, and the rule of Law is the foundation of Jurisdiction. Not even Fleet can stand against the verdict of the Bench for long, not without destroying the basic assumptions of our social contract. You know it."

The Bench had no significant police force of its own, and if the Fleet disregarded the Bench it could do so with impunity; but without the legal and administrative framework of the Bench, Fleet would find itself without supplies, without resources, without recruits—and challenged for local dominion by Home Defense Fleets like that of the Combine, or the Emandis Home Defense Fleet in Brisinje Judiciary.

Delleroy leaned one arm on the table's surface, sitting at an angle to the table to face her very directly. "I'll tell you what the foundation of the Bench is," he said, low-voiced and intent. "It's not the Judges. It's not the Fleet. It's not the clerks of Court of the planetary governments or system proxies, or any of those things. It's us. Plain and simple. We are the foundation of the rule of Law, Rafenkel, Bench Specialists. It's us who run the Bench anyway. What difference can it make who calls herself First Judge? It's the Bench Specialists assigned who do the real work."

That it was perfectly true in a limited sense did not mean that Delleroy had any business actually saying such a thing. "We're the hidden weapon of the Bench," she corrected, a little bit frostily. "And *only* a weapon or a tool. Mind your place."

"Come on." Delleroy's tone made it clear that he didn't have any patience just now for pious clichés. "You're the one who knows better than that, Rafenkel. It's our job, not the Judges' or the First Secretaries', to see what needs to be done and then make it happen.

Why are we here in the first place? Because each one of those Judges knows that no solution we won't support can stand. How about the way we rewrote the rules, for an example? Whose idea was that, anyway?"

Changing the strategy for attacking the debate, he meant. Rafenkel frowned a bit, thinking. "I heard from Balkney. He heard from Capercoy and was about to talk to Zeman. I don't know. Does it matter?" It had been a good idea. She could understand his curiosity, but she hadn't bothered to ask, herself. She'd thought she'd find out as things went forward.

"Of course it doesn't." Delleroy stood up. "Time to eat. We're going to need our strength. That Ivers, she's a tough one."

Maybe Delleroy was right. Maybe the Bench did run on Bench Specialists rather than the Judges. There were many Judges and few Bench Specialists—an enormous amount of power without well-defined limits in the hands of a small number of fanatically anonymous operatives, running things from behind the scenes. What was to stop them from simply taking the Law into their own hands and redefining it as they saw fit? What was to stop them from taking over?

Little things. Duty and honor, and the fact that their only excuse for what they sometimes had to do was that it was in the service of the greater good and the common weal. An historical understanding of the necessary fact that the moment people started to make up their own rules they lost their objectivity and began to act at cross purposes with one another, with inevitable negative consequences for the population.

Was Delleroy hinting that a Bench Specialist, and not some misguided Fleet high-level operative, had truly assassinated the First Secretary?

Would the Jurisdiction be in worse shape if it were being run by Bench Specialists? There would still be Judges, and the rule of Law— but no one single presiding, unifying voice. If the Judiciary were to be run by Bench Specialists, what was there to prevent some one Bench Specialist from plotting against the others, and ultimately establishing an absolute autocracy?

What was to stop any one given Judge from doing just that if there was no recognized highest-level authority, under Delleroy's confederacy model? Had Delleroy actually been sounding her out on building an influence base for Brisinje—or for Padrake Delleroy, when confederacy came to the Jurisdiction?

Delleroy was deep. It would be like him to be trying something like that just to demonstrate how seriously he took his assigned argument for confederation. What an operator, Rafenkel thought admiringly, and followed Delleroy out of the debate room to get her mid-meal in the kitchen with the others.

DIERRYK RUKOTA LOOKED down through the soundproofed clearwall into the pit of the Engineering bridge, resentfully. He would much rather have been down there with Wheatfields right now, looking at simulated fire patterns from weapons placement proposals. Much.

Instead he was up here on the observation deck that overlooked the Engineering bridge, which was entirely too crowded. First Officer. Intelligence Officer Two, she'd always made him nervous. Ship's surgeon with his arms crossed over his chest, chewing on the cuticle of his thumbnail irritably; and, of course, Brevet Captain Jennet ap Rhiannon, glaring eye-to-eye with Karol Vogel where he sat.

"And Koscuisko's auxiliary imager. And the micro-flints. And an entire storeroom, Vogel, and very nearly did a number on my weaponer as well, and that's not even getting to the real damage you've done this ship."

Her weaponer? That would be him, Rukota realized, impressed. He hadn't quite realized that Fleet warships ever carried weaponers for the ship as a whole, rather than the crew member assigned the role on the Wolnadi fighters. Here he had thought that he was just an irresponsible stowaway having the time of his life.

"Captain ap Rhiannon." Vogel sounded tired, and a little out of temper. "I can only assure you again. It was an accident. I had as much invested—no, I didn't. But appearances to the contrary notwithstanding, it was not a deliberate act of sabotage. Would I have to have died to convince you of that?"

Rukota could sympathize with Vogel's irritation. He had been very thoroughly bruised and rattled by the explosion, but was otherwise unharmed. Vogel hadn't gotten quite far enough from the blast-funnel made by the open doorway when the bomb exploded, and several pieces of miscellaneous Secured Medical had been picked out of his brain along with fragments of bone.

Koscuisko hadn't known about the borrowed—now destroyed—surgical set when he'd been operating. A good thing for Vogel, too, Rukota decided, with a sideways glance at Koscuisko's thunderous scowl. He'd never seen Koscuisko in a really bad mood before.

Ap Rhiannon looked thoughtful. "Might have been a good start, Specialist. Because without that Record, I don't know how I am going to protect this crew from Fleet, and that means that you may have cost me lives."

Vogel rubbed his forehead wearily, seeming not so much aggravated now as discouraged. "I can give testimony. I saw it. That should count for something. And we ran all of the checks. You can ask your weaponer, he was there."

Oh, no, you don't, Vogel, Rukota thought, and kept his gaze fixed firmly on the scene below. He could see the status boards. He could see the forward scans. The *Ragnarok* was due to drop vector; ap Rhiannon liked to watch. Vogel was not going to drag him into this if Rukota could help it. Vogel was the Bench Specialist here. He could just deal with Jennet ap Rhiannon—

"We know," Two said cheerfully. She had no other mode that Rukota had ever been able to determine. It was an artifact of her translator. Her normal conversational range was well out of reach for most hominid ears, and her vocal apparatus was not set up for Standard. "We saw you. Yes. Every precaution. And if it had been anybody but a Bench Specialist, we would have no doubt. You suffer from the reputation of your breed."

In a manner of speaking. Vogel rubbed his forehead idly, as though his head ached; it should, Rukota thought. The skin that covered it was halfway healed already, but the plate that Koscuisko had laid over the brain tissue to keep bone in place while it healed would not be fully metabolized for at least three months.

"I'm not in the habit of losing evidence," Vogel said. "It's just not what I do. I'm annoyed about this myself, I'll never live it down."

Not the way in which to introduce the subject of regret, perhaps. Rukota cleared his throat to draw attention away from Vogel's choice of words. "Coming up on a drop, your Excellency," Rukota said. "Go to audio?"

Ap Rhiannon seemed to think about it, but nodded. Rukota opened the feed. Wheatfields was talking.

"Shave a few off lateral. It's a loose vector, and we're hot. Calm it down, Tamer." The main display screen was a muted blank, but at odd intervals a speck of black seemed to fly out of the center and off-screen in an arc that was still so wide it didn't look curved at all, from Rukota's point of view. It was just a schematic, but it meant that they were nearing the exit vector they had targeted on entry.

"How many hours since we hit?" Vogel asked, sounding curious even past his basic apparently discouraged condition. "The man's a maniac."

Yes, they'd made a swift transit. Wheatfields had taken nearly two days off of the trip by keeping up his velocity as they hit the entry vector. There were limits to how useful that sort of risk could be—miscalculation could spike a ship onto a harmonic, and you might end up somewhere quite different from where you were going.

But the *Ragnarok* had been an experimental test bed, a proving model, and Wheatfields had been its Ship's Engineer for as long as it had been a functioning hull. Engineers didn't usually take risks. That was what Command Branch was for.

"He may be a maniac but he never blew up Secured Medical. And he had cause to," ap Rhiannon retorted. Rukota didn't think her heart was in it, though. She was watching the power oscillation monitors from over Wheatfields' shoulder, several lengths removed.

As if Wheatfields knew that he was being watched, he reached for the exact read that ap Rhiannon appeared to be examining, to make an adjustment. The key to successful vector exit was a smooth approach with no sudden shifts in the ship's momentum to throw the figurative stream of vector space into an eddy that would take the ship down with it. Nobody knew what "down" might mean, on vector.

When ships snagged on something on an exit vector, they were invariably torn to pieces by the shearing shifts in force, like a thin-skinned glass boat hitting a rapids. There was no particular reason why it had to be done slowly; just that the less time you allowed yourself to brake to exit velocity, the higher the possibility that you weren't going to be able to smooth your speed down perfectly, and come out of it alive.

"Set the index, Fan. Conner, take us down another three on that lateral. I want those engines recalibrated as soon as we drop vector. Careful. Sarend? What are you reading?"

Wheatfields did know that he was being watched, of course, Rukota reminded himself; he knew perfectly well that there were people on his observation deck. It had just been the illusion of cause and effect.

"The debouch's shifted a bit, your Excellency, we'll have another twelve to sneak up on it. I've sent a report out to Local. I read seven point six four by eight. It's not perfect, but it'll do."

Now Wheatfields stood, which brought his head almost uncomfortably close to the edge of the observation deck's overhang. Wheatfields was an unusually tall man, even for a Chigan—Chigan ran tall and thin to the Jurisdiction Standard to begin with. "Not good enough," Wheatfields said, firmly. "Need I remind you that our captain is watching? Nothing less than exceptional will be accepted. Recalculate, Sarend, vector in six."

Rukota couldn't see the technician's face from where he stood, but he knew how to interpret that set to a woman's shoulders. She wasn't in the least put out by the rebuke because it hadn't been a rebuke, but a compliment. A reminder. *You're exceptional. Be yourself. Show your captain what you're made of.*

"Seven point eight six nine by eight, sir, respectfully apologizing for point one three one variation due to yaw on section five outboard two. Confirmed."

Looking up over his shoulder to catch ap Rhiannon's eye, Wheatfields smiled. Rukota wasn't sure he'd ever seen Wheatfields do that, but he hadn't been on board for more than a few months. "Thank you, Sarend, Tamer, Fan, Conner. Tamer. Acquire the exit vector."

On the main screen those little black dots were flying less and less quickly, their arcs more and more pronounced. A thin border of accumulated black dots had begun to collect all around the perimeter of the forward screens like snow falling on a warmed windscreen. The *Ragnarok* was shedding speed.

"Up on twelve," Tamer said. "Down eight. Down eight. Down seventeen. Up six." It clearly meant something to Wheatfields' people, if not to Rukota. He knew the general idea—minute adjustments to impulse streams and main reactor core feeds, to make equally minute adjustments in the *Ragnarok's* precise velocity. Strictly speaking, it wasn't necessary to come off vector exactly as one had entered it but in reverse. Pilots and engineers prided themselves on backing off a vector—facing forward—nonetheless. Point of honor. And least wear and tear on the equipment from vector shear, that way.

"Drop vector in three," Wheatfields said. "Tamer, if you're going to fix that shift, now is the time to do it. Shade it for me—perfect."

Those little black dots were whirling out of the center of the screen as though they were bullets of black ink shot into a funnel, collecting at the sides, piling up. Thicker. Darker. Denser, almost moment by moment. Nothing was actually arching or collecting or congealing—it was just a schematic, but one whose data representations made an elegant and effective sort of a description of a ship on an inbound spiral off a vector.

"There it is." Wheatfields turned back to his chair and sat down, leaning well back with an expression of mild benevolent self-satisfaction on his face. "Your Excellency. We have Brisinje Jurisdiction, Emandis space. There is a communication waiting for you."

Ap Rhiannon keyed the transmit. "Thank you, Engineer, beautifully done, smoothest yet. Very impressive."

And it was, too, but ap Rhiannon was still talking. "That'll be Emandis Station telling me I can't have cannon. Route it through to my office, please, and Vogel can come with me to explain why we need to add a replacement surgical set and related equipment to an already full manifest."

"My pleasure, Captain," Vogel said with a gentle bow. He was lying, Rukota was sure, but nobody cared. Together, ap Rhiannon and Vogel left; once they were gone, Two hopped down off of the chair in which she had been perched and lifted her beautiful black velvet muzzle with its extraordinary array of very sharp white teeth in Koscuisko's direction and chattered with her mouth, stilling herself—as usual—before the translation was well begun, to wait. Looking up at Koscuisko expectantly. Not only was Two's dialect out of range, it was apparently significantly faster—or perhaps simply that much more efficient—than normal hominid speech.

"You have reviewed the record, Andrej," she said. "What do you think?"

Koscuisko didn't answer directly. He looked to Rukota instead. There was something going on behind Koscuisko's pale eyes that Rukota didn't understand but knew he didn't like. "I think that

Secured Medical has been thoroughly destroyed," Koscuisko said. "It will never be usable for its original purpose again. To that degree, Vogel has done me a significant service."

The words were pretty. But there was tension in them. "For which I cannot take credit, your Excellency, nor assign any to Vogel. Nothing that I heard or saw would lead me to suspect that he was up to no good." Except for theft of surgical apparatus, of course. That had been a little underhanded of them. "You saw the tapes. What's your professional opinion?"

Koscuisko shook his head, looking very discouraged all of a sudden. He sat down, brooding over the Engineering deck on the other side of the clear-wall. "There are no obvious signs of hidden intent, but Vogel is a Bench Specialist, and I would not expect to see any from such a man. I have seen him produce what amounted to a raw-pelted lie by inference and misdirection, and in a very serious matter, and I doubted my suspicions even when I knew that they were all but certain to be true."

That would have been an interesting thing to see, Rukota decided. What had happened at Burkhayden—where Koscuisko had last seen Vogel, by report of gossip—that could possibly have elicited such a remark? Or did Koscuisko have history with Vogel that went further back than that?

"But you have no suspicions in this case," Rukota urged, to cover the awkward silence.

Koscuisko shrugged, turning his attention back to Two—who was waiting patiently for her answer. "I have no evidence. Vogel blew it up. I have no reason to believe that Vogel had any ulterior motive that would lead him here with the intent of destroying the forged record. But it is so convenient for the Bench, and so inconvenient for the *Ragnarok*. You know that the captain means to make an announcement on all-ship?"

"Very soon," Two agreed with a crisp nod that came only halfway through the first word of the translation. "She does not trust her crew. She cannot believe that they are fully aware of consequences. It is insecurity."

Ap Rhiannon? Insecure? Rukota could have laughed at that, except that he could understand Two's point. He didn't like it. "See here, Koscuisko, what motive could Vogel have had? He's a Bench Specialist. Dedicated to the rule of Law."

"Yes." Koscuisko sounded somber. He was simply not in a very good mood, it seemed. He hadn't been in a very good mood since he'd come back off leave with a forged record. "The rule of Law, and the maintenance of the Judicial order. Both of which receive a very hard blow from the knowledge that a record has been compromised in order to incriminate innocent people. How are you to feel if you discover, after years of mourning, that someone you loved might never have even confessed at all—never mind endured inhumane duress—before he was put to death by torture?"

So Vogel might have destroyed the record because it was forged, because the injustice of condemning the *Ragnarok* as a mutineer and its crew to Inquiry was not as potentially grave a threat to justice as the introduction of proof that the record could be manipulated. "I'd be willing to swear to the sincerity of Vogel's claimed motive, your Excellency. I couldn't, of course, not under oath. But I'd be willing to."

Koscuisko nodded. "Vogel was interested in knowing whether there was a connection between two forged Judicial instruments. We can speculate therefore that Vogel did not himself create the forged instruments. But whether he was about to discover a link, and was prevented by the forger's self-defense mechanism; or had discovered a link and destroyed the record in order to protect somebody—an accomplice, perhaps—I don't know. I'd like to have him under a speak-serum. But without the captain's permission I have no authority."

Ap Rhiannon didn't care. The real importance lay in the fact that the forged record had been destroyed. They were naked and defense-less, and ap Rhiannon was much more interested in finding clothing than in determining whether Vogel had stolen her trousers. Time enough for that when she'd covered her back, Rukota supposed.

He could hear the clear-tone for the allship, and the voice of the captain: "Jennet ap Rhiannon, for the Command and crew of the Jurisdiction Fleet Ship *Ragnarok*. We are approaching Emandis Station for resupply. Down-leave will be granted according to policy with the First Officer's approval."

Was it his imagination, or could he hear her taking a deep breath before she went on?

"A recent accident has seriously compromised evidence that this ship was holding pertinent to its Appeal against Pesadie Training Command for inappropriate charges in the death of acting captain

Cowil Brem during evaluation exercise. While I remain determined to defend the honor of this ship and the loyalty of its crew until it is vindicated, I cannot conceal from you the fact that we have lost significant leverage."

That was an understatement if he had ever heard one. The crew could be under no illusions as to what it meant.

"I encourage you all to take advantage of the opportunity to take down-leave at Emandis Station to consider your personal options in light of this information. Jennet ap Rhiannon, away, here."

It was quiet on the observation deck. Two raised one wing to scratch behind her ear with the claw at the end of the second joint, thoughtfully.

Koscuisko shook his head. "Leave now, or forever wed your destiny to mine. She is an incurable romantic underneath it all. Someone permitted her to watch the wrong entertainment in her off hours when she was a child. If she had access to entertainment. If she had off hours. If she ever was a child."

Rukota snorted. Crèche-bred and romantic? "Well, I'm not going anywhere," he declared firmly. "She might just try to leave without me. And she needs me. The ship, I mean. Who'll look after her cannon? No. How about you?"

"There are deserts on Emandis," Two said suddenly, as though the idea had only just occurred to her. "With fat and juicy thermal columns. The maintenance atmosphere is not the same." Nor did the Ship's Engineer care for her using his maintenance atmosphere for soaring. It tended to unnerve his technicians. Who knocked into things. That knocked into other things. Rukota had heard more than one story about it. "And you, Andrej?"

"I believe she would be just as pleased to leave without me," Koscuisko said. "We have never been particularly comfortable with one another. I do not mean to leave these crew with an inadequate surgery." Was that a jab—Rukota wondered—or did Koscuisko have something else on his mind?

Koscuisko kept talking. "And still I cannot come all of this way, and not speak to Joslire where he rests. Where Joslire has gone, I cannot guess. His marker is here. I am simply going to have to risk it."

There seemed to be nothing more to say. Excusing himself with a polite nod, Rukota went away. The last thing he heard as the door closed behind him was Two's voice, Two's translator's voice. "And *Scylla* will be coming there as well. You have friends on *Scylla*, if I remember?"

But the door closed before he heard Koscuisko's reply, and it was none of his business anyway. He went out to his workstation near the docks in the maintenance atmosphere to check the manifest one last time, to be sure he hadn't forgotten anything on his wish list for weaponry from Emandis Station.

CHAPTER TEN
SHARP WORDS

"YES, I GRANT you that Delleroy surrendered most of his markers to Chilleau," Bench Specialist Nion said. "It's not a persuasive argument, though, is it? Only proves that confederacy is even less good an idea. Nothing more."

Jils sat at the side of the room, listening, watching. After taking an active role in the debate with Padrake—an exercise which had taken six full sessions, each one of them intellectually and even physically exhausting—it was as good as a holiday to do nothing more complex than sit and listen.

"Then you should simply extend that line of reasoning." Rinpen's voice was admirably calm in the face of Nion's almost-sneering one, Jils felt. Surely Nion's sneering at the very idea of selecting Chilleau Judiciary in any form had nothing to do with Jils' own feelings of mild aggravation. Surely. "We have previously established that selecting the Second Judge at Chilleau right now is better than confederacy. Selecting Chilleau Judiciary right now is less prudent than waiting for her administration to regroup, with Ivers' very professional help."

Nion rolled a pale eye at Jils and all but lifted her lip. There was something wrong with Nion, Jils decided. Andrej Koscuisko was a blond man of fair complexion and very pale eyes whose hair—fine-textured as that of Dolgorukij men who lacked chin-beards tended to be—was always falling across his forehead. Nion was so fair of face as to be almost blue with it, however, and her eyes were almost as pale as Koscuisko's.

So how was it that elements of physiognomy that interested Jils in Koscuisko's face moved her to nothing more than dislike when presented in an even more extreme form in Nion? Her hair was as fine as filament wire, all of the hair that fell to her waist still making up a single braid of no more than a thumb's thickness, tied up into a depressing little knot at the back of Nion's head. If it had been her, Jils decided, she would have gotten a weave, or cut her hair short. Something.

"Yes, of course. Specialist Ivers is undoubtedly a significant asset in Chilleau Judiciary's administration. I'm sure it's very nice, being Bench Specialist at the First Judge's seat. You should get Tanifer talking some time."

Nion, like Padrake, seemed to identify the specialist with the Judiciary a little more closely than Jils was accustomed. Padrake at least knew better. Bench Specialists were rotated precisely in order to avoid developing inappropriate relationships with any one Judge. Her own long association with Chilleau had been mildly anomalous, but she hadn't spent all of her time at Chilleau even when she had made it her base of operations at Verlaine's request.

Padrake's apparent assumption that Jils was personally committed to the Second Judge's cause was all the more puzzling in light of his own experience. They had teamed with each other five years ago. He had only been at Brisinje for two years or so, she remembered him telling her—she thought. No. Five years. No. Two years. Which?

Shifting in her seat Jils swallowed back a sigh of exasperation. If anyone was in danger of identifying too closely with the agenda of any one particular Judge, it was surely Padrake himself, on first-name terms with the First Secretary, and all. And these were not very comfortable chairs. They'd been brought in to the theater from one of the laboratory areas—light, flimsy things with a very thinly padded seat.

Why she shouldn't use the perfectly good seats that were already here in the theater room, Jils did not know, but the procedures they had all agreed on called for the observer to be seated at right angles to the axis of discussion and not more than five eights distant from the table with the tiles, and none of the rather more comfortable chairs already here could be pulled off of their anchors and placed correctly.

Since Jils was observing, Nion could make all the acid comments she liked without fear of reprisals; Jils was here to listen. Firmly pushing her pique away from her mind, Jils crossed her arms over her chest and leaned back in the chair, pushing off with one foot to tilt the seat toward the back wall and brace it there.

"But, and Ivers is much too well disciplined to mention this, Rinpen, she knows as well as anyone that Chilleau is compromised and corrupt. There are rumors that a record has been compromised, by a clerk of Court at Chilleau Judiciary—Verlaine's special pet, in fact. And more."

Balancing a chair between its two back legs and the wall could be delicate business. Jils used the opportunity it gave her to adjust and shift and cover her unhappy surprise. There was no doubt in her mind but that the Malcontent had controlled the information as carefully as possible, and the Malcontent was as good a secret service as Jils had ever seen. But secrets that were big enough couldn't be kept forever.

If Nion knew about the existence of the forged record, did that mean Nion knew that Jils had been there when the secret had been discovered? It could look bad. Sitting here in the theater of a research station deep beneath Brisinje, it suddenly seemed to Jils that it almost certainly looked much worse than she had imagined.

"There's no such thing as a Judiciary that has never been compromised." Rinpen's retort was gallantly fielded, but a little weak. "Citizens under Jurisdiction have already shown their willingness to move past the difficulties in Chilleau's recent past. The Domitt Prison. The Nurail. Even with Cintaro making a persuasive case out of the Domitt, the selection was in Chilleau's favor."

Well argued, but his heart didn't seem to be in it. Whether or not he'd heard about a forged record, he knew that there was an issue now. Jils shifted her weight in her chair, irritated. She could have said something—but not without interfering unnecessarily with the discussion. Nion knew that. Nion was taking advantage. Jils was beginning to not like Nion.

She was beginning to dislike her chair, as well. Its variety of functional ceramic tube-and-brace construction might well be durable and inexpensive, but it didn't feel quite solid to Jils in some obscure sense. Maybe she was just blaming it for Nion.

"A forged record," Nion repeated, maliciously. "In a Judiciary characterized by the close working relationship between the First Secretary and Bench Specialist detailed. What do you think the common citizen will make of the existence of a forged record, under those circumstances? Of the judicial insistence that a Fleet warship that leveled stolen battle cannon against Fleet defensive fortifications has committed no crime, when the only possible interpretation is that mutiny is being hushed up for the sake of the Dolgorukij Combine's tender feelings about its ancestral aristocracy?"

This was going too far. Arching her back to push against the wall with her shoulders, Jils opened her mouth to say something; Rinpen looked at her—clearly worried—and Jils settled the chair back into its leaning position, though not without effort. Maybe the entire station had settled, sited as it was on the shores of an ancient lake which might well be unstable, and which had certainly never suffered the indignity of a structure of any sort until quite recently.

Maybe the floor was uneven. The chair wobbled and was a little difficult to control, its structural tubing loose. Probably just needed an adjustment, Jils told herself. Her own attitude certainly did.

"Which Combine, and the Judiciary in which it is located, can be counted on to exert themselves to stabilize Chilleau to the maximum extent of their ability." Rinpen spoke slowly, as though he was sounding out his own argument as he spoke. He apparently found it persuasive, however, because his voice strengthened and grew more confident as he continued. Maybe he had just been afraid that she was going to attack Nion, Jils thought. It was a good idea. Nion clearly needed attacked, with her ghostly pale complexion and her watering eyes and her teeth that looked like milk-teeth and which were just wrong in an adult jaw, and not much of a chin either.

"The Bench expects its First Judge to show tact and discretion when dealing with local influential persons"—Jils set aside her irritation for a moment to listen; she was interested in where Rinpen's argument might be going—"and respects attributes that are important in minimizing conflicts that can lead to police actions."

Rinpen was sounding so self-assured now that it was almost as if he'd rehearsed this speech. Maybe he'd anticipated Nion's attack. Jils took a deep breath to calm and center herself, frowning at the way the chair's frame wobbled beneath her.

"Within limits," Nion insisted. "A Bench which enjoys the public trust and confidence will be granted credit by the other Judiciaries and the rest of Jurisdiction space, and only within limits. Chilleau does not."

That was perfectly true, but only as far as Bench Specialists and senior Bench staff went. Oh, and senior Fleet officers.

"Meal break," Jils said, with one eye on the station's master chronometer. "Please suspend your discussion until we reconvene, here, after mid-meal." She wasn't sure it was mid-meal. There was no sense of time in this station, not even with chronometers at hand. It could be dawn in Brisinje. It could be midnight. Here and now, whatever it was, it was time to go eat, so Jils leaned her head back to push off from the wall again and tilt her chair forward onto all four of its floor-points fore and aft.

The front floor-points of the chair came down on the carpeted floor of the theater with a sharp impact that startled Jils. She had just enough time to realize that the chair had not stopped tipping forward when its front bar had struck the floor before something sliced up between her body and her right arm, tearing the fabric of her uniform, tearing her flesh.

Ceramics, she told herself. The sharp edge of a shattered structural tube caught against one of her ribs, taking her breath away in a manner that was familiar but not any more welcome for that. Ceramics, brittle with age. She should have thought twice about leaning back in the chair. She should have noticed herself noticing that the chair didn't feel quite right.

She had a good long time to reproach herself as she struggled for breath against the pain in her side. She didn't particularly want to breathe, not really—she knew that the moment she did, the pain in her side would only be worse. But she did. She was not going to relinquish consciousness. There was more than just her failure to notice her own perceptions that was wrong.

Jils took a breath at last, and found a black-humored sort of satisfaction in the fact that it did in fact hurt worse than anything she could call immediately to mind. She knew she'd been hurt worse. She knew she had good reasons for not thinking about that. She lay on her back and panted shallowly, half-hearing Rinpen beside her. Nion must have gone for the medikit. Jils hoped Nion had gone for the medikit. She hoped Nion wouldn't try to use it on her.

"Can't leave you alone for a minute," someone said. It was Padrake. She was beginning to focus, but not particularly appreciating it. Padrake held a long jagged spear of crazed and shattered ceramic tubing up where Jils could see it. "Just missed sliding up into your abdominal cavity," Padrake said cheerfully. "Lucky you, Jils."

She didn't like the undertone of worry that she could hear in his voice. She knew how to read him. He was shocked, almost frightened. She'd thought that something was wrong. Now she knew she'd been right, but that didn't make her any happier than breathing had.

"Lift," someone said—Zeman.

Jils appreciated the expert handling of the people who were moving her onto the gurney. She also appreciated the fact that nobody had given her any drugs yet. There was a heavy pad of medical compress laced around her now, to staunch the bleeding; that hurt, too. They were going to have to move her. The sealers, the blood-fluid and the rest would be in the little clinic. Jils began to wonder how badly she'd been injured. The idea was almost more than she could bear to contemplate: Bench Intelligence Specialist Jils Tarocca Ivers, to be assassinated by an old lab chair?

"Ivers," Zeman said. "Long bad graze, bleeding pretty good, scraped rib-bones. If the shard had slipped just a little, we wouldn't be having this conversation. We need to give urgent care, but you'll be ambulatory again in about two hours. How about a dose of this or that?"

She hadn't been assassinated by a chair. That was what was wrong. Someone had watched her, seen her leaning back, had sabotaged her chair. Maybe not. Maybe she was imagining things. Maybe pain was making her paranoid. Paranoid was not necessarily a bad thing to be.

"Let me have one of this. And at least five of that." It was hard to choke out the words, because it hurt to breathe. More than that, though, part of her brain was desperate not to accept any drugs. It would be so easy, if she were drugged. She could have an idiopathic allergic reaction to a micro-fungus that had crept into the solution somehow. Her heart could absenmindedly forget to beat. It wouldn't take much.

"Maybe a fraction of the other thing," Padrake suggested. Jils hadn't felt the dose go through, but she could tell that it had, because her thinking seemed to sharpen and focus all at once. Jils knew that Padrake was worried. He'd keep an eye out.

Nobody who wanted her dead for the good of the Judicial order could decently murder her by stealth anyway; executions had to be announced. *Jils Ivers, in the matter of the crime of assassination of a senior Bench official, it is my judgment and my decision that you are at fault and are appropriately to be punished therefore.* Announced and then acknowledged; no games with chairs that had gone unused for too long, no tricks with drugs would satisfy the jury of a Bench Specialist's peers. She was probably safer right here, right now, than she had been since Verlaine had been murdered.

"Two fractions of the other thing." Jils held up two fingers to make her point, and then closed her eyes. Closing her eyes helped her concentrate on capturing her memories before they faded, before anesthetic drugs clouded her judgment.

While they moved her to the tiny medical unit, Jils focused her mind, listening only to be sure she heard Padrake from time to time. The furniture had been here as long as the station had been, though new equipment had been brought in to support the special needs of Convocation—secured communications transmission equipment, among other things.

The environment was stable, controlled humidity, minimal fluctuations. Structural tubing could fracture under stress, but there shouldn't have been the sorts of stresses that could lead to materials fatigue on such a level. She needed to have a look at that chair, what was left of it. She needed to have a look at the other chairs as well.

The shard had scraped up along her ribs to her armpit, or at least that was what it felt like. The pain was a dull ache, but they hadn't given her enough drugs to deprive her of consciousness. They'd known better than that. None of them would have wanted to lose consciousness in a situation like this. All of them were fully capable of having the same questions about the accident as she did, so how could any of them hope to get away with sabotage?

She was making assumptions based on expectations of common values that might not be universally common at all. How was she to know? Could she go up to Rinpen or Nion or Rafenkel and say, "Pardon me for asking, but if you were going to assassinate me, do you mind telling me how you'd go about it?"

Medical unit. Someone eased her arm up and away; someone cut her uniform blouse and exposed her side. She smelled a sterile field generator in action, felt a familiar prickling tingle traveling up her side as the quick-knit unit worked its way from point of entry to the endmost extent of the wound.

The transparent membrane would seal the wound and keep it clean while open for observation, and would gradually shrink toward its vertical midline over time, drawing the new skin back over the wound to heal without a scar—or without much of one. You could have the scar tissue peeled, and there'd be a new scar, but a fainter, thinner one. Two or three peels, and there was no scar left to speak of, but it was a tedious process for which Jils had never had patience.

The quick-knit's resonation was exquisitely uncomfortable against newly scraped rib-bones. Jils set her teeth and waited; it would be over soon enough. She'd take a break, sleep for a few hours. If there were something to be found out about the chair, she'd find out about it. If someone didn't want her to find out about the chair, she'd find that out, too.

And then she was going to find a way out of here. She had no intention of sitting quietly and waiting to be killed. Under the new procedure, her role could be safely terminated at the front of the process. The longer she could keep Chilleau's bid alive, the longer she would live; but if someone had just tried to kill her, they clearly weren't waiting. Neither would she.

There had to be other ways to get to the surface than just the lift-car. There had to be. She would find them, because if she didn't find something to do soon, some way to take charge of her own destiny, something that would give her the illusion of control over her fate, she was going to go to pieces. If that happened, she'd never know who'd killed Sindha Verlaine, and why.

"Timurcillium must be as close to untraceable as you can get," Rafenkel observed in as neutral a tone as possible. Ivers would already have noted that; it was hard to ignore. The chair had been carefully painted with an antiquing agent, something used extensively on the forged objets d'art market and otherwise mostly ignored because it was in everything—a component of packing materials.

For instance, the preheat packaging material, in an inerted form, could be pulverized and washed out with a mildly acidic solution to pull the substance from its inerting matrix. The packaging was pulverized in the kitchen after every meal service, and many of the things people mixed in their water yielded a mildly acidic solution. Kilpers was one of them.

"But only where the tubing meets the seat. And then only on one or two chairs," Ivers said, as if meditatively. They had found two other chairs in the theater treated in the same manner, the ceramic tubing carefully painted with timurcillium to create a line of weakness that would shear under sharp pressure and split off just such a spear as had nearly skewered her. They were out in storage now, tagged as hazardous, waiting for forensic examination.

They had all been grouped together, so that Ivers could easily have selected any one of them—or none at all. She had been observing a debate. Someone had moved the chair that had been there for the observer, but whoever had done it had waited until the theater had gone off-monitor. Ivers might have selected a treated chair anyway. Ivers liked to lean her chair up against the wall, and the more comfortable chairs didn't tip.

"Target," Ivers said. "The chair only fails on impact. It's still load bearing. And if it went when someone was just sitting on it, the knife-section of the tube wouldn't have enough momentum to do much damage. The only person likely to be actually hurt is the one who is letting her chair fall foursquare to the floor again. Me."

Rafenkel could see the argument; it was clear enough. Why Ivers might have rigged the accident herself was a little less clear, but to look at Zeman, he wasn't sure. Rinpen had been talking to Zeman. Rinpen had been talking to her, too, but she hadn't been able to buy the argument at all.

There was no need for Ivers to stage an attack to divert suspicion away from herself because, prior to the chair's collapse, there had been no other incidents in which Ivers had been suspected of anything—except for the problem of Verlaine's murder, of course. In that case, the incident did nothing to absolve Ivers of Verlaine's murder and everything to endorse suspicion of her guilt by making it clear that someone thought she might very well be guilty, and need killing.

"If there's anyone who could stunt that and stay off the record while they were doing it, it's probably a Bench Specialist," Capercoy said gently. He had a very agreeable accent, soft and warm and fuzzy around the edges with a bit of an occasional drawl to it that dropped the middle out of words from time to time, when it was least expected. "We're not likely to come up with an answer before Convocation is finished, Jils. The report's one thing; what we're going to do about it is another."

Ivers dropped her head, clearly struggling with frustration. Rafenkel could empathize. "If I thought it'd do any good to stand up on the table and solemnly swear that I had neither thought nor word nor deed in the killing of Sindha Verlaine, I'd do it," Ivers said. Her voice held little hope. "But nobody who already thinks differently would believe me. I wouldn't believe me, on principle."

Too true. It was part of the burden of the Bench Specialist never to believe what anybody told them. "Look here," Rafenkel said. She'd had an idea. "Maybe nobody was trying to kill you. Maybe it was a well-intentioned warning. Clumsily executed, yes. In poor taste, yes. But nobody's killing anybody until the Selection is decided. We can't do that unless Chilleau is represented, at least for now."

Ivers nodded, looking very tired. She wore no visible bandaging, but her movements were a little awkward. It had to be wearing on her. A slice up the side was no joke, and if it hadn't been calculated to kill her, the margin of error had been irresponsibly small.

"I was counting on that, Rafenkel. Thought I'd have a bit of a break. But then you decided to reroute the decision tree."

True enough, yet again. At the time, Rafenkel had thought it likely to be welcome to Ivers—get her in, get her out of a vulnerable situation as quickly as possible. The trick with the chair could have been calculated to encourage her to disqualify Chilleau and escape; because, if she was successful in defending the Second Judge's bid against Fontailloe's challenge, she was going to have to wait until the final decision had been made as to which Judiciary Chilleau would face in final debate. Was someone working on Ivers' nerves to persuade her to cut her losses, throw her own platform, and flee?

"All right, Jils," Capercoy said. "You're okay for the run. Cintaro will not accept the selection of Chilleau, not until the administrative issues are cleared up."

The gap left by Verlaine's murder, obviously. His successor could not hope to build the contacts and relationships of a lifetime in a single year. "And Fontailloe is simply not an option. Nobody believes otherwise except for Tanifer, and I'm not so sure even Tanifer does. So you'll be here till the end. And once Cintaro is selected, we can leave together."

Safety in numbers. She and Balkney had been trying to keep an eye on Ivers since Ivers got here. Balkney had apparently liked Ivers on the few occasions in the past that they had worked together; he was worried for her sake.

"Sant-Dasidar will endorse Cintaro if Chilleau is out," Rafenkel said. Capercoy was being very up-front and candid; she could do no less. Maybe full disclosure would reassure Ivers, at least a little bit. "But not otherwise. The Sixth Judge's story is that Chilleau is still the correct selection. She doesn't have to worry about Fleet giving her any problems."

"Fleet giving who problems?" This was a voice from the doorway. The door had been left open—nobody was saying anything that everybody couldn't hear—but Rafenkel was a little startled, regardless. She hadn't heard Delleroy approach. "Not Brisinje. She'll have the Emandisan on 'em so fast, but we've never had any issues with Fleet. Jils, how are you? Ready for the wars again?"

Ivers relaxed when Delleroy came into the room. She didn't slump or slouch; to the contrary, her shoulders seemed to have lifted by some degree, as though a weight on them had been lifted. Balkney and the Widowmaker had been forced to marry, in the end, and Widowmaker had gone onto the inactive roster—at least in theory. Delleroy and Ivers were going to have to face a similar decision sooner or later. It was too clear—at least to Rafenkel—that they responded to each other on a dangerously trusting level.

"How'd it go with you?" Ivers asked, affection almost blatant in her voice. "Balkney chewed your skinny ass?"

Delleroy shook his head. "I'm not doing very well, Jils. But it's not my fault. Confederacy just doesn't have the chops."

"I'll remember you said that," Ivers said. "I may be able to use it. I'd better go, gentles. Tanifer and I are going to start our talk about Fontailloe, and why Chilleau is clearly the better choice."

Or not, from Fontailloe's point of view. "I'll walk you out," Delleroy said. "We've been busy. Want to know how that scrape is doing. Later, gentles."

Given the mutual feeling Delleroy and Ivers appeared to share, Rafenkel felt perfectly comfortable letting Delleroy do the escorting.

"Later," Capercoy replied, on Rafenkel's behalf as well as his own.

Rafenkel stood and stretched. She was going to be glad to get away from here herself, but not as glad as Balkney and Ivers alike, always supposing both of them lived that long.

AP RHIANNON HAD asked him to come and review the surgical set requirements, but Andrej Koscuisko didn't think she had his surgical set on her mind. There had been trouble brewing between the two of them since he had returned to the *Ragnarok* to find her captain. It had only been a matter of time before an explosion occurred—one he had himself primed and ignited.

"The requisition is complete and correct in all material aspects, your Excellency," Andrej confirmed, setting his chop to the senior medical officer's certification of destruction of original issue. She was watching him as suspiciously as a scholar's assistant a too-confident intern, as though expecting the worst at any moment and more than ready to return grief for grief in generously compounded measure. "I hope there is no question of fault to be found with my stores and issues. The equipment was taken. Pure and simple."

She shook her head. Leaning well back in her chair in her office—the captain's office that had been Lowden's before her—she put her feet up on the desk and squinted at the toe of her right boot. "Stolen, Koscuisko, no question. No. I've never had cause to doubt the professionalism and the attention to procedure and detail that you have nurtured in Infirmary."

That sounded like a compliment, and made Andrej nervous. "Very kind, your Excellency. Fully deserved, the praise of Section, with no merit accruing to me thereby. It is their doing."

Now she put her hand back to rest on the top edge of the chair's neck supportand gaze up at the ceiling. "Oh, but praise is due, your Excellency. You lead by example and indirection. Bad example. What really impresses me is how well they do with you there to mislead them."

Well, that was a rebuke burnished and brilliant. He could appreciate it for what it was. "You're too kind." Of what did she intend to accuse him this time? There was so much. And yet he had an idea that he knew where she was going.

"Not at all, Doctor, I have no difficulty in recognizing superlative performance despite its unfortunate implications. This is a ship at war with its own Command, Koscuisko. We can't hope to survive without trust. I agreed to trust you to come on board and rejoin your crew. I respected your motives. I'm sorry to see you have extended no such trust to me."

Tricking a sheet of plain-form out from underneath a stack of flat-files, she pushed it across the desk at him. Andrej took it. His personnel request to cover his planned leave at Emandis: all of his bond-involuntaries. Even Robert. Robert had known Joslire. Of all people, Robert should be allowed to go and gaze upon Joslire's memorial tablet.

"Explain to me, your Excellency, in what way have I disappointed you?" Andrej was genuinely confused. Surely Stoshi hadn't gone so far as to speak to the captain before he'd left. That would have been—well, actually, something one might expect, from a Malcontent. "With regard to my requested leave, I have shared no confidences with anybody on board this ship that I have withheld from my Command. At the same time, one might be excused for having thought that his reasons for wishing to visit a man's memorial tablet might justly be considered personal."

She blew her breath out between clenched teeth, making a sort of a frustrated sound, rolling her eyes at him with transparent disgust. "If you say so. I'm not going to let whatever personal issue you might have with this office interfere with my professional duties toward this ship. You have reason to mistrust the captain of the *Ragnarok*. I can respect that."

Pulling her chop on its chain out from underneath her blouse, she reached for the release and endorsed it, then passed it back. "For that reason, Koscuisko, you're going to Emandis on leave, and you're taking every bond-involuntary troop on my inventory with you. We are in more dangerous a situation than ever. We've lost our sole protection, such as it was. The record is gone, and nobody who trusts a Bench Specialist to do what she wishes they would deserves to live. If letting you steal these troops is what it takes to get you off this ship, then I say steal away, Doctor."

Oh, now he was getting angry. Had she no respect for the regard in which he held the people who had seen him through horrors of which she could have no immediate knowledge? "You have determined that, with the record no longer available, I seek the first opportunity to run away from my duty." That was what she had said. More or less. "It's true that I worry about my gentlemen. Somebody ought, and I am considerably obliged to them. To you not at all."

That was a little harsh. He was obliged to her for sending the wrong team of Security home to Azanry with him, months ago— an action born of what he had to admit was justified paranoia that had saved him from a plot to take his freedom, if not his life—and still what was missing between them was respect. She did not credit him with having feelings. Self-interest seemed to be as far as she would go in attributing motive to his actions.

"The feeling is mutual," ap Rhiannon retorted sharply. "You are, by repute, among the finest battle surgeons in Fleet, or at least you were when Lowden let you alone to do your job. I've seen you in

Infirmary. You could be a significant strength to this Command, Koscuisko, and that's why I can't afford any ambiguity over why you're here. If that insults you, I'm sorry."

She was angry herself, so much was obvious. She didn't seem to have noticed, however; her tone remained fairly level and her language moderately temperate. Maybe she was simply telling the truth. It was possible.

"I have said that I mean to stay with my Command, your Excellency. The ship is yours but Infirmary is mine. You do insult me when you suggest that I am looking for ways out."

Not until the *Ragnarok's* appeal had been heard and sustained. Verlaine was dead, but the documentation Verlaine had signed and sent to him on Azanry was still legal and binding, fully executed: relief of Writ. He could go home and strive to live up to his son's inflated image, and dread the day when Anton would find out. He could be free, his family had half-forgiven him for quarreling with his father already, and he had much to do to repair the damage he had done to alliances and trading relationships when he had married Marana.

Until the *Ragnarok's* appeal was accepted, he would do none of those things. It was a point of honor. The crew of this ship had persistently treated him like a human being, as well as merely an officer, during all of the years that he had been here; it almost convinced him that he was one, and there was no sacrifice that he could make that would begin to balance out the gratitude he felt toward every soul who declined to spit or make a sign against spiritual contamination when he walked past them in the corridors.

"Would you just listen to yourself?" Her voice had sharpened. He had succeeded in annoying her past her self-discipline at last, as it seemed. "You're the inheriting son of the Koscuisko familial corporation. You have a clearly communicated abhorrence for your Inquisitorial function, and an unfortunate history with Fleet Captain Lowden, deceased."

Leaning over her desk with her hands folded—as though to prevent herself from throwing something—she stared at him ferociously as she spoke. "By any measure of rational evaluation, by any sane measure, you have more to lose than the entire crew of the *Ragnarok* combined, and you get insulted when I suggest that you cannot be relied upon because there is too large a gap between what you say and what anybody, anybody at all, can see with their own two eyes."

Well, if she put it that way, Andrej supposed he could see her point. She was crèche-bred. She knew nothing of honor as Andrej understood it. Her entire life had been an indoctrination into the lowest common denominator of peoples' desires and convictions.

"For this reason, you release the bond-involuntaries to go with me to see Joslire, because you wish to remove any obstacles in my path, so that I may leave."

She didn't answer; she didn't need to. He could see her endorsement in her eyes.

"You surprise me, Captain. Bond-involuntaries are valuable resources. To throw them away—just to be rid of me—"

"They're good troops." She was the captain. She could interrupt him. But she didn't do it the way Lowden had. She wasn't making a point about her rank or about Andrej's subordinate status, about how careful Andrej had to be to avoid provoking her into assessing sanctions against the bond-involuntaries. She was just interrupting. "I hate to lose them. Under any other circumstances, I wouldn't allow it at any cost. Cost is the issue."

Well, that sounded reasonable, and she sounded calm enough as she continued. "You've wanted to take them for a long time. You can do me much more damage by staying, and being unhappy about it, than by taking six bond-involuntary troops. We'll need the Wolnadi crew, and we won't be able to replace them, but they're not going to be needed for Inquiry *while I'm in command of this ship*, so take them and go and don't come back."

That wasn't likely to be a very long time, was it? While I am in command of this ship, she'd said. Once the *Ragnarok's* appeal had been accepted, once the ship had been cleared of wrongdoing and restored to active status, ap Rhiannon's career was over. It wouldn't matter that the appeal had been upheld then. She'd thrown it away the moment she'd decided on her course of action. It was too bad that she wouldn't let him respect her for it.

She'd given him an order. What was he going to do? He had a sudden temptation to refuse, just to be spiteful—but then all of his arranging would come to nothing. No. He had to get them away. He'd known when he'd performed the surgeries that to expect a man to bend his neck to a governor twice in his life was simply not to be entertained. Even if she meant to strand him on Emandis

Station, he had to go so that the Bonds could get clear of Fleet before Fleet found out what he'd done with them.

Maybe it would be for the best if she did strand him; it would tend to support the idea that she had not known what he was doing. Nobody knew what he had been doing. He had told nobody. They were welcome to guess what they liked, and he knew very well that the guesses of his staff were not likely to have hit far from the mark, but he had said nothing.

"I will. Thank you." She could have held them on board. She could have kept some of them back as hostages for his good behavior. She was going to let them all go, and if it hadn't been for her explanation, he wouldn't have been able to believe it. She wasn't letting them go. She was sending them away, in order to be rid of him. "A final question, Captain, with your permission."

"Of course."

"If I should come back without them, your Excellency, will it be to find my boots and baggage on the loading docks?"

It was a challenge. They both knew it was. She only considered it, however; she did not rise to her feet and throw the half-empty flask of brutally red wine that was a constant feature of her desk at him.

After a moment of careful deliberation, she replied. "I am willing to put up with a great deal from you, Koscuisko, to have your services for my crew. No. I won't throw you out. But I'll believe it when I see it."

They had exhausted all their available topics for conversation, Andrej decided. He bowed, doing his best to make it an honest salute.

"Very well, your Excellency. Thank you, and good-greeting."

"Enjoy your leave," she said, and turned away to study a report scan as he left.

He'd find out soon enough whether she meant what she'd said, or not. But for now, he had to go and tell Stildyne to muster his bond-involuntary troops to go with him to Emandis Station, to accompany him to Joslire's gravesite. It would be the last duty they would ever be called up on to perform. It was fitting that it should take place in a graveyard.

CHAPTER ELEVEN
PRIVILEGED RELATIONSHIPS

THE CAPTAIN'S SHALLOP was a small sturdy craft that would carry up to thirty-two souls in ease and relative comfort. It had come down to Emandis Station from the *Ragnarok* with half that number. When their errand was done, Stildyne would proceed down to Emandis itself—the port city of Jeltaria, in the arid zone between the sapphire Sea of Genet and the thorny brown-black hills of the Minto Range—to command Koscuisko's escort to the place where the memorial tablet of Joslire Ise-I'let stood over the dead man's ashes in the glittering white ground.

"Brachi, I'm nervous," Koscuisko said, staring up at the great rolling globe of Emandis in the sky above the depot station with a look of longing on his face such as Stildyne had seldom seen. "I have not seen him for all of this time. I wonder if I should not leave them behind. Joslire doesn't know them. Except for Robert. And you must come as well."

Robert St. Clare had known Curran, a man Stildyne himself had never met. Up until quite recently, he had been half-convinced that he hated Koscuisko's Emandisan bond-involuntary for the affection with which Koscuisko remembered him.

But then he'd analyzed Koscuisko's back-sheathe, bit by minute bit, on the thula during their trip from Azanry back to the *Ragnarok* after the assault on Koscuisko these weeks gone past. There was no way in which the catch could have slipped, no explanation for how the knife had fallen free and into Koscuisko's hand when he lay helpless at the mercy of his enemy. For Koscuisko's life, Stildyne could forgive the dead man the fact that Koscuisko loved him.

"No, it'll be all right," Stildyne said, still surprised when Koscuisko used his personal name. They'd had words about it. Cultural differences. Koscuisko was trying to observe Stildyne's preference, at the expense of his own behavioral expectations; staggering. The effort said more to Stildyne about the value that Koscuisko placed on him than the use of his personal name could touch, satisfying though that was. "They're Bonds. They might have been his shipmates if things had been different. You know how they look after one another."

It had been a good thing to say, apparently. Koscuisko seemed to relax all at once, and smiled very cheerfully. "A telling point," he agreed. "Thank you. If we are not careful, First Officer will leave without us. Let's hurry."

Mendez' business was with the depot master. Emandis Station had declined to pre-clear for load-out without a personal visit. She was well within her rights to do so—it was munitions that the *Ragnarok* was after, and in significant quantity—but they were all unhappily suspicious that she was simply stalling for as long as she could. *Scylla* was en route, with three attendant corvettes. If Emandis Station held them here until *Scylla* arrived, and *Scylla* was unfriendly—

Scylla wouldn't lay a finger on them. The *Ragnarok's* legal status was unresolved, but the fact that Captain ap Rhiannon had lodged a formal and acknowledged appeal was not in question. There were no Fleet intelligence groups at Emandis Station. Emandis Station was run by the Emandis Home Defense Fleet, EHDF, as a semi-autonomous enterprise under contract to provision Fleet, and licensed to obtain and store controlled items.

Fleet couldn't put an interrogations group down without permission. And Jennet ap Rhiannon had made herself clear on allship: they had nothing to hide or to explain; they would stay out of trouble, and trouble would stay away from them. If Fleet wanted to wrangle with the *Ragnarok*, it would need a pretext to do so when it was in a Home Defense Fleet depot. Their captain expected them all to refrain from supplying a reason.

Stildyne followed Koscuisko to the mover where Mendez sat waiting, and they were off for the depot's administrative center. Emandis Station was clean and bright and beautiful, standing several hours off of Emandis itself and rejoicing in a generated atmosphere—a very gracious grid—and all of the amenities for rest and recreation of crews in transit. It was a short ride down wide tree-lined lanes from the docking site to the depot master's office. Koscuisko said little, watching the planet high overhead; Mendez said nothing at all.

The depot master's office was small but well furnished, very clearly the workspace of a busy woman who had neither time nor patience for external rank-signals. The depot master rose to her feet as they were buzzed through to her office, nodding her head once in response to Mendez' formal greeting, but letting Mendez know straightaway that there were to be some issues to resolve.

"Your Excellency," she said. She didn't sit down; she didn't suggest they sit, either. "I'm sorry you had this trip for nothing, sir. Emandis Station cannot release this stores manifest."

In fact, First Officer had come in person because Emandis Station had already suggested that it could not release the requested stores. Jennet ap Rhiannon did not take "no" for an answer, unless it were in response to "Any problem with that?" Mendez was clearly not at all surprised at the depot master's claim. He folded his hands in front of him and protested: quietly, calmly, logically.

"Our requisitions are all Fleet-standard, Depot. And I need those stores. Especially the munitions. On what grounds do you decline to execute your mission and release these supplies?"

Now she sat down slowly, and invited Mendez to rest himself with a gesture of her hand. She wasn't Emandisan, Stildyne decided. She was tall and almost blond and a little sunburnt. All of the Emandisan that Stildyne had seen represented were slender people, not tall, dark-eyed and dark-complected. Singularly elegant and superlatively self-disciplined, which was not to say that the depot master wasn't.

"Release of replacement equipment must be accompanied by surrender of the equipment it is to replace, your Excellency, you know that." Polite, but inflexible. A civil servant from somewhere else in Brisinje, perhaps, responsible for the depot and very sure of her procedures. "You have failed to present appropriately endorsed waiver documents. Unless you carry them with you for surrender here and now, I cannot release the munitions you demand."

Koscuisko hadn't been explicitly invited to sit down but he did so, quietly and unobtrusively. Stildyne stood. The only time he sat down in the presence of his officer of assignment was when they were playing cards in quarters after shift. Or in the sauna. Or when Koscuisko came to his tiny cell of an office, which did not happen often.

"You are in receipt of a preliminary copy of our duly logged exception document," Mendez noted mildly. "It's at the headquarters of the Home Defense Fleet even now. We don't want to create any friction here, depot master, but we need our stores. My Captain doesn't want to see me back without them."

The *Ragnarok* needed guns. It was an experimental test-bed that had never been issued its full complement—or, if the artillery had been issued, it had never been delivered, much less installed. Maybe it was being held somewhere for the day when the *Ragnarok* would be formally commissioned as a ship of war. Or maybe someone had sold it off on the invisible market. After all, that was how the *Ragnarok* had acquired the single battle cannon it could deploy—they had liberated it from the invisible market, where it had been sitting in inventory as a case of deck-wipes.

The rest of the stores would be welcome but, as it was, the ship could not defend itself against more than one or two of the warships in its weight class if Fleet decided to assert itself. Shooting their way out of Taisheki Station had been an act of mutiny—technically speaking, anyway.

"You know the exception report must be endorsed at Fleet headquarters level, your Excellency. The Home Defense Fleet's authority in this instance is limited. I cannot in all good conscience release a primary equipment load of this level without more explicit instructions, First Officer, I trust you will forgive me. Will that be all? Your crew will be welcome to stand down for rest and recreation, of course, once your bond has been—excuse me."

One of the alerts on the depot master's desk had gone off, blinking at her with a brilliant blue urgency. Frowning, she keyed her receive; whoever it was, whatever it was, she started to say something angrily, glanced quickly at First Officer and Koscuisko sitting in her office, decided against saying a word. She closed the comm with a sharp and irritated gesture and stood up, her chair rolling back to hit the wall behind her and bounce forward again in reaction to the vigor of her action.

"Excuse me," she repeated, and quit the room without another word. Very strange. Mendez looked back over his shoulder at Stildyne and Koscuisko then put his hands to the arms of his chair, clearly preparing to leave.

"We'll have to consult the captain," Mendez said. "I don't care to go back without a loading schedule. No reason to put you through that, though, Andrej, you're already cleared for planetfall at Jeltaria. Why don't you and Stildyne just—"

The door to the depot master's office opened, and someone entirely different came in: an Emandisan in the uniform of the Home Defense Fleet. If Stildyne knew his rank markers, this was a senior officer in the logistics branch, stores and supplies. The officer seemed to hesitate, very slightly, as he passed the place where Koscuisko—who was looking a little confused, from Stildyne's angle on him—still sat in his chair; but continued toward the desk with such brisk dispatch that Stildyne decided he'd imagined it.

"We're in receipt of your requisition, your Excellency," the Emandisan said. His Standard was perfect. "Also of the exception document. I've been instructed to treat it as a fully endorsed Fleet instrument. We can begin to load out in five hours' time. Will that be acceptable?"

First Officer settled back in his chair warily, looking if anything even more uncertain than Koscuisko. "Very acceptable, and thank you. But this would seem to be a reversal of sorts. A man can't help but feel a little concerned. What's going on?"

It could be a trap, Stildyne supposed. Yet what could the Emandisan Home Defense Fleet have against the *Ragnarok?* The quarrel ap Rhiannon had with the Fleet was just that—with the Jurisdiction Fleet. Home Defense Fleets tended to keep well clear of any Jurisdiction entanglements.

"Depot Master Seprayan is a very conservative administrator," the Emandisan agreed. "Intelligence indicates, however, that it is not reasonable in this case to demand surrender of resources never issued. We will cover it with Fleet if we have to."

It sounded reasonable enough, if not for the fact that, moments ago, the depot master had been adamantly unreasonable about it. Taking a clearly determined breath, Mendez challenged the reversal head-on. "To what do we owe this unusual accommodation, Mark Captain?"

Mark captain. That was right, Stildyne thought, impressed. He hadn't taken the spacing of the bands across the man's right shoulder into account.

"In all the history of Emandis, there has never until now been an alien who has worn Emandisan steel," the mark captain said, looking at Koscuisko almost hungrily before focusing his attention back on Mendez. "As you may be aware, First Officer, a knife-fighter's five-knives are cultural artifacts that we consider to be of defining importance. A man was wronged. We owe it to his knives to make it up to him, any way we can, and an officer assigned to the Jurisdiction Fleet Ship *Ragnarok* is the lawful custodian of those knives; who can expect every cooperation from Emandis Station, accordingly."

Koscuisko had sat forward and was staring at his boots, with his hands folded in front of him and the knuckles showing white. Mendez eyed Koscuisko a little cautiously before he responded to this rather startling, if welcome, statement.

"I see, Mark Captain. Very well, we'll be glad to take advantage. Doctor Koscuisko has been cleared for transit to Emandis proper, to the city of Jeltaria. We were hoping for a local pilot."

There was an unusual sort of tension in the mark captain's voice as he replied. "The local pilot who was scheduled to perform that service has been delayed at Brisinje, your Excellency." He was talking to Koscuisko now, Stildyne realized, not Mendez at all. Mendez outranked Koscuisko, but didn't seem to mind. "We have another man waiting. We're sorry. We understand how anxious you must be to meet your brother, and he you, but it can't be helped. He is a pilot first, and a man with family second, as are we all."

Koscuisko's brother? Stildyne frowned. He hadn't realized that Koscuisko had any brothers in the Emandisan HDF. The Combine's Home Defense Fleet, yes: Koscuisko's brother Lo, the next youngest after Meeka, older than Nikosha by some years. It wasn't impossible, of course. Only one of Koscuisko's brothers—Nikosha, the youngest—had been there when Stildyne had accompanied him to Chelatring Side to meet with Koscuisko's parents.

No, not Koscuisko's brother. Curran's brother. Ise-I'let's brother. Koscuisko wore Joslire Curran's knives. That clearly made Koscuisko family, in some sense. Reasonable enough, Stildyne decided. Totally unexpected, but reasonable.

Koscuisko stood up, as though suddenly incapable of fully controlling his emotions. "I wish to be taken to the place as soon as possible," he said. "I have been waiting since I found out we were coming here. I will hope we can still meet. But I can't wait. I need to go."

The mark captain nodded with grave and evident respect. "Of course, your Excellency, and it may yet be that Ise-I'let gets away from Brisinje before your ship leaves our station. In the mean time, First Officer—"

Mendez signaled his attention with politely raised eyebrows, and the mark captain continued.

"In the meanwhile, we invite your ship to enjoy the hospitality of Emandis Station until that time comes, whenever it should be."

That meant more than it seemed, Stildyne realized. Once the load was complete, the *Ragnarok* would typically have a limited period of time to clear the system: the Bench wanted no conflict between Fleet and civilians. The mark captain was indicating that the *Ragnarok* was welcome to remain in Emandisan space, for a little while at least.

It was as much as saying that the *Ragnarok* was being offered the protection of the Emandisan Home Defense Fleet. In light of the current tension between the *Ragnarok* and the rest of the Jurisdiction's Fleet, that was a particularly interesting privilege to have extended. Was it really just because Koscuisko had Joslire's knives, or was there something else going on?

The *Ragnarok* would get its commissioning issue of arms and munitions at last; Koscuisko would have a chance to sit with Joslire's people and mourn. If everything was actually to turn out to be as easy and as satisfying as that, they would all be happy: the captain, the First Officer, the Ship's Engineer, Koscuisko, everybody. *If.*

But just in case the Emandisan didn't intend Koscuisko's knives to leave, Stildyne was prepared to fight.

GRUNTING A LITTLE—her side hurt where she'd been injured, and the ventilation shaft was by no means sized for a traveler—Jils pulled herself head-and-shoulders out of the primary ventilator access and into the air-well to shine her lantern up into the blackness of the shaft above.

"Do you see anything?" Balkney asked, his hands around her ankles to anchor her and his voice muffled by the barrier of her own body in the conduit. Jils scanned the sides of the air-well, playing the focused beam of the lantern from wall to wall of the naked rock shaft as far up the walls as the light would reach.

"There's a lot of rock." Just beneath her, though, she could see rungs fixed in the wall. The floor didn't appear to be far. She hoped that perspective did not deceive her. With only artificial light, the chances of confusing the eye with shades of gray were uncomfortably high. The rungs gave her a reference, though. They seemed to be about the same, and within an arm's reach beneath her. "Let loose of me, Balkney, I'm going down."

She felt the lifting away of his grip on her ankles, and wriggled forward. Awkward. Balkney could do it, maybe Capercoy, any of the women. Padrake would never fit through here, though—he had altogether too much shoulder.

Turning onto her back as she worked her way forward, Jils took hold of the rung just above the access and pulled herself out, into the air-well. As she began to climb down, Balkney reached his hand for the lantern, leaning over the air-well from the vent-conduit shaft on his elbows to train the light on her route. Yes. Not very far down. If they had been on the surface, the vent-access might have been the flat roof of a one-story building. Reaching the bottom, Jils dusted her hands together, looking around.

"I don't see any other access," Balkney said, from above. He'd angled himself over to one side to shine the lantern up along the wall that rose into the darkness above the shaft, rung after rung, into obscurity.

Jils shuddered. She didn't want to think of how far down they were.

"What do you think?" He had the light. She was at the bottom of the air-well. He could back up into the shaft and lock the grill and leave her. She could try to climb out. Maybe if she did, she'd fall. If she were lucky, she'd fall from high enough to die on impact. That would be better than starving to death. There was no water here. What had she been thinking?

"Catch," Balkney said, and let the lantern drop. She had an emergency glim on her; he probably did as well. He might have stopped to let someone know where they were going, between his meeting with her in the kitchens after session and their rendezvous outside the generator station. If both of them disappeared, someone might know where to look for them. She could hope. She hadn't really thought this through, impelled to the experiment after hours spend brooding over how deep they were and how unhappy it made her to think that there was only one way out.

Balkney was a sober married man, but he still climbed like a cat, jumping the last few feet to land sure-footed with his flexed knees more than equal to the force of the impact. He barely made a sound when he landed. The air was still; sound didn't carry. Why was the air still? Maybe she just didn't feel its current. This was an air-well. There almost had to be some sort of an air current, whether passive or actively generated.

"I think it's a long way up," Balkney said, staring up into the gloom with his normally sharp face practically knife-edged in his concentration. "It was a long way down. Seemed to be. Hard to judge from inside a car. I'd want protection if I were going to try to climb that ladder. Assuming it goes anywhere else than another vent-shaft, of course."

"If this is the one, the schematic seems to imply it goes all the way up." There did have to be air-wells, almost necessarily. They were deep enough that the air would not refresh by normal exchange quickly enough to sustain human life where none had ever existed. A doorway into a lost world, and someone had put in an air-well? It was a guarantee of contamination. She hadn't decided what the station's founders might have been thinking, either, but she remembered why she'd wanted to get Balkney alone.

From the inside pocket of her blouse, she pulled the piece of paper that she'd been carrying around with her for days. "While you're busy looking at things, Balkney, have a look at this."

He took the paper by one corner and held it up, shining the light from the lantern full on its surface, frowning—but a frown that smoothed over into surprise—and then a kind of amused recognition. "Hah," Balkney said. "Well. Interesting. I found a bookmark in a text that turned up in my queue, myself. Didn't bring it, sorry." He handed the sketch back, the little drawing Karol had done of the Hangman. Not guilty. "I didn't connect it with Vogel at the time."

Balkney had said that he hadn't heard anything about Karol's whereabouts. He could easily have been lying, but that wasn't the way Balkney did it. He didn't tell lies. He simply avoided making statements that were counter-factual in such a way as to facilitate whatever assumptions he didn't mind being made. And he'd made a positive statement of negative contact with Karol Vogel.

"So what'd yours say?" Jils asked, interested. The walls of the air-well seemed to be moving, drawing in on her. It was an intriguing effect, but not one that she particularly appreciated. "Here, you can tell me on the way out."

Moving slowly and deliberately, she turned toward the rungs on the wall, listening and waiting. It would be so easy to leave her here. He wouldn't have to lay a hand on her. And he was a Bench executioner; it was his job to make people disappear.

"It said Ivers didn't do it," Balkney said, his voice measured and thoughtful from the bottom of the shaft. He couldn't possibly be having reservations about his own position, could he? She climbed up past the access in order to swing into it feet-first, and back down the shaft on her belly as she had come. It hadn't been so long a trek from the corridor to the air-well, but it took longer to crawl than it would have taken to walk. She could see Balkney jump up lithely to take the first rung, and stayed to watch—just in case he was wondering if she had murder on her own mind.

"At least that's what I decided it meant. You tell me." She had to hurry backwards to give him room to get in. His boots were a little on the worn side of relatively new, Jils noted. Leather soles. The stitching would need attention in another few months.

What was she doing, getting distracted by shoe-leather? Leather soles didn't grip like some other materials, nor were they as quiet. Balkney hadn't intended on sneaking up on anybody or on having to dance if he did. Shouldn't she be listening to what he was saying?

"It was a peculiar piece of cutlery, with a solid line on the curved edge. Shadowing the blade, but not the edge. I thought it might be Vogel's style, but it took me some time to decipher the message. Ivers is clean."

Backing down the vent-conduit on her hands and knees, Jils realized suddenly what Balkney wasn't saying. Battle-axe. The image caught her by surprise and she laughed, a short sort of a barking sound that startled her almost as much as it seemed to have startled Balkney.

"Right," she agreed, to let him know that everything was under control. "I understand." The edge was sharp and clear, no clean-up necessary. Battle-axe. It had been a long time since anybody had called her that. Balkney might be one of the few people left in service who would connect it to her.

Or Balkney could be making it up. He'd said he had nothing to show her, but if he'd brought the sketch with him, she'd have suspected that, too, and wondered if he'd fabricated the sketch in order to mislead her. For that, Balkney would've had to know that she was going to find a doodle on a courier from Chilleau to Brisinje. That was stretching it. Unless he'd planted the doodle, but that was stretching it even further.

"So what's next?" she asked. Balkney hadn't said anything, busy working his way down the vent-shaft after her. He knew she trusted him to a limited extent, and she knew he trusted her. She could have left him at the bottom of the air-well just as easily as he could have left her there. "Something I need to know?"

He stopped moving in the shaft. "Nion," he said. "Has a new sort of way of thinking, a little like Delleroy and maybe Rinpen and possibly Tanifer. Privileged model."

So it hadn't been just her imagination. It was good to think that she hadn't just been seeing things, but not good to think that Padrake could have lost his focus to such an extent. "Why do you say that?"

Balkney had started to move again, but slowly. They were near the entrance to the shaft. "She spoke to me," Balkney said. Though Jils couldn't see his face, the tone of his voice made her think that he was trying to pick his words very carefully. "Maybe to some of the others, I'm not sure. About executing a Writ. She'd heard stories about me. She seemed a little too interested in some of them. Mosch, for one."

Bench Intelligence Specialist Elipse Mosch. She'd lost her way amid the lawless confusion of the Lettel uprising sixteen years ago, and started to behave like a warlord rather than a guardian of the Judicial order. Balkney had removed her for the good of the Bench and its citizens, but it hadn't been easy—or without controversy.

Some people still affected to believe that Mosch had been a Bench-sanctioned agent provocateur, but Balkney's point—Jils supposed—was that the hit had made his reputation, in the small secretive community of Bench Specialists. Now Balkney wanted her to know that Nion might be looking for a target of opportunity whose acquisition might do the same for Nion.

"Whoever killed Verlaine is mine." She had no intention of meekly surrendering her revenge to bolster the reputation of a young Bench Specialist. Showing her throat would be as good as a confession of guilt anyway. Reputations were to be earned by hard work and personal achievement; assassination was the easy way out, a shortcut. "I mean to have satisfaction."

They were back at the corridor, Balkney dropping out of the vent-shaft to land lightly on his feet beside her. His expression remained mild, but betrayed a little surprise. Yes. She supposed she was angry. "I won't be getting in your way," he said. "I've got a wife and children to think of. I think Capercoy is solid. Maybe Rafenkel. Just watch yourself."

It wasn't much to ask, and had been well intentioned. It wasn't his fault she was so keyed up. "Thanks," she said, and offered her hand. "I appreciate it. But how are we going to know about the air-well?"

Shifting the conversation back into neutral territory, careful to ensure that nothing was said that couldn't be safely overheard. Balkney nodded in apparent appreciation of the tactic and started down the corridor with a quick firm grasp of her hand.

"The question would be how deep it was capped off, if it's been capped. We could come back with a crawler, but those things are slow." Because the little mechanical climbers were very safe, and proceeded cautiously in order to successfully navigate difficult terrain. Vertical surfaces, for one, but the air-well had been dressed rock for at least a portion of its depth, and that would be relatively easy for a crawler to negotiate. "Maybe if we look at the station's life support protocols we'll find something."

That was an idea. If life support had a safety consideration hidden away somewhere in its library, it might tell them whether the original builders had made any allowances for a catastrophic failure of transport or ventilation. If she had built this data station, she would certainly have wanted to be sure about that, but these people had done some rather odd things. Light-wells. And were those light-wells wide enough for an adult hominid to ascend?

It was a welcome distraction from the issues on her mind, and looking for ways out helped her to manage her discomfort at being more or less trapped. There was only the one lift that anybody seemed to know of. If something happened to that—she supposed someone might climb the elevator shaft, but there was no way of knowing even if it was a straight line of ascent, and an accident could as easily have jammed the escape routes as anything else—

"After third-meal," she suggested. "In the maintenance area." This was not so large a station that it took very long to walk from place to place; they were coming back into the living area already. Balkney would have to go and observe Capercoy versus Rinpen on whether a new Judge should be raised from the subordinates available at Fontailloe. She was due to argue Chilleau against Zeman, with Padrake watching.

"See you, then," Balkney agreed, and turned off down a side corridor as they neared the kitchen. Jils stopped in mid-corridor, listening keenly to the sound of nobody near her, nobody at all. Padrake. Balkney had said that he thought Capercoy was solid, and Rafenkel probably. Nothing about Padrake. Was that odd?

Was that a data-point that contained information, or just noise? Had he not mentioned Padrake because he assumed Jils had come to her own conclusions, or had his remark been a little more deliberate than that?

Suspicion was a Bench Specialist's friend, but it could become a liability if it was not carefully controlled. There was sometimes a thin line between healthy caution and paranoia. Jils meant to stay on the sane side of it, if she hadn't strayed too far already.

Putting the question in her mind away for the time being, Jils went though into the kitchen to take mid-meal and prepare her thoughts to challenge Zeman for the honor of Chilleau Judiciary.

THE SIGNS WERE not good. First Officer was pacing like an animal held in close confinement, her eyes fixed fiercely on some spot on the floor always three-eighths ahead of her no longer quite flawlessly shined boots, smoothing her light brown hair back across the rounded top of her narrow head with a gesture that stopped only barely short of clutching at hairs in sheer frustration. Calleigh Samons had seen this behavior before. First Officer was in danger of blowing her retard circuits past any hope of immediate recovery.

"Munitions packs. Expired propulsion recharges. Quantifiable rounds. Nothing else? Are you sure? A spare shallop, perhaps, for ap Rhiannon to use to send out for fresh sellats out of season?"

The depot master kept to her seat behind her desk, calm and imperturbable. She didn't seem unsympathetic. In fact, she seemed quite aware that she was throwing propellant packs into the conversion furnaces, almost glad of the conflagration Calleigh feared would explode upon them soon.

"Well, battle cannon, First Officer, and a spares set for five Wolnadi fighters since the basic issue is more than ten years old. The *Ragnarok* asked for nothing less than a full munitions load, accordingly approved for release by Emandis Station's Home Defense Fleet Administration."

First Officer stopped at one side of the depot master's office to look into the watch monitors Loading docks. Container after container after container, munitions and stores and consumables and perishables and new boots for everyone, and—standing in the middle of a small clear space on the docks on one monitor—a very tall man and a very large bat.

He was easily twice as tall as the bat, and he wore a uniform. Calleigh didn't think First Officer could actually discern the *Ragnarok's* ship-mark on the man's shoulder, not on watch monitor, not from here. There was no doubting his identity, all the same: Serge of Wheatfields, Ship's Engineer, Jurisdiction Fleet Ship *Ragnarok*. And the Intelligence officer, assigned same.

First Officer Saligrep Linelly swore and spun on her heel to put the clearly irritating sight behind her. "Don't get me wrong, depot master," she said. "No intention of butting into your business, fully satisfied at all times in the past with the professionalism and performance of the Emandis Station depot. I just can't help wondering how ap Rhiannon rates. We wouldn't dare dump a requirements ticket as deep as that one had to be on you, not without adequate warning. And very good reasons. And negotiations with the supplier chain further on up."

The depot master nodded in solemn agreement, and closed her portfolio. "I appreciate that, your Excellency," she said. "And to be fair to the *Ragnarok* I can understand, abstractly at least, why they have to have so much right now. They never did get primary load, in all likelihood. It's never been formally commissioned as anything but a test bed. I told them to wait for Fleet clearance. I was overruled, First Officer."

And resented it, too, the depot master made no secret of that. There was no reason why she should. A person was welcome to feel as much resentment as she liked over incidents that could properly be resented, so long as a person didn't let it interfere with her duty.

"Overruled." First Officer sat down, a little heavily, and folded her hands across her belly, slumped in her seat. "In what way? By whom?"

"By the Emandis Home Defense Fleet, your Excellency. Having apparently elected to accord the *Ragnarok's* chief medical officer the status of an Emandisan knife-fighter, it is the duty of the Emandisan fleet to oblige him with defensive supplies as he sees fit."

First Officer let her hands drop to the sides of the chair, letting them hang dangling in mid-air. After a moment she spoke, very calmly really, Calleigh thought. "The *Ragnarok's* chief medical officer is not Emandisan, so far as I know."

The depot master nodded solemnly. "No. The *Ragnarok's* chief medical officer is not Emandisan."

"He is in fact Dolgorukij, I believe," First Officer suggested, and the depot master nodded again. She was beginning to think about smiling, Calleigh thought; it was lurking in the corners of her eyes. It wasn't a malicious smile by any means, no, it was a cheerful supportive smile a-borning. *Yes, you are right. It makes no sense.*

First Officer took a deep breath and seemed to be weighing her next words carefully, but said them all the same. Once she started to speak, the words gained momentum and passion and life and brilliance until they shimmered in the air.

"He is in fact Andrej Koscuisko. Andrej-freaking-Shoeskoe. Andrej never learned in all of these years and about to get himself killed and his entire command with him Shoeskoe. Andrej how one poor crèche-bred brevet captain be expected to make a dent in his thick Dolgorukij skull Shoeskoe. Andrej Captain Irshah Parmin is really going to regret not having killed him when he had the chance Shoeskoe—"

"That's the man," the depot master agreed. "The first man from an alien bloodline to carry Emandisan steel in the history of Emandisan steel, and the history of Emandisan steel is the history of the Emandisan. So they tell me. Gone downplanet to visit some people he knows, I understand. To talk to someone he used to know, at the memorial site."

Of course. Joslire Curran. "Well, I heard," First Officer said, looking back over her right shoulder at Calleigh—who was glad she'd left her team outside the office, and not just because it wasn't over-large an office. "I heard that Koscuisko didn't even know it was Emandisan steel. Didn't have a clue. Carried five-knives for more than three years and never once wondered about them."

It was true. And of course it was hard to believe now that the story was out. Why should Koscuisko have wondered? Curran had provided them. Only a man with considerably more ego than Andrej

Koscuisko would have suspected that he'd been made bearer of a priceless artifact. Koscuisko's ego was perfectly healthy, but he had not been prone to delusions of grandeur in the time that Calleigh had known him.

"I was there," Calleigh said in response to First Officer's implied invitation of a remark. "I saw it. It was Curran who made them sacred to Koscuisko. All of the rest about Emandisan steel, I don't think that ever meant as much to him as the fact that Curran's life's-blood was on those knives."

"You know, Koscuisko used to be under Irshah Parmin's command," First Officer said to the depot master, thoughtfully. "Maybe if we let the Home Defense Fleet know that, we'd get clearance to draw from reserves. Worth a try, anyway, don't you think?"

No, the depot master didn't. She didn't seem to have much of an opinion either way. Calleigh knew what First Officer had on her mind, though: *he was ours before he went to the Ragnarok, and if having him is the key to Emandis Station's depot, well, we can arrange that. The captain wants to sit down for a talk with Koscuisko anyway.*

First Officer covered any potential awkwardness by standing up, talking as if the question had no answer. Perfectly true, in a manner of speaking. "Well. Thank you for your candor, depot master. We'll be in touch, and if you would go ahead and initiate load of what you can release to us, we'd appreciate it. Crew's been anticipating extra shifts required to stow supplies all the way from Brisinje. Hate to disappoint them."

This was something that the depot master clearly understood, and she seized it all the more happily for being a return to business as she was accustomed to it. "Very good, First Officer, slips four-eight and five-one, and as far away from the *Ragnarok* crew as possible. We can begin to load in about eight, your Excellency."

Not that there was much left to load on First Officer's manifest, not after the depot master had run it against stores available. Calleigh could find it in her to resent it a little bit herself. *Scylla* deserved the stores. What was the *Ragnarok* going to do with a munitions load, unless it meant to defend itself against its own Fleet using its own Fleet's own resources, as it had at Taisheki?

Peculiar things had always happened around Koscuisko. Failure of Writ at the Domitt Prison. The Emandis Home Defense Fleet shaking the whole purse of the depot out for Jennet ap Rhiannon to pick and choose what struck her fancy, because Andrej Koscuisko wore Emandisan steel.

The captain was going to have a thing or two to say to Calleigh's former officer of assignment, and she followed her First Officer out of the room, her sense of resignation warring with her presentiment of peculiarities yet to come in Andrej Koscuisko's wake.

CHAPTER TWELVE
HOME IS THE HUNTER

IN THE DEPOT master's office, Andrej had heard the Emandisan officer speak with increasing distress; and now, as he stood on the landing field at Jeltaria, his feelings of foreboding deepened into an anguished conviction that everything was going to go wrong. Horribly wrong. Irreversibly wrong. Stoshi could have warned him; Stoshi had said nothing. Two could have tipped him off; had she actually tried to do so? Hadn't she told him that transport was arranged, and that he would be met?

Fool that he was, he had taken her to mean that there would be someone to make local arrangements. A guide, perhaps someone who had contacted the family on his behalf and negotiated a meeting, someone who could tell him about Joslire's family and how things were and what he could expect. He'd been mistaken.

There was a welcoming party waiting for them: maidens with flowers, a cavalcade of ground transport cars, and six people standing on a large golden carpet of beaten reed-fiber—local handicrafts, pots of flowering plants.

Chairs and attendants, and Andrej hadn't known what he was going to say to Joslire's people in the first place and could not call to mind even a single one of the ideas he might have had, under the stress of being so suddenly confronted by aged women of Joslire's family. They had to be. They could not be anybody else.

In the overcast hush of the waiting launch field, Andrej stepped down the loading ramp to take his place in the Security formation. Something caught his eye as he came forward: a twitch of a finger. Lek Kerenko. Finger-code, the milk maid's daughter. Lek had been with him on Azanry, at the Matredonat, when he had outraged propriety and astonished his Marana by marrying her. It was a good point. A man capable of so brazen an act as he had committed at that time, and in that place, had no right to feel nervous just because a private pilgrimage had turned into a media event.

Stildyne marched them all across the thermal sheathing that blanketed the launch field's surface. It wasn't a standard formation by any means—that would be six, and they were eight—but his gentlemen rose to the unusual occasion like the superlative soldiers they were. There was a young officer waiting for them just short of the room-sized reed mat. Andrej couldn't decipher her rank, but she made her function explicit at once.

"Your Excellency." Something seemed odd about her accent. Andrej realized that it was the fact that she didn't seem to have one, not that his ear could detect. Her Standard was flawless. "A very great honor, sir. If I might translate for his Excellency. My name is Piross, and I'm to make introductions, at his Excellency's will and good pleasure."

Security spread out with solemnly measured tread and posted themselves along the near edge of the reed mat and its sides, facing out. Facing away. Making the room defined by the reed mat a private space. There was no breath of wind; the air was as still as though there was no such thing as a wind in Jeltaria, and the clouds were gray and thick and heavy with rain. They would not let the women of Joslire's family sit in the open in the rain, surely?

"My Intelligence officer said that I would meet with his surviving relatives," Andrej said to Piross. "If one of them is Joslire's mother, I have not been warned, and fear an embarrassment. It is a terrible thing in my home world to come face to face with a man's mother and not demonstrate appropriate respect."

Piross nodded sharply, as if acknowledging an instruction. Covering for his confusion, Andrej thought gratefully. "His mother's sister, your Excellency, and his father's mother. His eldest sister. The son of another of his mother's sisters, the son of one of his father's brothers, and the wife of his surviving brother, with her firstborn child."

The Emandisan officer at the depot had said Joslire's brother was not there. It was so strange to look at these people and see Joslire in their faces.

"What am I to do?" They were looking at him, those old women, hawk-eyed and merciless. *Where did you come from. Why are you here. What business can you have, you too-pale man? Why are we troubled with your presence?*

"You give her the knife and show her your hand. She may prick your hand. She will give you back the knife. Then we'll all go to the orchard, and they'll open the gate for you."

Knife? What knife? Which knife? Of course he had brought them. They were Joslire's. "But which is the right one?" he asked in a low voice, trying to control his panic. That knife, perhaps. Of course it would be that knife. It could be no other, the one that he wore between his shoulderblades when he wore it at all, the one that he tended to wear even when he did not feel the need to go fully armed to a staff meeting. He didn't wait for her reply. He had enough to go on, and he was the son of the Koscuisko prince after all. He had generations of ritual bred into him.

"Mister Stildyne," Andrej said, unfastening the secures of his duty blouse—black, because he was one of the *Ragnarok's* Primes. It was a particular black whose use in uniform was restricted to officers of senior rank. Of course his under-blouse was clean, and in good repair. If it were otherwise, he would have no choice but to be humiliated in public—and the Saints only knew in what broadcast and record and rebroadcast record—by appearing in disrespectfully slovenly dress.

Stildyne would never have let such a thing happen. He stood at Andrej's back to take the blouse. In his shirtsleeves, Andrej stepped onto the reed-mat and crossed its padded surface to where the old women sat. They looked much older than he had at first taken them to be. It was not the creasing of facial skin that spoke of the years, but the shining of the bones of the hand beneath the skin, the fingers thin as a bird's wing.

These women represented the blood that had been Joslire's life, and their dead—the missing generation, Joslire's brothers and sisters if he'd had any—had fallen victims to the same cruel treachery that had enslaved Joslire. Andrej knelt, because they were women and they were old and they were not to be asked to rise by a man who had any respect for his mother.

Down on both knees, he bowed his head, raising his hand to draw the knife. Flattening his palm, Andrej considered it—this was the weapon that had taken Joslire's life—and presented it to the oldest of the women, who sat like an abbess with her hands to her thighs, watching him closely with her dark eyes.

"Tell her that I have brought these back," Andrej said, not looking at Piross. "They have saved my life on at least one occasion, and freed Joslire for him. He should have them back. They belong to his family."

The translator spoke. The oldest woman leaned forward and drew Andrej's hand toward her with the knife still across its palm. She seemed to squint at the scar on Andrej's palm—where Joslire had pushed that knife through, back to palm, and pinned his hand and Andrej's hand together—then picked it up.

Holding it to the cloud-diffused light of the sun at midheaven, she turned it slowly from side to side, as if she were evaluating its condition, and then she spoke. Her voice was quavery with age, but firm and self-possessed for all that.

"Tell him he is mistaken," Piross said, from behind Andrej. "The knife does not follow the family, grandson. The family follows the knife."

The old woman leaned forward again as the translator was speaking, reaching out for Andrej. To touch his head, and give him benediction? Andrej bowed his head, but she was going for the back of his neck instead. The sheath. She sheathed the knife between his shoulderblades, and it felt warm to the touch all along its length as if it had absorbed a day-long dose of full sunlight during its few moments naked beneath the cloudy Emandisan sky.

Then she stood up, and beckoned to Andrej to do the same. "Now we will go and meet the family," she said through the translator. "But put on your costume, and bring your people. We want to be sure that your ancestors understand who you are, so that they'll know you when they see you, the next time."

What was he to do?

Grandson, she'd called him—or whatever she had called him, Piross had translated it that way, and Piross' command of Standard was excellent. Unchallengeable. What was expected of him, what—

Look to the second son. His mother's housemaster had told him that, early and often. In someone else's house, look to the second son and guide on him. The first son is the inheriting son, and if you do as he does, you may commit a mis-step. The worst thing that can happen to you if you look to the second son is that you gain a reputation for being over-careful to avoid giving offense, and there is hardly a thing as an excess of politeness where the inheriting son of a great house is concerned. Look to the second son, and you will do honor to your father's name and your mother's nurture.

There was no second son here; there were only Joslire's cousins. Andrej turned his head to find one of them, to discover what he should be doing. Lead? Follow? What?

One of Joslire's cousins caught Andrej's eye just as Piross started talking. "His Excellency is expected to walk behind the women of the family but ahead of its other men," she said. "You will not travel in the same cars."

Joslire's cousin seemed to acquire the scent of Andrej's confusion at once. He grinned so broad and open and unguarded a smile—there in an instant and gone almost as quickly—that it struck Andrej to the heart. He'd seen that smile before. Not very often, but he'd seen it, and the pain staggered him where he stood.

Stildyne was behind him with his blouse, holding it to help Andrej dress himself, steadying him at his back as he had been doing for all of these years. Andrej stood for a moment longer than was perhaps strictly necessary. Stildyne stood with him with, his hands to Andrej's shoulders as if in the act of smoothing the fabric to lie perfectly flat.

Hadn't the Emandisan officer suggested that Andrej's brother was hoping to meet him? Why hadn't he noticed? Because the reminders of this place, of how much he had learned from Joslire and how much lost when Joslire had claimed the Day, deprived him of his capacity for rational thought. He had to rethink his arrangements. How was he to make this work?

The cars would be waiting, and there were elderly women. Even if they had not been the knives' family, they would still be old women who had suffered much and who should not be kept waiting while one man brooded over his difficulties as if he were the only person here who'd had any in his life.

Straightening his spine, Andrej nodded to Stildyne over his shoulder, and turned crisply on his heel to follow the women to the transport that was waiting—with a full police escort, name of all Saints—and the translator with them.

ON AZANRY, KOSCUISKO's planet of origin, burial places were great gleaming stoneworks let into the ground; Stildyne had seen pictures. Not everybody was buried in such splendor, but in the burial places of the old aristocratic families you could sometimes walk down row upon row of stone boxes underground before you reached that which had once held the founder of the line.

Dasidar himself was buried in the dead-house of the Autocrat's court, Dyraine of the Weavers beside him. There were tours available on remote. They had to recycle the space, in the older families; there wasn't room for everybody, any more. The first, the last, and four parents remained, and everybody else was moved off into much smaller boxes that contained just bones in disarray. Dolgorukij funeral customs fascinated Stildyne. Many of the things about the Dolgorukij interested him. Koscuisko was as good as a hobby, that way.

This was no huge stone house of the dead, no anonymous envelope of residue from an industrial funeral. The transport cars drew up beside a long white wall and, through the gates, Stildyne could see that the wall ran up the slope of a modest little hill on either side. There was a plantation of some sort. The translator had said orchard, hadn't she?

Stildyne got out of the car on one side while Koscuisko and the translator exited through the other. There were Security everywhere, Emandisan security. The port authority apparently took Koscuisko much more seriously than Koscuisko had expected, or Stildyne either. Stildyne didn't know yet whether or not there was going to be a fight about Koscuisko's knives, though the old woman's actions coupled with the translator's explanation did seem to imply that the knives were to be left with the officer.

Jeltaria was arid and dry, for all that it was on the banks of an inland sea. The apron in front of the gate was covered in crushed white rock that caught the light and sparkled in the clear air. The clouds had lifted a little, it was even warmer than before—Stildyne could feel himself sweat.

Curran's family was holding the gates. Koscuisko was to go through. The oldest woman said something; Stildyne looked to Koscuisko's translator. "Come into the orchard and meet your ancestors," the translator said.

There was all this police presence. Would Koscuisko want his people to go in with him?

Koscuisko gave him the nod, and Stildyne started the Security detachment through the gate, past Joslire's family. Nobody stopped Security, so it was clearly all right. Once they were through, the two cousins closed the wooden gate behind them. The oldest woman headed off down the main axis of the orchard, talking as she went. Koscuisko hurried to catch up, which meant Security hurried and Stildyne hurried, and the translator hurried, as well.

"There have been more than thirty-five generations of the knife in our family." The old woman, but the translator's voice was that

of a young woman. It was a little confusing. "Not all of equal dura-
tion, of course. I will show you the first to take your knives into his
hand. And then you may go and speak to your brother."

The orchard garden was a regular matrix of white graveled
pathways and earth boxes on the ground, four or five feet high, two
or three times as long, half that length deep or wide. Each of the
raised beds contained a tree with ripening fruit: yes, an orchard. The
old woman was headed up the hillside at a determined pace with
Koscuisko following after.

"What are these trees?" Koscuisko asked the translator, who
translated the question for the old woman's benefit—just so she
would know, Stildyne supposed—but answered it herself, not
waiting for the old woman to do so.

"They're a slow-growing hardwood, your Excellency, a nut-
bearing tree. The peculiarities of the Madic tree include the required
proximity of juvenile as well as past-bearing trees for successful
fructification to occur, and they are hungry for flesh in the first years
of their growing."

They weren't beautiful trees. They were looking more sinister to
Stildyne by the moment, as a matter of fact, but vegetables had that
effect on him in general. He'd never seen a tree but in pictures until
he'd been a grown man of twenty, and even then it had been a tame
tree in a zoological gardens. He could remember the first time he'd
seen wild ones. The experience had been very unnerving.

"You feed them on the bodies of your dead," Koscuisko said.
There was something in his voice that made Stildyne almost want to
shudder, and it took a great deal to have an effect like that on a man
who had to face Brachi Stildyne in the mirror every morning. "What
is it of the tree that earns it so much honor?"

The old woman had led them to a place halfway up the slope
of the little hill. The walls of the raised beds there were old and
primitive, piled stones that had been gradually collapsing over who
knew how many years. The tree that still stood there was long
dead, bleached and scoured and polished by wind and dust and
sun and time.

"This is the first man who ever kissed the knife that you now
wear." The old woman was looking at Koscuisko, though it was the
translator of course who put the words into plain Standard. "Touch
his hand, grandson. Know your ancestor."

Taking Koscuisko's hand, she climbed up the little rubble of rock into the raised bed where the dead tree stood, and put Koscuisko's hand—his scarred hand—to the trunk of the tree. Koscuisko snatched his hand away as if out of the thermal exhaust of a conversion furnace.

"Holy Mother," Koscuisko said, but it was sometimes hard for Stildyne to decide whether he were swearing or praying. This was one of those times. "It sings." And carefully Koscuisko put his hand back to the dead trunk of the tree. "It is humming. Alive. Breathing."

The translator said nothing, but the old woman who had named herself Koscuisko's grandmother smiled as if she knew exactly what he had said. Maybe she did. There was no particular reason to assume that she couldn't understand the spoken word perfectly well, or well enough, even if she didn't actually speak it.

"We had no body to feed a tree when Joslire came back to the orchard," the old woman said. "There was only ash, and bits of bone. We worked it into the earth around the ancestor, so that Joslire would have the strength to find his way. Here he rests, Koscuisko of the others."

No tablet. No marker. No stone. Stildyne knew that Koscuisko had expected some object to look upon and call a grave, and there was none, only the dirt and debris around the base of an old tree, and little bits of something cinder-looking. Not what Koscuisko had expected, not at all. Stildyne wondered why. Koscuisko was a thorough man, he should have been better prepared; or was this a closely held secret, permitted to Emandisan families, not widely published in tourism documentation?

Koscuisko put his forehead to the trunk of the old—dead—tree, and was silent. The old woman nodded, as though she was satisfied about something.

"You do not need the translator to talk to your own brother," the old woman said—and the officer who Koscuisko did not need in order to communicate with Joslire Ise-I'let translated with evident care. "I leave you with your people. We do not allow others into our orchards, grandson. Use your time wisely."

Whatever that meant. Leave for Koscuisko to be here with off-worlders, perhaps, in the middle of a private family orchard. There were a lot of the trees here. Joslire's family had apparently been around for a long time.

The sound of old and young women walking away down those graveled paths was clearly audible in the orchard's stillness. When Stildyne could no longer hear their footsteps, Koscuisko raised his head, and spoke.

"Gentles, I have something to say to you," he said to the tree trunk, "and there cannot be very much time." Turning away from the tree, Koscuisko accepted the nearest helping hand—Robert's, as it happened—to climb down out of the raised bed, standing with his back to the containment wall.

"Brachi, I would ask you to forgive me if I believed that you did not know my purpose from the start, even if I did not dare to tell you. Perhaps you have heard from Lek that I was offered my freedom, on Azanry, gentles. The First Secretary at Chilleau Judiciary has granted relief of Writ."

Nobody stared. So they all knew, not surprisingly. Koscuisko nodded, as if accepting this as an answer. "Very good. It means I do not mean to stay for longer than I must, on board the *Ragnarok*. We stand here in the presence of a man I loved, and killed so that he could be free."

Clearly wasn't proposing that he kill them, Stildyne knew—or hoped. There would have been no reason for Koscuisko to take such risks to tinker with their governors if all he wanted to do was kill them.

"There is a small freighter at the launch field where we came in, a respectable beast from the Khabardi shipyards. I know that you will be as shocked as I to hear that there are people even in the heart of Jurisdiction who have dealings with the outlaws of Gonebeyond space."

"Sending us away, are you?" Robert said suddenly, almost vehemently. "And why d'you assume that we'll just go? My duty was not of my choice, your Excellency, but it is my duty, and you should not insult us. After all."

After all that they had been through together. After all that they had learned from one another. After all that they had meant to one another.

Koscuisko shook his head. "I will tell you a secret, Robert, and you will understand. I could not live in Fleet without your help. All of your help," Koscuisko added, looking at Stildyne, right at him. "I will not be able to live in Fleet at all for very much longer." Koscuisko seemed clearly determined, but to be thinking twice even so. He took a deep breath, and continued.

"If you do not leave now, someone in the future may be able to compel you to admit that I murdered Captain Lowden in Burkhayden, and set fire to the service house to burn the body so that he could not come back to it. I was not thinking very clearly at the time."

No, Stildyne thought. *You can't tell them that. You can't tell them. Nobody is supposed to know. I don't know. Nobody knows. How could you tell them*—and then he understood, even as Koscuisko spoke on.

"But now I have told you, and betrayed your trust by giving you a terrible secret. You will not dispute with me. You must go away. Please. There is little enough in Gonebeyond, but I am assured that there are neither governors, nor facilities that could impose them without killing if they tried."

Well, that was a comfort, wasn't it? Stildyne asked himself. Maybe it was. He'd worked with Bonds for almost his entire life in Fleet. He'd seen the things a governor could do, and at Burkhayden he was the man who had done them.

"If you can take the chances you've taken," Pyotr said, "we can have some too. The tax collector also must pay taxes."

Koscuisko nodded. "And I can't make anybody go. I have no cause to believe I know what is in your hearts, because you have been prisoners in my presence all of these years. But here, in the place of the dead, I ask it of you. I have owed my life to Joslire. I have owed my life to you. My cousin has a place for you to go, in Gonebeyond. He says it will be deficient in the luxuries of life, but you will be free."

His cousin? So that was where Stanoczk had gotten himself off to in such a hurry. Stildyne hadn't minded Stanoczk's precipitate departure, no, of course not.

"But you're not coming," Hirsel pointed out. "Have I got that part right?"

Stildyne could see sweat running down the side of Koscuisko's neck. It was uncomfortably warm, and close—but his face was pale.

"Good enough for us, but not for you? What kind of an offer is that?"

"The ship needs me." It was immediately obvious that the suggestion was not to be accepted. Koscuisko raised both hands, palms outward, making hushing gestures. "It needs you, too, but we have other Wolnadi crews. We can cope. We have no other neurosurgeon. You are not needed to work in Secured Medical. And also I mean to keep the truth hidden for as long as possible: there is Security on the vector."

"What's the plan, then?" Lek Kerenko asked, a little skeptically. "Better dead than Bonded, your Excellency, but if I can avoid both at the same time I will."

What Koscuisko was offering could not but be fraught with danger and promised hardship; he was clearly grateful to Lek for making the most positive response yet.

"And I mean both to be avoided, if there is any way that I can make it so. We are going to the service house, gentles, and in the early morning a car will come to take you to the launch field. I have sent you on an errand. The freighter has a cleared departure, and I will simply have to stay in bed until the ship has acquired its vector. Well into the morning. Nearly half a day, to be safe."

"What if we don't all go?" Godsalt asked, frowning. "Pyotr is so close to Reborn. Not to get personal, man."

"If you don't all go, I will only have sent some of you. First Officer will not press the issue as long as he has the say about it." Which could not be very long, of course. That was part of what had been on Koscuisko's mind all along, clearly enough. "But I hope you may all decide. You will need each other. You are the only people who could understand what you have endured."

Pyotr was about to say something, but Hirsel put his hand to Pyotr's shoulder. Robert took a half a step back and caught Garrity's eye; Godsalt nodded. Lek shook his head as though discouraged, but he said nothing.

Koscuisko turned his back to them all and raised his head to stare up into the dead branches of the tree whose roots were dressed with the mortal remains of a man Koscuisko still loved. "I would wish to have you with me always if I could," he said. "But my motive would be selfish. It would be for my sake and not yours. I don't know how I am to do without you."

It was at that moment that Stildyne understood that he was going to go with them. He didn't think Koscuisko realized it, yet; Stildyne had only just now seen the logic of it for himself. He couldn't unsee it. There was no acceptable alternative. Koscuisko loved these people. They'd need someone who understood their situation, someone who could stand between them and the rest of the world and smooth out the rough spots until they had had time to learn again what it was to be free.

When Koscuisko continued, he had apparently found a new strength of determination, his voice strong and steady, if pitched low. "I only tell you this because I could not bear to send you away from me without at least once acknowledging how much I owe. I ask you to do this knowing that it is a risk and that life will not be easy, even if you get cleanly away. I have watched you suffer for these years. Please. Take the only chance that you may get to be away from suffering, at least of that particular sort."

In the still air, Stildyne was half-convinced that he could actually hear himself sweat.

"Why aren't you coming? And tell us the truth of it. It's owed," Lek said suddenly.

Koscuisko looked back over his shoulder, but didn't turn around. "Six renegade bond-involuntaries lost in Gonebeyond are not worth the effort it would take to return them," Koscuisko said. His voice was harsh and hopeless. "I can't go. Fleet would have no choice but to report a kidnap or an absence without leave, and follow in force. There would be a bounty. There would be no disappearing, no new life."

Koscuisko had a point. Stildyne hadn't thought about it, because the course of action that Koscuisko had suggested was taking its own sweet time to sink in. They'd all known that Koscuisko was up to something, or he understood nothing of these men, and they were by definition intelligent men with the psychological resilience it demanded to be forced to become an instrument of torture, to live in fear of torture, and yet live. They were probably smarter than Stildyne, with the possible exception of St. Clare.

"Thought of everything, he has," Robert said to Godsalt, who stood next to him. "It's like him. Here's what's left of Jos, though. You didn't know him, and I did. I didn't get to say good-bye to Joslire, either."

Koscuisko winced, and closed his eyes. But when he opened them again and turned around to face them, the expression on his face was resolute—almost cold. "Good-bye, Robert," Koscuisko said. "Thou hast been very good to me, and had little but abuse and care for thanks. I pray to all Saints that you will be free. Lek. Good-bye. I will explain your absence to my son."

There was a solid core of merciless determination in Koscuisko's nature. Stildyne had seen it once or twice before. It made him shudder now, too. There would be no turning Andrej Koscuisko from his purpose, regardless of the cost.

"Pyotr, good-bye, and thank you for the care that you have had of me. Godsalt. Good-bye, I will miss you, and so will Soft Tissue Displacement, I will have to answer to my staff for it. Hirsel, good-bye, and may you have better luck in the future than you have ever had in the past. Good-bye, Garrity, I can only hope that you can forgive me when I say that I hope I never see you again. Ever. After tonight."

Stildyne had never known another man who could make up his mind like Koscuisko. It had been one of the things that had intrigued him from the start, well before he'd realized that Koscuisko's opinion had begun to matter to him much more than it ought to have done. "Fall back," Stildyne suggested. "Give the officer some room."

Koscuisko turned his back again. One hand on the retaining wall of the raised bed to steady himself, Koscuisko reached down, just at hip-height, and took up a handful of the earth that was there. What he did with it Stildyne didn't know; he was occupied in moving Security off to a respectful distance.

Koscuisko hadn't said good-bye to him. He wasn't going to get to say good-bye. He was going to have to just get up and go, and never see Koscuisko again. It was hard. But that was life. It was even funny that no one else appeared to have realized that Stildyne had no choice but to leave Koscuisko if he loved him, and he had long since been forced to accept the awkward fact that he did.

Then, like fluid coloring when Koscuisko dripped a catalyst into a flask in his pharmacology lab, the air filled in an instant with a fine mist of soaking rain. There was no seeing Koscuisko at the tree. Did he know where they were? Could he find them? It came on so suddenly that the scent of moisture followed after the drenching mist.

Stildyne wondered if he should send out a scouting party, but no, here was Koscuisko back again, walking slowly and contemplatively with his head bent toward the ground and the rain coming in little rivulets across his face and shoulders. What was the hurry, after all? Stildyne asked himself. They had already been wet from the inside out, what sense was there in hurrying to avoid getting wet from the outside in? It wasn't as if the rain was cold. It was warm rain. It was almost exactly as hot as it had been before the rain had started.

The thick mist of rainfall obscured walls and boundaries and the skyline of the city in front of them. They were alone, for these few moments, all alone, with each other.

No one spoke. Moving at a meditative pace, they walked in an appropriate formation out of the orchard into the street, and loaded into the ground transport cars to go to the service house as Koscuisko had arranged.

THE WELCOMING PARTY was still waiting. Andrej couldn't face them, not just now. He was ashamed—there were old women and a young mother, he'd kept them waiting—but he had reached the utmost tolerance of his psychological resilience. He should have done more research. He had no one to blame but himself.

Even before he had realized the opportunity this would give him to send his gentlemen away, he had long dreamed of kneeling down at Joslire's grave, in front of Joslire's marker, and telling the silent earth how much he missed his friend. There had been no grave. There had been no marker. He had trodden in his boots on sacred ground, and not known it. Yes, the tree sang of itself, but right now Andrej could find no comfort in that.

"Beg for me the pardon of these people," he said to the translator. "My heart is full. I can't speak, I'm not fit for company, and there are my gentlemen. Only one night. If it is disrespect of the dead—I don't know what I will do—"

She was every eighth the professional; there was no hint of surprise or disapproval on her face or in her voice. "It is understood," she assured him gravely. "His Excellency's accustomed practice. They are only making sure that you don't need to talk right now, sir."

It was all right, or at least being overlooked in dignified silence. In front of the family of the murdered man, he was to go directly from the burial ground to the service house. He had done that on the night of Joslire's death, as he remembered, but they had stopped at the port's hospital first, to dress the wounds that the others had suffered—and to burn the body, sending it up in smoke.

Joslire had been there when Andrej had discovered that he had an appetite for torture. Joslire had kept him company, and given him comfort. Andrej hadn't realized how much difference it made. He'd been alone in Port Rudistal, watching the temperature gauge of the hospital's incinerators. Then there'd been the furnaces at the Domitt Prison—

Andrej shuddered. He was alone now. He had sent them away and they would go, even Robert whom he loved also. They would go because he bade them, and then he would be alone.

"I'd like to get the officer changed," Stildyne said to the translator. It was a voice that put a hand to Andrej's shoulder to steady him. To comfort him, in a different way than Joslire's friendship had strengthened him, but Stildyne was a different man and Andrej owed him much more than he could possibly repay. "If it wouldn't give offense to the family."

The translator bowed politely one more time, but Andrej had remembered who he was, and crossed the wet concrete apron before the orchard gate to bow in turn to Joslire's family. The least honor he could do to them was to make his own excuses.

"I'm honored to see the place where his ancestors are." And that was true. "I need some time to settle my own mind. And I have wished my Security to have the opportunity to take recreation, and will be sending them back to the ship on an errand for me tomorrow. I ask to be forgiven."

If he didn't go with them, they couldn't go to the service house. Not under ordinary rules. And since he claimed to be sending them off in the morning, this was their only chance to have a little fun.

The youngest woman spoke, her expression anxious, her baby fretful in her arms. "Does his Excellency leave in the morning?" she asked in rather less fluent Standard than that of the translator. "Shona I wish to have the chance. Joslire was his brother."

This Andrej could promise honestly. It would be two or three days before the *Ragnarok's* load-out was completed, and whether the *Ragnarok* would let him back on board at all was to be seen. "I mean to stay in port as long as I may be allowed," he said. "If all Saints are generous, it will give us both the chance, your husband and I. Will it be possible to visit with your family tomorrow?"

The translator spoke for him. The oldest woman smiled. There was a ghost there, too. "Required," the old woman said; the translator actually blushed as she said the words. "Transport will come for you, grandson. You have not seen your house. We have not seen you in your place."

She had just put him in his place, though, and decisively if kindly enough. Yes, he would be forgiven if he went elsewhere tonight. No, he would not be forgiven if he failed to be a dutiful adopted son tomorrow. Even as heartsore as he was, Andrej had to smile.

"I will prove that I can take instruction, and do my utmost to shadow in his place in such a way as may do honor to his memory," he promised. "Please excuse me now."

Security were loaded in the cars already, all except Stildyne; and there were Emandisan Port Authority security to protect his Security while they protected him. He hadn't been so flamboyantly secured in his life.

Sitting in the ground car on the way to the city's public house, Andrej leaned back against the padded cradle of the seat and closed his eyes, listening to the pain that was in his heart and mind. Joslire was dead. It had been a mistake to come. It had reminded him, and Joslire was dead all over again, fresh dead, new dead, gone and gone and gone and gone. He'd forgotten how much it hurt. He'd thought he'd put the agony away. There had been the Domitt Prison; he had not had time. Had that been his error? Had he never truly mourned his friend?

Not a mistake. It was his second chance, to feel the loss as though it was just done and suffer for it without the need to master his emotions and turn his mind to work. "When we arrive," he said, knowing that Stildyne would be listening, "If you would make the arrangements, Brachi. I can't face the negotiations now. Convince them."

Arrival at a service house too often caused an uproar, and all manner of misunderstandings founded in his personal notoriety. He was the Ship's Inquisitor on board the Jurisdiction Fleet Ship *Ragnarok*; he clearly could not be offered any ordinary accommodation.

Pain-workers would be called for, and if he could convince the housemaster that in fact he did not wish to reproduce in his intimate behavior the regrettable activities of his professional life, they were all too ready to conclude that he desired a beating.

Once upon a time, he had grown so weary of trying to make himself understood that he had agreed, *oh, very well*; it had not been a successful experiment.

The animal portion of his nature did not experience sharp sensation as pleasure, and the professional portion of his nature could not be silenced from making a technical critique. The last thing he needed when he wished to engage was to be so forcibly reminded of exactly what he was in all of its grim horror, and things had simply not gone well at all.

He'd felt so sorry for the woman, he'd tipped her outrageously, but she'd known. He'd been able to tell. It was a part of his curse: he could tell. He had learned the lessons of patient interface too well, in school. When people were distressed or suffering, he could smell it like a drug.

"I'll see to it," Stildyne promised. "If you're going to sit up, do you want a game of cards, later on in the evening?"

Stildyne would do that for him. When Stildyne was done with his own enjoyment, he would come and sit with Andrej in the officer's suite at a service house, and keep him company. Andrej thought about it, but shook his head.

"Thank, you, Brachi, but not this night." Stildyne would only remind him of the fact that there were men in a different area of the service house that he would never see again. Not dead, but going away from him regardless.

Which reminded him—"I didn't dare say anything." He owed Stildyne trust and confidence, and had showed him neither. "And Stoshi only finalized arrangements when he came on board. I do not ask if Stoshi said anything to you. I only ask your pardon for reserving my confidence. I believed it necessary."

"I should have guessed," Stildyne said. He sounded more than usually meditative to Andrej, and meditation wasn't usually something he associated with Stildyne. "Only myself to blame. It's a useful reminder, of how things can be perfectly obvious in hindsight, and to all intents and purposes invisible in plain sight all along."

Yes, Stildyne was right. "I'll have my supper," Andrej said. It was getting to be evening, by the sun. "It's nice to be alone, once in a while. Maybe they'll have something of interest for you."

Officers had orderlies, someone from Security detailed every night to stand outside their quarters and attend to whatever chore might need doing: boots, fetching supper, playing cards with drunken officers. On board the *Ragnarok*, he was never alone—or never far from the company of another soul. It was not the same thing.

"We'll see," Stildyne promised, sounding a little amused. It wasn't as though he believed for one moment that Andrej didn't know— surely not. "Don't worry. I'll take care of everything."

"You always do," Andrej acknowledged. Then the ride was quiet until they reached the service house, and all went in.

"I DON'T BLAME the depot master," Captain Irshah Parmin said thoughtfully to his cup of bhan. "I'd be angry too. I've been angry. I never met a man who fried my breakfast ungreased like Koscuisko could, not ever in my life. An accomplished officer. Yes."

But it was clear enough to Calleigh that he was seriously unhappy. He had the Intelligence officer's report in cube in front of him: rumors, gossip, innuendo, report. From what he'd shared with them all—Ship's First, Intelligence, Doctor Weasel-Boy, Calleigh Samons—there was a very peculiar dynamic at work in Fleet these days. Koscuisko had been notorious almost from the beginning of his career, and now the stored-up anxieties of certain elements in Fleet appeared to be attaching themselves to Koscuisko, rather than to the woman who had done more to earn Fleet's resentment honestly and fairly.

Calleigh could feel the injustice of it, for ap Rhiannon's sake. Koscuisko had a reputation, but it wasn't difficult to acquire one in his line of work, especially with Verlaine doing his best to raise Koscuisko's profile by persecuting him relentlessly. It would have taken all of the faculties of a much more subtle man than Koscuisko to avoid acquiring a name for himself in Fleet.

It was ap Rhiannon who had taken the *Ragnarok* and left Taisheki—Koscuisko merely executing his orders, by reliable report— and still people who should have known better, who did know better, affected to believe that Andrej Koscuisko was the cause and the ring-leader of disaffection on board the *Ragnarok*.

"It's not your problem," First Officer reminded him. "Koscuisko was reassigned years ago. So you feel that you missed a chance with him. He's not yours to nurture and cultivate. It's no reflection on *Scylla*."

The captain laughed short and sharp and sudden, losing control of a moderate amount of bhan as he did so. "What? Jennet ap Rhiannon is going to develop Koscuisko's professional presentation? Don't make me laugh." Ignoring the fact that First Officer just had, Calleigh noted, but kept the thought to herself. She was here on sufferance. The captain only involved her at all because she'd been Koscuisko's chief of Security while he had been here on *Scylla*. They had grief in common. "She couldn't professional deportment her way out of a—That's unfair. I take it back. They're well suited, now that I come to think of it."

Doctor Weasel-Boy sniggered, but everybody affected to ignore him. He kept shut.

"You could just as easily turn quietly around and go back to Brisinje," First Officer pointed out. "Pick up a few stores for the sake of appearances. Now is not the time to make issues with Emandis Station."

The captain scowled. "Emandis Station has decided to make issues with Fleet, it seems to me," he observed, not unreasonably, in Calleigh's opinion. "Who's to say there has to be any trouble? He's a Fleet resource, I'm a former commander. I haven't seen him. Isn't it my bounden duty to try to get him to see the error of his ways?"

"Maybe you'll get lucky," Doctor Weasel-Boy suggested. "Maybe he'll try to talk some of your crew over, and he can be shot while escaping. Making lewd and unseemly suggestions to a senior Security warrant with intent to debauch. I know I would."

And had, on a fairly frequent basis, since he had come on board. It didn't really bother Calleigh, not all that much. She'd been dealing with the impact of her body on the opposite sex since she'd been six years shy of her maiden voyage. The other sex, too, but the women Calleigh had known had usually been significantly subtler about things.

"Just go borrow him a bit, Chief," the captain said to her, not bothering to look at Weasel-Boy. "Leave his Security out of it. He frets about them. Tell him I'd like the favor of a word or two in my office. He'll understand. You won't have any trouble."

Yes, Koscuisko would understand—he understood force and coercion much better than the average medical officer, force and coercion being his stock in trade. No, she wouldn't have any trouble with him if she could keep clear of his Security. "Shall I leave word at the desk for ap Rhiannon, sir?" There was no need to specify which desk; Intelligence knew where Koscuisko was expected to be.

Men who were subject to the threat of death had no business being predictable, but Koscuisko would always go first to a service house to turn his Security over to the service staff for a little of the sort of recreation that didn't usually come with much of a rest. She'd been to a service house with Koscuisko herself, on one memorable occasion. The man knew what he was doing with anatomy.

Irshah Parmin made a face, his lower lip thrust halfway to his chin. "N—I—yes. Yes. All right. The officer is paying a call on the Command and general staff of the Jurisdiction Fleet Ship *Scylla* at the request of a former commanding officer. Something like that, Salli, what do you think?"

First Officer didn't think much of it, by the looks of her, but apparently she could see the humor anyway. "Better than a ransom note," she admitted. "Try to stay away from any guns-for-surgeons suggestions, Chief. And you know Koscuisko as well as anybody here, after all."

Except for Code Pyatte, that was to say—the only bond-involuntary left on board who had been here during Koscuisko's tenure. She'd better leave Code behind. Asking a bond-involuntary to kidnap a former officer of assignment would probably upset his equilibrium; the conflict could have an unpredictable effect on his governor, and Koscuisko would never forgive that. Never.

"Very good, your Excellency," Calleigh said. "With respect, sir, and only for the sake of clarification. Your instructions are to escort the chief medical officer of the Jurisdiction Fleet Ship *Ragnarok* to *Scylla* from wherever I find him in an Emandisan port, whether he likes it or not. Without being noticed by the Port Authority, if I can help it."

"You make it sound as though there was something unusual about it," the captain complained. "Yes, Chief, precise and correct, as always. Thank you."

Calleigh saluted with a bow. She was done here. Turning to leave, she heard Doctor Weasel-Boy speak up one more time. "I've got some good stuff for Dolgorukij," Doctor Weasel-Boy said. "If he doesn't want to talk to you when he gets here, I mean. I could help you with that. Maybe I should go with Chief Samons, your Excellency, much less chance of Koscuisko kicking up if he's unconscious, we'll find a big enough box—"

"Shut up and get out," the captain said. "Thank you, First Officer."

Calleigh had to hurry if she was to be far enough ahead of Weasel-Boy to be able to credibly ignore him if he called after her.

She took long steps as quickly as she could without actually running, thinking all the while. She had her instructions. No harm was threatened or likely to befall him. Koscuisko was likely to be angry, but he wouldn't blame her personally.

There were people on board *Scylla* who remembered Andrej Koscuisko. If the captain decided to hang on to him for a few days, where would he be quartered? And would there be visiting hours? A sign-up sheet? Come and see the Inquisitor, very rare Dolgorukij senior officer, only one known in captivity?

The captain had Koscuisko's best interest at heart, if only in his own way, although Koscuisko was unlikely to see it the captain's way.

But it would be good to see Koscuisko again. Calleigh had seen a lot more of him at his worst than she had of other officers, and on balance she liked him anyway.

She wondered how she was going to get around his Security. He'd have sent his Bonds downstairs to recreate themselves, but Security Chief Stildyne was no slouch—

Koscuisko would have sent Stildyne off to find amusement, as well. She'd figure it out when she got there. The middle of second shift, on *Scylla*, so it was coming up evening in Port Jeltaria—it would be six-eights on toward morning already when they got there. She'd see what the situation was then.

Mulling over her team composition, Calleigh hurried away to her tiny office to issue a warning order for involuntary escort, senior officer, leaving immediately.

CHAPTER THIRTEEN
NEW BEGINNINGS

"PRIVACY," STILDYNE SAID firmly, with his back to the common room. "That's what's wanted. Privacy and dinner. If a professional is wanted later, one of them will call. Thank you. But no players. Just feed them and leave them alone."

The floor manager looked confused, but Stildyne had left her no room for further protest. He knew that the Bonds had a great deal to think about. If he'd been Pyotr—only a few years away from an honorable retirement, and a future as a privileged citizen—what would he do?

He didn't know. And he couldn't guess. What the governor did to a bond-involuntary was all but unimaginable to a free soul. It had only been in the past few days that Stildyne had begun to realize what Koscuisko had been seeing all along: that, after all these years, these men were strangers to him. He hadn't begun to know Robert or Lek or Garrity or Godsalt or Hirsel—or even Pyotr. He had known bond-involuntaries, respected them, valued them, but hadn't known the men at all.

The floor manager nodded. "Very well, Chief. Dinner it is. I'll go put the order in. Any dietary restrictions? Liquor?"

Why don't you ask them, Stildyne thought. He knew the answer. They were slaves; they had no competence to speak on their own behalf. That was his job. "Mister Kerenko?"

Turning back to call for Lek, Stildyne's eye had caught one of the house staff coming out of a niche with an armload of linen. There were private cubicles arranged around the perimeter of the common room, eight or ten of them. If Stildyne had to guess, it would be that the bed linen would be as crisp tomorrow as it was right now. It would take a man with nerves of stalloy to sleep, after what Koscuisko had said to them.

Lek came forward, to the doorway in which Stildyne stood talking to the floor manager in the corridor. "Chief."

"Lek, I'd like you to go with this woman to the kitchen, and make the pull. Mister Kerenko knows everybody's likes and dislikes, he'll be able to help you. I should go check on the officer now, Lek, all right?"

Kerenko nodded and then bowed. If Stildyne hadn't known, he would not have guessed that Kerenko need no longer fear punishment for any minor failing, however slight. On the other hand, although it was true, Kerenko didn't really know it yet either, perhaps. On a higher-function conscious level, he knew, but Kerenko had undergone the same careful indoctrination as the others: operant conditioning, perfection or punishment.

Koscuisko had to realize that. Koscuisko had to know that he was sending Stildyne into Gonebeyond space with these men. He had to.

Koscuisko wasn't going to get away with it, not without at least saying good-bye. If Stildyne was never going to see Koscuisko again—and he couldn't really pretend that he was going to—he was going to demand the same consideration Koscuisko had extended to his gentles, that of having his departure acknowledged with regret.

He wasn't going to worry about Kerenko and the floor manager. Bond-involuntaries knew how to act the part, and none of them were stupid. "Carry on," Stildyne said. "I'll see you all in the morning." The very early morning. He wasn't going to ask them. He was just going. It was for Koscuisko's sake, not theirs, that he was going. He had no intention of giving anybody any rash ideas about consensus.

Walking away—before anybody had a chance to challenge him on his promise, statement, insinuation—Stildyne made his way through the service corridors to the next-to-uppermost floor, where the senior officer's suite would be located. Service houses were standard built, standard run, regulated and taxed by Jurisdiction; there were a limited number of floor plans. He knew his way around a service house. So did Koscuisko.

Had he known all along that Koscuisko had killed Lowden, Stildyne wondered? Yes, he knew perfectly well what Robert St. Clare had done. If Koscuisko hadn't convinced him and Karol Vogel alike that Robert himself had no idea, Stildyne would have killed Koscuisko's favorite at the first opportunity, just to keep him from a death by slow torture and the consequent anguish that would inflict on Koscuisko. He knew with equal perfection exactly what would, or at the very least could, happen to Koscuisko himself, if the story ever got out.

The story would get out. Koscuisko had told them all. No matter how careful they were, compromise was bound to occur, sooner or later. Koscuisko had told them in order to convince them to leave. Which led him back to the vexed question: did Koscuisko understand that Stildyne had no real choice but to leave as well?

No. If Koscuisko had, he would have said good-bye. He had not said good-bye. After all of this time, Koscuisko didn't understand that loving him meant seeing to his needs and concerns first, and consulting Stildyne's own preferences fifth or sixth.

Yes, his preference would be to stay, where he could have Koscuisko's company—on a fairly intimate level—even if he could never have Koscuisko. But the bond-involuntary troops were not, for all the perfection of their discipline and the beauty of their martial competence and the strength of their character, grown men who could be simply sent way with their governors off-line.

They had been conditioned to live within cruelly narrow boundaries. They would need help. They would need him. Koscuisko loved them; therefore, Stildyne had no choice but to do what would be best for them.

Should he say something? Koscuisko would thank him for his sacrifice. Koscuisko might possibly embrace him—as a man, not as a lover—and tell him that his sacrifice was noble and admirable, when in fact it was neither, at its base. Koscuisko would be surprised. If he were not surprised, it would mean that he had counted on Stildyne to exile himself in Gonebeyond for Koscuisko's sake, expected it, planned on it, decided it and never so much as mentioned it to Stildyne himself, taking the only gift that Stildyne had to give him for granted as his. Already his.

Koscuisko wouldn't do that to a bond-involuntary. But there was a chance that he would do that to Stildyne. Koscuisko had been raised to mastery, and could have no doubt after all these years that Stildyne was his man to direct and command.

Stildyne was just deciding that he could not take the chance of finding out when he opened up the door between the service corridor and the main passageway, and discovered the housemaster and her assistant in the passageway, arguing between themselves in muted but passionate tones.

"It'll never work," the assistant was saying. She was the short plump one, and Stildyne liked women plump when he had to choose among women. "The very idea, asking a customer to provide services. They say he's sensitive about it, too. He'll have us dismissed. We'll lose our pensions."

The housemaster herself was not too very much taller, but she was much less generously padded, and the way she wore her red hair gave her something of a vaguely predatory air. "He's a doctor, here's a patient. And we'll just ask. We could lose our license if we can't provide services on demand, just as easily as—Chief Stildyne."

She changed her tone and her demeanor the moment she noticed him coming down the hall. "Is everything arranged to your satisfaction, Chief? The men decently put away for the evening?"

"No complaints." The assistant housemaster had a document in her hand that looked vaguely familiar to Stildyne for some reason. It was just a legal document or a medical record: yes, a doctor's order. A prescription. "May I see that?"

He'd surprised them, and they hadn't been very comfortable with whatever it was in the first place. It was the most natural thing in the world for Stildyne to reach out and pluck the doctor's order from the assistant's sweaty grasp.

"Ah, no, Chief, if it's all the same, private document—really, I protest—"

Yes, it was a private document. Not as if he was going to say anything to anybody about it. He was leaving in the morning; he was going far far away and he wasn't coming back ever again. Of what possible interest was a doctor's order to him? It was a Fleet document. That was interesting. It was executed and authorized by Koscuisko's own Chief of Psychiatric. That was even more interesting.

One word, and Stildyne passed the document back. He understood. He understood more than he really wanted to, but that was his own fault. "Well, well. Caught with two cruiser-killers standing off, and your pain-worker's on vacation."

"Had to go home very suddenly, we haven't had time to find a back-up, it's not like it's a common specialty. And you know how strict the licensing authority can be—" the assistant started, a little crossly. The housemaster trod on her assistant's foot with passion, and the assistant shut up.

"Medical requirement," the housemaster said firmly. "These things aren't passed out like port freedoms, Chief, you know that. It's got to be hard enough for her to come here with something like this. I really don't want to contemplate the grief it'll give her to come here hoping, and to go away again—without."

There and then Stildyne decided that he wasn't going to say good-bye to Koscuisko., in case it turned out that Koscuisko had been assuming he'd be going all along. It was a small risk, a slim chance, but the potential reassurance was not much greater than the possibility for disaster. Since he was going, he'd go with his illusions intact. And he wouldn't meet the Bonds in the morning as they left, either—that could intimidate them or give them second thoughts, make them wary about whether they were being set up. Paranoia was an occupational hazard for a bond-involuntary.

He'd meet them on board the ship, when it would be obvious that he was going, and everybody who had decided to come would have made that decision as freely as possible beforehand, without any spoken or unspoken influence from him.

For that, he had to find the ship. This was a respectable port, but by no means a major mercantile hub; there was only the one launch field. Koscuisko had said that it was a Khabardi freighter. Stildyne had all night—he could find it. What he needed was to find the ship with the Dolgorukij accent, and if it wore a red halter around its neck, he would not be in the least surprised. There was the chance that Koscuisko's cousin Stanoczk would be coming with them.

"Good luck trying," Stildyne said sincerely. "I'd lean on the soul-in-need angle, if I were you. You'll be lucky if he doesn't throw you out bodily."

"But there's a chance?" the assistant asked eagerly, being apparently recovered from her trodden toe.

Stildyne nodded. "He's been approached before, but in different contexts. Twice as awkward that she's on the same ship. It could be construed as fraternization. Captain frowns on that." So did Koscuisko. He was prickly about relations between ranks, because of the power inequities that existed.

Koscuisko had explained it to Stildyne as proof that no man could exploit a bond-involuntary for selfish gratification and call himself a man—long before Stildyne had confessed to Koscuisko that he had done just that, in his past. A bond-involuntary was not in a position to give consent because a bond-involuntary could not refuse a superior officer anything. That was the reason they were exploited, of course—Stildyne had thought at the time that that should have been staggering clear to Koscuisko.

When circumstances had made it necessary for Stildyne to tell Koscuisko what he himself had done, Koscuisko had replied that Stildyne's previous abuse of bond-involuntaries was not as important as his current abstention from abuse. It was a nice thought. Stildyne believed that Koscuisko meant it.

Now he was going to find out whether it was true. He was going to Gonebeyond with people he'd had parties with for his personal amusement, before Koscuisko's time, when Lowden had expected it. Almost required it. He'd find out whether having *stopped* was important enough to make amends for having *done* in the first place when they got to Gonebeyond and those men came to realize that they were free and Stildyne outnumbered.

"We must try," the housemaster said. "We've a duty."

Stildyne nodded again. Yes. She did have a duty. Service houses were to maintain adequate staff to provide services as needed on request. A doctor's order was a particularly important request.

"Remember that he's a doctor, and you may be able to make it work," Stildyne said. "A woman is in pain. He won't like that. I've got things to attend to."

If he couldn't find the right ship on his own, he would have no choice but to come back here and wait with the others. He didn't know how much time he had before someone came for them; so, if he didn't intend to be left behind, he had better get started. He didn't have time to talk to Koscuisko anyway. Yes. That was right.

The housemaster stepped up to the door to signal for admittance, and Stildyne slipped back into the service corridor and away before Koscuisko could catch him mooning about in the halls and ask him what he thought he was doing.

ANDREJ KOSCUISKO STOOD at the viewing-wall looking out across the low-roofed city of Jeltaria, toward the launch field. He couldn't see individual craft, not from here, and he didn't want to take the chance of calling up a detail. It might seem suspicious later.

There was no telling how long it would be possible to keep knowledge of the bond-involuntaries' departure from interested parties—or from parties that would interest themselves, parties that would become interested once they found out. If that happened too soon, they might track the craft and intercept it before it reached the vector. It was four hours between Emandis Station and the dar-Nevan vector. He had checked. A fraction of a day, starting tomorrow morning. Sighing, Andrej turned from the wall and touched off the view.

There were no actual windows in the officer's suite of most public houses, for two reasons: one of them being the requirement to be able to get around, to get at the various rooms in the suite from all angles, and the other being the need for security. Not that it had done Lowden the least bit of good. Threat was anticipated from outside; that an assassin would approach through the public accesses, come to the front door—that was not included in the planning process.

To be fair, there were no instances of officers being murdered by subordinate officers in service houses that Andrej had ever heard of. Now his gentlemen had all heard of it, though, and Stildyne as well. Where was Stildyne? Andrej wanted to talk to him, to beg his pardon for not having included him in planning at a much earlier stage, among other things. He could have used Stildyne's help. Even now there were probably things that Stildyne could think about that were beyond Andrej.

On the other hand, they were at a service house and Stildyne had his appetites, just as any man might. Much less opportunity than some of the bond-involuntaries to find appropriate avenues on board ship, however. If Stildyne thought of something suddenly in the middle of the night, he would come and tell him. Andrej could be confident of that. He decided not to bother him. Among the staff here at the service house, Stildyne might have already found a genial young man of the general type that he preferred,.

There was a signal at the door. His dinner, perhaps. Without Stildyne to play cards with him, the evening was likely to drag a bit, but Andrej couldn't see calling for companionship. He had visited with Joslire in the graveyard, and sent his gentles away. He was going to be no kind of company at all.

"Step through," he called. The door hadn't opened as it might if it was just house staff with his meal or more towels or something of the sort. House staff would come through the service corridors anyway, wouldn't they? Was there a problem?

It was the housemaster and her assistant. She had greeted Andrej upon his arrival. Now she bowed very properly and took a deep breath, shot a glance at her assistant, and spoke.

"Very sorry to disturb his Excellency, who has made his preference for solitude very clear. We have an unusual situation, sir, a problem. May we trouble his Excellency to entertain a situation report?"

They were already troubling him, but his dinner wasn't here. That they wanted him to do something for them was obvious; they would not have come to see him just to tell him about their lives and difficulties. "I will sit down," he said, and turned his back to go into the little sitting room to the left of the suite's reception and dining area. "Yes, come."

Neither woman would cross the threshold into the sitting area, however, which rather amused him, although it kept him on his feet out of baseline politeness. In his experience, women with red hair had not been characterized by reserve and shyness. The housemaster was a red-head with a very pale complexion, and her teeth were not to the Jurisdiction standard—some cosmetic defect that she'd never bothered to address, clearly enough. Her teeth were a bit crowded at the front of her mouth, and put him in mind of a river-wolf, somehow.

"His Excellency is not the only soul from the *Ragnarok* to honor us this afternoon," the housemaster said, from the doorway where she stood. "The port authority notified us, of course, and we've taken the usual measures to prepare to accommodate a cruiser-killer class warship. Two."

Scylla and *Ragnarok*, she meant, Andrej assumed. And she was probably not talking about the bond-involuntaries or Stildyne when she spoke of other *Ragnarok* crew. "And this has to do with me what, please?"

"With respect, sir, believe us, profound and sincere, and not wishing to give offense in the slightest. Your Excellency. There's a prescription here to be filled. And we can't provide. The only pain-worker we have on staff has had to take an emergency personal leave."

Pain-worker? They wanted him to beat somebody for them. There was something in him that leapt at the offered opportunity with savage delight, but Andrej had no intention of acknowledging that appetite.

"I'm on holiday, and I'm not interested. I give you the benefit of the doubt and trust that you do not mean to insult me. Good-greeting."

Get out. The housemaster looked to her assistant; her assistant bit her lip but seemed to think of something, all of a sudden.

"Yes, sir, of course, your Excellency. But it is a doctor's order, sir, and we are unable to oblige. The patron is clearly in significant distress. Could you not consider it, your Excellency? Doctor?"

As if a doctor were required to inflict recreational beatings in a brothel. No. Services houses had pain-workers for that—trained professionals who had studied the careful management of intense physical sensation to elicit a pleasurable or ecstatic response, people as far removed from the genuine practice of Inquiry as an actor was from a murderer. As he was from an honest man.

"Let me be blunt." Since they weren't taking the hint. "I have no experience in whatever is required. My expertise lies in far more destructive fields than any appropriate to a service house. I cannot oblige you. Good-greeting."

The housemaster shook her head, her close-cropped hair catching the light as she did so. "The patron is fearfully nervous, sir. We understand completely if you don't care to become involved, it's an extreme imposition on our part to so much as suggest it, sir. But she's gotten this far, and if we turn her away, who knows when she'll have the opportunity? Or the nerve to take advantage of it? If you could just look at the order, your Excellency. It's more than awkward for us; a woman is suffering, and craves relief."

With a sigh of resignation, Andrej put out his hand for the housemaster's scrip, and carried it over to sit down with it at the table and have a look. This entire interchange was offensive in the highest degree, but it was unquestionably a distraction.

The patient's name he did not recognize, but the authorizing physician was his own Chief of Psychiatric: "After careful evaluation, a therapeutic exposure to traditional stimuli in a controlled atmosphere is recommended in order to confirm diagnosis by treatment. Appropriate access to a licensed pain-worker is therefore prescribed the named patient under the provisions of, billing code thus-and-such. By direction, Somerstrand Farilk, Chief of Psychiatric, Jurisdiction Fleet Ship *Ragnarok*."

No, it was not possible that Farilk had sent a patient here in order to encourage Andrej to consider the proposal that Farilk had

made. If Farilk said that one of Two's under-technicians suffered
from some psychological deficit that might be usefully addressed by
a pain-worker, then it was so. Andrej had worked with his clinical
staff for too long not to have an informed respect for each and
every one of them.

They weren't on the *Ragnarok* because their professional qualifications were wanting. Fleet could, and did, integrate mediocri-
ties successfully at every level of operation. They were on the
Ragnarok because they wanted to be there, or couldn't fit in to
the political environment of the Commands in which they had
found themselves prior to their frequently involuntary transfer.

The housemaster was right. A woman was suffering. How could
they suggest that he venture into territory that lay well outside his
area of actual expertise?

If he did not, they would send her back to the ship depressed
and desperate, without comfort, as though unworthy of consideration because her need was outside the normal parameters of the
Jurisdiction standard.

He'd taken extreme measures to relieve suffering before. She
was not a bond-involuntary, but did she deserve less of his consideration because of that? Officers did not consort intimately with
lower ranks, not on Jennet ap Rhiannon's *Ragnarok*. And yet he was
not long for the *Ragnarok*, one way or the other. Either the Selection
would be decided, the *Ragnarok's* appeal resolved, and he would be
free to go home a civilian; or ap Rhiannon could just as easily
refuse to let him back on board of his own ship, and solve in that
way the problem she apparently had believing his commitment to
the Command.

If he stayed here, he would brood. He would pace, and struggle
with a selfish instinct to seek out Stildyne for companionship and
conversation, which could only embarrass Brachi if he were in bed
with some blond. "I make no promises," he said. "And it is highly
irregular. Show me to the place and I will see what I can do."

If it was true that he had accidentally been bound to St. Andrej
Malcontent rather than Filial Piety at his naming, then he should consider the teaching of the Malcontent. The Malcontent had never
cared whether a person's need was odd or unusual, acceptable or
unacceptable. The Malcontent only cared whether people were fed
and clothed, and had a dry place to sleep, and got whatever it was

that they needed to understand the mystery of the Holy Mother's plan for them in this world.

He would try to do his duty to the Saint. He owed the Malcontent for many favors already; for the freedom of the bond-involuntary troops he loved, as just the latest example. He would go and talk to the patient, they would negotiate, and if the Holy Mother used him to bring peace to another soul—whether or not it was a Dolgorukij soul—it would be a small start on the very long journey that lay ahead of him, if he ever hoped to make reparation for crimes that could not be undone.

THE SIGNAL CAME at the door very early in the morning, but nobody had slept. "Good-greeting," the floor manager said. "Your car is waiting."

Robert looked around him one last time: walls, benches, beds in rooms on one side or the other, littered with the remains of two large meals. Little drink. A man wanted to be sure he knew what he was doing when he left the world as he knew it.

"Very good." In Chief Stildyne's absence, Pyotr acted as their Chief. He had more years of service than Chief Stildyne did, and it was no particular secret that if he had not been a Security slave he would have made Chief Warrant years ago. First Officer had certainly never taken exception to anybody's tendency to treat Pyotr as though he were one. "Formation, gentlemen. Let's go."

It wouldn't do to keep the officer waiting. The officer wanted them out; he'd made that painfully clear. No last words or parting embrace, and still it was a wrench. He had followed Andrej Koscuisko all the way from Fleet Orientation Station Medical, and lucky for him, too.

It hadn't been his doing. Koscuisko had happened on a secret that he hadn't been supposed to have, and it would have meant the end of young Robert had Koscuisko not got stubborn about it. All of these years, and nobody here knew what Koscuisko had done to save Robert's life.

Nobody alive knew Koscuisko better than he did, which was why he knew that there was no help for it, no help at all. Koscuisko wanted them gone. They'd go. It was the last time they'd ever do what Koscuisko wanted.

There hadn't been much left to discuss, last night—they'd got most of the chewing done before, as the implications of Koscuisko's surgeries became more and more clear. Koscuisko had always wanted rid of them, for their own sakes. He never would give himself the credit he'd earned honestly for doing what he could to protect them from the bullies of the world, and shield them from the horrors to which they'd been condemned.

Robert had written long speeches in his head to be delivered to Koscuisko once the Day had dawned and he was free to speak. They'd go unspoken now, forever, and it was probably just as well, but it was a shame. He had some good lines in there: pointed remarks about men who cherished guilt, which was after all a form of vanity that did not become a man; about men who cared for people by whom they would not accept being cared for without a fight. Things of that nature.

It was short of dawn. The air smelled sweetly of damp dust. It was already hot outside, or at least warm, and oppressive with humidity. Fog lay heavily around the streets and alleys that their transport passed on the way to the launch field. Nobody spoke. Robert wondered if the others were disappointed that they hadn't had a chance to say good-bye to Stildyne. They knew more about Stildyne than Robert did—they'd all been here longer than he had, except for Godsalt, who was new. But even Robert had seen for himself the change that Koscuisko had wrought in Brachi Stildyne, and honored him for it.

Maybe it would have been too risky, too much of a compromise. Stildyne was going to have to explain to First Officer where his troops had gone. First Officer wasn't going to be interested in listening to Koscuisko about it. Stildyne was responsible to First Officer for keeping track of troops; he'd be in for an interesting interview.

It was a shame not to have a chance to take his hand, though. Koscuisko had been considerably harder on Stildyne than on any of the rest of them, and for Robert's part, he appreciated how Stildyne had borne up under Koscuisko. Stildyne had been good to them. It was hard to go without saying good-bye.

It was hard to go. There was no future for them under Jurisdiction; Koscuisko was right about that. He was right about many things. When he was wrong, it was generally in holding a belief that there was no way around one thing or another. Robert had noticed this about him a long time ago.

It was hard to blame Koscuisko for the failing of his imagination, though, when it was so richly peopled with horrors that were real and not imagined at all. Koscuisko could be excused some shying away from consequences because he had a so much better than average understanding of what those consequences were.

It only made it more impressive, in Robert's mind, that Koscuisko had made up his mind finally to hazard the extreme consequences of declining to exercise his Writ ever again.

Those consequences made flight to Gonebeyond a rational strategy, and that annoyed Robert at Koscuisko's insistence on not going with them; but he was done being annoyed with Koscuisko. There was no reasoning with the man when he had his attention fixed. The closest thing that Robert had ever known to the ferocity of Koscuisko's concentration was that of a professional herding dog, but he'd never said as much to Koscuisko. People who weren't herding people couldn't be expected to understand.

The launch field was brightly lit but uncertain in the outlines of its lanes and outbuildings because of the fog. The traffic control gate checked their report papers and waved them on through: party of six to report to Khabardi freighter *Kavkazki Pass* to receive cargo on instruction, his Excellency Andrej Ulexeievitch Koscuisko, Jurisdiction Fleet Ship *Ragnarok*. Very normal and unremarkable.

They left the ground-car that had brought them from the service house at the field transport barn and took a mover out onto the launch field itself, heading for the material handling lanes where the freighter they were to board was to be found. Someone might eventually notice that they'd never called for transport back from the launch field to the service house, but they were all bond-involuntaries under orders, and it would simply be assumed that they were doing as they had been instructed—as was in fact the case.

A Khabardi freighter was a Combine ship. Surely that would be suspicious after the fact, but Koscuisko did not seem to intend to attempt to conceal his complicity in their flight. How could he? Flight was impossible without his direct intervention, surely—oh, yes, they were technically speaking all on Safe, but Koscuisko's not-entirely-secret surgeries were bound to come out after this.

And it was Koscuisko's choice and Koscuisko's decision, Robert reminded himself, following Pyotr up into the belly of the beast, hearing Lek behind him. There was a man standing in the cargo bay of the ship waiting for them; nobody Robert knew.

"Pyotr Micmac?" the man said. He was a big man, big hands, knobby shoulders, deep voice. Accent. "Kazmer Daigule, I'm to be your pilot. How many are we taking on board?"

Someone had come into the doorway between the cargo bay and the interior of the ship as Daigule spoke; short, female, Robert thought. Pyotr looked past Daigule with mild curiosity but said only, "There are six of us all told, pilot. When do we leave?"

"Come on, then, so that we can secure and clear. We're leaving as soon as we're locked and loaded. No time to waste, come on. You've got a pilot? Kerenko? Come with me, pilot."

Well, that was a familiar note in a welter of unreality—come on, hurry up, let's get going. Wait. Robert could understand that. He stood to one side as the others boarded—Godsalt, Hirsel, Garrity. It was an intelligent ship, this Khabardi; it sealed up promptly and efficiently then said something in some Combine dialect or another that sounded almost like something Koscuisko said when he got impatient to be off.

"Clear," the woman said. "This way. We'll seal down here. Introductions and explanations once we're off." Since she was apparently one of the crew, it was likely that she'd know if the loading ramp wasn't happy with the job that Robert and Garrity had done of securing it.

There were the universal telltales to consider—there was no room for linguistic misunderstandings where things like security doors for space flight were concerned—and the u-t's looked perfectly happy to Robert, so he followed the woman, and Garrity followed him, out of the cargo bay and up to the freighter's main access and into the front of the ship up by the wheelhouse. It was a small wheelhouse; freighters liked to use all available space for freight, not like a courier ship, not like that luxury model that had come to Pesadie to take Koscuisko home on leave.

"Get strapped in," she said, and went forward into the wheelhouse. Robert could hear her over the status-line that ran to all of the passenger shells, the little alcoves lining the corridor just short of the wheelhouse where people who weren't actively engaged in flying the ship were expected to secure themselves while the freighter made space.

Garrity took a place across the corridor from Robert. Robert could see his face in the dim light of the shell, but not his expression. Ducking his head out for a last quick look, Robert counted quickly. Six or seven passenger shells on a side, and his was the furthest from the wheelhouse. This freighter would carry fourteen to twenty souls then, since there were usually two to four souls running loose even at launch to make sure everything came off as it was expected.

"Packages all loaded," Robert heard the woman say. "Ready for departure, Kaz."

The pilot switched the shells into braid, so that they could listen. They weren't on transmit; only the wheelhouse transmitted on approach and on departure.

"Launch control. Khabardi freighter *Kavkazki Pass* requests final clearance, outbound for dar-Nevan vector to Oma. Please confirm."

"We hear you, *Kavkazki Pass*. We'll have a clearance for you in just a moment. Did you have any last minute callers? The gate thinks someone might have come looking for you." Launch control sounded a little bored, actually. Clearly not very excited about anything that might be happening this time of morning, but the launch had been carefully timed, Robert realized: the second half of first shift, long enough in for people to have gotten all of their routine shift-initiation checks out of the way, but before they started to perk up and take an interest in their environment, looking for the end of their shift.

"Been and gone, Launch Control. Permission to initiate launch sequence."

"Transmitting clearance codes, *Kavkazki Pass*. Hope you enjoyed your stay. Come again, and thank you for selecting Jeltaria Field for your in-transit requirements. Launch Control, away, here."

The freighter started to move. There was a rolling tone built in to the background noise, a subtle audio cue as to what the craft was doing—moving into launch position, angling for launch, launching. Robert knew that he wasn't actually hearing the sound of wheels against pavement or anything of the sort. A person's ear still strained to hear, and the rolling tone was provided for its psychological effect.

The pilot had switched his transmit off, but Robert could hear voices from the wheelhouse almost as easily—narrow corridor. "Are we related?" Lek was saying.

The pilot replied, "I'm not your cousin, if that's what you mean. No. No more than any two Sarvaw, Kerenko, and our mutual cousin Maritzj here, she's Arakcheyek. Comm officer. Have you done the dar-Nevan vector before?"

"Not for years," Lek said. "Cousin Maritzj." It was hard to read the sound of Lek's voice; Robert couldn't quite figure out the tone. The woman was a Malcontent? He hadn't known there were any female Malcontents.

"We're going to angle for a spin that would drop us at Oma, but sharpen the approach in the last fractions. We're not supposed to know how to reach Gonebeyond from Emandis Station, but I've done it before. No worries."

The pitch and intensity of the rolling tone had changed. The freighter had reached its slot on the launch field; the tank had attached. Robert done this time and again since following Koscuisko— not often on a freighter, no, but often enough. This was different. This was the end. This was taking them away, and they would not be coming back here, ever.

"Yes," the pilot said, apparently in response to a question Robert hadn't heard. "Five tanks. People are used to Combine freighters taking the high road. We've got perishable cargo, or at least that's our story."

Five tanks. Robert was impressed. Five booster tanks from Jeltaria Field would get them up and through atmosphere and spank them smartly on their way to the vector, too, before falling away to land themselves quietly at depot for refueling. It meant the freighter would be using much less of its own fuel to get out of Emandis space. The idea filled Robert with a sudden nearly nostalgic sort of anxiety. Who knew how far the freighter's fuel would have to carry them, to get to wherever they were going in Gonebeyond?

"Final clearance confirmed," the pilot said. "*Kavkazki Pass* away here. Good-greeting, Jeltaria, and we look forward to seeing you again, some time."

No shielding in known Space would damper the roar of five tanks lifting something as large as a Khabardi freighter from the ground. There would be no overhearing conversation for several minutes, so Robert closed his eyes and took a deep breath and tried not to worry about the fact that they were leaving the officer all alone, by himself, and only Chief Stildyne to keep after him for ever after.

When it got quiet, he knew that the tanks had detached, which meant they'd cleared atmosphere. They were outbound. No need to be strapped into shell any more.

The woman came down the corridor from the wheelhouse, talking as she went. "We'll leave Kaz and your man in the wheelhouse for now. Come along, I'll show you what I can about where we're going and what we expect to find there. Follow me. Common room is just this way, a bit cramped right now but we needed all the space we could get for cargo."

That made sense. Robert unstrapped, and waited for the end of the line. Pyotr. Godsalt. Hirsel. Garrity across from Robert stepped out but then stopped, looking back toward the wheelhouse with an expression of astonishment on his face.

"You heard the comm officer," Robert heard a familiar voice say. "Get a move on, man."

It was their Chief. Robert pushed away and out of his niche. Stildyne. As big as life and twice as ugly, which meant actually very ugly, since it was Stildyne. "What are you doing here?" Robert asked, feeling delighted but unable to understand why. "Who's minding the officer?"

"Koscuisko can take care of himself," Stildyne growled, but not too sincerely. "Unlike you. Get along, Robert. There's a briefing to be had."

Stildyne. Stildyne had come. Why? Why hadn't he told them? Had he been afraid that they'd decline to take him? Robert supposed they could have. But it was academic. Stildyne was here. Life would be easier, with their Chief to look after them.

Gladdened by the presence of a familiar note in the middle of all of this strange new music, Robert went after the others into the common room and squeezed himself between crates and boxes, and listened to what the comm officer could tell them about what the future might hold for them when they reached Gonebeyond.

A FAMILIAR SOUND in the outer room woke Andrej, and he took a moment—not moving—to collect his wits. Where was he, and what was he doing here? Unfamiliar bed, but familiar enough: a service house, the bedding a careful balance between luxury and practical attention to the commonsense requirements to clean and freshen on a daily basis. Or even more frequently. Someone in bed with him, what was that about? Oh. Yes. Her. She wasn't a house professional, or she wouldn't have taken the liberty of falling asleep in a patron's bed, not unless she'd been invited—or instructed—to do so.

Not a house professional. She'd come with a medical order, that was right. And he, he had agreed to see what he could do; and there they were. If he meant to take a status check, he had better move quickly. Security were in the outer room, come to collect him for one reason or another or perhaps simply to see to his fast-meal—an intimacy Stildyne permitted himself to which Andrej took no exception. The woman lay on her side with her back to him, one arm tucked beneath her head. Turning onto his side, Andrej lifted the bedclothes away from her body.

There were ways around the Protocols. As soon as there had been Protocols established, people had found ways around them; and there were strict limits on the degree of damage that a judicial officer was authorized to inflict directly or by proxy without evidence or confession. Wherever there were limits, there were cheats, ways to hurt a man without harming him, without leaving evidence of abuse outside of Protocols. She was substantially unbruised, the skin unbroken. Andrej knew that he had been fierce with her, and could see very little evidence.

She'd been fierce with him as well, in her own way. Hearing Security behind him, Andrej covered her over again, drawing the covers well up behind her head on the pillow. Stildyne might recognize her if she stirred, and that would be awkward.

It was awkward enough as it was. He was going home, but she was a member of the same command as he. Jennet ap Rhiannon did not care for the fact that he was a member of her command at all, and he certainly would not be, if the captain ever found out that he had spent the evening in a service house engaged in intimacies conventional and unconventional with one of Two's intelligence analysts.

Stildyne could step lightly when he wanted to, something that Andrej had always admired—it was no small thing to move so large a muscle mass so quietly—but something wasn't right.

He turned his head to look back over his shoulder toward the door. For a moment, he relaxed, scolding himself. *There, you see, Andrej? Nothing out of the ordinary. Your chief of Security. Yes. That's all.*

Then he froze in the bed and stared in horror, because it was a chief of Security, but it was the wrong chief of Security, even if she was carrying a curt-robe in a completely harmless manner.

"Sorry to wake you, sir," she said. "Captain Irshah Parmin particularly requests the favor of an interview. If his Excellency would care to step into the next room to get dressed, please."

He held out his hand for the robe, wondering if he was dreaming. Calleigh Samons. He hadn't seen Calleigh Samons for how long? Not as though he didn't think about her, from time to time, because she was unquestionably one of the most desirable women he had ever met in his life, as well as being a thoroughly professional chief of Security.

In fact his fish, his masculine nature, portions of his anatomy better left unacknowledged in polite company, were greeting this sudden apparition with unseemly interest, even though they had been thoroughly exercised very recently. "What is the meaning of this intrusion?" he asked, because it was expected of him. She couldn't possibly imagine that she could simply amble into his bedroom and demand that he get dressed without some protest on his part.

"Outside, if you please, sir," she repeated firmly if still quietly. "We'd just as soon not create an alarm. No sense in embarrassing your gentlemen, your Excellency. This way."

His gentlemen. His Security. His bond-involuntaries assigned, whom she would presume to be sleeping off an evening of their own two levels down. If there were an alarm, they would be expected to respond to it. What time was it? Had they left? Were they still here? Because if they were still here, he couldn't let an alarm go off. It would destroy any chance of moving them quietly and unobtrusively to the launch field. Someone would notice if they left suddenly.

And if they had left already, he couldn't afford anybody noticing that, either. The longer nobody noticed that they were gone, the longer they had to make for the vector undetected, innocent and uninteresting cargo of an innocent and uninteresting freighter. What was he going to do?

The woman rolled over in the bed, seeking his warmth. Andrej slid out and away from her carefully, doing his best to avoid waking her up. Samons stood to one side, watching the woman carefully. Andrej watched too, belting his robe around his waist, watched as she stretched and settled her head on the pillow and stilled back into a profound sleep again. Her eyes. Andrej was almost certain that she'd opened her eyes, but if she had she hadn't really seen anything; beause she closed them without any sign of alarm or surprise.

Hurrying through into the next room, Andrej waited impatiently for Samons to close the communicating door. If the woman woke up, Samons might take it into her head to borrow them both for an interview with Captain Irshah Parmin; she'd said she didn't want an alarm—she clearly didn't want anybody realizing that she was taking him. He was being kidnapped. If the woman came, too, they would all find out that he'd been in bed with one of Two's people, and the woman would be humiliated, and much more harm than good was sure to come of it.

"Well," he said quietly so that she would know he didn't mean to kick up a fuss. "What have you done with Stildyne? He is not going to be happy, Chief, and I won't stand between the two of you. You will be on your own. I'm not happy either. I hope Captain Irshah Parmin has some very good reasons to share with ap Rhiannon, or there will be some serious irritation at Emandis Station."

He would normally have washed before he dressed, and had his fast-meal as well. He was hungry. He had had an unaccustomed amount of exercise last night. Chief Samons might well remember his personal habits from the years that they had spent together on *Scylla*. If she did, he could hope for fast-meal at some point, when she could manage it, but that point was clearly not now.

He turned his back on her and started to dress. She'd seen him stitchless often enough before, but a man had his pride. Besides, it had also been several years—she might imagine him to be more impressive in his person than he actually was, and if so he had no intention of disabusing her of any flattering notions that she might be entertaining.

"All quiet in the service house," she said. "Special escort, we told the house security. They know *Scylla's* ship-mark when they see it. I need us to be out of here before anybody comes knocking on your door with your morning rhyti, your Excellency. Best all around."

Andrej accepted the trousers that she held out for him, stepping into the one leg then the other, fastening his waistband over his under-blouse. "I've never heard of officers kidnapping each others' chief medical officers," he said, partially to keep the conversation going and partially because he couldn't quite believe what seemed to be happening. "Isn't this an act of piracy? I'm sure Irshah Parmin outranks ap Rhiannon within Fleet, but she is the captain of the *Ragnarok*, and I am medical resources assigned. He has no right."

"Can't be helped, sir." Andrej thought he remembered that tone in Samons' voice, thought he recognized it. "Command direction received. You know the captain's always been a little irrational on the subject of Koscuiskos. I'm sorry."

She handed him his boots, and he sat down. Yes. Captain Irshah Parmin had always been a little irrational on the subject of young Andrej Koscuisko, no longer quite as young as he used to be. Andrej had had good reason to be grateful for it, too. He'd known at the time that Irshah Parmin was being very patient with him. He hadn't understood until later, until he'd had to deal with Captain Lowden, how horrible his life and that of his bond-involuntaries assigned could have been had Irshah Parmin not made generous allowances for foolish young officers with no real understanding of their position in Fleet. Very generous allowances. Far more patient than Andrej himself would probably have been, had the roles been reversed.

That didn't make it all right for Irshah Parmin to send Security into Andrej's bedroom to take him off in the middle of the night and leave his own Security behind.

But in light of the fact that Andrej could not afford any disturbances that might interfere with the stealthy departure of his gentlemen or expose that departure prematurely, it couldn't hurt to concentrate on reserving judgment until he'd heard what Irshah Parmin had to say.

She shook out his duty blouse for him, very formally indeed. Andrej settled the shoulders and shot his cuffs and made up his mind to make the best of things, at least for now.

"Somebody's going to have to write a note to Stildyne for me," he said, and nodded to signify that he was ready to go. "Because I'm not trying to explain this to him on my own. I give you fair warning."

"First Officer will apologize in person," she promised with a bow. "If the captain won't, that is. Thank you, your Excellency, this way, and it is good to see you again."

Well, yes, it was.

There were people waiting in the corridor outside—nobody Andrej recognized—and all wearing *Scylla's* ship-mark. No bond-involuntaries. He wondered if there were people that he knew, still on board *Scylla*.

"So tell me, who is running the Infirmary these days?" he asked, and went off down the hall under Security escort, a detained man, to go and have a word with Irshah Parmin.

CHAPTER FOURTEEN
REUNIONS

KOSCUISKO WAS WHAT seemed to Calleigh to be uncharacteristically quiet on the trip to the launch field, and on the courier. He sat in the passenger compartment, and then in the courier, with his face turned to the window. Not speaking. He'd asked a few general questions at the start—information gathering, and well done at that—but then he had lapsed into silence. She couldn't say exactly what she had expected from him but it wasn't stillness. She remembered him as having been a man moderately restless in spirit, always curious. Always inquiring.

It had been years since she had seen him last, though. He'd lost weight, or gained weight, or maybe his weight had shifted. He looked a deal older than she remembered him, but she remembered him as having looked very young, and he still didn't look quite his age in Standard years. Dolgorukij were a long-lived subspecies of hominid. They took that much longer to start to look mature in years. How old was he? Closing on forty, she thought, but she couldn't remember.

When the courier came to rest in the maintenance atmosphere of *Scylla*, Koscuisko rose to his feet and left the passenger cabin as though he were returning to his duty post, and not come against his will under Security escort. Why not? Calleigh thought. There was only one of him. It wasn't as if he could make an escape of whatever sort. Nodding to her mildly confused Security, Calleigh formed them up, and followed Koscuisko out onto the docks of the maintenance atmosphere.

Koscuisko paused for a moment on the loading apron, looking out past the cargo-handling drones to Emandis Station and Emandis itself beyond. Was he looking for the *Ragnarok*, Calleigh wondered? *Ragnarok* was there, but had taken the central loading slips by right of first arrival. *Scylla* made do with one of Emandis Station's auxiliary docks, and Irshah Parmin was just as happy about that as he was about everything else that had to do with the *Ragnarok*. If Koscuisko was wondering about setting off a distance flare, an appeal to his people, he gave no sign of it.

Turning, he started into the maintenance corridor, heading toward the captain's office. There were people in the halls who knew who he was, but Koscuisko gave no sign of noticing that either. Calleigh knew that the news would be all over the ship within moments.

That was all right. They knew Koscuisko was here, but they didn't know why, nor did they realize that he was here under armed escort—though some of the crew might put things together. Koscuisko was not accompanied by his own Security escort but by one of *Scylla's*, properly speaking Doctor Weasel-Boy's. There were words there for those with the learning to read the language.

Koscuisko knew where he was going, and he made no attempt to divert in his progress toward his goal. When they reached the captain's office, though, he didn't signal; he went straight through, and if Calleigh hadn't given a quick warning from her point behind the detachment, Koscuisko might have succeeded in surprising Irshah Parmin.

As it was, the captain looked startled when Calleigh saw him, following close on Koscuisko's heels. Koscuisko stopped a precise distance from the captain's desk and saluted, bowing, before he assumed a modified position of attention-wait and looked at the captain in silence. That was rude. Koscuisko should say something, but kidnapping him had been even more rude, and Irshah Parmin didn't seem much taken aback. The captain had been accustomed to Koscuisko being rude—just not on purpose. By accident, which was almost excusable, most of the time.

"Good-greeting," the captain said, standing up. "Thank you for coming. Apologies for the less than customary method of extending the invitation, Doctor, you know the First Officer I think? You won't know Doctor Lazarbee, our chief medical officer."

Koscuisko nodded to First Officer, but only just glanced at Doctor Weasel-Boy—didn't even nod. Calleigh suppressed a wince. Doctor Weasel-Boy was a man to sniff out a slight and cherish it; they were off to a good start, they were.

"First Officer," Koscuisko said. "Captain. If there is any precedent for making off with another command's resources by force of arms, I have never heard of it, your Excellency. You must have very good reason for spitting in my captain's face."

His captain? Ap Rhiannon? Irshah Parmin frowned. Calleigh could feel herself flushing with annoyance. "His" captain, indeed. But it wasn't her argument. She'd been sent to bring Koscuisko; she had brought him. She was not here to argue with him on the relative merits of the two ship's captains.

"Turnabout's fair play." The captain sat down slowly. "Care to be seated, Doctor? I'm worried about you. Ap Rhiannon's just the cosmetic code. But it's bad enough even so, I'd have thought you'd be anxious to get away."

Koscuisko sat, but he didn't relax. "I was anxious enough to get back to my ship. Why would I want to get away? I mean no disrespect, your Excellency, but you have your own chief medical officer—Doctor Lazarbee?—and I am posted to the *Ragnarok*."

The captain walked his fingers along the edge of his desk, contemplatively, before he answered. "Yes, well, in point of fact, the *Ragnarok*'s annoyed me. Why can't I get my stores loads, I ask, and they tell me it's because the *Ragnarok* has a prior claim in. When I ask why Emandis Station is willing to release not only primes but seconds and terces to the *Ragnarok,* they give me some inarticulate nonsense with the word 'Koscuisko' in it."

A muscle jumped, suddenly, in the side of Koscuisko's face, near the hinge of his jaw. A grin. "And you thought if you had the right stores-chop you could get some supplies transferred? Redirected? I don't see it happening, your Excellency."

Captain Irshah Parmin spread out the fingers of his hand in an expansive gesture. "We won't know until we try it, will we? I'm not asking for much. We'll send you back to the *Ragnarok* as soon as they notice you've gone missing. In return for a satisfactory conclusion to a dialog, of course."

He should just come out and say that he was worried about Koscuisko and wanted to make sure that Koscuisko had a chance to brief with *Scylla's* Intelligence officer. He should just say that. But Koscuisko had set him off balance, Calleigh supposed, and Koscuisko had always been exceptionally good at annoying the captain. Or maybe he just didn't want to talk in front of Weasel-Boy.

"You probably shouldn't expect any immediate reaction." Koscuisko gave no sign of softening toward the captain's proposal, either explicit or implicit. Koscuisko had to know that Irshah Parmin hadn't borrowed him as a marker in a stores dispute. Irshah Parmin had just so much as said so after all. "I was granted several days' down-leave, and expected to sequester myself with Joslire's family. You remember Joslire. He has a brother that I am anxious to meet."

"They'll have noticed you're missing by the time they want to leave, surely." Yes, Irshah Parmin remembered Joslire. He didn't react to Koscuisko's remarks, however, possibly because there was no answer for Koscuisko's not-very-indirect rebuke. "Tell you what, go and visit around for a bit, catch up on old acquaintances. Chief Samons will escort you."

As opposed to Doctor Weasel-Boy, that was to say. As *Scylla's* posted chief medical officer, Weasel-Boy might have reasonably expected to have that responsibility, and Koscuisko was a celebrity of sorts in Fleet. Maybe that was why Irshah Parmin wanted Weasel-Boy kept out of Koscuisko's way. Or maybe it was just that, without a Security escort, there was nothing standing in Koscuisko's way should he decide to go down to the maintenance atmosphere, commandeer a crew, and leave—or at least attempt to send a distress call.

"You understand that I object to having been brought here, and to being kept here," Koscuisko said. "I put you on notice that the captain may not be as anxious for an exchange of hostages as you flatteringly suggest. And that you are keeping me from making the acquaintance of an Emandisan family to which I apparently belong, or who possibly belong to me, by virtue of Joslire's knives. There is, apart from all that, no arguing with you, your Excellency, and I should like my fast-meal, if I may."

"Oh, feed the man his breakfast," Doctor Weasel-Boy said suddenly. "Priorities, after all. I'll hunt up Conner to take you through my infirmary, Koscuisko. Conner remembers you—can hardly stop talking about you, in fact. Captain, if I may be excused."

Captain Irshah Parmin had turned his head to stare at Doctor Weasel-Boy with an expression of mild incredulity that was almost exactly the same with which Koscuisko was regarding his counterpart. Calleigh wanted to laugh, it was so perfect; but she was technically responsible to First Officer for Weasel-Boy, and managed to contain herself. Weasel-Boy was easy to alienate, and she already did so on a regular basis. It was best to avoid exacerbating the problem, if possible.

Irshah Parmin turned back to Koscuisko. "By all means, Doctor," the captain said. "I'll send First Officer to you in officer's mess."

Where First Officer could have a heart-to-heart talk with Koscuisko without Doctor Weasel-Boy in attendance. First Officer didn't care for Weasel-Boy. Nobody did. First Officer wouldn't want to share sensitive intelligence with Koscuisko in Weasel-Boy's company, in order to avoid raising any questions that she had no intention of answering about sources of information.

"Thank you, your Excellency," Koscuisko said, apparently reconciled to a few hours spent on *Scylla* now that he had registered his protest. It would be only a few hours, too, Calleigh was sure of it. Koscuisko's Security would wake up, his Chief of Security would form them up to go and fetch their officer, and then they'd find out that Koscuisko wasn't there. They wouldn't be keeping him from Joslire's family for more than the forepart of the day.

Maybe she could go with Koscuisko when they returned him to Emandis, and meet those people herself. There were Security still on board who had known Joslire Curran, and one who had been there the night that Koscuisko had killed him.

"What's that about your new family, sir?" she asked as she left the captain's office with Koscuisko and his escort. "And there's a brother?"

Koscuisko was annoyed, but his temper would improve once he'd been fed. It almost always had. "With wife and child," Koscuisko confirmed, heading down the hall toward the officer's mess. "Grandmother, elderly aunt, two cousins, older sister. Not much of a family resemblance—they all look Emandisan to me—but I've seen Joslire's smile and I never thought to see it again. There's an orchard."

If Koscuisko said so. She wasn't sure she'd ever seen a bond-involuntary grin; certainly never, outside Koscuisko's immediate company. She'd worried about whether Koscuisko's influence on bond-involuntaries would trip them up in the service of less sympathetic officers, but Koscuisko's successor Doctor Aldrai had been genially willing to ignore Security entirely, and First Officer was having none of Weasel-Boy's periodic complaints of insolence or insubordination—perhaps because Weasel-Boy complained as much or more frequently about other officers as about bond-involuntary Security assigned.

"I should wait to ask you for the details, sir." She needed to go round up some Security. Code was on sleep-shift, but Code wouldn't mind; Code might even be on his way to the officer's mess right now. Someone would have told him. "If you'll give me your parole of honor, I'll go speak to the First Officer. While you're eating."

"Go and speak away, Chief," Koscuisko said. "I'm not going anywhere until I've had my rhyti. I hope there's decent rhyti. I remember what we used to have to put up with."

She was not in a position to judge. She didn't drink the stuff. She left Koscuisko to his fast-meal and went down to Security to collect the people who had worked with Koscuisko when he'd been here, and who might want to hear about Joslire Curran's family.

IT WAS UNQUESTIONABLY the case that one officer's mess was very like another, yet Andrej found himself almost uncomfortably aware that he was not on the *Ragnarok* as he ate his fast-meal. The rhyti was all wrong. He didn't know the Security. First Officer Linelly he remembered, of course; at the bottom of it all—he decided—what he liked least was the fact that they remembered him.

They seemed to have been fond of him, in some sense, and that was better than to be held in contempt, as the current chief medical officer apparently was. He hadn't heard anything one way or another about Doctor Lazarbee, not even to know what his clinical concentration was. There was no use pretending that Doctor Lazarbee hadn't heard of him, and that was the reason that being remembered was a problem.

When he had been among the crew of the Jurisdiction Fleet Ship *Scylla*, there had been hope for him. He had not yet fallen into the depths at which Captain Lowden treated with Ship's Inquisitors. He had been a sinner, but not damned, and it was doubly painful to think back on his innocent self-assurance in those days, knowing what he knew now about his addiction.

If he'd had nothing but captains like Irshah Parmin, he might have found redemption, given time. He might have ended his service and gone home without a thirst so savage in his heart that he did not dare to name it. If only, if only, and yet he had only himself to blame. Hadn't Irshah Parmin tried to teach him, before it was too late?

Hadn't the captain greeted him with genuine sorrow on his return to *Scylla* from Rudistal, to tell him that he was to be transferred and that no bond-involuntaries assigned were to be allowed to follow him—with the single exception of Robert St. Clare, whom Irshah Parmin was not permitted to keep?

And yet he could not have kept silent and held his peace about the Domitt Prison. Even if he had known what ruin would come into his life, what atrocities he was bound to commit, what was to become of him, once he had looked upon the pitiful fuel to the furnace fires of the Domitt Prison he could not have said nothing, not without embracing a damnation even more detestable than that to which he was fairly condemned.

"Rumor has it that there was a warrant out," First Officer was saying. She'd cleared the room. It was just three of them: First Officer, the Intelligence officer—Bassin Emer—and Andrej Koscuisko. Fast-meal, but neither of them were eating. "And an assassination attempt, first at Burkhayden. Then on home ground. And definite undercurrents of unhappiness in some senior Fleet quarters. He's worried about you."

Irshah Parmin was a good captain. Perhaps that meant he took occasional liberties with ethical behavior—and doubtless he wouldn't mind if it turned out that ap Rhiannon wanted Andrej so much that she'd trade stores or munitions to have him back—and argue the legal points later. That hadn't been why Irshah Parmin had sent Samons to kidnap him. Andrej was trying to respect the captain's charitable impulse, but it was hard to feel reasonable about anything with the freighter carrying his Bonds still short of the exit vector, by his reckoning.

"There was no assassination attempt at Burkhayden." He was in a position to know, though he wasn't going to tell. Robert had murdered the man who had brutalized his sister. He himself, Andrej Koscuisko, had killed Captain Lowden, and he should have done it very much sooner than he had, too. There had been a warrant, but he couldn't verify the existence of a warrant without leading intelligent people to wonder about the assassination of Griers Verigson Lowden, officially on record as a Free Government terrorist attack.

How many other Free Government terrorist crimes had actually been Bench-sanctioned actions? There was a Free Government, he knew that, but nothing he had ever heard or seen in his personal experiences as an Inquisitor would support its existence as anything more than a small, stubborn, desperate, only very loosely organized resistance movement.

If there was a grand plan and a command structure and an authority hierarchy, Andrej had never heard of any such thing first-hand from persons in a position to know. Maybe that was what was really dangerous about the Free Government, though. If it didn't represent genuine population unrest, it wouldn't keep on cropping up spontaneously.

First Officer was watching him, waiting. Andrej frowned at himself, and refocused. "Assassination attempt on home ground, yes, but I have good reason to believe it was an isolated act. A deranged Clerk of Court." There almost had to be conspiracy behind the forgery of the record, but he wasn't going to get into that. He certainly wasn't going in any direction that might lead an intelligent person like First Officer to conclude that the evidence of that conspiracy, the forged record, no longer existed. Had been destroyed under circumstances that were ambiguous, at best.

"And for the rest, the captain has never been very happy with me, either. So there are no new issues there." His principle antagonist, First Secretary Verlaine, had declared truce, and sent him documents for relief of Writ. Verlaine was dead, and Andrej had told Specialist Ivers to hold the documentation until the *Ragnarok's* appeal had been resolved, so there were complications—but no surprises. "There, we are done. May I go back to Jeltaria, now?"

He was tempted to add that his Security would be wondering where he'd gone, but he didn't want to raise the issue of Security in anybody's mind. The longer he could avoid people starting to wonder where his Security had gone the better, and for that he had to do what he could to prevent people from noticing that they were missing. They weren't missing. He knew exactly where they were, if only in a general sense. That was between him, and Security, and Chief Stildyne, though—and there was a thought: Stildyne would cover for Security. He knew that Andrej wanted those troops away.

How Stildyne felt about his plan was something that Andrej had yet to discuss with him. He'd wanted to talk to Stildyne much earlier, and been prevented. He didn't think he was looking forward to the interview, but it was unquestionably owed. How could he, of all men, have exiled his own people to Gonebeyond, sent bond-involuntaries out on their own to make a new life in an environment about which they knew next to nothing?

After years of impressing on Stildyne how seriously Andrej took protecting his people, how could he send them away unprotected, abandoned them all with a wave of his hand and an it's-been-good-to-know-you? Stildyne would never accept such be-havior without remark, rebuke, objection.

"Not my call, Andrej," First Officer said cheerfully. "I can't swear to Captain that you show evidence of understanding the gravity of the situation, and the peril in which you appear to be. Reflects badly on a man to have his subordinate officers murdered, he feels—even if they're not his subordinate officers any more. You can't possibly expect him to believe ap Rhiannon is in a position to protect you."

No, indeed, especially given the fact that ap Rhiannon didn't like him. Or didn't trust him. Or something. Andrej poured himself an-other flask of rhyti, since there were no Security here to do it for him. "Cold as it may sound, Salli, it is no longer Captain Irshah Parmin's business. I'm very annoyed. I have people to see, down-planet."

He could almost hear Stildyne's voice, mocking and scornful. *Yes, sir, of course, sir, spend six years—twelve years—talking about how people ought to treat troops, and then decide that it's for other people*. Right. Almost, but not quite. There was something about the imagined sound of Stildyne's voice that puzzled him. He was missing something.

"I'll tell him. But he's pretty annoyed himself, I don't mind tell-ing you. The depot's not stripped bare, exactly, but all of the sexiest goodies are gone, and you know how Irshah Parmin feels about Home Defense Fleets to begin with."

Yes, he knew how Fleet felt about HDFs. They were useful political tools, sops to proud world-families or systems; they were cost-effective reserve resources that Fleet could, and did, deploy when it didn't want to spend its own money. They were a means to an end, a way to encourage continued investment in research and development that Fleet could direct and profit from, again without having to pay for it. But to the extent that they represented an excep-tion to Fleet's otherwise absolute monopoly on the lawful use of force of arms, Fleet distrusted them all, in principle, as opponents just waiting for a good excuse to cause trouble.

And if you expect me to accept this without an argument after all the years I've spent trying to figure out what you wanted from me, you've got an over-rated reputation for psychological acuity. With respect, your Excellency.

What was it about the unusual tone of Stildyne's imaginary voice in his head? It sounded like Stildyne—half-disgusted, laying down the law—but Stildyne indistinct around the edges. Fuzzy. Distant. Halfway to the exit vector.

Andrej jumped to his feet as though the seat of his chair had suddenly bitten him in a very delicate place. Distant. Halfway to the exit vector. Stildyne had gone, he had exiled himself to Gonebeyond to take care of those troops—to stand between them and their conditioning, to ease them back into the life of free men. Stildyne. Gone.

Why hadn't he guessed it? Why hadn't he realized that once Stildyne knew, Stildyne would make exactly that decision?

Was it because he had gotten so used to Stildyne that he hadn't envisioned a life without him? Or was it—to his shame—that after all that Stildyne had done to be what Andrej wanted, Andrej still expected him to fall short of expectation?

"Something the matter?" First Officer asked carefully, dropping a napkin onto the table to soak up the rhyti Andrej had spilled when he'd stood up so suddenly.

"Nothing new." It was true. He should have at least wondered, he should have tried harder to talk to Stildyne about it, and now Stildyne was gone and Andrej was ashamed.

There had to be a dancing-master. Reborn men were never simply abandoned to their freedom without the careful assistance of people who could teach them to be free again, the same people who had taught them to be slaves in the first place. What had he been thinking? "I am as immense an ass as I have ever been, Salli, and the captain is quite right to be annoyed with me. I should be locked up for my own safety, in the Saint Andrej Thick-Headed Refuge for the Hopelessly Oblivious."

He sat down again, slowly. Gone, without a word. Why should there have been one? Stildyne would assume that Andrej would speak if he had something to say. Andrej had not spoken. But Stildyne had gone anyway, true to the calling he had embraced. Andrej had been in enough trouble already for accepting Stildyne's service without acknowledging its motivation or ultimate source. Now he was in so much more trouble with Cousin Stanoczk, just because he disapproved in principle of men who enjoyed other men, when the man that they sought to enjoy was him

Stildyne had never made anything like an improper advance, not after the first one. All of these years, Andrej had blamed Brachi Stildyne for being what he was; but Stildyne was an honest man who had changed and grown and sacrificed with no hope of reward—or even recognition—and now there was this.

"If you say so, of course." First Officer sounded a little bit dubious, but not disposed to pry. "Finished with your meal? There are people out there who are eager to see you, Andrej. Doctor Lazarbee has made himself unpopular. I'll just turn you over to Samons for the time being."

First Officer pushed herself away from table and stood. Andrej folded his napkin and matched the gesture, gazing at the debris on his plate with a bowed head. "I'm sure Captain has only my best interest at heart," Andrej said. "A man doesn't care to be handled quite so casually. But I was unquestionably among the less responsive of his junior officers, and he was far more charitable to me than I could have deserved. I'm not minding seeing you again, Salli."

"Nor I you," First Officer said, and grinned; held out her hand with a sudden spontaneous gesture, and clasped his very warmly. "Come around after third-shift and you'll hear more than you probably need to know about Lazarbee. If Captain made allowances for you, you spoiled this ship for all but the very highest standard of medical administration ever after, and Weasel-Boy is not it."

That was kind of her. There was nothing he could do at this moment to repair the injustice he had done to Brachi Stildyne except to dread what his cousin Stanoczk would have to say to him about it. The best he could do now was to keep people busy, keep them from wondering why there was no alarm from Emandis Station about officers gone missing from service houses.

The longer he could hold off the inevitable questions, the better chance they had of successfully acquiring the dar-Nevan vector for Gonebeyond space. And no matter how careful the planning, there was always the possibility of an error—the chance of a mistake—

No, he wouldn't give it life by thinking about it. Andrej waved to the Security who stood outside the now-open door to the officer's mess, calling them in. "Tell me who is wearing green-sleeves on board of *Scylla* these days," he suggested, "and all of the gossip about Chief Samons. Before she gets back."

Where Calleigh Samons was concerned, he needed all the help that he could get to fortify himself against her elegant lithe body and her beautiful eyes, and the fact that she could probably break him into two pieces as easily as though he had not been Dolgorukij at all.

IN KOSCUISKO'S ABSENCE, Jennet ap Rhiannon had had the Chief of Psychiatric in, to represent Medical at her staff meeting. It was not a regularly scheduled staff meeting; ap Rhiannon was in undress uniform, and had lowered the horizon in the flask of strong red wine that she was drinking by an appreciable margin within the past hour. Rukota had to grant that she showed no signs whatever of being under the influence.

Different categories of hominid reacted differently to given intoxicants. If his suspicions about her genetic background were correct, she should be as vulnerable to that wine as anybody. Perhaps that was why she drank so much of it—to keep up an habituated, if relative, immunity.

"She slept how long?" ap Rhiannon asked Doctor Farilk, with a tone of slightly outraged incredulity in her voice. "So she hadn't been to a service house for a while. What had she been doing all night to sleep till halfway to sundown? Why didn't they turn her out?"

"Your Excellency," Doctor Farilk said, gently. "With respect."

Yes, the woman had slept that long. She'd had a physically intense experience of whatever sort, perhaps the first opportunity she had had to sample a particular form of recreation that made no sense whatever to Rukota—but neither did the idea that his wife loved him, out of all the men and women that so beautiful and intelligent a woman could have had for the asking; and yet it was true.

They hadn't turned her out of bed because she'd been sleeping in the officer's suite, and the house staff hadn't had any instruction to rouse her. For all that the house staff had known, Koscuisko had intended to come back.

But above all, it was none of the captain's business, and an invasion of privacy to speculate. Ap Rhiannon rubbed her eyes with a weary gesture, and nodded. "Of course, Doctor Farilk. Please excuse my indelicacy."

That wasn't a word Rukota would have expected to hear out of ap Rhiannon. He frowned. What was in that wine? Ap Rhiannon was still talking, though, and sounding enough like ap Rhiannon to allay any fears he might have had about drugs in her liquor.

"So *Scylla* sent troops to take Koscuisko away, and we have a witness who can attest to the ship's-mark, which the night staff also confirm. But she was asleep at the time, and by the time she woke up, it was much later than she had expected. She found no Security from the *Ragnarok* on site. So she came back to report, and *Scylla* is probably wondering why nobody's sent for their chief medical officer back yet."

Just exactly so. The night staff was also in a position to attest to the fact that Koscuisko had ordered transport for his people out to the launch field, after which they'd not been seen again. Nor did Stildyne seem to be on the job, though nobody appeared to have seen him leave. They had left; so much was almost screamingly obvious.

Koscuisko had jacked the bond-involuntaries' governors and sent them away, and they'd either killed Stildyne or taken him with them. Rukota didn't think they would have murdered their Chief, but he had almost as much difficulty imagining them inviting Stildyne to come on a picnic with them to Gonebeyond—which was their only possible destination, under the circumstances.

"If somebody doesn't say something soon, somebody is going to really wonder," First Officer Ralph Mendez observed. Rukota liked Mendez. Mendez was a very comfortable man to be alone with, in the sense that you could be with Mendez and completely alone at the same time. "We've got to make some noise, your Excellency."

"One of the best battle surgeons in the inventory," Karol Vogel added quietly from where he sat at the far end of the table savoring some bean tea. "You'd almost think you didn't want him back. And if a ship doesn't want its battle surgeon, it's because it doesn't think it's going to need one, which means no battle, which means conflict avoidance."

Which all added up to Gonebeyond space all over again, though Vogel wasn't so rude as to come right out and say so. The *Ragnarok* had no intention of being held at Emandis Station, however. Their escape from Taisheki had been narrow enough, and loss of life had been avoided by lucky accident alone. They weren't likely to have any such luck again, and they were still all one Fleet. Any casualties inflicted by one ship upon the other would be casualties inflicted upon itself, in a very real sense.

"Koscuisko knows how I feel about him, Vogel," ap Rhiannon retorted. A lot of people didn't care for Inquisitors as a class, but Rukota didn't think that was ap Rhiannon's problem with the man.

"He hasn't convinced me to trust him differently. He has more to lose than any twenty of the rest of us combined. He's better off well clear of *Ragnarok*, and *Ragnarok* is, consequently, better off well clear of him."

She did have a point. Rukota's very limited experience of Andrej Koscuisko had led him to conclude that Koscuisko was as stubborn as ap Rhiannon, and to suspect that the equivalence was at least partial explanation for ap Rhiannon's distrust; but it was abstractly true that Koscuisko was to be a very important man in Combine affairs, and could buy even the Jurisdiction Fleet Ship *Ragnarok* for a garden-ornament, if he decided that he wanted one.

"There is a ship." It was Two. She'd been very quiet; Rukota had almost forgotten she was there. He was getting used to sitting with giant bats, perhaps. "One that is still several hours from acquiring the exit vector, unlike another ship similar in some ways that has almost reached the vector even now. If the captain determines that the ship is carrying contraband, she could very well go in pursuit of it."

"The *Ragnarok* leaves Emandis Station, *Scylla* will follow after it—" Rukota started to object. Two lifted up the flange of her wing for silence, and Rukota shut up.

"Emandis Station is not pleased to have *Scylla* borrowing other peoples' officers without prior clearance. It seems to communicate a lack of respect, I am told. And also Andrej wears five-knives. Emandis Station will not facilitate *Scylla's* pursuit, from analysis. It is possible that *Scylla's* departure might even be impeded. Shocking."

"So we can get out if we don't mind leaving Koscuisko," the Ship's Engineer said with no little degree of self-satisfaction in his voice. "What's not to like?"

Disgusting. "Well, Koscuisko might have thoughts on the issue," Rukota pointed out. Koscuisko wasn't here. He had nobody to speak for him. It was almost too bad, how willing they seemed to be to leave Koscuisko to his own devices—except, of course, that a man with Koscuisko's money had a much wider range of devices available to him than the Jurisdiction Fleet Ship *Ragnarok*.

"I'd better go down," Vogel said to ap Rhiannon, letting Rukota's protest pass without comment. "It'll be expected. And we really can't have Home Defense Fleets in open conflict with Fleet resources. Jils Ivers is at Brisinje; she and Koscuisko have history together, and I've got to get to Brisinje anyway. Maybe I can call on her for help."

Well, it wasn't anybody's history with Koscuisko that mattered so much as the almost irresistible temptation that something like this would present to the Emandisan fleet to take advantage of the situation to assert some autonomy. That was a problem for Bench Specialists, though. Vogel was right enough about that.

Ap Rhiannon nodded. "Yes, thank you, Bench Specialist. General Rukota will meet you on the docks to see you off." She waited until Vogel had gotten up and made his salute and gone away. Then ap Rhiannon leaned across the table and looked at Two. "That ship?" she asked. Two shook her vulpine velvet-pelted head with sharp decisive clarity.

"Of course not, your Excellency. But so long as we are chasing a ship as if it had bond-involuntaries on it, honest port authorities will be doing their best to clear the vector approach so that a fugitive may be safely fired upon. Distracting authorities from bothering to question any other ships that might be approaching the vector at this moment. We are to abandon Andrej; it seems the least that we can do."

Chase a ship, create a decoy. Leave Emandisan space. Get away. Ap Rhiannon sighed. "I'm not completely happy about that," she said. "He is unquestionably a good surgeon. And he runs an efficient Infirmary. But better him than us."

Well, if that didn't restore his faith in ap Rhiannon's enlightened self-interest. Yes. The ship did profit from Koscuisko's medical skills. She had to cut her losses and run, though, and Rukota couldn't argue too much with that.

"I'll go make sure Vogel gets off," Rukota suggested. "Good-greeting, your Excellency. First Officer. Engineer. Two. Doctor Farilk."

He needed to find out what Farilk liked to drink, Rukota decided, on his way out of the room. He had an idea that Farilk's take on staff meetings might be very different indeed than what Rukota thought was happening in them; and there was a vector transit in their near future, with nothing to do between here and Gonebeyond but gossip about one another.

CALLEIGH SAMONS STOOD at attention-rest behind Andrej Koscuisko in the captain's office, trying hard to calculate how indebted she was to Koscuisko for giving her a spectator's ticket to a show such as she could scarcely have imagined. Three senior officers from the Emandisan Home Defense Fleet. A Bench intelligence specialist. First

Officer, Captain Irshah Parmin, Andrej Ulexeievitch Koscuisko, and even Weasel-Boy was here—though what his excuse might be she couldn't guess, and nobody else had bothered to ask.

"Fleet Captain, with all due respect. Emandis Station and the public mercantile ports of Emandis proper are the lawful responsible of the Emandis Home Defense Fleet. You have breached a public trust by your ill-considered actions. In earlier years it would certainly have been considered a direct insult."

They had been called to the captain's office when the delegation from Emandis Station had docked; Koscuisko had been offered a chair, and had sat down. The Emandisan officers had similarly been offered chairs, and had declined to sit—one among them bowing gravely in Koscuisko's direction as they politely refused to be accommodated. Or accommodating.

Nobody had asked Weasel-Boy to sit, and Calleigh wouldn't have known what to do if anybody had asked her. First Officer had taken her post behind the captain, to his left. First Officer's posture was perfect. Koscuisko's posture was respectful and attentive, but confused—if she still knew how to read Koscuisko.

"Provost Marshal Jenner." Irshah Parmin spread his hands out on his desk in a gesture of solicitation and propitiation, but it was a carefully controlled gesture—one that preserved the dignity of the office. "Surely that's stating things a bit strongly. Even your merchant ships have a right to police up their own crew, though I grant you that we failed to go through proper channels to notify you first."

"He's not your crew. He's the *Ragnarok's* crew. And he's an Emandisan national besides. You sent a team of Security into a public service house, your Excellency, to grab a man out of bed and terrorize an innocent young woman—our apologies, your Excellency, for the reference," the provost marshal said to Koscuisko, as if an aside.

Then he faced back to where the captain sat waiting, clearly aware of the fact that the provost marshal wasn't finished with him yet. "And in front of a Bench Intelligence Specialist, Captain. We consider this a very serious affront. If there was a First Judge presiding you would not be so ready to violate the integrity of the Port Authority, I think."

Strong language. The Bench Specialist referred to—a man of middling height with an iron-gray moustache and a fine physique, his battered old campaign hat tucked into the plaquet of his uniform, which looked so new as to create suspicion in Calleigh's mind that it had been made specially for the occasion—made a little gesture with pursed lips, glancing down and away from the provost marshal, as if finding the odor of the Emandisan's irritation a little high. He hadn't said much beyond the polite exchange of greetings, though he and Koscuisko apparently knew each other.

The captain gathered his hands into a carefully arranged clasp on his desk in front of him, and spoke to his thumbs with equal care. "If there were a First Judge presiding, the Emandis Home Defense Fleet might be a little more cautious in its accusations, provost marshal. Koscuisko is a Bench resource, not an Emandisan national. No disrespect was intended toward the Emandis Home Defense Fleet or the Port Authority or anything to do with Emandis Station. I failed to consider that a simple administrative act might be so interpreted."

He was telling the truth, too, Calleigh knew. First Officer had had reservations from the beginning. First Officer stood motionless and silent now, giving no sign of having any I-told-you-so sorts of thoughts. Calleigh had to admire her professionalism.

"Koscuisko carries five-knives." The Emandisan provost marshal had gone a little pale, in Calleigh's estimation. It was hard for her to tell with Emandisan; they were darker-complected than many hominid subspecies, something like an average between the too-fair Dolgorukij and a Gilzirait as dark as the luminous shadow of an earth across the face of one of its moons.

She'd never learned to really interpret Joslire's expressions, but when he had been dying, his skin had seemed the color of a shark's skin beneath the cold streetlights. "And five-knives are a cultural artifact of signal importance to our community. By virtue of the knives, he is an Emandisan knife-fighter, and the operant term in this instance is 'Emandisan.' Furthermore, he has family in Port Jeltaria who have waited for a long time to talk about his relationship with his teacher."

Would that be Joslire, Calleigh wondered? And the provost marshal wasn't through with the captain yet—"We demand his immediate restoration, your Excellency. You have no right to hold an Emandisan citizen against his will, unless you accuse him of crimes against the Bench."

Koscuisko stirred; he put his head down, covering his face with one hand, elbow leaning upon the arm of his chair. Was that a quiver or a twitch she saw disturb the fabric of the duty-blouse across his broad back? Was he laughing?

Captain Irshah Parmin was not insensible to the humor of the situation, even if the Emandisan themselves betrayed no sign of being anything less than absolutely serious. "Well, he was a Bench resource first," the captain said. "Met his man Joslire in orientation, didn't he? So he belongs to Fleet first, and Emandis second. And he's got people of his own, I understand, but they're not complaining, so forget them."

The captain stood up. "While regretting having given offense, Provost Marshall, I repeat that we view this as a strictly internal Fleet matter. One in which the Emandisan Home Defense Fleet should not interfere or attempt to intervene. Specialist Vogel?"

What the captain meant to ask or expected to hear from the Bench Specialist were fated to remain forever unknown. Before he had a chance to more than say Vogel's name, the talk-alert cleared its attention-tone, and the Intelligence officer's voice resounded throughout the room.

"With respect, your Excellency, and my apologies for the interruption, sir. The *Ragnarok* has cast off its freight-lines and is preparing to leave the docks. Stated destination, the dar-Nevan vector, to leave Emandis system for an undisclosed location."

Koscuisko put his hands to the arms of his chair and half-rose out of his seat, his shoulders practically radiating mistrustful fury— glaring at Specialist Vogel.

Specialist Vogel didn't look surprised. And neither did the Emandisan. That fact did not escape the notice of Captain Irshah Parmin, who raised his eyebrows at Vogel and growled. "What is this, Bench Specialist?"

Vogel raised a loosely clenched fist to his mouth and coughed with polite diffidence. "Oh, yes. That. Some of the *Ragnarok's* troops have gone missing, seven in all. The *Ragnarok's* Intelligence officer has credible evidence that places them en route to the exit vector even now."

Calleigh did a quick mental calculation. It was nearing the end of third-shift in a very eventful day; she had borrowed Koscuisko from the service house this morning. Early this morning. Had they even been at the service house when she had done the thing? She'd been worried about Koscuisko's bond-involuntary security, and they hadn't even been in the service house at all.

Had that been why the house staff hadn't challenged her story more strenuously—because they knew that Koscuisko's Security had already left, or were leaving? Had they assumed that Calleigh's team had been replacements for Koscuisko's security, *Scylla* and *Ragnarok* taking turns to husband a valuable resource?

Koscuisko closed his eyes with a grimace that Calleigh could not interpret, and slumped back in his seat. The Emandisan provost marshal nodded.

"Requested clearance to go in pursuit," the provost marshal said. "Load-out was at a status break, so there wasn't much of an issue with terminating the load without completing the inventory, though it does leave the ship without its third redundancy in dry-goods. We're told that evidence puts the fugitive ship on an approach vector that could place them in Gonebeyond."

"There's a ship, is there?" the captain demanded, harshly. "Wait, let me guess. It's an Emandisan. No. Wait. A Combine ship."

"Neither, by report," Vogel replied, calmly and with measured regret in his voice. "Some fairly general-purpose rental fleet ship aroused suspicions when it logged an unusual angle of approach to the vector, and it doesn't seem to behave quite like a ship of its class with a standard-components propulsion system. I'm sorry, your Excellency, this must come as a blow; I've heard that you were close."

"Robert," Koscuisko said, as if he was agreeing with something that Vogel had suggested. "Robert, and Lek, and Pyotr—who would have thought—"

"Hah," Doctor Lazarbee said. Calleigh only just barely didn't jump; she'd forgotten he was in the room, but here he was, coming forward to stand beside the chair in which Koscuisko sat. "So much for the Koscuisko mystique, eh? Put the rascals on Safe, and they're out of here. Maybe it was a mistake to bring 'em with you, Koscuisko, reminded them of what sorts of things happen to your Security— stabbed, wasn't it?"

Koscuisko stood up from out of his chair altogether too quickly, pivoting on the heel of one foot as he came and pushing with the ball of the other to provide the impetus for his movement.

Calleigh saw the black-clothed arc of Koscuisko's right arm raised with swift but controlled power too late to intervene before his clenched first made contact with the side of Weasel-Boy's jaw and sent him staggering backwards to fall over a chair in the captain's conference area and collapse.

Calleigh was impressed. Koscuisko had always been strongly left-dominant when she'd had the training of him. Stildyne had clearly been working closely with Koscuisko to balance out his available lines of attack.

"You released the *Ragnarok?*" the captain asked the Emandisan provost marshal. From the tone of his voice, he already knew the answer. The provost marshal did not shrug—he was more polite than that—but the shrug was in the air regardless.

"Load-out terminated by request, inventory duly signed over, we have no reason to wish to detain a ship ready to depart," the provost marshal said. In the corner of the room Calleigh could see Doctor Weasel-Boy struggling to rise before subsiding into a helpless crumple once again. Nobody seemed to be paying much attention.

"I have an unresolved issue with the *Ragnarok*," Irshah Parmin pointed out very reasonably and calmly. "The ship is also under appeal of very serious charges, guilty of mutiny in form at best. If I let the *Ragnarok* depart from system with a full munitions load, I fail in my duty to the Fleet and to the Bench. We leave immediately to intercept the *Ragnarok*, First Officer, mark and move."

Koscuisko sat back down, rubbing the knuckles of his right hand absentmindedly, thanking Calleigh with a nod when she handed him a white-square to wipe his hand. His skin was bleeding. Just as well, really—blood cleaned a wound. "She's going without me," Koscuisko said to Vogel. "Damn her. And damn you, too, for letting her, that's my ship, Vogel, those are my people."

"We'll begin the disengage immediately, of course," the provost marshal said to Irshah Parmin. "If I recall correctly, we're in the middle of the potable water cycle, though. We won't be able to shift until we can complete the cycle if we don't want to risk a major spill. Probably half a day, Fleet Captain."

"No, disengage now. If we wait half a day we'll never catch that ship, the *Ragnarok* can probably make the vector in half a day—"

It certainly made things convenient for the *Ragnarok*, Calleigh thought, Koscuisko's Security deciding to make a run for it. Too convenient? No, Koscuisko seemed genuinely rattled by Vogel's revelation. A lucky accident, then, for the *Ragnarok*.

"I'm sorry, Fleet Captain, but we must insist. We don't like to disengage mid-process at all, it's dangerous to try to stop mass load sequences once they've been initiated. Taking any shortcuts cannot be countenanced. No." The provost marshal sounded sincerely regretful, utterly serious. There wasn't the slightest hint of any gleeful cackling in his tone of voice, his expression, his body language.

"We'll start to cut *Scylla* loose as soon as possible, but it will be at least sixteen hours. Perhaps twenty. You are in the middle of your reloads sequence, but we won't have to handle too much by way of munitions recall. That will be a help."

Captain Irshah Parmin stood up and leaned over his desk. "So we don't have a chance. All right. Send some of your corvettes. Stop the *Ragnarok* short of the exit vector. I wouldn't put it past her to take the entire ship into Gonebeyond on pretext—what a nightmare—"

The provost marshal shook his head. "I'm sorry," he said, "but it's an internal Fleet matter. We have no brief to intervene, and may not act on behalf of Fleet without direction from the Ninth Judge at Brisinje."

"Which direction I will forward as soon as possible," Vogel added in a reassuring tone of voice. "I'm borrowing a courier from Emandis Station to take me to Brisinje immediately. I may even beat the *Ragnarok* to the vector. I don't know, though. The Engineer can shift that hull with admirable efficiency. Experimental technology, as I understand. It's got a great future from what I see of it."

"Infamous," the captain said, sitting back down. In the corner, Doctor Weasel-Boy was still waving his arms and legs around in the air, very much like a beetle on its back. "You're all in this together. Vogel. Provost Marshall. Koscuisko, for all I know. Well. If that's the way you're going to play it."

The provost marshal bowed with perfect respect and precision. *Yes. That's exactly the way we're going to play it.* The captain nodded in disgusted resignation and continued.

"Go to Brisinje, Bench Specialist, tell First Secretary Tirom that we'll be held over here for a few days. Never mind sending the Emandisan fleet instructions, though, I don't want to encourage anybody to throw themselves away in Gonebeyond. Koscuisko. You're orphaned, it seems, and there are no Security resources on Emandis

Station rated for specialty escort. After all, we had you picked up and packed off before anybody even noticed."

That was unnecessary, Calleigh thought. But the captain was angry, in a calm understated Irshah Parmin sort of a way. Koscuisko had done it again. "So, with apologies, Provost Marshall, we'll just keep him safe with us until Fleet can decide how to dispose of him. Koscuisko stays an internal Fleet matter. Will that be all?"

"Objecting once again in the strongest possible terms," the provost marshal said to Vogel. "To repeat. Emandisan national, and a uniquely privileged citizen. Fleet has no authority to detain Koscuisko or to place his knives in bondage. We will be unable to permit the *Scylla* to leave Emandis Station so long as Koscuisko remains on board, unless of his own free will."

Worse and worse and worse—almost absurdly so. "Do I get a say in this?" Koscuisko asked the captain.

"No."

"Just asking," Koscuisko replied politely, and seemed to relax in his chair. He at least knew what was going to be happening to him in the near term: nothing.

"Jils Ivers is at Brisinje," Vogel said to Koscuisko. "I'll see if she can be spared to mediate. If you think it might help."

"I will look forward to seeing Dame Ivers again." No, there was still something else going on with Koscuisko, Calleigh decided. What was it? Something to do with Ivers, whoever she was?

"If you're quite finished, Koscuisko, you can clear out. Provost Marshall, go, Specialist Vogel, good-greeting. Intelligence, put the *Ragnarok* on monitor." Just so that the captain could cultivate his aggravation by watching the *Ragnarok* leave, Calleigh supposed. "First Officer. Send someone to pick up Doctor Lazarbee, would you? Very kind."

Fleet Captain Irshah Parmin didn't trouble himself over-much with things he couldn't help. This situation was one of those things.

But he was unquestionably as angry, in his calm resigned fashion, as Calleigh thought she had ever seen him in her life.

CHAPTER FIFTEEN
INTERVENTION

"IF FONTAILLOE CAN'T seat the next First Judge from existing Judicial resources, then Fontailloe can't seat the Second Judge from Chilleau," Jils said firmly. "The issue remains the same."

"There may be no single judge at Fontailloe ready to assume the role of First Judge, true." Jeru Tanifer had grown old in the service of the Bench. What would become of Tanifer under the new administration at Fontailloe was anybody's guess. "All the more reason to provide on-site guidance during a difficult time."

"Fontailloe has to promote a judge either way," Nion said suddenly. Jils was startled to hear it. Nion was observing; she wasn't supposed to be engaging in the debate, in any sense. Turning her head toward the window, Jils examined Nion's face in reflection— belligerent in expression. Tanifer had turned his head as well, but to look at Nion, apparently as surprised as Jils.

"Inappropriate interjection," Tanifer said reprovingly. "Ivers. Your call. The point is one that I might have brought into discussion. I'd rather not have to abstain from making it."

Nion's point was hardly one that hadn't occurred to people before, though. With one last long look at the reflection in the window—Nion, Tanifer, Ivers—Jils turned back to face Tanifer. "The point is in fair play," she agreed. "To return to your point. On-site guidance might be for the long-term good of Fontailloe, using the Second Judge's experience as a resource to develop a newly promoted judge's confidence. Such an accommodation has not been felt necessary in the past, however. And who's to see to Chilleau if we move its Judge?"

Nion had folded her arms and was staring out the window with evident frustration and disgust. The only direction in which there was anything to see from the observation float was toward the station. The station's lights illuminated its walls, and the walkway between the shore and the float was lined with gleams. In every other direction there was nothing but black water, the cave's roof disappearing into the darkness, and the far shores of the lake out of sight.

It was nighttime in Brisinje, Jils realized. No light from the surface shone through those light wells to give any definition to the world outside the float. There was only the dark, and the station.

"A new First Judge from Fontailloe could be perceived as outside the Bench's entrenched interest," Tanifer said thoughtfully. "Promote at Fontailloe, send the new judge to Chilleau while Chilleau's new First Secretary comes up to speed."

"That's the worst of both worlds." It was a prescription for disaster, and Jils meant to write the dosage instructions out carefully. "Meanwhile, you pull the Second Judge out of the Judiciary that she has made her home for an entire career and place her at the mercy of the First Secretary of the old First Judge, a man loyal to the memory of na Roqua den Tensa and accustomed to doing things the previous incumbent's way. There will be inevitable resentments if they feel they are having a Judge imposed on them, especially if she is just going to be there for a few years."

In fact, the only thing that Jils could think of that would be worse than sending the Second Judge to Fontailloe would be not declaring a new First Judge at all. As far as Jils was concerned, Confederacy still took the prize for the single worst solution to the situation they were in.

Tanifer sighed. "I need a personal functions break," he said. "Want anything from the kitchen? Coming with me?"

Jils declined with a polite wave of her hand. She didn't particularly need to stretch her legs just now. She'd save her break—she might want it later on in the session. They were three hours into this session, and it was the second day they'd been arguing. Two, three hours to go, and then they'd pick it up again after a sleep break.

Tanifer rose to his feet and left the room without looking at Nion. Jils stayed sat, running through their progress in her mind. She wasn't sure they were much closer to agreement than they had been days ago.

"Look at that," Nion said suddenly. Jils pulled herself out of her concentration to see what she was talking about. Standing up from her observer's post, Nion took the six steps required to cross the room to stand at the outermost angle of the room, staring into the blackness. What did she see?

Jils didn't feel like standing up. She was tired, and her ribs hurt. Nion was an unpleasant person. Jils didn't like her. Her teeth were all wrong—baby teeth, baby teeth grown to adult size in an adult jaw to grotesque effect. Jils had to shake her head at herself. Nion's teeth were a part of her lineage, not a moral failing of any sort. But Jils still didn't feel like standing up. "Look at what?"

"That," Nion repeated and pointed.

Wearily, Jils rose to her feet—there wasn't any point to being gratuitously rude, after all—and went to stand beside her, a little behind Nion and to the left. It was a habit. It was just a habit. Most hominids were right-dominant. Their instinct was to turn to bring their right hands into play against an enemy standing to their left. It didn't work with Bench Specialists, or with anybody else who had trained much in hand-to-hand; but it was still a default.

Facing away from the station into the darkness, all Jils could see was the interior of the room, mirrored in the glass. "I'm not getting you. I don't see anything except for our reflections."

"While I see a traitor to the Bench." Nion took a step to the right, turning so that she and Jils faced each other. She had a hand-harpoon, a light little crossbow handarm-sized that could be folded flat and carried almost anywhere concealed in a sleeve or a boot. "And the person who will restore the honor of the service. You killed First Secretary Sindha Verlaine, Ivers. Die for it."

Nion fired. Jils feinted right—if Nion was right-handed, it would be her instinct to follow an attempted escape from right to left in her own frame of reference—and dropped to the ground with a push to the left, trying to move as much of her body out of the path of the harpoon as possible. Pocket-harpoons didn't have much range, by and large, and made up for the lack by carrying poison in the cutting edge of the barbel-headed point. Nion didn't have to deliver a traumatic wound to kill her, so Nion would—had—aimed for the body.

It was a very slim chance, but it was the only one Jils had. There was only one round to a pocket-harpoon. It had no target tracking system; part of the reason that the weapon could be successfully concealed was its lack of an intelligence of its own. If she could confuse Nion's aim enough, and move fast enough, she might escape a fatal cut. She reached out for Nion as she dropped, hoping to set Nion off balance; she got her ankle, pulled it sharply, and Nion lost her footing and fell.

Had she been hit? Jils couldn't tell. She didn't have time to check, either. Nion would have used a fast-acting poison, one without a readily available antidote. Nion's best hope of having her act accepted as a killing for cause lay in being sure that the "killing" part of it was already accomplished before the question came up. Once Jils was dead, the precise reason why she had been killed receded somewhat in importance. Jils knew how that worked.

She didn't feel a cut; the sharp pain in her scraped ribs when she hit the ground distracted her. If she hadn't been cut Nion would, necessarily, try to cut her again. From the moment Nion had drawn the weapon, it had been Nion against Ivers to the death. If Jils was going to die at the hands of someone with such unnatural teeth, she was going to do her damnedest to take Nion down with her. Self-respect demanded nothing less.

Nion fell, but before she hit the ground Jils rolled away, curling her body into the space in which Nion had been standing. The harpoon lay on the ground behind Jils. Maybe it had sliced her as it passed but, if it hadn't, she wasn't about ready to lie still and wait for Nion to pick it up.

Nion had scrambled to her hands and knees, reaching for the harpoon. Jils kicked once to send it clattering away from them, and then again to connect with Nion's throat. Nion wasn't paying attention. She wanted the harpoon. Jils didn't have one.

She had a fraction of one second to think about her alternatives while Nion lay gasping for breath on the floor with her hand to her throat. Jils wasn't armed because they were all to have left their weapons on the surface. That was to her advantage. Nion was distracted by the loss of her harpoon.

Jils started to rise to grab a chair and see if she could break a tube out of the frame to serve as a bludgeon; started, but her ribs had other ideas and sent her back down to the floor with a gasp of surprised pain that was only intensified when Nion—having struggled to her feet, now, in the time that Jils had let escape her, handicapped by the pain from recently scored bone—kicked her in the ribs where the cut had been. Then she stumbled across the room; for her harpoon, Jils supposed.

She couldn't breathe, and her ribs hurt like little she could call to her mind for comparison. It didn't matter. If she didn't do something, she was much worse off than hurt—she was dead. She caught at the leg of the chair by the table, the one she'd been sitting in, and managed to push it into Nion's pathway as the woman turned on her with harpoon in hand like a knife.

It would work very well for a knife. All Nion had to do was to cut her, but Nion fell over the chair that Jils sent across her path of advance and crashed to the ground. Nion did not loose her hold on the harpoon.

Jils couldn't let Nion rise again, not if she was to have a chance, any chance at all. Staggering to her feet, Jils put one foot down on Nion's hand to fix it in its place and dropped down heavily onto one knee, which landed in the middle of Nion's back. She was off balance; Nion almost threw her, fighting, snarling with an inarticulate cry of rage.

Jils smelled blood, and knew it wasn't hers. Nion had been cut by the harpoon, poisoned by her own weapon, but that wouldn't stop her from using the last few moments of her life to take Jils out with her. Jils couldn't not afford to gamble on whether she could get out and defensibly away from Nion before Nion got her. Not in her condition.

Jils took Nion's hand between her two hands, got Nion's jaw cradled into her left palm, and twisted. Something snapped. The body went still.

Now finally Jils could crawl away from Nion, so long as she kept to the other side, away from the hand that held the harpoon. Nion was not dead yet, though she would be losing consciousness quickly, but she was no longer capable of coordinated movement or directed action. Jils had broken Nion's neck. It was over. They didn't have the medical equipment here on station to stabilize so serious a compromise, and the poison on the harpoon would be doing its work as well.

Had Nion killed her? Had she been cut by the harpoon? Was the white-hot aching anguish in her side just the protest of her recently injured body?

Jils sat down at the table, her movements slow and clumsy. She tried to remember the sequence of the attack to give herself a list of things to check, places to look for her death warrant incised upon her skin by the poisoned edge of a hand-harpoon. She couldn't remember. Was she dying already?

The door to the room burst open with a sudden furious force, and Padrake came through with fragments of structural beams decorating his shoulders. He had beautifully broad shoulders. Jils had always particularly admired them.

"Harpoons," Jils said to him, hearing the slurring at the edges of her own words. "One down. Don't know about self."

"Can you walk?" Padrake asked, his eyes moving from point to point as he took in the particulars of the scene.

Jils shook her head. "Not sure. But I don't want to fall into the water." There were others coming in behind Padrake. There was Tanifer, for one. Capercoy. Balkney. Rinpen. "Not confident of swimming."

She didn't want to breathe. It hurt to even think about swimming. "Medical," Padrake said firmly. "Sorry about this, Jils, please don't kill me—"

If he'd tried to take her up in to his arms to carry her, she would have. It was too absurd. His innate sense of self-preservation served him well; he shouldered her instead, one arm hooked around a thigh and the other supporting her shoulder. Being carried like a sack of spent grains was marginally better than being carried off in a litter, Jils supposed.

She was very tired.

She concentrated on breathing past the pain in her side and was pleasantly surprised when she did not, in fact, die on her way to the station's tiny medical area.

IN THE PAST seven days, Shona Ise-I'let had worked double shifts for material management and then recreated himself in the warehouse moving stores with cranes and auto movers, sleeping when he had to, and eating whenever he paused to think about it.

The launch fields of Brisinje proper were still fully enveloped in the fires that had started days ago. A huge black stinking stain in the atmosphere had reached the brilliant clear blue skies of Imennou, the night fog leaving sooty streaks on the white walls as it lifted in the morning. The flowers were dying, poisoned.

People who worked outside had to wear respirator masks and wash carefully as soon as they were indoors; people with respiratory illnesses were not to stir out-of-doors at all. The public services in Imennou were stretched to their limit to see to the welfare of such people, young and old alike.

If people couldn't get out-of-doors, they couldn't get to the markets. If people couldn't get to the markets, they began to run short of provisions. Provisions were beginning to thin, though there was still enough food. The local crops had been almost exhausted, but there were still areas the smoke had not reached, and fields that continued to yield. Local transport could still sustain them.

One of the old quarters of Brisinje had been burned as well. There'd been a rumor that some of the saboteurs responsible for the destruction at the launch field had been found, and a mob of frustrated, fearful people had gone in to take the most primitive kind of revenge on guilty and innocent alike. There needed to be an answer. There needed to be a Selection. That a riot could light fires in Brisinje within eyeshot of Bench chambers was a horror too profound to be described.

Shona had worked—with Brisinje out of operation, all of the cargo handling had to be absorbed through smaller facilities well removed from the source of the disaster—but Shona had been counting, as well. Seven days. The *Ragnarok* had almost certainly left Emandis Station. He had no hope.

His family had met Andrej Koscuisko. They had taken him to where Joslire's ashes had been scattered into the sacred earth. Then they had heard nothing more of him. They had been told that Fleet had jurisdiction problems, that the Port Authority had lodged a complaint; but they'd not seen the man himself but the once.

Shona had resigned himself, almost. His crew, the others on board of the courier, had done what they could to help him along, alternating between attempting to distract him and leaving him strictly alone.

He could not honorably put his private thirst—to meet the man to whom his brother had given the most precious thing on all Emandis—above the fact that cargo had to move and trade continue or else the suffering caused by the burning launch fields of Brisinje would extend far beyond the boundaries of Brisinje Jurisdiction. Could not. Wanted passionately to be able to, and worked as hard as he could to manage his piercing sense of deprivation—or at least to dull it, with fatigue.

Six days, and Shona was sitting in the launch controller's function room in front of three schemers, juggling alternate projections to find a launch sequence for ships of varying sizes that would maximize the weight that they could lift in the next thirty-two hours.

Things were relatively quiet; and in every quiet moment, a man consulted the schemers on the question of re-arranging the launch

sequences. There were always adjustments that could be made. There
was always new information coming in. The entry lines were out on
a courier coming in from Emandis Station. Shona heard the ship's
identification without paying attention. He was tired.

Someone came and handed him a launch-ticket, and he sighed
in resignation: *Priority redirect, depart for Brisinje immediately, and depart
from there on arrival of passenger or passengers for Emandis Station as
quickly as possible, all available means to be employed to speed the transit.*

He punched the orders into the nearest schemer, watching the
ship's identification scroll across the reader while he waited for the
schemer to calculate the delay that this would create for everybody
else at Imennou. Yes, that was an elite Emandisan courier. Yes, it
could clear in very little time. Yes, the crew was on site. Yes, he could
bring it in to Brisinje, there were places you could put a courier
down if you really had to—somebody really had to—

Wait. That was his courier. His ship. He was the pilot there, on
the manifest. Courier pilot Shona Ise-I'let, in support of Bench Specialist Vogel. Imennou to Brisinje to Emandis Station, special priority, departure—immediate.

Shona jumped to his feet and turned away from the schemers
toward the room to shout out his discovery—his good fortune.
They were all waiting for him, staring, smiling. He couldn't help
smiling back. Koscuisko would be gone well before he could possibly get to Emandis Station—it was two days' transit—but he was
going home. As much as he appreciated the need for extra help at
Imennou, he wanted to get home. He'd been on one mission or
another for too long. His baby would have forgotten what he
looked like.

"You'd best go get some sleep, pilot," the shift leader said, her
voice full of mischief. "You've got to ferry a Bench Specialist to
Brisinje. We don't dare put you on a priority mission with less than
your full preparation cycle, do we?"

As if he was going to be able to sleep. Yes, he would be able to
sleep, because he had to. No responsible pilot would attempt a difficult entry through Brisinje's local atmosphere with anything less
than all his faculties, let alone a run to Emandis at top speed.

Could it be—might it be possible—was there any chance—

He couldn't afford to think about it. He smiled again—showing
his teeth, almost rude, where Shona came from—and hurried out

of the room, helped on his way by the cheers of the people who had been his companions for these days of desperation struggling to absorb the freight, process the inventories, get the cargoes to where they needed to be.

His family had at least met the man. His wife would tell him all about it. He was going home. He'd missed his chance, the only one he might ever have, but he was going home. Joslire would understand.

His brother knew that necessity brought sacrifice better than any living man of Shona's acquaintance. With that comforting thought, Shona sought his billet and lay down, and chanted himself to sleep with the words in his mind. Home. Home. Home, home, home. He was going home.

"Leaving," Jils said with determination, forming the words with care. The painkillers were making her groggy, and she couldn't afford groggy. They could kill her much more easily that way. How many of the people here wanted her dead? Had Nion been the only one? Were they all just waiting for a chance?

Possibly. But to lapse into paranoia was to surrender her reason. She had to make up her mind to at least act as though she could trust anybody here, anybody at all. Padrake. She could trust Padrake. Surely Padrake knew her as well as anybody yet living—Balkney, she could trust him too, Karol had said so.

"Delleroy's contacted Tirom," Balkney assured her, not preventing her from standing up—exactly—but standing so close to her in the tiny medical area that there was no way she could attempt to straighten from her seated position without becoming much more intimate with Balkney than she had any intention of doing. For one thing, Jils was afraid of his wife. Any sane person would be.

People said that the Hangman was a cold, ruthless assassin, a man who could kill without his pulse changing. She didn't believe it. He'd been paired with his wife for quite a few years and both of them still living, as well as the children.

She lay back down on the bed in frustrated resignation. All right, she was going to trust Balkney, but she was still shaken and weary, injured and in shock and full of all kinds of drugs. Antidotes, in case she'd been scratched. Pain medication. She wasn't sure what. Nion was dead, her corpse in a locker in a storage room. What they were going to do with it down here, Jils couldn't imagine.

But she couldn't stay. It was not possible for her to continue to function in this environment. She had no intention of giving anyone another chance. The next assault would end it for her for certain; she was weak now, and vulnerable.

"Apparently you're needed at Emandis Station, Ivers. Conflict between the Home Defense Fleet and Fleet rapidly escalating toward critical mass, and you're the Bench Specialist to defuse it, lucky you." Balkney had turned to the bedside chair to seat himself, once she lay back down. Once she surrendered. "You're to go up with Delleroy. He's to accompany you, represent the Ninth Judge, and so on. It's two days to Emandis Station, not much less with even a really good pilot. Plenty of time for you to rest up. Jils."

Balkney said her name with an unusual emphasis, almost as if it was something he'd still been deciding whether or not he was going to say it until it was actually spoken. He surprised her; he'd never used her personal name. "What?"

"You keep your eye on Delleroy. There's something that doesn't feel quite right to me. If you were my friend, I'd be right here with you." And he was; and he was. "If you'd been my lover, I wouldn't be letting you alone with anybody, not even a sober abstemious married man like me. Particularly with a sober abstemious married man whose primary role under Jurisdiction has been as an eraser of redundant lives. I'm not happy about this."

Well, that was just ridiculous. She knew Padrake; Balkney didn't. Padrake was actually doing his imitation of a man almost demented with worry and distraction, really. It could be hard to tell, sometimes, that was all.

"Since we are alone together," she suggested, feeling the cumulative effect of drugs and excitement, fatigue and pain slowly but certainly begin to overwhelm her. "I'm blaming any snoring on you. I'm gone, Balkney. Sorry. Can't help it."

"I'll be here."

His voice faded into a twilight as sudden as it was profound, and ceased to impart any meaning.

She'd just gotten past the initial disorientation of waking after having fallen asleep under the influence of drugs when she heard Padrake come into the room, singing out cheerfully. "Up and at them, Jils, we've got a lift to catch. They're waiting for us topside. Let's go. Are you okay to walk?"

"I'm tired," she replied, her eyes still closed. "Not crippled. Where are we going?"

Someone had a hand at her shoulder, helping her up. Her entire body still ached, and her ribs—oh, yes. That was right. Her ribs. That had been earlier. The hand at her shoulders didn't feel particularly Padrake-like; Jils opened her eyes just as Rafenkel turned away to reach for a flask of water.

"Topside," Padrake repeated. "'Emandis Station needs you. We've got a courier on standby. Chilleau's sent someone to speak for the Second Judge in your absence. Ready?"

"Stims," Rafenkel murmured to Jils, showing her a small handful of pills that Rafenkel was holding in the palm of her hand. "Garden-variety, caffeine and ferridose. It's only been a few hours. And you can sleep on the courier."

Rafenkel said they were stims. They looked like the common run of freely used stimulants; could be poison, of course. But she'd settled her mind, as she'd slept, on the subject of paranoia. Wasn't going to give in to it.

"Thanks." She took the pills—they tasted like common stims, too, that bitter metallic tang that was intended to discourage overuse and prevent accidental ingestion—and drained the glass of water. Could be poison in the water as well. On the other hand, at any moment there could be an earthquake—Brisinje was still geologically active—the entire cave could collapse, and she'd be just as dead.

She'd survived an assassination attempt, maybe two, and these were her peers—Bench Specialists. Maybe Nion hadn't been quite up to speed, and made careless by arrogance. The fact remained that Nion had tried to kill her, and failed, and if anybody else meant to they'd have had plenty of chances by now, and she was not—was *not*—going to surrender to fear. "Who's come for Chilleau, Padrake?"

She pushed herself carefully up to her feet, feeling wobbly but intact. Her ribs hurt. She didn't mind them hurting. Pain was useful—it reminded a person that she was still alive. It could also be a distraction; but she'd be sleeping on the courier, as Rafenkel had suggested. Padrake would be there as well, wouldn't he? He'd said "we." So that was all right, then.

"I'm not actually sure that Chilleau sent him," Padrake admitted. "But Arik's checked, and the Second Judge will accept the substitution, under the circumstances. Let's go."

What circumstances were those, exactly? Those of having been almost killed, and having no intention of whatever sort of staying in this dangerous-to-her environment for a moment longer? Or of the Second Judge being disgusted with her for her failure to find out who had killed the First Secretary, frustration that was trending unquestionably toward a conviction that Jils had done it herself?

She wasn't interested in thinking about things. She settled herself in the lift and waited for her mind to clear. Not until the lift started signaling the end of trip—nearing surface, arriving, clearing atmosphere, opening doors—did it occur to her that, in the combined distraction of her physical state and her concerns and reservations, she couldn't remember what answer Padrake had made to her question about who it was that Chilleau had found to send here in her place.

"Who are we meeting?" she asked Padrake, who had been resting himself with his legs stretched out and his arms folded as his eyes closed. "Anybody I know?"

He opened his eyes with an expression of mild confusion. "It's sure that you know him," Padrake said. "Vogel. Missing for months, just turned up in Emandis, but his affidavits are apparently in order or Chilleau wouldn't have agreed. I'd like to get the story on that, but we're not going to have time, I'm afraid."

The lift had stopped and cleared. The doors slid open. Karol. In uniform, no less, but he had his old jacket and older campaign hat in his kit, or her name was not Jils Tarocca Ivers.

With him was First Secretary Arik Tirom, frowning anxiously moving forward to offer her his hand as she exited the lift, with the apparent intention of assisting her. "Dame Ivers. Very unpleasant for you, Bench Specialist. Completely undeserved, I'm sure it goes without saying."

They smelled. Karol and Tirom both did, ever so subtly, of soot and smoke. The launch fields were still burning, then.

"Thank you." She couldn't be rude to Brisinje's First Secretary—not without good reason; she didn't have it in her to be rude for the sake of being rude. Not like Nion. "Academic now, sir. Karol. Where've you been?"

No, that wasn't right. She should ask *how have you been*. She should. He looked a little worn around the edges, and twenty years younger at the same time. *How've you been, what do you mean by disappearing and strewing cryptic little sketches hither and yon, what do you think you're up to?* She couldn't. She'd gotten close to Karol, they'd worked very well together, she'd felt his disappearance as a personal loss and a professional handicap, and she was in pain and not in a very moderate state of mind.

"Plenty to tell you about that, Jils," Karol said. "But later. I came to ask you to go to Emandis Station. *Scylla's* taken Andrej Koscuisko, Emandis claims him for a native son and objects to *Scylla's* misappropriation of valuable cultural artifacts, and the *Ragnarok's* left the system, so *Scylla* doesn't know how it can let Koscuisko off the ship without losing face."

And as angry as she'd been at Karol for more than a year, as angry as she was at him right now, she had to step back in the privacy of her own mind to admire the succinctness with which he gave her situation, problem, background, and probable unfortunate outcome to be avoided, by implication. They were good together—as agents, never as lovers, but there were ways in which she was closer to him than she'd been to any lover.

Even Padrake? Padrake was standing behind her with his arms folded again, and the vibrations in the aether from the Padrake sector toward the Karol direction were not in particular warm and friendly. Best if she avoided any comparison of degrees of intimacy in her mind while she was standing between the two of them.

"I can get him out," she said. "But only if he'll come. All right. I'll see what I can do." She knew things about Koscuisko's exact legal status with respect to Fleet that no one else around here might know. Verlaine had known, Verlaine had obtained a grant of relief of Writ for Koscuisko, but Verlaine was dead. The clerk at Chilleau who had processed it and the Second Judge might remember, but they weren't here; no Fleet Captain would let himself be dictated to by any clerk of Court, and the Second Judge had other things on her mind. "Have you been briefed, Karol?"

"First Secretary's given me the brief packet," Karol said. "The rest of it I'll have to figure out as we go along. Where are we?"

"Ask Balkney." Karol might not know who was part of Convocation. "So far, all I'm really sure of is that everybody thinks confederation is a sub-optimal solution and Fontailloe is out of the question, either as a temporary home pending re-architecture of Chilleau's administration or as the base of a newly elevated First Judge. Balkney can tell you, though. I'm prejudiced."

You can trust Balkney. Maybe Capercoy; maybe Rafenkel, and nobody else that she cared to name. Karol had already made up his mind about that, though. She didn't add anything more, and Padrake spoke over her shoulders to the First Secretary.

"Two days there and two days back, Arik, if we're lucky. With Vogel coming on line, we could lose a few days while he gets himself calibrated, but some of the disputation can be settled in the mean time. I'll be back inside of five days."

Jils looked at him—What did he mean, he'd be back? Padrake tilted his head down to meet her eyes, and seemed almost to blush.

"You're to go on to Chilleau, Jils, once we're done at Emandis Station. The Second Judge doesn't care to interrupt the process a second time."

No, the Second Judge didn't care to have Jils represent her in Convocation, not if she had anybody—anybody at all—to use instead. That wasn't quite fair, though. Karol was as good as she could have hoped to be, his only handicap his lack of immersion in the problem and its possible solutions over the recent months.

And who knew? Maybe that wouldn't be a handicap after all. Maybe a man who had not been inside the problem would see the way clear to a best possible solution that would otherwise escape them. She could hope. Since she was to have no further opportunity to contribute to the process, hope was all that she was to be able to do.

She was going to Emandis Station to mediate between Fleet and the Emandis Home Defense Fleet on the subject of Andrej Koscuisko. She was going in person, to signify the importance that the Bench put on pursuing good relations between the two—and perhaps because she had the authority to tell a Fleet Captain what to do, but only if she was actually there. She was going to remind both parties that the Bench was still the ultimate authority. And she was going because the Second Judge had dug up Karol Vogel from somewhere and sent him to replace her as quickly as possible.

"Very well," Jils agreed. "Let's get going. But you owe me an explanation, Vogel." For too many things to be mentioned here and now. He knew it, too, because he nodded. And then gave a little start, the way he did when a thought turned a corner in his mind and burst into the forefront of his consciousness, surprising him.

"Oh. There's one more thing. Koscuisko's angry with me. But it wasn't my fault. It was booby-trapped. Ask him about it."

What could that possibly be supposed to mean—but Karol hurried past her into the lift, and the First Secretary followed. To effect the introductions, Jils supposed, not really required but necessary for the sake of the formalities. History was watching. What would history make of this mid-process switch-out of the personnel?

As if it mattered. No Bench Specialist was under any false impression as to what history might say about him/her, if he/she ever turned up in history at all. To an extent, it was a failure to turn up on any sort of a public record, if one was a Bench Specialist.

"Let's go, Jils," Padrake said softly, as though in sympathy with the turmoil in her mind. Karol turned up out of nowhere, with some vague protest about Koscuisko. Something booby-trapped? What could he possibly be talking about?

What else could he be talking about except the Record, the forged record whose patently false evidence was to have formed the keystone of the *Ragnarok's* defense of its crew against accusations of mutiny and murder?

She was cold. She could wait. Ask Koscuisko, Karol had said. She'd do that. She would. "Let's get out of here," she agreed with a nod, and led the way out of the blockhouse to where the ground cars were waiting to take them to the launch field, and thence to Emandis Station.

THIS WASN'T A convocation, Rafenkel told herself, disgusted. This was a circus. The chair collapsing under Ivers might have been a practical joke gone awry—might have been. Might. But Nion was dead and, while there was unquestionably a harpoon in evidence, who knew for sure where it had come from or who had attempted to deploy it?

If she had been Ivers and wished to kill Nion, she certainly wouldn't have used the harpoon herself. She would have shown it, let Nion take it away from her, and then killed Nion in self-defense. She would have. There were problems with that approach, of course.

"Specialist Vogel," First Secretary Tirom said. He had come as far as the airlock but was not, apparently, going to address them in the theater; this wasn't a formal visit on behalf of the Bench, but an administrative errand. "Some of you may already know him. Chilleau Judiciary has agreed to transfer its proxy to Specialist Vogel, in Specialist Ivers' absence."

The first problem would be that it was a risk. Nion was younger than Ivers, and Ivers had been recently injured. If that had been the plan, it was unnecessarily hazardous, as well as unnecessarily complicated.

"I know Vogel," Balkney said. "Who's to speak for Brisinje, though, First Secretary?"

The larger problem lay in what Ivers' possible motive might have been. Rafenkel couldn't come up with any that satisfied her. Why would Ivers want to kill Nion? It was understood that, under the circumstances, such a frame might successfully hold, since it was easy—well, relatively easy—to understand why Nion might have wanted to kill Ivers. But Bench Specialists didn't waste killings.

"Padrake's expected return date is in approximately five days," Tirom said. That would be two days out, one day to resolve the problem, two days back. "We're hoping his absence doesn't delay things. Vogel can speak for Chilleau."

"That isn't why I came, though," Vogel said, suddenly. Maybe not suddenly—no, his tone of voice was temperate and his body language perfectly calm and respectful—but it surprised Rafenkel; and Tirom as well, apparently.

Vogel nodded his head in response to Tirom's questioning look, and continued. "I'm glad to be here to speak for Chilleau Judiciary. But I was actually coming to introduce a new element into the deliberations. There are nine Judiciaries represented here, First Secretary, and yet nobody speaks for a developing market that stands in as much need of regulation of trade and preservation of civil order as any. Maybe more."

Tirom was staring. Rafenkel thought she might be staring too. She knew perfectly well what Vogel was saying; she just didn't quite believe it.

"Launch fields are burning," Tirom said. "Cities are in a state of anarchy. Entire economies have been thrown into a state of chaos.

And you want to talk to us about Gonebeyond space? There is no Tenth Judiciary, Vogel."

Vogel shook his head. "No, First Secretary, you're absolutely right, there is no Tenth Judiciary. But there will be. And the Selection we make will define Judicial policy for the next twenty to sixty years." Depending upon the choice, and the individual chosen. "The new First Judge will have to deal with Gonebeyond. The previous incumbent's policy is no longer appropriate in that respect."

The previous incumbent: that would be Fontailloe. Tanifer, who stood toward the back of the small crowd at the airlock, looked thoughtful to Rafenkel, but made no remark. None was required. They all knew that Fontailloe's approach to Gonebeyond had been to ignore it.

"It's not a formal position," Balkney said to the First Secretary. "But Vogel's right, as well. We haven't been putting as much weight on that element as perhaps we should, in light of the population expansion in Gonebeyond."

Yes, it had come up, and no, they hadn't made a tile for it. They had too many problems within Jurisdiction space to care much about Gonebeyond, which after all presented no challenge to Bench markets. Still, Vogel's point was well taken. Gonebeyond was a market. And the new First Judge was going to have to decide how to deal with it as things changed and developed over the years.

Tirom seemed reluctant to accept Balkney's remark—though it was clearly reasonable, and nobody objected to it. After a moment he nodded his head, slowly. "Very well," Tirom said. "And on behalf of the new First Judge, whoever she may be, thanks for raising the issue, Specialist Vogel. There should be no real delay to process, I hope. If all of the Judiciaries represented are willing to hear Vogel speak on behalf of Gonebeyond space, Brisinje has no objection."

Again, nobody spoke, so nobody was objecting, either. The small detail of Supicor being unrepresented with Nion dead went either unremarked or discounted as overtaken by events.

"Thanks," Vogel said to Tirom, at least in part to end an uncertain silence in which nobody seemed willing to speak up. "We'll get right on it, First Secretary."

Go away now and leave us alone, we've got work to do. Well, maybe not so much *leave us alone* as *we'll get back to it.*

Whether Tirom took it in the former or the latter sense, Rafenkel couldn't tell. There were no hints in his tone of voice or his expression; maybe that was the answer right there, though. In whichever sense Tirom interpreted Vogel's words, he was not obviously offended.

"Thank you as well, Specialist Vogel. The Bench appreciates your willingness to step in at this time of need. You know how to reach me if you need to—" They'd all just tested that, with the crisis created by Nion's assault and death, but it was something to say, Rafenkel supposed. "Till later, then. I'll see myself up, yes, thank you."

He had brought Security with him, waiting in the lift-car, but they all knew what he meant. Once the airlock had closed, once the light on the wall had reported that the lift-car had begun its ascent, Capercoy raised his voice. "Let's all gather in the theater," Capercoy suggested. "We probably need to brief Vogel. I wouldn't mind a briefing myself."

"Two eighths," Tanifer agreed. "Time for a beverage break. What'll you take, Vogel?"

This was actually not so much a polite request as a subtle signal: *I for one don't feel like I need to watch this man every moment.* There was more than one kind of baseline being established.

"Bean tea, if you've got it." Vogel's response in turn was similarly coded: *and I don't mind not watching you fix my beverage.* "Kavene if you don't. Thanks."

Bean tea, indeed. Some Bench Specialists had an exalted notion of what was available in small scientific research stations. It was a pretty safe bet that there were few enough sources of bean tea in Gonebeyond. Rafenkel shook her head, and went off to open up the theater.

CHAPTER SIXTEEN
RESETS

"WE'RE OPERATING AT a disadvantage here, Vogel," Rafenkel said frankly, once everybody had assembled. The theater was much the same as the last time Rafenkel had been here—the table at the end of the room, the three ranks of chairs in tiers, the secured communications console behind the table on the far wall. "So we're just going to have to do our best and let things fall out where they may. I'll start. The Sixth Judge is for Chilleau. She won't have Fontailloe. She'll take Cintaro if she can't have Chilleau, but she'd rather claim it for herself than admit a confederation."

This wasn't what anybody had planned; they had wanted something more formal, more professional. Nion had taken that away from them. It was a good thing she was dead.

Balkney sighed. "Ivers has kept Chilleau alive to date; we've been unable to disqualify the Second Judge and move on. Haspirzak is willing to accept Chilleau, but not Cintaro. Haspirzak believes that any other choice will bring chaos."

"And Ibliss is afraid that selecting Chilleau will bring chaos, and wants to go with Cintaro," Rinpen added with dispassionate regret. Maybe it was good to sit down and lay things out in plain speech. They'd been talking around it so carefully that the situation hadn't been as clear as it might have been.

Now that she sat in the theater and listened, it seemed clear to Rafenkel that there had been little real movement on anybody's part since they'd got here. If anything, peoples' opinions seemed more—and not less—polarized than when they had begun.

"Supicor believes she has a chance as a compromise consolidation," Zeman said. Zeman was here for Eighth, not Seventh, but there was no one to speak for Seventh and Zeman had spent the most time with Nion in discussion to date. "Eighth just wants an answer. Any answer. She'd even go for confederacy if she had no choice, but that's Delleroy's position."

Vogel nodded. "I can speak for the Second Judge," he said. "Though I'm sure Jils has been doing a better job of it than I can. I can tell you with a fair degree of confidence that Verlaine wouldn't have accepted any solution that included Fontailloe, and he didn't like Cintaro either. To the extent that I'm representing Gonebeyond as well as Chilleau, I'm going to have to insist on that."

Strong language. Bench Specialists usually didn't issue ultimata, not amongst themselves.

"What's your reasoning?" Capercoy asked. "Verlaine's dead."

Vogel nodded. "Dead, but I can still hear him clearly enough. More Judiciaries and more local authority, he'd say. And Fontailloe was to blame for making torture an instrument of State, he'd say, and Cintaro was right there with her."

If this was true, Verlaine had been much more radical in his thinking than anyone had guessed—or at least more so than Rafenkel suspected. "Explain," she suggested. "More Judiciaries?"

Vogel nodded again. "Yes, each with a reduced span of control. It's all a control issue at the heart of it, obviously enough. And when did we start getting in to Inquisition in a big way? Fontailloe felt that it was losing control. Feeling the lines of direction and administration beginning to slip. Jurisdiction's gotten too big for nine Judiciaries."

Which would explain Vogel's reference to a non-existent Tenth Judiciary, Rafenkel supposed.

Balkney shook his head, as though there was something in his ear that he was trying to dislodge. "We're not going to argue dead men's protocols, Vogel," he said firmly. "What's your agenda?"

"Chilleau," Vogel replied calmly. "Behind Ivers all the way. With a sideline in the future of Gonebeyond space. Whoever takes the Selection is going to be presiding over a crucial point in the history of the Bench. We're going to need a Judge with the flexibility to face a whole new set of challenges. It's not going to be like it's ever been before. Gonebeyond's too big to just send in the Fleet and hope for the best."

So Cintaro was out, from Vogel's point of view, because Cintaro wanted more prisons and more emphasis on the Protocols. Vogel's point—to the extent that Rafenkel thought she understood it—was, among other things, that opening a dialog with Gonebeyond would take a Judge who was capable of understanding what had forced people to flee in the first place. No administration identified with the maintenance or furtherance of Inquiry was going to get very far in persuading Gonebeyond to consider any sort of integration into Jurisdiction space.

"Well, we knew from the start that the default solution was Chilleau, if it could be done," Tanifer said. "Ivers and I had been discussing whether the Second Judge could be moved to Fontailloe. Supicor, I think we can all agree that Supicor wasn't going anywhere. Am I right?"

Nobody disagreed, so Capercoy spoke. "Down to Fontailloe, Cintaro, Chilleau," Capercoy said. "If it's not Cintaro, the Judge will very possibly claim a degree of independence, with all that means. If it is Cintaro, we overrule the clearly expressed majority opinion, and that means even more of the same."

Capercoy didn't finish the thought. He didn't have to. They all knew where it was going.

They couldn't pass over Chilleau Judiciary—her administration couldn't hold the Bench together—but they couldn't select Cintaro, who would elect to respond by turning her back on the rest of Jurisdiction space There was one solution that acknowledged the weakness in Chilleau's administration and minimized the damage that would be caused by a Fifth Judge deciding to make her own rules—

"Forget Fontailloe," Rinpen said to Tanifer. "Fontailloe is not going to happen. If we all work Chilleau versus Cintaro, we may have a solution by the time Delleroy gets back. We can't wait any longer than that. We don't dare."

Tanifer nodded. Rafenkel was almost certain she knew what he was thinking.

There would have to be a newly promoted Judge at Fontailloe no matter what; and if it turned out that the confederacy model was their least-worst choice, there would be a new First Judge at Fontailloe—because all of the Judges would be First Judges, in their own jurisdictions.

If they were forced to consider confederacy , after all the sport they'd had with Delleroy on the issue, she was never going to hear the end of it from him.

"TAKEN?" PADRAKE ASKED, coming forward into the wheelhouse where Jils stood looking over the pilot's shoulder at his schematics.

Two days from Brisinje to Emandis Station. Karol had come in person—so the *Ragnarok* was at least two days gone. Koscuisko was two days detained. She wondered—no, she didn't—what sort of a mood he was going to be in when they got there.

"That's what it says," she agreed, passing the briefing sheet to Padrake. "They pulled him out of the service house between late supper and early breakfast. Did it so quietly that there were no alarms for his Security, except that his Security had apparently already left by the time it happened."

Padrake leaned up against the bulkhead to one side of the entryway into the wheelhouse, shaking his head as he scanned the brief. "Protest from the *Ragnarok* against unauthorized detention of personnel assigned. Counter-argument from *Scylla* for overdraw of Fleet resources at depot, but it's the EHDF that runs that depot, isn't it? And the *Ragnarok's* left without him, so they can't be that upset that *Scylla's* got him. A little bit insulting, that, wouldn't you say, Jils?"

"It's better not to make any assumptions where Koscuisko is concerned," Jils said, shaking her head. "He's got his own standards. Some of which I like, and some of which make no sense to me. You might want to be sure you come with me, when we get there, I've heard rumors about Koscuisko's vocabulary that we may find substantiated. We're going to need a record, a heat-resistant one—"

"With respect," the pilot said. It was the same pilot who had brought her here from Chilleau, and she'd been under the impression that Ise-I'let had been anxious to get home. What had happened? "If you'd clear the wheelhouse, Specialist Ivers, Specialist Delleroy. Vector transit to calculate, Specialists."

The pilot's voice was firm and clear, but there was tension in it that Jils didn't understand. Karol always got a little unhappy about his vector spins, though—not because there was ever anything wrong them, just because it was the way that he was. Maybe the pilot had already done his calculations when she'd joined him at Chilleau. It didn't really matter why. He wanted them out; they'd leave.

"Sorry, Ise-I'let," Padrake said, straightening up. "Gone directly. Jils. I'll be in my cabin. Got a little bit of a technical problem to chew on."

Right. "You go right ahead." No, she didn't need his company, not in the same room. The bed-cabins on a courier were small. She had work to do. "Let me know when you have a moment, though, courier pilot. I have a question. Thanks."

Out. He didn't have to say it. The word lay writ large across the tension in the fabric of his uniform across his back. Something was eating at him. It was a good idea to leave people alone when they were calculating vector spins. She followed Padrake out of the wheelhouse and through to the middle portion of the corridor, where the bed-cabins were. Padrake's was across the hall.

Padrake closed his door behind him, with one last concerned glance at her as he did. She winked at him—she wasn't going to be fussed over, no matter how much of a guilty pleasure it was—and went to the small locker in her bed-cabin to pull out the data she'd been carrying with her since she'd left Chilleau. She left the door open. She was tired of feeling enclosed.

She hadn't gotten very far with it before. She'd just kept on starting, realizing she couldn't recall a word she'd read, starting again. She started at the beginning one more time, re-reading those long dry bits of ships going one way, ships going another. Cargoes. Passengers. Fleet movements.

There'd been a battlewagon at Ygau, and Fleet presence at several other vectors besides—Burig, Ktank, Upos, Wellocks, Panthis. She found that she remembered more than she'd realized; and was just marveling, again, at the casualty rates that the Terek Vector assessed against its traffic when the pilot rapped with his knuckles on the frame of the open door to announce himself.

"You had a question, Dame Ivers?" The vector calculation seemed to have taken it out of him; he was pale, which was not in the least attractive on an Emandisan.

Jils had to pull herself up out of the traffic at Terek and think for a moment. Yes. She had wanted to ask the pilot. "Thank you, courier pilot. Personal curiosity. You ferried Specialist Vogel from Emandis Station?"

The pilot shook his head. "From Imennou, Specialist. We've been lending a hand at the launch field there, trying to handle the overflow from Brisinje."

He wasn't going to volunteer any information—discreet young man, a good choice, for a courier pilot. She'd thought his name was familiar; why was that? "I was interested in whether you'd seen Specialist Vogel before. I'd found a piece of paper in the exercise wheel on the way from Chilleau that appeared to have come from him, but I hadn't realized at that time that he was anywhere in particular."

The pilot smiled, very easily, very engagingly. "Specialist Vogel told me that you would be wanting to know," he said. "Yes. I'd seen him before, but he'd been acting as a port inspector at the time. Some weeks ago, and it was at Panthis, I think."

Miserable tanner that he was. A port inspector. Karol didn't like port inspectors; he took advantage of the role to act out everything he found objectionable in the breed, and sometimes she thought he had a little too much fun doing it, too.

"I hope he didn't make things too difficult." Though if the pilot remembered Karol he was likely to have reason.

The pilot smiled again, but there was something hurt and hungry creeping into his face that made Jils anxious for his sake. "It was a memorable occasion, Dame. He pretended that there wasn't anything wrong with our documentation, and that he was furious about it. No chance to kick up. Free liquor at Panthis for as long as we care to drink, kind of him. You know, there's always something wrong with the documentation."

Yes, she did. And she knew exactly how Karol had played it. "Something on your mind, pilot?"

"You and Specialist Delleroy." The words came out in a bit of a rush. "I do my best not to overhear conversations that are none of my business, Dame. But I'd resigned myself to the fact that Andrej Koscuisko was gone and I was not going to get to see him, after all."

It couldn't be that the courier pilot had been looking forward to catching a glimpse of Koscuisko the way a man went to a zoological garden to see a venomous snake—or a botanical gardens, for that matter, to wander in amongst the poisons. There was some personal reason behind Ise-I'let's interest, Jils was sure of it, and chose her words accordingly.

"If it's confrontation you had in mind, I'll have to warn you." Not as though it would surprise Koscuisko himself. She wouldn't be surprised if he'd got bored with it: *you inhumane monster, you killed my father—my brother—my wife—my child—my friend.*

She could almost hear Koscuisko's voice, cold and clear and as cutting as ice for all the soft edge of some of his characteristically Dolgorukij diphthongs: *Yes, yours and those of better men than you.*

What do you want from me? An apology? It would be hypocritical of me to tender one. I am in the abstract sense sorry for your loss, but I decline to attempt to pretend to you that I did not enjoy it. At least probably. You can't expect me to keep your murdered dead apart from all the others. There were simply too many of them. Now do get out of the way, and if you wish to pull a knife, you will have to clear it with my Security.

She shook herself with a little scowl, annoyed—too easy by half. The pilot was waiting for her to finish her thought. "You'd be best advised not to initiate a confrontation on board *Scylla.* He used to be their chief medical officer. They might take it amiss. That, and one is expected to wait one's turn in line, and it's a prodigious long one."

"He is at Emandis Station?"

Had he heard her at all? Was he even listening?

She nodded. "Yes, on *Scylla.* In protective custody, I gather. My job is to get him off the *Scylla* without provoking armed confrontation between the Emandis Home Defense Fleet and Fleet, and I think I have just the approach, too." The EHDF, that reminded her. What had Karol told her? Emandis Station claimed Koscuisko for a native son?

The pieces fell into place. Ise-I'let. She should have remembered. Koscuisko had lost a man at port Rudistal, a bond-involuntary who had been with him since his earliest days at Fleet Orientation Station Medical. Joslire Curran had been an Emandisan knife-fighter; that meant five-knives.

And at the point of his death, under honorable circumstances in the performance of his duty and by his choice to spare the Bench the expense of rehabilitating him, his legal status had reverted to that of a free man with full citizenship—and his name to the one he had carried before his condemnation. Ise-I'let. The courier pilot was related to Koscuisko's man, and in all likelihood meant to demand the return of the knives.

"Souls under Bond have no families," the pilot said. "No contacts, no communications. Nothing. But I've asked everywhere I've had any chance at all, and from what I've heard Koscuisko didn't just restore our honor and our position when he killed Jos. He loved my brother. I loved my brother. We have things in common. I thought I'd missed my chance to talk to him."

That was all very well and good as far as it went, but Jils wasn't sure it went far enough. Koscuisko had peculiarities—"Excuse me if I'm speaking of things that I don't understand," Jils said, as gently as she could. "Does Koscuisko want to speak to you?"

Koscuisko was on *Scylla*. How could she promise this earnest young man that he'd have his chance when she had no idea whether Koscuisko would be willing to engage in a conversation?

The pilot nodded. "I heard from my family, Dame. They met him at the launch field in Jeltaria, and took him to the orchard. Then the *Ragnarok* left, and they believed he had gone with them. My wife and child have never touched the holy steel."

He shut up abruptly, as if he had said too much. Five-knives, all right, Jils decided. That was between Koscuisko and his man's family. It was none of her business.

"Dolgorukij value kinship ties, as a general rule." Whether Koscuisko did was anybody's guess, but in many ways he was a traditionally conservative Dolgorukij—his family was among the more conservative of the great families, among other things. "I think you have a good chance of seeing him." On shipboard only, of course, in case there was an issue about the knives and Koscuisko decided not to give them up.

Where were Koscuisko's five-knives? On board the *Ragnarok*, which would mean gone? She had the feeling that, given the apparent willingness of the Emandisan to get sticky about Koscuisko, the news that the knives had left the system without their escort would not go over well. Would Koscuisko have taken them with him to visit Joslire's family? She could hope. Traditional, and ceremonial-minded.

"These days I have been struggling with it," the pilot admitted. "It will be a great thing in my life. Thank you, Dame Ivers."

It was little enough to have done. Jils waved him away cheerfully enough, then turned back to her data. Wait a minute. The pilot had said he'd seen Karol at Panthis? She went to the door and put her head out into the corridor.

"Ise-I'let. Sorry. Tell me again. How many are some weeks, and had you ever seen him before that?"

The pilot had turned around when she called to him, and stood now in the corridor, considering her question. "Well, Dame. Let me think. I started Brisinje to Ygau to Terek, lay over in Sashama, then through Burig to Wellocks. That would have been about the time the First Secretary died, I think. We heard the news coming off Wellocks to Terek again. Then we were had a mission to Upos from there, on to Panthis, where Specialist Vogel came on." And left her a message. "So that was just before we went back to Chilleau on standard courier. Three weeks before I carried you from Chilleau to Brisinje, Dame."

It was hard to follow the pilot's line of thought, but Jils could see the reasoning, rehearsing his travels: *if this is six weeks ago, I must be in Panthis. If Karol had heard about the death and started his own investigation, he would have had time. If Karol had done the murder, though—*

Now the door to Padrake's bed-cabin opened to reveal Padrake standing in the doorway with his collar and cuffs undone, a stylus in his hand. "What's going on?" he asked. "Garrile to Nabmedor, Fellau and Warbay and cold Boglynn shore?"

No, Wellocks to Burig to Upos, and—Jils shook her head, annoyed. It didn't matter. She'd only been interested in the one piece of information. The pilot apparently recognized the reference, because he grinned; and then he sang—very surprisingly, but in a very nice voice really, in a middle register. "'As a boy, then a man, then a master of men.' Jetorix, anyway. With respect, Specialist Delleroy."

"You just go on back to the wheelhouse, my lad," Padrake said, with his accent as rich and plummy as it got only when he was drunk or being silly. "I've business to transact with this fair maid blithe and bonny. Away with you, now."

A very appealing smile, the pilot had. He bowed and turned and closed the door between the wheelhouse and the corridor. Padrake straightened up, his head dangerously close to the lintel of the door— he was a tall man—and cleared his throat.

"And now, me proud beauty, how are you feeling?" His voice returned to its more normal speaking tone as he crossed the hall to follow her into her cabin.

"Tired and irate," she said, consideringly. "And sore. So don't you get any ideas, my man. There is a time and a place for everything. And this is neither."

"But I'm an intelligence specialist," he argued, closing the door. It was not a large bed-cabin. It was even smaller with two people in it. Between the bed, the table with the data, and the two of them, it was fairly well filled as spaces went. "It's my mission to collect and analyze information. Tired? In what way? Irate? About what? Sore? Exactly where, exactly precisely where, exactly precisely and uniquely where?"

Tired of watching her back and wondering about everybody who crossed her path. Irate and angry that she'd been attacked, twice, she'd had to kill to save her life and she could never stop herself from wondering if there had been another way around the problem that she just hadn't seen in time. Nion hadn't deserved to die for ambition. Well, maybe she had, and any Bench Specialist displaying stupidity deserved the same. Nion had been stupid, incautious, overbold, grandstanding—

"Mostly my ribs." She was tired. She could use a little recreation. She and Padrake had been lovers before, and his hawk-hooded eyes, his leonine mane had grown more decorative over the past few years. He'd always been a very attractive man, and there was a good deal of him in the appropriate places in appropriate measure, too. "Here."

He started to move but then drew back, as though he had suddenly thought of something. "Oh. Wait. Rafenkel gave these to me. I'm supposed to try to get you to take some. How about it?"

Painkillers. She took the mediflask and looked at its contents. "Fast-acting?"

"No, I don't think so, sorry, standard issue—Oh."

Yes. Oh. She opened up the mediflask and shook out the standard dose: one each, repeat on the third hour until asleep or stupefied, whichever came first. She usually had a good hour, maybe more, or—with the condition of her body to consider—maybe less.

Taking the mediflask into the tiny lavatory, she swallowed the dose with a flask-full of water to help it dissolve, and then she joined Padrake again in the bed-cabin. Handsome Padrake. Attractive Padrake. Padrake whose body already knew things about hers, whose body hers knew and wanted, again. Maybe she'd never entirely stopped wanting him. That had been one of the reasons she'd put distance between them in the first place, after all.

"Mostly here," she repeated, pointing. Padrake took his cue. He put his arms around her, one arm laid carefully across her shoulders so that the arm that went around her waist did so on the unhurt side.

"Not here," he said, and touched his fingers to the hollow of her back where her spine lay in its channels. "Not here." Where her uniform fell from the waist to the hip, smoothing the fabric with all due deliberation over her backside to make absolutely sure that nothing hurt there. "Not here either, I hope, Jils. Let me know."

He wouldn't hurt. She didn't have to worry about him. She knew the fragrance of his flesh, and the soft touch of his body hair and the way the muscle of his back and shoulders felt beneath her fingertips. She knew the taste of Padrake's mouth, and he remembered how to kiss her, too, just the way she liked to be approached with lip and tongue. He knew. She remembered. It was good.

She laid aside her troubles with a contented sigh, and surrendered to the pleasures of a careful hour spent between lovers who had history to cushion their caresses.

Later—Jils didn't know how much later, but it was later, she was blissfully relaxed and boneless in the bed, and her ribs didn't hurt at all—later he left her, standing up to dress and go back to his own bed-cabin. There was only room in the bed for one and one-half people, and Jils had to sleep either on her back or on one side; it left little room for Padrake. And he hadn't taken any pain medication.

One eye half-open, too lazy and sleepy to turn her head, Jils watched Padrake dress, admiring his back. Those beautiful shoulders. The taurian power of his neck, the way the muscle tapered— not too much, he had a figure, but not too extreme a waist—down to braid into the strong set of his hips. Yes. A fine figure of a man. She closed her eyes, smiling.

When she opened them again, it was because she had heard something, and might have been alarmed had she not seen Padrake's familiar back. Still dressing, apparently, she had dozed off for mere moments. She hadn't heard the clicktone of a scroller at all—she'd heard him fastening his trousers, or something. The data was on the table, he might have accidentally nudged it, what did it matter? He was dressing; she was asleep. She felt wonderful. Wonderful. Hadn't felt this good since she could remember when.

She closed her eyes again and didn't open them till hours had elapsed, Padrake long gone.

"Tell me," Andrej said gently, tossing a token onto the pile in the middle of the table. "I hope to hear that things go well with you, Code?"

Code Pyatte had been one of the bond-involuntaries assigned when Andrej had served on *Scylla*. He considered the tokens in his array and discarded, rather more sedately than Andrej had. "It's been quiet, your Excellency. Quiet is good. I mean in specific quarters, sir."

There were other bond-involuntaries here in the small cabin, none of whom Andrej knew, though they'd claimed to know of him. Technically speaking, they were on watch. He'd been under confinement to quarters since he'd struck the chief medical officer. What was his name? Weasel-Boy? No. Lazarbee. It was hard to sit with Code and know that there was nothing Andrej could do for him. He couldn't even tell Code that Robert had escaped. Code was under Bond, and would suffer for hearing the information.

"I understand." He knew exactly what Code was saying. Captain Irshah Parmin had kept his chief medical officer clear of special assignments, and Secured Medical as empty as possible. Andrej hadn't understood how careful Irshah Parmin really was about that, either.

It was another area of the life of a Ship's Inquisitor in which Captain Lowden, late and emphatically unlamented, had opened Andrej's eyes and left him wishing he'd remained half-blind forever. "Morrisey, your call, I think. Your Doctor Aldrai has a good name in circles, from what I understand. One of our best burn specialists, if I remember?"

The other bond-involuntaries were not as much at ease with him as Code was, and there wasn't anything that Andrej could do about that. He couldn't send them away, not when they wanted to be here. Chief Samons had already let him know that their eagerness to pull the duty had not pleased Doctor Lazarbee.

Morrisey—that was Efitt Morrisey, Andrej had heard Code call her by that name but he didn't care to push her comfort boundaries by presuming intimacy—grabbed a token and let it fly, with a confused murmure "This troop—ah—begging his Excellency's pardon—" that Andrej let pass without remark.

It was hard. He remembered too clearly how a bond-involuntary could suffer out of simple confusion. And there was nothing he could do except to be as calm as possible, and notice nothing.

"Aldrai was all right," Code said quietly, waiting for his teammate to make the next move. "She was willing to stay on, too. She liked the company. It seems that Fleet had other ideas. There were officers who were particularly interested in coming to work for *Scylla*, as the gossip has it."

Four-handed spanners was not an intellectually challenging game, but it didn't have to be. Andrej had never been good at cards. Dice, bones, stones, or rollers he could manage with adequate skill and sometimes a fair degree of luck; cards he could deal in a very ordinary way, on a good day.

It had made him popular in school. Many people who might otherwise have had reservations about socializing with Dolgorukij aristocrats had discovered themselves perfectly capable of trying to take his money in a cheerful and convivial fashion, once they'd made up their minds that there was no unfair advantage on either side.

Andrej considered Code's careful phrasing while he studied his array. Why would someone want to come to *Scylla*? The command was a good one, yes, but Brisinje was a quiet Judiciary, or had been before the troubles had broken out. Safe, quiet, uneventful. "Perhaps someone felt he needed a vacation," Andrej proposed, picking up a token. If he could get three more in the same family, he'd win the hand, for the first time all day.

Code shook his head. "That would be a reasonable supposition," Code said, with a peculiar weight on the word "reasonable" that made Andrej's ears prick up. "The officer claims to have been sent on a mission, as it were. Worked closely with the Bench Specialist in Brisinje in the past, by his report. You didn't want to give me that token, sir."

Code lay his tokens out in array. Five. Seven. Nine. Eleven. Reefers. It was a relatively modest array, to be sure, but it was a complete one; and beat any array-in-progress by definition.

"Name of all Saints," Andrej swore, without much rancor. "Some octave I may beat you, Code, but it is not going to be at any time in the near future. Look at this, look. I could have had such a nice series. Really, it grieves me deeply."

Out of the corner of his eye, he saw Efitt Morrisey almost smile before she remembered who she was and sobered, quickly, with a sidelong glance at Andrej to see if he had noticed. He'd noticed no such thing. Code collected tokens from the table, sorting them out into the starting array.

"Pulled strings, and got into a comfortable billet?" Andrej asked, after a moment's sad contemplation of the hand he might have had. "I wouldn't have connected a Bench Specialist with any kind of reasonable people, myself."

He had to be careful with that because, although he and Code had been close to one another once, it had been five years, and a man did not lightly suggest that a bond-involuntary had cast aspersions on the integrity of a Bench Specialist.

"Just what is said by some, sir," Code replied. He was thinking, too. If it was hearsay, he could report it so that the officer would know that it was being said. "Posted here from the Galven at Ygau, possibly eight months ago, sir. Willing and eager to do his Judicial duty, but the captain has had no calls of his own and declined others."

Andrej thought about this, somberly, looking at the tokens in his newly distributed array. An opportunist. Chief medical officers who were eager to do their Judicial duty were either willing to do whatever it took to further their careers—at the expense of truth and mercy—or else they were sadists, people who gloried in the inflicting of pain for its own sake. People like Andrej Ulexeievitch Koscuisko.

"Our captain has always been an extraordinarily stubborn man," Andrej said, by way of reassurance. "The more he's pressed, the more he digs in his heels. Such men are very good to find in command. *Scylla* is lucky to have him."

Importune chief medical officers aside, Captain Irshah Parmin was a conservative man, and no supporter of the Protocols past their point of usefulness—which ruled out most of the apparatus. He had protected Andrej. He had protected the bond-involuntaries. He would protect them still. And because of Captain Irshah Parmin Code had never seen the *Ragnarok*, not from the inside, not when Lowden had been in command.

"I'll tell the officer that the officer said so," Code said, with a broad grin in his voice and his eyes, and a little smile on his face.

It was a rebuke—a loving rebuke, Andrej realized—and smiled back, delighted. Code was telling him that he should be more polite to the captain than he had been. It was true that he had not comported himself in the captain's presence as a man truly appreciative of all that Irshah Parmin had done for him. To be scolded by Code about it was wonderful.

There was a signal at the door. One of the other Bonds went to see what it was, engaging the talk-alert. The talk-alert was on muted standby in token of Andrej's status as a man in confinement; that way he didn't have to listen to the administrative chatter on board.

"Bench Specialist Jils Ivers, your Excellency." It was Chief Samon's voice, and it was strained. "With pilot. To see you, sir."

As if he had any choice, but the troop at the door did him the courtesy of waiting to be told. Andrej nodded, and the troop opened the door. Specialist Ivers, well. He hadn't seen her since the *Ragnarok* had broken out of Taisheki Station, and sent her away on the Malcontent's thula.

The door slid open. There was Chief Samons. There was Specialist Ivers. Chief Samons was pale, though, and Ivers looked a little tense herself. Andrej stood up to greet he. She had been the bearer of very good news as well as very bad news, in his life, and there was something about her personality that he found very appealing, though he had never given much thought to exactly what it might be.

"Your Excellency," she said. "I hope I find you well, sir. May I introduce to you Joslire Ise-I'let's surviving brother."

She stood aside from the open doorway, and the man who had been behind her stepped forward. Andrej felt the skin across his shoulders prickle as though his uniform were full of static electricity. It was a young Emandisan of average height and build—and average appearance, too, for all Andrej knew—but there was his brother in that man's face, and Andrej had and still loved Joslire with gratitude for the enrichment of his life and companionship in evil hours, and sorrow for his loss.

"I have been very anxious to make your acquaintance," Andrej said, and could hear a tight sort of longing in his own voice. "I am Andrej Koscuisko, and I loved your brother. But he only ever called me by my name once in his life that I know of, and we are family now, the old woman said. Will you come and embrace me, for your brother's sake?"

Code had risen from the table when Andrej had stood up, as had the others—it being a concession on their part to sit down with him in the first place. Now Code drew his fellows out of the way, to the side of the room.

The Emandisan, Joslire's brother, advanced with an uncertain step. "Shona," he said. "Shona, your Excellency. Very glad—to meet you—very—"

An Emandisan—and in the uniform of the Emandisan Home Defense Fleet, which Andrej could recognize by now—

an apparently responsible person, and with a wife and child. For one moment, he was overcome. In that moment, Andrej took Joslire's brother to himself, and kissed him for his brother's sake, weeping. He hadn't expected to meet Joslire's brother after all. He hadn't been prepared for this.

But Emandisan were a people of dignity and sobriety. Releasing the man, Andrej stood for as long as it took for him to fumble for a white-square and wipe his face. By the time he had thrust the dampened cloth away, both he and Joslire's brother had recovered themselves to a degree, however temporarily.

"And what brings you, Dame Ivers?" Andrej asked, a little breathlessly. He was in control of his emotions. Yes. He was. He would not look at Shona Ise-I'let, or he would lose his composure. "Grateful as I am to you for bringing this man to me, you must have some other object as well, I am sure."

She stepped across the threshold and into the room, keeping her distance as if unwilling to interpose herself. "Even so, your Excellency. You are a situation, sir, single-handedly creating a point of contention between local and Fleet authorities, no less potentially dangerous for its unexpected nature. I have to speak to the captain on your behalf."

She was serious about the danger of friction, but not about his fault. He could tell. "Take your time." He was not yet in control of his emotions; he had to pause and wrestle with them. "If Shona will humor me, I have many things to say to him."

She nodded. "You'll have plenty of time, your Excellency. On our way to Chilleau for your documentation." She must have seen the sudden realization in his eyes because she grinned at him cheerfully, ruthlessly. Oh. Yes. Documentation.

The captain claimed him for Fleet; Ivers knew he was one thin brief away from being a civilian. She didn't know that the record that could protect the *Ragnarok* had been destroyed, and the ship's best chance for vindication with it. "If I may leave my pilot with you, Chief, I need to join Specialist Delleroy. I don't mean to keep the captain waiting."

Chief Samons bowed. Ivers went out of the room. Chief Samons waved two of the bond-involuntaries after Ivers—on escort, Andrej supposed—and turned her attention to the pilot. Shona. Joslire's brother.

"Not wishing to intrude," she said. "We all know you were close, sir. But there are others. Permission to let them know."

Others who had known Joslire, like Code, desperate to not to be noticed and sent away. How could he send Code away? Joslire had been his man, bound to him of his own free will. *Be of Koscuisko, forever.* But Joslire had been Code's teammate as well.

"You will not mind meeting others who also loved your brother?" Andrej asked, just to be sure. He didn't need his answer in so many words; he could read it in Shona's honest Emandisan face. Shona was not Joslire, but, oh, he looked like him in ways that went beyond his face and form. "By all means, Chief. Send to us the people who were here. And, if it isn't cruel to ask, Code will help me tell about the night when Joslire died."

It would be good to talk about Joslire with other people who remembered him. So long as he was to have his time alone with this Shona, Andrej would share the wonder of Joslire's brother with an ungrudging heart, and be glad for Shona's sake.

CHAPTER SEVENTEEN
VECTOR TRANSIT

YES, ONE SHIP was very like another, and yes, she knew where she was going. The *Scylla's* security escort was politeness, not guidance. The last time she'd been on board one of Fleet's cruiserkiller-class warships it had been the *Ragnarok*, a substantially newer ship than *Scylla*, and *Scylla's* corridors looked just that little bit more worn by comparison.

Scylla had been to war, and the *Ragnarok* never had. There was no such wear and weariness about the uniform or carriage of *Scylla's* crew, however. In that, at least, *Scylla* and *Ragnarok* were similar. Both crews seemed to have a sense of their identity as a Command, and to care for how they represented themselves to one another.

At the one critical turning, the Security pointed her toward the captain's office rather than toward the officer's mess. Jils nodded—as much to herself as anybody—and took the indicated route. They didn't expect too many people, all together. Who did they really need? The captain, his First Officer most like, and the representatives from the Emandisan Home Defense Fleet that Padrake had stopped to collect from Emandis proper as she came directly on to *Scylla* to have a word with Koscuisko, if possible, before negotiations were begun.

Koscuisko looked well. She hadn't really given him much of a chance to speak, however, not springing his man's brother on him the way she'd done; nor was she sorry. The relationship between Koscuisko and Joslire Ise-I'let had been unusual enough to excite remark from its beginning, and it had only gotten more interesting when Koscuisko had taken Curran's life and inherited Emandisan steel.

Padrake was waiting for her in the captain's office when she arrived, Captain Irshah Parmin standing up to nod politely as she entered the room. He was not a tall man, and very broadchested; most of the hair had gone from the top of his head and seemed to have migrated to his eyebrows, giving him a very owlish look.

His First Officer was taller than he was, sturdily built, and looked vaguely annoyed. *Scylla's* chief medical officer was there, as well—the man had no neck to speak of—and something gave Jils the impression that it was the chief medical officer, and not the three Emandisan officers, who annoyed Saligrep Linelly, Ship's First Officer.

"You made good time," Jils said to Padrake, by way of greeting.

Padrake bowed to her with an expression of satisfaction on his face. "I've borrowed one of Emandis' couriers. I like flying with the Emandisan. They're the best. I'll be needing to leave as soon as we have a satisfactory resolution." Turning toward the captain—who was waiting—Padrake raised his voice, and got down to business.

"Since we are at this moment involved in very critical negotiations at Brisinje, your Excellency, the Ninth Judge hopes that we will be able to resolve this dispute in an expeditious manner. We've asked Specialist Ivers to accompany us because she has a particular past relationship with the officer and his Command—although that won't do us as much good as it might have done, since the *Ragnarok* has left the system."

"Was allowed to leave the system," the captain corrected, calmly. "Gentlemen. Would you care to be seated?" This was directed at the Emandisan officers, who declined with shakes of their heads. Jils wasn't about to sit down. She'd been sitting down all of this time. On the other hand, her ribs hurt. Padrake had been very careful, and her ribs still hurt.

He couldn't have received instruction from the Ninth Judge, though, so he was making that part up, but it was well within his brief. She wouldn't have brought the Judge into it, but Padrake was here specifically to represent her, since the dispute was within her jurisdiction. Everybody played fast and loose with attributions from time to time, when the situation called for it. Everybody.

Padrake kept to his feet, maintaining solidarity with the Emandisan officers. "These officers state that Andrej Koscuisko is an Emandisan national," he said to the captain, clearly opening his argument. "You removed him under armed escort and in secret from an Emandisan port, in violation of police protocols. He should be returned because you should not have taken him. You further have no authority over him in his capacity as the custodian of Emandisan five-knives."

Padrake couldn't exactly call Koscuisko a knife-fighter. Koscuisko wasn't, not in the Emandisan sense. Someone who could fight with knives, yes, he had proved himself there—and she'd seen him.

"I regret the inadvertent impropriety I committed when I had him escorted to *Scylla*," the captain said, choosing his words with evident care. "I had not anticipated that my action, an internal Fleet redirect, would be interpreted as disregard of the Port Authority in any way. This was a failure of judgment on my part for which I am prepared to apologize."

One of the Emandisan officers nodded; they'd been over this ground before, as it seemed. The captain wasn't finished, though, and the Emandisan officer apparently knew it—they'd clearly been over that as well. "However, Andrej Koscuisko is a Bench officer with a sworn duty to the Fleet. Whether the Emandis nation wishes to embrace him as their own is not at issue. He is a Fleet officer. Now that his command of assignment has left the system, this is the only appropriate place for him to be."

Jils could see the argument. Unfortunately, she was sure that the Emandisan could see its implications as clearly as she could. The unspoken "where he can be protected" was shimmering in the air. She was going to need to intervene before people got even more annoyed with one another than they were already.

"You're holding him against his will," one of the officers said. "In an environment in which he is exposed to insult." This was said with a meaningful glance in the direction of the unprepossessing person wearing the rank of chief medical officer coupled with *Scylla's* ship-mark. There'd been friction there, Jils surmised. "He is the custodian of the knives. There is enough residual hostility over the circumstances surrounding the unprecedented enslavement of the steel in the first place, your Excellency. We earnestly advise the minimization of anxiety over their present disposition. His family is waiting for him."

His family? Koscuisko's family was waiting for him—that was true enough—but nowhere near Emandis Station. Jils shook her head to clear it: she had to concentrate. And her ribs hurt.

"Permit me to intervene," she said, firmly. "Specialist Delleroy is here for the interest of the Bench. We can't afford conflict between Fleet and the EHDF, gentles, especially now when we are experiencing such increasing difficulty with keeping the peace. I was asked to come to represent Koscuisko's interest, though he didn't send for me. There's something you don't know, Captain, with respect."

They were all looking at her. She took a deep breath. She was going to have to shave a few curls off of the truth to make this work; was she going to be able to pull it off?

"Before his unexpected death, First Secretary Verlaine sent me to Koscuisko when he was home on leave to offer him relief of Writ, in acknowledgement of some irregularities surrounding his renewal of his term of service with Fleet. Koscuisko has executed the documentation, and I have witnessed it. He requested a delay in filing while the legal status of the *Ragnarok* was in question—a matter of loyalty to his Command."

And a matter of the legalities surrounding the custody and placing-into-evidence of a record with forged evidence. But those were details whose disclosure was not required under the present circumstances, and which could only raise more questions than they answered.

"Koscuisko is a citizen again?" the chief medical officer said loudly—the adjective "brayed" sprang to Jils' mind, but she suppressed it sternly. "Then he's in violation for wearing the uniform, isn't he? Told you, your Excellency, there's something about your precious Ship's Inquisitor that just isn't what it ought to be."

Professional jealousy could be an ugly thing. It was particularly ugly in its immediate incarnation. The captain exchanged a quick— frustrated?—glance with his First Officer, but said nothing.

"Specialist Ivers, surely we can all agree that any such charge would be very poorly timed as far as the cause of political stability is concerned," one of the Emandisan officers said to her, very seriously.

She couldn't afford to let him continue. She was afraid that he'd say something that would be difficult to overlook, something that might come too close to appearing to be an overt threat. She held up her hand, and the officer fell silent.

"Koscuisko is not at this moment a citizen. It is only a question of filing, however. So you see that there is no need for you to offer Koscuisko a berth on *Scylla* pending a new assignment, your Excellency."

There was a wistful expression on the captain's face for one fleeting instant. It was gone so quickly that Jils wondered if she'd imagined it. "If you put it that way, Dame Ivers, I suppose not," the captain said. "Pity. We could have used him. Damn fine battle surgeon, I never saw a better one."

"Better rid of him, your Excellency," the chief medical officer said so suddenly; Jils started—she hadn't exactly forgotten that he was there, but she certainly hadn't expected him to contribute to the conversation after the captain's wordless rebuff.

The First Officer looked either annoyed or disgusted, or maybe both, but let him talk.

"He's a disruptive element, he is. Encourages insubordinate behavior on the part of troops assigned. If I didn't already know that he can do no wrong in your eyes, I'd have some issues to discuss at Captain's Mast, but I will content myself with pointing out his history of resisting his Judicial duty."

Captain Irshah Parmin stood up. "Disruptive," he said, with a sort of an almost affectionate disgust in his voice. "He's always been that. True enough. Specialist Ivers, if this is so, why did it require your personal intervention? You could have told us so. He hasn't mentioned it."

The captain was not suggesting that she'd made it up—not exactly. Padrake clearly had a slight touch of the uncertainties himself, however; and Padrake already knew that sending her personally was partially due to the sensitivity of the situation, and in larger part simply a face-saving approach to the fact that she had to be gotten away from Convocation before someone else decided to attack her.

"Koscuisko has no reason to mention the matter because it is in process—not complete. Until his ship of assignment left the system without him, he was probably content to wait out the appeal, and now that the ship has gone, I am the only person at Chilleau who knows where I have put his documentation."

She'd had plenty of other things to think about when she'd gotten back to Chilleau Judiciary. Koscuisko had told her to put off filing the documentation. Whether he'd be willing now to take the freedom that Verlaine had offered him and go home was probably going to depend on how he felt about the legal status of the evidence that the *Ragnarok* held in custody. She'd talk with him once they were on their way to Chilleau. Away from here.

"If Koscuisko is in transitional status, you cannot hold him, your Excellency. And we would not wish to, either." The Emandisan spokesman seemed to grasp what Jils was trying to do, and was apparently willing to put the face-saving solution forward. "We will provide you with transport to Chilleau. We'll need to call up a fresh crew. The one you're carrying has been on extended assignment. It will be a few hours. Captain?"

"I can release him to the protection of a Bench officer without prejudice to Fleet's interest," the captain conceded. "Will you be wanting anything else?"

A formal apology for the disrespect he'd shown when he'd had Koscuisko kidnapped, Jils supposed. He had said that he was sorry.

"Quite all right, your Excellency. Professional respect, not the time to indulge too nice a sense of prerogative. Thank you." The point had been made, Jils had to admit. The Emandisan Home Defense Fleet had protested against the Fleet's behavior, and Fleet had been made to stop and consider and make concessions. They could afford to let Koscuisko go, now. "We'll send you some fresh crew, Dame Ivers. The pilot is not going to want to be deprived."

Indeed not. Shona Ise-I'let and Andrej Koscuisko clearly had a good deal to say to each other. If he'd been able to get off Brisinje days ago, when she'd arrived, maybe none of this would ever have happened. Oh, she would still have been attacked—and would still have killed her attacker, if she'd been lucky.

"I knew his brother as well, Provost Marshal," the captain said, his voice much more relaxed and genial now that the sticking point had been resolved. "No, not nearly as well as his fellow Security, but I'm curious. Would it be an imposition? I'd like to meet the man."

The Emandisan officer's expression was frankly and honestly appreciative. "There's a lot of balance to be restored with that family, your Excellency. I don't think it would be unwelcome in the least. You honor the memory, in fact."

Well, this was certainly tidy. Padrake was looking at her with peculiar intensity, as though he was trying to decide whether she had made it all up; but he was clearly sensitive to the mutually felt desire to get clear of this awkwardness as soon as possible, and turned his attention to Irshah Parmin.

"Very satisfactory solution," Padrake said. "On behalf of the Ninth Judge and First Secretary Arik Tirom alike, I thank you both, Captain, Provost Marshal, for your willingness to meet halfway. I'll just go get my kit and be on my way. Got to get back, Specialist Ivers."

Yes. It was better if they didn't try to say good-bye in private. He'd be delayed again. She'd forgotten how easy it was to exploit his presence for the comfort of her body. She thought the success with which they had revived their terminated relationship had surprised them both equally. A reprise of the quarrels they'd had years ago was not required to prove the wisdom of leaving well enough alone and going on, grateful for a brief but not to be repeated interlude.

"Good speed, Specialist Delleroy. Show Vogel no mercy, he deserves none." Where had he been, and what had he been doing? Bench Specialists didn't say good-bye. It was bad luck. "If you would like to come with me now, your Excellency, you can ask Koscuisko for yourself. About his relief of Writ."

Padrake had been on his way out. Now he hesitated, and looked back over his shoulder at her. "And then you can see yourself to Infirmary, Specialist," Padrake said. "You've wounds to tend, and the finest facilities in Fleet right here. Doctor—Lazarbee? Yes, thank you, your Excellency, Doctor Lazarbee. I appeal to you to see that Specialist Ivers does not escape this ship without a thorough going-over."

She swallowed back a snort of fond irritation. There were drawbacks to being with people who knew one a little too well. Karol would almost certainly have left her to report herself—and she would have done it, too.

"As soon as I've spoken to Koscuisko, Specialist Delleroy," Jils promised. *Now get out, you tiresome person.* "Captain, First Officer, Provost Marshal. Shall we all go?"

The change of crew would leave the courier empty, but the data that she had on board was secured there. It was safe. She would go to Infirmary; she wouldn't mind a status check. It had only been two days. She suddenly felt as though it had been just two hours, but that was the way of it—the body waited until after the crisis had passed to relax and start to mend, and that was what really hurt. Mending.

Well, six days between Brisinje and Chilleau to sleep, and then it would be back to the wars for her. A few hours to wait for fresh crew from Emandis Station, a visit to Infirmary, and then she would have nothing more to worry about beyond who had killed First Secretary Sindha Verlaine, and why.

NOBODY COULD AFFORD to trust anybody—that was one of the rules of a Bench Specialist's life. The other side of the balance on that one, though, was that Bench Specialists above all needed to be able to decide who they were going to trust amongst themselves. Erenja Rafenkel didn't know Karol Vogel; she didn't think she'd ever met the man. She trusted Capercoy and she trusted Balkney, as far as that went. Balkney trusted Vogel, and Balkney had more reason than most to be cautious about where he bestowed his trust.

It was two days after Vogel had come down with Brisinje's First Secretary to vouch for him, and Rafenkel was practicing her knives on the black beach of that obsidian lake, while Balkney retrieved knives and Vogel did nothing helpful whatever.

She could see the floater from here, the observation station on the lake in which Nion and Ivers had fought. Tanifer and Rinpen were there, arguing Fontailloe against a deferred Selection. Zeman was observing, Nion was dead, Delleroy and Ivers were gone—so with Balkney and Vogel and Capercoy all here interfering with her concentration, the full complement of Bench Specialists in convocation was accounted for.

"That's interesting," Capercoy said to Balkney as Rafenkel set up her array for her next round. "Because he told me that he'd heard it could only be Cintaro, in the end. He told the Fifth Judge that, too. She believed him."

There was more light in the observation float out on the lake than there was here on shore. Rafenkel doubted that anyone in that room would be able to see what any of them were doing very clearly. Capercoy stood with his back turned to the float even so. His body had the kind of roundness to it that combined youth and muscle; toothsome, the effect, or maybe she'd just been down here for too long.

"Didn't tell me anything," Vogel said. "Of course I've been out of the country. But it does sound like something may be going in an interesting direction here. You say your Judge won't have Chilleau or Fontailloe, Cape?"

Delleroy had been busy, for a man who hadn't joined them until Ivers had arrived. Much of his work had apparently been done before anyone came down here, from what they were beginning to piece together. Told Balkney that it was almost certain to be Chilleau. Told Capercoy that there was no question about the Fifth Judge's eventual selection—what could he have hoped to gain? Division? Whose partisan was Delleroy, if not Brisinje's?

"She might have done before Delleroy got to her." Capercoy sounded sour about it, too. "Inappropriate influence. Told her that in light of the questions about Chilleau, it was her duty to take the wheel and guide the Bench through the stormy seas into calm waters. Persuasive man. He had me, too."

If she thought about it, she could find it in her heart to be offended, Rafenkel thought. Delleroy hadn't approached her with any inappropriate suggestions. Or had he? What was that he had been saying about who should be running the Bench? "If she won't accept Fontailloe or Chilleau, we have a problem," Rafenkel said, just in case no one had noticed. "Because a lot of people feel it should be Chilleau. No matter what its First Secretary had proposed."

Vogel let his breath out in something that was halfway between a snort and a sigh. "Verlaine was a visionary," Vogel said. "The frustrating thing about that is that he was ahead of his time, but only just. I had a lot of respect for Verlaine. Not that we didn't have our differences."

"You know," Balkney said to her, walking a set of knives from the target back to where she stood with her weapons laid out in array on a podium in front of her. "Vogel seems to have told me that Ivers didn't do it. Vogel seems to have told Ivers that I didn't do it. I haven't heard Vogel say that he didn't do it. Where have you been? Not out of the country. Not for all this time."

"Well, not offing senior Bench officers, if that's what you mean," Vogel said scornfully. "But no. Not out of the country for quite all of this time. I thought I'd take a vacation, if you must know—and if Verlaine thought I was off on an errand, so much the better, but he didn't send me."

"Vogel's got a woman in Gonebeyond," Capercoy said to her. "Wanton red-headed wench, as I understand." The way in which Capercoy chose to phrase his remark made her laugh; she missed her grouping. Balkney shook his head at her, sadly, and went to collect the knives for a do-over. She considered completing the partial grouping with him in it, but stayed her hand.

"I'll have you speak respectfully of Walton Agenis," Vogel warned, his voice light but careful enough to put them all on notice. He was serious about this. "I'd heard Verlaine talk about Gonebeyond in the abstract. Have you ever been? Interesting things happening, out that way."

Balkney brought Rafenkel back her knives. "Concentrate this time," Balkney said. Between your shoulderblades, Rafenkel thought, but she didn't say it.

"Well, that's nice," she said instead. "What does it have to do with the selection?" Two days, and Tanifer couldn't see his way clear to give up. It couldn't be Fontailloe. Even if there hadn't been history against it, Chilleau with a seasoned Judge and a new administration was to be preferred to Fontailloe with a seasoned administration and a new Judge.

"Someone's manipulating judicial documents," Vogel said. "You've heard the rumors, I'm sure. Manipulating judicial documents is only the first step toward manipulating Bench policy, even authority. I'd have stayed in Gonebeyond and been happy if Fleet had taken Verlaine out, but I don't think Fleet did it."

That meant Vogel thought Ivers did it? No. Not Ivers, not Balkney. "We're just not getting a piece, somewhere," Balkney said, stepping well clear of Rafenkel's line of fire. "Frustrating. I'm having that just-out-of-reach-solution feeling. I hate that."

"Analysis," Capercoy suggested. "Speculation only. Verlaine was killed to prevent him from implementing his proposed reforms, assumption one."

"Or that's just the obvious motive and it had nothing to do with Verlaine's reforms," Rafenkel said, weighing the knife in her hand. "The immediate effect is to put the selection on hold. Verlaine's reforms may still be adopted by the new First Judge, whoever she is. Verlaine's murder cripples Chilleau."

"With Cintaro the benefiting party," Capercoy agreed. "But Cintaro had resigned herself to not winning."

"You said that Delleroy talked to her," Vogel reminded Capercoy. "In what context was that?"

Capercoy was silent, thinking.

Rafenkel threw the knife. One. Good hit.

"Setting up convocation." Capercoy spoke slowly, clearly concentrating. "She didn't have much of a mind about it before, willing to step into the breach but not about to defy the majority call. It could have been a subtle long-term plot, of course."

Balkney apparently didn't think so. "Cintaro wouldn't have been able to predict the convocation. If Cintaro had done it, she'd have laid claim to the title by default a lot sooner than this. Fleet's done its best to milk the Bench dry for privileges and tax revenues, but they'd have made their move if it had been a Fleet plot. Same reasoning."

This was the sort of random-fire exercise that could lead to breakthroughs or a dead wall. Rafenkel knew which one she felt they were heading for. "What else had been going on around there? Apart from the obvious. Verlaine's reforms were a threat. But he would have had to negotiate them."

"No, Bench Specialists would have had to negotiate them," Balkney countered. "As always. It doesn't matter what the Judge gets up to, it's the Bench Specialist who gets stuck with the work. That's the way of things."

Rafenkel's knife went wide of target again. Vogel made a show of moving carefully up-range; she ignored him. "Bench Specialist privileged model," Rafenkel said, almost to herself. She hadn't thought about it, not like this. "What would we usually do? Step in, wouldn't we? Help the new incumbent out until he had his feet underneath him?"

"But Jils couldn't do it," Vogel said. "Especially after she discovered the body, she was the obvious suspect. And I was out of the country. Jils had a murder to solve. Chilleau would need help from someone else."

"Help or annexation." Capercoy sounded as though he wanted to be sick to his stomach. "Delleroy's due to move on, he's been here five years. Brisinje is quiet. Vogel was gone, and Ivers had worked with Delleroy before."

It was a huge and horrible accusation. And there was not a shred of evidence to support it. None. "So he's been preaching confederation because he's sure it'll fail?" Rafenkel asked, dubiously. "And doing it wrong, because I'm convinced?"

"Working with Cintaro so he can be the man to manage that," Balkney said. "The man of the hour. But it's all supposition. Doesn't change our immediate task."

He was looking at something. Turning her head, Rafenkel saw the debating party on its way out across the lighted causeway between the observation float and the shore. Since Nion's death, they had all gone into the observation float together and left it as a group.

"Cintaro's determined," Capercoy said, one last time. Just in case they'd gotten distracted, Rafenkel supposed. "I don't know whether Delleroy could manage that. Maybe he can. But it'll come to shooting."

As ideas went, the suggestion that Padrake Delleroy, and perhaps some others who had been heard to speak to the issue of privilege and Bench Specialists, was responsible for the death of Sindha Verlaine was new and terrible and too convincing to be summarily dismissed. But Balkney was right. They still had a primary mission that was independent of who had murdered Verlaine and why. They still owed Jurisdiction space a solution to the problem of selection, the best solution they could find.

Delleroy would be back inside of three days. With Zeman and Tanifer and Rinpen out of debate, they could all gather in the kitchen. Vogel could regale them with stories of the Langsarik fleet in Gonebeyond. They could criticize each other's eating habits, and keep an eye out for pointed daggers falling from the ceiling or chairs splintering into spears or hand-harpoons appearing in the starchies where they had no business being.

"Let's eat," Rafenkel suggested. She took the knives Vogel returned to her and wrapped them up in their case for safekeeping. Three days from now, Padrake Delleroy might have some questions to answer.

In the particular Emandisan sub-culture in which Shona had been raised, the dead weren't much spoken of except as they served as anchors or reference points in history and kinship: *in your great-grandfather's time*, or *she's your sister's daughter-in-law*. When a man needed the companionship and the advice of his dead, he went to the orchard and sat down beneath a tree and meditated.

Shona himself hadn't had that opportunity. The first years of his life had been spent in poverty and isolation. He could see, now that he was a man, how kith and kin and complete strangers had taken what quiet steps they could to better the family's plight—even at risk of sanctions themselves, on occasion.

He had not been allowed to enter the family orchard until he had carried Joslire's ashes there, and held the container while his grandmother had parceled Joslire out amongst the trees. To fruit, they needed minerals and organic compounds found in the remains of dead animals, and all of the trees had fruited in the following year.

It had been an additional sum of money, quite a substantial one, because the fruit from a family's orchard was held to impart some of the strength of the family itself, and sold at a premium comparable to proprietary pharmaceutical drugs. It had been just one more wonder in a year full of wonders—before the year was out, the government had fallen and the orchard walls had been restored at the administration's expense.

He'd been too young to understand what they meant to do to his brother when they had arrested Joslire. At that time, he had been more immediately affected by the execution of his other brothers, his father, his uncles. Later, he'd understood that a clean killing had been merciful compared to the imposition of the Bond. He remembered rather little about Joslire. Joslire had been away from home for most of Shona's life anyway; the discipline of the knife-fighter did not account for family ties.

But these people remembered his brother. It was more than just the chance to meet Andrej Koscuisko at last; more even than finding in Koscuisko no shimmering madman with an obscene appetite and the curse of the truth-sense upon him, no demonic spiritual entity whose glance could wither babies in their mother's womb, but an ordinary officer—perhaps an extraordinary officer, but an ordinary man—who felt his emotions keenly, and who had loved Shona's brother so much that he was prepared to love Shona as well for Joslire's sake. More than that.

There were people here who wanted to talk to him about Joslire: officers, crew, the captain, the First Officer, the chief of Security. One of the bond-involuntaries on board had known Joslire and the others had heard about him. The medical technicians in Infirmary, where Shona had gone with Specialist Ivers at her suggestion possibly for just that reason, remembered Joslire. Some of it was just the natural instinct of good-hearted people to fondly reminisce about the dead, but that fond reminiscence was exactly what was left unspoken and private, among Emandisan.

When the time came to leave, Shona was anxious to get away. He needed to be by himself for a little while to rest and store up all of the things he had been told, so that he could tell them in the orchard where his child could hear when his child was old enough. The provost marshal and the Port Authority's representatives had commended him to his duty and left; Koscuisko, Ivers, the new crew, they were all on board of the courier, and free of *Scylla's* maintenance atmosphere at last.

It was a trip that Shona had made before—ferrying Specialist Delleroy—but this time it was not his responsibility to do the vector calculations, so he only went to the wheelhouse out of habit, really. And because his heart was too full to speak further with Koscuisko just now. The pilot that Emandis Station had sent was an older man, Nairob; Shona knew him, if not intimately, and greeted him with a cordial salute as he stepped across the threshold from the corridor.

"Pleasure to be carrying," Nairob said cheerfully, his hands on his boards as he ran his baseline calibration. They were clear of Emandis Station. "Four hours to the exit vector, and then Chilleau in four days after that. Enough time?"

Shona opened his mouth to confirm that supposition, but thought again. Four days from Emandis Station to Chilleau Judiciary meant shaving a little more than two days off the usual transit by taking Emandis to Chilleau direct, which could only be done with a courier but was only seldom if ever attempted by larger craft—there was a risk involved.

Any time a man made a vector transit, there was a risk. It was a fact of life, but Chilleau direct—if the calculation went wrong, they could be killed. They could be worse than killed. They could be lost. Lost, killed, it made little difference to most people, but Andrej Koscuisko was traveling on the courier this time—and Andrej Koscuisko was carrying five-knives.

They were Joslire's five-knives. If they were lost in a vector mishap, it would be the end of a line of direct transmission that went back to the days of open-fire forging in the desert. Koscuisko was a man, but those knives were part of what it meant to be Emandisan. It had been a crime to have ever let them leave Emandis, a crime for which the government that had persecuted his family had been punished. To put the knives at risk would be worse than a crime: it would be a betrayal.

"No." He couldn't do that. It was no fault of Nairob's that he made the suggestion; Shona was personally notorious for taking slightly riskier approaches and getting away with it. Nairob was only doing as he not unreasonably expected Shona to have done in his place. "Let's take the slow transit just this once, Nairob. More time to talk. We've got knives on board."

The expression on Nairob's face changed from one of mild confusion to one of moderately horrified understanding. "Knives," Nairob said. "You're right, Shona. Six days it is. Dar-Nevan to Brisinje, to Chilleau via Anglerhaz."

Shona nodded. "We'll be bored," he said, with gratitude for Nairob's quick comprehension. "Or maybe your people will be bored. But we won't be sorry. Thanks, Nairob."

He knew where Koscuisko was—in Delleroy's bed-cabin. He knew where Specialist Ivers was, too. It was an unusual feeling to be a passenger on the courier rather than its pilot; but he was a passenger, and he was going to take advantage of the privilege to go and lie down. He had six days. He had time.

When he got home, he was going to write down everything that he could remember, and then he'd go and tell it to the trees.

"I WASN'T SURE you'd go along," Ivers said. She didn't want to play cards. She claimed she had work to do, and she probably did. She was who she was, after all, while Andrej wasn't himself. He was what he was, yes, but as to who he was—that remained open to debate. "I appreciate your willingness to contributed to a non-violent solution."

He shook his head. Unlike Specialist Ivers, he had nothing to do, nothing whatever. His personal effects were on board the *Ragnarok*, and who knew where the *Ragnarok* was? He wasn't sure he wanted to.

Scylla had provided him with appropriate uniform, clean linen; but as far as new translations of the corrupt and confusing text to the controversial "Apiary" section of the story of Dasidar and Dyraine went, *Scylla's* on-boards had had nothing to offer. That was hardly surprising.

The work was still too raw and unpolished; the Autocrat had yet to authorize its release, nor would she until and unless a consensus could be reached on whether Dasidar had slept in the meadow in the summer sun dreaming of the sweetness of Dyraine's lips, or had simply broken open somebody's skep to rob the bees of honey to sweeten his drink.

Andrej had his own opinions. Stealing honey might well be less noble an occupation than dreaming of lost love, but Dasidar had been starving all throughout the "High-mountain-song," and a man who didn't have the sense to eat when he was starving fell a few pegs on the estimability scale, in Andrej's mind.

"I've no choice, really." He was sitting at the tiny worktable in his tiny bed-cabin with a recent issue of proceedings from a conference at the surgical college on Mayon. The controversy of the day was whether surgical interventions that remediated the results of simple aging were too obviously reasonable to be considered twice, or an affront against nature and religion and morality and the dignity of persons needing but unable to afford such interventions to address deficits resulting from poverty, illness, or trauma. Andrej was not much interested in it. "My ship's gone off without me. And Vogel has probably told you about the record. So you see."

No, she didn't see. Vogel hadn't told her. In which case Andrej wondered whether he should have, but it was done now. "No, your Excellency." She didn't need to call him that, but it was the title appropriate to his civil rank, as well as the military or judicial rank he was ready to surrender. "Karol said something, but I wouldn't have connected it. Where did you find him, anyway?"

She was sitting opposite from him at the table, which was so small that their knees periodically touched. She was leaning just the slightest fraction of a little bit. The tech on *Scylla* had told him that Ivers had a genuinely nasty scrape all up on one side of her ribcage, and scored bone hurt—especially ribs, because they were always moving when a person didn't expect them to be.

"It wasn't my idea. I don't think he likes me." Though Vogel liked him well enough, or disliked him little enough, to have covered up the murder Andrej had done at Port Burkhayden. If he started thinking about that, though, he might accidentally say something about it. "My cousin Stanoczk came with letters for me. Vogel arrived with him."

The Malcontent wouldn't be interested in the controversy at Mayon, either. To a Malcontent, the solution would have been obvious: let those who wished, and could afford it, purchase such services at a premium, to fund the surgeries for those whose need was not a matter of relative convenience and who could not otherwise afford to seek healing. There were ways in which life made sense from the Malcontent's point of view. Let all souls under the Canopy of Heaven contribute what they can, and be provided what they need.

"Did he say anything about where he'd been, or why he'd gone?"

Andrej thought about this. Could he answer it without compromising himself? "He told the captain that he had evidence of the subversion of the Judicial process to accomplish individually motivated acts of vengeance not sanctioned by Judge or required for the upholding of the Judicial order." Yes, that was right. Vogel had said that to ap Rhiannon. "Then my disgusting cousin told him that there was a record that contained false evidence in the custody of the *Ragnarok*. He wanted a look at it."

She wasn't saying anything, waiting for him. He sighed. "Which he was granted. The record blew up, Specialist Ivers. We lost one of the surgical imaging sets, which was annoying because, you see, nobody had mentioned to Medical that one was to be borrowed. The record is gone. The *Ragnarok* is judicially naked. And ap Rhiannon does not like me."

Was it just him, or did he sound as though he was whining? Yes. He was whining. He shook his head at his hand lying on top of the table, discouraged.

"That's good," Ivers said. "You're off the hook. Security has taken off for parts unknown, your ship has gone after them, and the record no longer requires the presence on board of a Judicial officer to preserve its legal integrity as evidence. You can go home."

Except that his Security had gone off to parts unknown, and the *Ragnarok* had gone after them, and the ship had no Judicial officers on board to give legally valid evidence of what he knew about the motives and actions of the captain and its crew.

Oh, and the fact that he longed for the environment he had believed that he sought to escape, addicted to the pleasure that the beast intrinsic to his being had learned to take in the suffering of captive souls. He could go home and hang himself and, if he were lucky, it would be before anybody offered to show Anton Andreievitch some tapes.

She apparently misinterpreted his abstraction, because she added a gently voiced, "Does he remind you very much of Curran?"

He knew exactly what she meant, though it was hard not to smile at the turn her questioning had taken. "Joslire has been dead for many years." He had no wish to embarrass her. "I'd forgotten how much I missed him, and Shona—I beg your pardon, Courier Pilot Ise-I'let—is not so much like him in appearance as in manner. I know that Joslire is dead, and to see a man out of the corner of my eye who moves in the same way is disconcerting."

In fact, there were ways in which he could have wished that he had never met Joslire's brother, because it freshened his awareness of bereavement. The pain was older now, though. The ache of it was familiar enough to almost be a comfort in itself. "And he is his own person, which is helpful. Also I have much to tell him about his brother and the debt I owe. Six weeks would not be enough time for that."

Six days in transit, the pilot had said. Andrej wondered whether the *Ragnarok* was off vector, wherever it had gone. He wondered if his people had arrived in Gonebeyond, and what welcome they had found there.

"When he approached me first, I thought he meant to confront you," Ivers said, rubbing at the back of her neck with one hand. She was clearly weary, but was being difficult about medication. In that way she was like her compeer Vogel. These people simply lacked a basic respect for pain and its effects on their own bodies and, as a doctor, Andrej could not approve. "Took me a moment to remember. And you did kill his brother, after all."

People did not need to keep reminding him. He knew what he had done. He had been there, she had not. "Begged him to stay," Andrej said, remembering. "The Captain had told me that he had petitioned for revocation of Bond. He might have come home a free man, and known his brother. He would not agree."

"Loved him, and killed him anyway?" she asked. "My apologies for the intrusion, your Excellency. I should get back to work."

Yes, it was an intrusion; yes, she owed him an apology. But on the other hand she had always been honest with him, as far as he knew, and had held up her end of it when he had asked her not to file the documents that would have taken him away from the *Ragnarok* so long as he could do it any good by staying there. He would tell her. Somebody needed to understand. No, somebody else; the Emandisan seemed to know all that there was, as it seemed to Andrej.

"Killed him because I loved him." He hadn't wanted to. He could have made Joslire stay. It had been in his power, even his authority, to do so. And had he denied Joslire for his own selfish reasons, his shame would be even greater than it was already. "It was his wish. To do less would have been to dishonor the service he had done me. Not despite, Specialist Ivers. Because."

She should understand that, if anybody could. On the other hand, in her line of work, perhaps one of the reasons for avoiding personal ties was precisely to avoid a conflict between duty and devotion. She nodded, as though accepting his assertion without necessarily understanding it; and left the table to go across the narrow corridor to her own bed-cabin. She had data to examine.

In a few hours they would be dropping off vector to make for Anglerhaz out of Brisinje space, and then to Chilleau. Shona was giving the crew a hand, in between talks, fleeing to one chore or another as the weight of memory and reminiscence overpowered him and Andrej alike, one in receipt and the other in transmission. Andrej wished that Robert could have been there. There were important ways in which Robert and Joslire had been as close, or even closer, than Joslire and Andrej, and there were things about their life outside of their officer's company that Andrej knew nothing about.

But that had gone as Andrej had desired it to do, and Stildyne had gone with them. With them they'd taken his last credible excuse for wishing to remain with the *Ragnarok*. There was nothing left for him on board ship any longer but duty and honor and the welfare of people to whom he was indebted.

He had no way of following his ship, no way of rejoining the *Ragnarok* now. Ap Rhiannon had won. There was nothing left to him to do but go home, and be damned.

J ILS I VERS CLOSED the door to her bed-cabin and sat down at the table, ignoring the aching of her body with grim determination. She was being sent back to Chilleau. She needed to get away from the claustrophobic intimacy of Convocation, but she had no prize to take back to Chilleau with her.

She'd headed off an unpleasant confrontation between Fleet and Emandis Station, yes, she was escorting Andrej Koscuisko to Chilleau Judiciary to be relieved of his Writ at last, but he wasn't entirely happy about that. Nothing had been solved. The *Ragnarok* was gone, not vindicated, and if she had been Jennet ap Rhiannon she would not be coming back at any time soon.

She had no news of the Selection, and was no closer to solving the problem of Verlaine's death than she had been when she had left Chilleau eighteen days ago. As a Bench Specialist, she had learned early in her career that if she tried to judge her impact on the world in terms of success or failure she would fall into error; it was sometimes as important for the good of the Judicial order that she fail as that she succeed.

But she was tired, and losing hope. There had to be a solution to Verlaine's murder, but was she ever going to see through to find it? She'd failed. Had failed, was failing, and could not see anything ahead of her but failure in the future.

It wasn't a good feeling, nor was the sickening sense of futility and familiarity that she experienced when she opened up her locker and took out the data that she'd carried with her from Chilleau to Brisinje to Emandis Station, and now back to Chilleau again.

She'd at least put the first part of her analysis behind her. She'd scanned the first portion of this traffic record so many times that she almost felt she could write it from memory. Traffic incoming and outgoing at Wellocks, where the saboteur had successfully destroyed all of the records on site and only the presence of the Jurisdiction Fleet Ship *Shikander* had kept order for the crucial hours between the discovery of the destruction and the resumption of normal operations. At Burig. At Upos.

The traffic on all adjacent vectors, some of it just there to provide an index in magnitude of activity, some of it maybe holding information. Panthis. Ygau. Terek. The casualty rate on Terek before, during, and after, as aggressive young pilots in expensive couriers gambled their lives against bragging points for speed and daring and against each other; Pintabo and Mirag, Fleet's adjutant courier service, desperately poor family-owned ships trying to make delivery premiums, Home Defense Fleet and Combine ships and—

Home Defense Fleet? Emandisan Home Defense Fleet. Jils scrolled up eight and sixteen views on her data reader, confused.

How could she have missed that? The pilot was identified, as well as the craft and its class and cargo; she'd come out with Ise-I'let on the courier. This courier. She would have noticed it on her way to Brisinje. Had she not gotten this far before Karol's note had distracted her?

It must have been. It wasn't the sort of thing a person would overlook. There it was, plain as day, Shona Ise-I'let had been on the Terek vector outbound from Chilleau the day after the murder had been discovered, a day and three-eighths after it had been done. A good pilot in a fast ship could get from Chilleau to Terek in so long if he pushed it, though it wasn't what the vector authority would assume.

Except she clearly remembered some of the ships further down the manifest, partially because one of them was named after a politician that Jils despised. She remembered that. She didn't remember having seen Ise-I'let's courier in the data. She had to have gone right past it.

She'd been over the same data at least three times, on her way to Brisinje, at intervals during her stay in Convocation, again on her way from Brisinje to Emandis Station. She hadn't missed it. She wouldn't have missed it. She was stressed and distracted and unhappy, but her brain hadn't stopped working. She'd have seen it and taken it up to ask Ise-I'let what he'd been doing—who he'd been doing it for, exactly—

Standing up suddenly, Jils felt the pain in her ribs that reminded her of the fact that she'd sustained a painful if superficial wound even before Nion had tried to kill her. She had to fall back to lean against the wall to catch her breath. She hadn't seen it. So it had not been there. Someone had tampered with the data, but the data was protected. It had its own secures. Who could have gotten the data to open itself to be read, let alone managed to insert a record, without the data-reader itself realizing that something was wrong?

She'd kept the data in her locker at convocation. Anyone might have gotten access to it. Anyone. Nion, perhaps.

But she'd looked at the data on her way to Emandis Station. She'd been looking at the data when Ise-I'let had come back from the wheelhouse to talk to her. If that line of information had been there, she would have put her finger to it and asked him then and there. She hadn't done that. So that line of information hadn't been there.

It had been added to her data between the time she had carried it on board and now. There was only one person who could logically have done it, who had the skill and the specialized knowledge and the daring to do it, but Jils couldn't stand to think of what that meant.

There was a way to find out. Picking up the data reader, she opened up her door and stepped into the corridor to signal at the opposite door, to see if Ise-I'let was in there, talking to Koscuisko.

CHAPTER EIGHTEEN
SMOKE AND CLARITY

KOSCUISKO HAD INVITED him in almost eagerly, and closed the door—out of respect for his privacy, Shona supposed, and was grateful. He wasn't sure how he felt being so close to the man in such a small space. Whether it was knowing who Koscuisko was, or knowing that Koscuisko wore the knives, Shona didn't know, but it was there. This man was to be watched and warded. He was dangerous. He meant no harm to Shona, of that Shona was convinced; but there it was. Koscuisko had the ghost of the wolf in him. Joslire must have seen it, and known that Koscuisko was fit to wear Emandisan steel.

"No," Koscuisko said. He had a bottle on the table, two glasses; Shona had accepted the offer of a drink politely, but hadn't taken more than a few sips. Koscuisko's cortac brandy was a taste not commonly cultivated among Emandisan. The bloodlines lacked the ability to metabolize the poison in the drink. An Emandisan could share a sociable glass if he was very careful and took no more than a fraction of the flask, but if he forgot himself in a misguided fit of camaraderie after sunset, he would be deathly ill before the sun rose in the morning.

Koscuisko had to know that. He did not press Shona to drink, and when he poured for himself and tipped the bottle to top up Shona's drink, he let the gesture go with a clink of glass to glass each time, and did not raise the level in Shona's glass by so much as one drop. It was only the ritual, for Koscuisko. Shona was content to sit and taste the brandy in small sips from time to time, and listen.

"No, we never really talked about that. I suppose I could have asked him, but I didn't want to ask him, because if I did, he had to tell me. It didn't seem that it could possibly be something he would wish to discuss. When he mentioned any family it was too obvious that the memory gave him very great pain."

So all of this time Koscuisko had known that there had been family, but no more than that. Of course Joslire couldn't have explained to Koscuisko about the knives. It would have been as much as an admission that Joslire had put them on Koscuisko, and Joslire—as Koscuisko told the story—had enjoyed the joke of that until the very end.

"It's one man in a generation, your Excellency, chosen by aptitude and willingness and temperament, and endorsed by the ancestors. Those who have gone before had my brother singled out from the day he was born. So goes the story, at least." Koscuisko needed to understand. It was important. Shona felt an anguished ache in his heart that Koscuisko should understand, and wondered if the brandy was affecting his emotions.

"There are Malcontents, on Azanry," Koscuisko replied in an encouraging and contemplative tone of voice. "The Holy Mother has marked them from the moment of their birth, because it goes without saying that no one would chose that path if there were any other. But it is between the soul and the Holy Mother. Sometimes it is clear that a man is for the Malcontent, but at other times it comes as a surprise to everyone."

Including the individual concerned? That did seem to be Koscuisko's point. "The knives themselves will not stay sheathed for a man they do not accept. He would have known when he first sheathed one against your body. If the knife did not jump out of the sheath, it meant that it had tasted your spirit and decided that you would carry it with honor."

Koscuisko looked concerned and wary at once, as though he wasn't sure of what he meant to say next. "I have wondered how I could carry them in that way," Koscuisko said. In what way? Shona wondered. With honor, perhaps? "To take them with me, everywhere I have gone, Shona. Everywhere. Many times have I decided I dishonor his gift and made up my mind to leave the knives behind. I do not wear them often on shipboard, but—other times—I want to have them there."

Koscuisko couldn't know what he was saying. He didn't know. The fact of the knives aside, he was no more Emandisan than Shona was Aznir Dolgorukij. Shona took a deep breath to steady his voice. "May one ask whether his Excellency ever—used them. With respect. Sir."

For a moment Koscuisko looked confused, and Shona concentrated on not holding his breath. He couldn't imagine it. No one in custody of Emandisan steel could, not what Koscuisko was tasked to do. Then Koscuisko's face paled and he started back in his chair, and Shona knew that it was all right.

"May all Saints turn from me in my final hour if I could ever have done so mean a thing to Joslire." Koscuisko knew what Shona had meant. Exactly. "I am a sinner, Shona, a murderer of men and women, and there have been those that I knew to be too young and killed anyway, as quickly as I could. Joslire's memory I have never soiled in that manner. They're the only clean things about me, and I do not wish to give them up."

Shona closed his eyes for one brief moment of relieved gratitude. Joslire had known what he was doing. It hadn't been an accident of circumstances and opportunity.

"No one could dare to request them of you," Shona said. "They cannot be alienated from you, by law and the ethic of the holy steel. You don't need to be concerned about it. Trust me on this."

The talk-alert at the door signaled before Koscuisko could reply, and the doors opened without any polite interval to wait for an invitation. It was Dame Ivers, and she had a flat-panel data display with her—a reader of a sort that Shona recognized, from seeing Specialist Delleroy with them.

"You," Dame Ivers said to Shona, who stood up when she came in but who had no idea what might have excited her. "Ise-I'let. You were at Terek after Verlaine was killed?"

The question was unexpected; Shona had to think. When exactly had Chilleau's First Secretary died, been killed, when had he heard of it? Coming off of Wellocks at Terek, hadn't it been? "I'm not sure, Bench Specialist," Shona admitted. "Is it important?"

"These are traffic records from Terek," she said, brandishing the data reader. "They say you were at Terek. They didn't say that before. The data's been compromised. I need to know if—"

There was a voice behind Specialist Ivers now, though, in the hall, and although Shona couldn't see who it was he recognized Nairob's accent.

"With your permission, Bench Specialist. We're coming up on the vector debouchment, Dame, I'd like to ask for Ise-I'let's presence in the wheelhouse, if he can be spared."

Nairob would drop vector by himself if he had to; Shona had done it on more than one occasion. Prudent and responsible pilots backed each other up, however, and Shona was the one who had reminded Nairob that there were five-knives on board. Or were there? Koscuisko had not offered to let him see them—they'd been in company before, and it hadn't seemed to occur to Koscuisko since.

Shona hadn't thought about it either, until just now. Maybe Koscuisko didn't actually have the knives with him. Maybe the knives had left with the *Ragnarok*—but how could that be? He felt comfortable with Koscuisko. Koscuisko smelled like family. He had to be carrying the knives.

Specialist Ivers nodded—if a little reluctantly, as it seemed to Shona—and stepped aside. "Of course," she said. "There'll be time later. Please feel free, courier pilot."

So now, of course, he did have to leave the room and go with Nairob to the wheelhouse, wondering. Trying to remember. Where had he been? Terek? He'd picked up Specialist Delleroy at Ygau where Delleroy had been on board of JFS *Galven*, that was right. Delleroy had been working with Fleet and vector control to help contain the panic when they'd found out that the traffic offices had been sabotaged. That had been before anybody had heard about Verlaine's death.

As Shona crossed the threshold into the wheelhouse, he heard Koscuisko suddenly raise his voice, behind him, in the corridor. "It's a bomb!" Koscuisko shouted. "All shields. Now!"

There was a sound of something falling to the floor on the other side of the corridor—as if from Specialist Ivers' bed-cabin—but Shona couldn't stop to think about it. All shields, Koscuisko had said. The nearest mechanism that could be used to engage the courier's blast containment defenses was on the outside wall, though, just outside the wheelhouse; Nairob was already at his console and looking up—alarmed, concerned—as Shona turned back to the corridor.

Nairob would have to make the vector drop by himself after all. Shona had to engage the blast shields, and once the wheelhouse was sealed off, it would stay that way until the courier was boarded.

Half-a-step toward the open doorway to pull the plunger-rod and close the circuit, manually, but Koscuisko had reached and thrown and something sank into the outside wall facing the corridor, sank deep into the emergency containment access and quivered there, ringing with the force of its impact.

Shona started back on instinct—it was too close to his face, he reacted without thinking—and that reflexive recoil saved him from being crushed as the blast shields fell with brutal force and the speed of desperation.

Shona stood there staring at the now-sealed connecting door between the wheelhouse and the rest of the ship. All over the ship, the blast walls would have fallen, sealing the courier off into nine separate life-sustainment zones, each quarantined from the others to minimize whatever damage might have befallen them. The rest of the crew would be wondering what had happened. Shona himself was wondering what had happened.

"Did he say a bomb?" Nairob asked. Shona shook himself out of his temporary paralysis and turned back to the boards. The knife. That was what he'd seen. Koscuisko had thrown the knife. That was how Koscuisko had engaged the blast shields. He'd seen it, and he hadn't seen it at all. What was going on?

"I'm not sure." He couldn't remember what he thought he'd heard Koscuisko say. He was shaken by the brutal suddenness of it, by the fear that gripped a man when the blast shields came down, knowing that something had gone terribly wrong and that their lives were at the mercy of luck and chance. "He may have said a bomb. I didn't see a bomb. Did you see a bomb?"

Nairob reached for a control on his console, scowling. "No. No sign of one in health monitoring, either. We'll drop vector and then we can try to figure it out. Check my calculations? I'd appreciate it."

Shona was good at vector calculations. It was a natural aptitude that had served him well in the past. "He seemed perfectly rational just now," Shona said, calling up the model. "There's no telling, I guess."

He'd wondered if Koscuisko had the knives. Koscuisko did. Shona had seen one.

Was it still there, outside the wheelhouse, sunk deep into the structure of the ship? Did the emergency containment initiation sequence generate enough heat or other energy to damage the blade, to destroy the knife, to obliterate something that carried the lives and souls of all of its custodians with it, lost forever?

He was shaken to the pit of his stomach. His hand trembled as he picked out threads on the console to test the patterns of force that would work upon the courier as it dropped from vector transit back into normal space. Concentrate. The needful task now; speculation later. The knife. Koscuisko had thrown the knife. Shona had seen her. It had to be her. It couldn't possibly have been anything else.

Something knocked all at once against the sealed doorway between the wheelhouse and the corridor, as though the courier had been a gigantic melon that some huge hand had just slapped to hear how ripe it was by its resonance. *Tock.*

It felt like something hitting Shona in the head from all directions at once, sending him sprawling across his console while Nairob actually fell forward into the narrow space between the consoles and the viewing-port. One blow, one giant's fist, and then the alarm system on the inboard health monitors started up all at once, orange and venomously green and red: the upper lining of the ship below the hull; the atmospheric integrity of the cargo bay; the power-plant where two of the crew were on duty while a third sat on the communications boards.

Something had hit the courier, but from the inside out. From the monitors responsible for the passenger cabins just outside the wheelhouse, from the corridor itself—there was nothing.

Nairob dragged himself to his feet, clambering up and over the console. "A bomb" Nairob said. "Do we have navigation? Do we have propulsion? Can we see?"

The view-ports were still registering, but the modeling projections had gone blank. There was nothing there. The consoles claimed that the courier was still at speed and on its course, some minor perturbations, nothing that couldn't be addressed; but the ship was blind.

There were no projected schematics, no visual summaries, no sense of whether the course that Nairob had scheduled would drop them where and when they were expected. Shona took a deep breath. It could be done on manual. Nairob had had the calculations done, and the ship could still tell them what they had to do to correct for what had just happened.

He'd never wanted to drop vector by hand, but once they'd got past this they would never have to do it for the first time ever again. They'd get past this. They would. The courier was a good piece of machinery, a very capable craft, and Nairob was good. He was good.

Koscuisko had given the knife to the ship to try to save them all. There was no report of any sort from the part of the ship in which Shona had left Koscuisko and Dame Ivers, and one of the skin-sensors thought that they might have begun to lose just the tiniest bit of atmosphere, which was just the tiniest bit more than they could afford.

"We need to get back on course," Shona said firmly, setting his console to rights and sitting down. "We don't have much time. We'll start the distress beacon once we're off the vector. Can you give me a calibration on the course deviation?"

They were going to bring this courier off vector safely whether or not there had been a bomb. There were six souls on board this ship, even if he didn't count Koscuisko and Ivers. He didn't dare include them, in his mind. He had to concentrate on the lives that they could save. There was nothing he could do about Koscuisko and Ivers until they could get help.

"It's slow," Nairob said. "But it's coming. Here. Deviation on linear acceleration, mark."

If he could not so much as bring lives that Koscuisko had tried to save to port, he would not dare to step into the family orchard, ever again.

JILS IVERS CRAWLED over the debris of the bed-cabin wall painfully. The emergency sulfurs were glowing. The light gave everything a ghastly green-yellow hue, the shadows flat and deceptive. No depth perception: in the dim light she could make out nothing amidst the wreckage on the floor except for something rounded and lighter in color than its surroundings that could be the back of a man's head.

The relative positioning was right—Koscuisko had been between her and the door when the bomb had gone off—but she couldn't tell for sure. She was going to have to get to him somehow, and she hurt. Nothing was broken so far as she could tell—the joints that weren't working were refusing to work in a manner characteristic of a sprain or torn muscle, not a broken bone—but one of the other things that she knew from experience was that it frequently came as a surprise, later, to realize the extent of an injury.

She'd had a rough time of it, recently—the collapsing chair, Nion's harpoon, now this. Lovemaking with Padrake didn't count, and she wasn't going to think about it now. "Koscuisko. Hey. You. Anders. Wake up. You've got explaining to do."

He hadn't gotten much done in the short space of time between his decision to seize the data reader and throw it across the corridor into her bed-cabin, and the explosion itself. If he had, she'd lost it in the haze that being blown sideways could cast over events immediately prior to a traumatic accident.

She hadn't gotten the exact reason why, but Koscuisko's conviction had been absolute. Between the two of them, they'd gotten the intervening doors closed, and they'd deployed the interior barrier wall, before they'd been interrupted. If they hadn't gotten those things accomplished, it might well have been a termination, not an interruption, so she was just as glad.

"You. Andrej. Up, and face the world. Wake up. Are you bleeding, can you tell?" It was slow going, crawling across the floor. She had to stop every few moments to catch her breath, but she was beginning to worry about Koscuisko because she couldn't see any movement in the rubble. There was very little of the barrier wall left. If he were underneath it, there would be digging to do.

The heap of rubble with the possibly blond head rumbled a bit like the ground in a seismic aftershock; subsided, buckled like the swell of a rising river, and said something in a language that Jils could identify as probably a Combine dialect of some sort, possibly High Aznir. She couldn't translate it, but if he felt anything like she felt, it was probably just as well.

"That's the ticket." She said it as cheerfully as she could manage, but she couldn't afford to relax yet. There was no telling. He was apparently alive, but in what sort of condition? "I hope your kit is somewhere you can find it. I've got a headache."

Slowly, the rubble on the floor hove up and fell away, and Koscuisko rolled over toward her to lie upon his back, making small grunting sounds. Very disgusted grunting sounds. She could hear him shift against the debris on the floor, a little a time. He was testing, she realized it by the pattern of sound. Feet, knees, hips, hands, elbows, arms.

"Nothing feels splintered," he said, but his voice was very strained. "I don't think I'm bleeding. How do you find yourself, Bench Specialist?"

"I can crawl fairly well." The inbred formality of the aristocratic class of Aznir struck her as more amusing than it probably actually was; they had just been blown up together, and he was calling her by title. "Just point me at the probable location. I want a drink of water."

No, she wanted his medical kit, because stimulants and painkillers seemed clearly the order of the day. "Far wall," Koscuisko gasped. "Farthest from the wheelhouse. I don't know what direction that is, right now. Regrets."

Yes, she had regrets too, and the fact that she was going to have to keep moving was worth a series all to itself. Koscuisko had been between her and the corridor. If she turned around and crawled the other way, she should find the far wall, and the bed-cabins were small. They were lucky the bomb hadn't breached the hull. If Koscuisko hadn't gotten the blast shields deployed, it might have done. What had Koscuisko used to set the sequence off? A knife?

"Bedding," Jils announced. "Fabric, anyway." So she was on the right track.

Koscuisko coughed. "Go left. Small trunk. Maybe destroyed." His voice was sounding stronger. Weren't there emergency stores in the hull somewhere? She was feeling better as well, but it was important not to take that as a sign that nothing was wrong. They were undoubtedly both in shock. That was in turn probably why she wanted water.

She took it slow and easy, and by the time she'd found Koscuisko's trunk, he had come dragging himself over the remains of walls and furnishings to join her and help her dig it out. A good third of the upper part of the case had been smashed in, but Koscuisko didn't seem to mind. Prying the trunk open with an effort visible even in the low sulfur-lights, he searched the interior then grunted in evident satisfaction.

"Well done," he said. "Thank you. Water?" His voice had the strained and gravelly sound of a man trying not to cough, because if he started he wouldn't be able to stop. Jils had done her coughing. She wished Koscuisko luck with the attempt.

There was no predicting some of the exact impacts of any one blast. This one had taken the doors off of the emergency stores that had filled one wall between bed-cabins on that side of the ship, but left the stores themselves more or less intact. She pulled out items as she located them—water, oxygen, the medical set. It was hard work even with Koscuisko to help her, and she wasn't at her best just now.

He didn't seem to be bending his right hand or any of its fingers, but that could be a trick of the light.

"Enough," Koscuisko said, and lifted the seal on a water flask. "Here. Take these." He had a small assortment of tablets, pills, capsules in his left hand, passing them to her awkwardly with the flask held between two fingers.

She accepted the offered medications, and the flask; but paused to toss them in the palm of her hand, weighing them up. "What's this?"

"Later." Koscuisko had turned back to his kit to sort out a set of drugs for his own use, washing them down with a second flask of water. She wondered why she was taking drugs in this form, but then she realized that the dose-styli were usually kept in the lid of the kit, and the lid was damaged. Maybe they were smashed. Maybe Koscuisko didn't trust them. "Shut up and drink."

Nobody had spoken so bluntly to her for a long time. It made her smile. Koscuisko was not to be questioned in his own field. It took her most of the flask to get the pills down, one and two at a time, with her throat as raw from coughing as it was. When she had finished, she sat still in her temporary resting place and closed her eyes, waiting for something to happen. Was it getting cold? No. She was cold because she was in shock. There were emergency blankets in stores, perhaps, but she didn't have the energy to find them.

"What happened?" Koscuisko asked, after a while. "I can't quite remember. Do you?"

She thought about it, appreciating the fact that her body was beginning to not hurt as much and that she was feeling much warmer and that it seemed easier to breathe. Had he given her an altitude booster? "There was something in the data I wanted to ask Ise-I'let about. That started it."

"You came to ask him whether he'd been at Terek when—something." Koscuisko spoke slowly, but there was less and less slurring to the edges of his words as he spoke on. "Shona had to leave. You said that the data had been tampered with."

It was beginning to come back to her. "I'd have remembered it. Not the first time through, no, I might have missed it once, not made the connection. But I'd looked at that exact data at least three times. It wasn't there before."

"And it seemed to me self-evident that the data had been booby-trapped as well as tampered with," Koscuisko said, contemplatively.

"I don't quite remember—let me think." He reached out for another flask of water. She passed it to him, remembering for herself while he drank and thought.

Yes. He'd been very definite. *It's a bomb*, he'd said, and torn the data-reader from her hands. Tossed it through the open door of her bed-cabin, closed the door on it, pushed her very vigorously into his own—she'd fallen across the table, she remembered—and thrown something, before he'd jumped into the room and closed the door and put his back to it to catch his breath before he'd suggested that she help him deploy the inside wall, with such convincing urgency that she had.

Then nothing had happened. Nothing. They'd been sealed into the small bed-cabin with nothing to do but stare at one another, since Koscuisko had thrown her data into the next room and there was to be no getting out of this until they'd dropped vector and called the vector traffic control. Koscuisko had had some explaining to do. That was what she'd been thinking when the bomb had gone off.

"I don't know if Vogel told you," Koscuisko said. "When he tried to coax the secret out of the record that Noycannir had brought to Chelatring Side, it blew up in his face, which fortunately had been similarly assaulted in the past so that there was scar tissue that protected him. When the record realized that someone was suspicious of it, it destroyed itself."

Koscuisko had told her at least part of that before, but maybe he didn't remember. She wasn't exactly sure what was new and what repeated. "I hadn't tampered with the data-reader, though. It wouldn't have known I was suspicious unless it was carrying an ear, and a thinker as well."

Both relatively sophisticated organics. It was possible.

Koscuisko, however, shook his head. He had shifted himself to put his back to what was left of the bed, and in the yellow light his expression was very difficult to read. His voice sounded increasingly confident, though.

"You wanted to ask Shona something. The new data raised an issue in your mind. Therefore, it was placed there to send you to Shona. Therefore, once you and Shona stood together, it would explode. It wasn't meant to destroy the courier, necessarily. It only had to kill the two of you."

No, he was reaching. That didn't make sense. She knew his reputation for making sometimes unnervingly precise intuitive deductions, reaching conclusions that seemed prescient or occult; she didn't believe this was any such thing. So there was a reason that Koscuisko thought as he did.

"Help me out on this," she suggested. "I'm not getting you. Data could be planted to incriminate Shona, or to mislead."

She thought he might have nodded. "I'll be honest with you, Dame Ivers, I'm not quite sure of that myself. But why would someone have wished to incriminate Shona? It is Bench Specialists that he ferries—Specialist Delleroy, a great deal of the time. And if you were to ask me who my first guess was for a soul who could tamper with a data record, I might say 'any given Bench Specialist.'"

Padrake. Koscuisko had no way of knowing where her suspicions lay; she hadn't shared the crucial timing with him. "Placing him at Terek at the wrong time would just lead to suspicion, though. And what if the next person who saw the data had no access to Ise-I'let?"

"You are to return to Chilleau, Specialist Ivers. You will not be using this data record. It will be wiped and reconfigured. But if Shona was in a position to place Delleroy at Terek, he might have said something to you. You might find out independently. Then, if you found that the data was not there, you would surely suspect a flaw in the source record. As it was, you brought it to Shona direct, as I recall? I have a headache."

She was getting sleepy. It wasn't Koscuisko's fault. He sounded a little drowsy himself, and maybe sleep wasn't such a bad idea. If they were to live, the rescuers would wake them up; if they were to die, it was surely better to die in one's sleep, because if she stayed awake she'd be forced to confront how all the pieces trended toward a fit.

They didn't all mesh, no. She needed to sit down with Ise-I'let to see what he could tell her. They simply all fit around a missing piece in the puzzle she had been trying to solve for months now, the problem of who had killed Sindha Verlaine. There was still that hole in the center of the picture. But, as she put things together, the outline of that missing information looked more and more like Padrake Delleroy.

"He always was good with his hands," she said sleepily, and then woke up with an embarrassed start to the implications of her own choice of words. Koscuisko wouldn't know. But she did. There was a problem. There had to be a problem.

She could find a way that it could not have been Padrake. She would, even if he had spent as much time as he could get alone with her. She'd thought it was because of old times, maybe to protect her—had he only been waiting for a chance to see the data all along, in order to subvert it? "But the record was a Judicial document. Where would he have—"

She shut herself up as she realized the connection she had made in her own mind, while she had not been watching. Koscuisko didn't seem to have noticed a lack of obvious connection between the two issues, the sabotaged data-reader and the forged record. Koscuisko was still thinking only along the lines of the idea that the same people had been responsible for putting bombs in both of them. Wasn't he?

"One of my gentlemen on *Scylla* said to me that their new chief medical officer had powerful friends, at the very highest levels. He even said the words 'Bench Specialist.' This was the gossip network's explanation for the unexpected and unwelcome displacement of Doctor Aldrai in Doctor Lazarbee's favor. Both officers of course have custody of a Writ to Inquire, as do I—for now at least. If a man wanted a favor, he could provide a blanked record and authenticate evidence that was not there. One with a Writ could then add to the evidence, but if there had been no evidence, the record might be convinced that no addition had been made. Conceivably."

No, Koscuisko was thinking back to the circumstances in which that damned record had been forged in the first place. The record hadn't been forged. It was an honest record. The evidence had been fabricated, and the record tricked into accepting it as original and authenticated data. Someone had authenticated the data, or the data shell, someone with an active Writ—unlike Mergau Noycannir, who didn't have access to records to carry around. Someone like the chief medical officer currently on board of the Jurisdiction Fleet Ship *Scylla*.

"Padrake seemed not to know him," Jils insisted, thinking back. "Where did he transfer from, did your Security tell you that?"

Her voice was more accusing, challenging, than she had intended. Koscuisko didn't seem to notice. He'd taken medication too. "I think Code said he'd come from the *Galven*, if that helps."

It did not. It didn't help at all. JFS *Galven* had been at Ygau when the traffic records had been attacked, apparently unsuccessfully, but now she knew. The traffic records at Ygau had been altered to remove one single entry: Padrake Delleroy coming from Chilleau, met by Shona Ise-I'let piloting the courier.

Padrake wouldn't have needed anybody's help to engineer an apparently failed attack on traffic records. So the favor he'd owed Lazarbee hadn't been that, but the provision of an authenticated record to be forged, a record that Padrake had provided to Mergau Noycannir for her own purposes. Padrake had no reason to wish Koscuisko dead. Padrake didn't care about Koscuisko, one way or the other. Why should he?

No. Padrake had provided the record in exchange for something else. Security codes. Noycannir had sold Chilleau's security codes to Padrake for the instrument of her revenge against Andrej Koscuisko, but he hadn't needed any but a very specific set. Koscuisko had killed Noycannir; Padrake had assassinated First Secretary Sindha Verlaine.

Why?

The room shook. Koscuisko made a sound of startled pain, followed by a series of shallow gasping grunts. He was more hurt than he had seemed to be, possibly more hurt than he had realized. That was the way of it. And frequently it was the relatively minor injuries that really hurt.

"What's happening?" Koscuisko asked, his voice a little choked in his throat. The room hadn't shopped shaking. If it was what Jils thought it was, it was going to get worse instead of better.

"We're dropping vector." That had to be it. "And if we're lucky we'll make it in one piece. Hang on. This may not be fun."

There was nothing to hang on to, but Koscuisko didn't argue back. Maybe he had other things to think about. She knew she did. First Secretary Arik Tirom had said that Verlaine's proposed reforms would destroy the entire Bench if Chilleau became the seat of the new First Secretary. Padrake hadn't seemed to disagree. Padrake, and Nion, and who knew whom else, had all seemed to believe that Bench Specialists were the natural authorities under Jurisdiction, that Bench Specialists should be running things.

Jils closed her eyes and concentrated, and if she wept she knew it was just pain. And that was all. What Padrake meant to do in

Convocation, she couldn't imagine. She was simply going to have to go back, and find out.

Things got quiet.

They were either off the vector or they were never getting off vector, because the ship was losing atmosphere and the oxygen generators wouldn't last forever. They could try to drop vector again, she supposed, but if they'd missed at Brisinje, it could be another six or seven days before they reached a debouchment point. She didn't think they had that long. To keep her mind way from grief and horror, she concentrated on her original problem, because she needed all the focus she could get.

Padrake had killed Verlaine in order to prevent Chilleau Judiciary from being selected. That done, why would he stop at further shaping of the Bench's destiny? He believed that he was properly the man to shape the Bench's destiny, he and other Bench Specialists—but only right-thinking Bench Specialists, clearly enough.

He'd used favors from Doctor Lazarbee to get the codes he'd needed to get in and out of Chilleau, and if Koscuisko hadn't killed Noycannir, Padrake would almost certainly have had it done himself, and Jils couldn't believe that Lazarbee had much of a future.

Padrake would do what had to be done to keep Lazarbee quiet until the danger had passed, and then Lazarbee would meet with some unfortunate accident or another, or be accused of falsifying a record for personal gain, to the detriment of the rule of Law and the Judicial order.

It could be Karol. It could be. Koscuisko had said that the forged record had exploded when Karol had tried to find out its secrets, but who was to say that Karol hadn't destroyed it to prevent its secrets from ever being plumbed? Karol had disappeared—no one had heard from him, no one knew where he was. Karol. Karol could have done it.

No, he couldn't have. Karol had had no possible access to the data-reader. Karol could have killed Verlaine, but Karol could not have gotten past all of Chilleau Judiciary's Security to do it without leaving visual evidence or setting off the alarms. Karol's talents in security codes and bombs were respectable and solid, but well short of the genius class. That was Padrake Delleroy.

But Koscuisko had also said that Karol had come on board with a Malcontent. Koscuisko didn't trust Malcontents, but had absolute faith in them; he was Dolgorukij, and could be wrong. But the Combine was a conservative economic power, and would have no interest in the destabilization of the Judicial order and the disruption of trade. But wasn't that just what Arik Tirom had claimed to fear would happen if Chilleau Judiciary took the Selection?

The Sixth Judge at Sant-Dasidar had endorsed Chilleau's candidacy with the Combine's full approval, but the Malcontent didn't answer to the Combine. The Malcontent answered only to its founder and patron saint, who had been dead for some time.

It wasn't outside the realm of possibility. The Malcontent had the resources to have engineered it all. It would mean that the Malcontent had risked Andrej Koscuisko's life—but only risked it—and it had been a madwoman from Chilleau Judiciary who had threatened it, so couldn't that have been part of the Malcontent's plan?

Karol wouldn't have set a bomb that could destroy the courier. There were other crew here beside her and Ise-I'let. Karol killed when he had to, they all had, but Karol did his best to minimize the collateral damages. It was a personal quirk of his. Or he could have set the bomb to destroy the courier, knowing that she would believe by that token that it had not been him, if something went wrong and she survived.

He'd set that fire in the service house in Burkhayden the night he'd killed Captain Lowden, after all, to put a good face on the cover story. That had been something so uncharacteristic of Karol that she'd had problems with it ever since, and had half-convinced herself that he'd fled in shame and self-disgust.

No one had been killed in the fire. The gods looked after fools and drunkards, favored the oppressed; Karol could not have counted on that, though, not when he'd set the fire. Unlike him. Absolutely unlike him. Why had he done it?

He hadn't done it at all. That was why. Karol had brought Andrej Koscuisko in off of the streets that night and put him to bed at Center House, and gone back out. The story was that Karol had found Koscuisko wandering in the streets too drunk to speak, alone and unaccompanied. That was the story. Maybe it was true, at least that part of it.

Karol hadn't set any fires in Burkhayden that night. So Karol hadn't set any fires to cover up his murder of Lowden, so Karol hadn't murdered Lowden, whether or not it had been Lowden's name on the Warrant that Karol had been carrying—and suddenly Jils was irrationally convinced that it had not been.

Karol had been in a sour mood from the beginning, at Burkhayden, and particularly sour about Lowden—and Koscuisko. It wouldn't have perturbed Karol out of the ordinary to have an assassination order on Lowden; Jils wouldn't have minded if the task had been hers to do, not apart from the basic unpleasantness involved.

Karol had been annoyed about Koscuisko. Not *at* Koscuisko— *about* Koscuisko. The warrant had been out for Koscuisko. Koscuisko had killed his captain. Karol knew it. Did Koscuisko? Had Koscuisko been so drunk that night that he didn't remember?

Because—if he did—why hadn't Koscuisko called on the Malcontent to get him out of Jurisdiction altogether, knowing as he did the penalty for such a crime? Had that been why Koscuisko had sent the bond-involuntaries ahead—

The room shook again, but only gently this time. It was enough to sharpen Jils' focus. She'd let herself get distracted, fantasizing.

"Voices," Koscuisko said.

Jils closed her eyes, her heart full of gratitude. It was a warm feeling, but it hurt. They had been found. They were rescued. They were going to be safe. She could hear the voices, too. The impacts that they felt were the containment walls coming away, lifted out of the courier if they couldn't be re-stowed.

They'd cleared the vector. One of vector traffic control's emergency response ships had them in its maintenance atmosphere, and was coming through to see what might be left of them.

The voices were coming clearer, closer. From the direction of the wheelhouse, now, and Jils could hear Ise-I'let in the lead. "Through here. Look at this mess. We don't know—we lost our intership in the explosion. They'd be here, I think—"

"In here," Koscuisko called then coughed. Jils could almost hear him swearing at himself for raising his voice, but it did the trick. In an instant, the ruins of the little room were full of rescue workers, lights, Shona Ise-I'let, stumbling across the debris that lay knee-deep on the floor toward where Koscuisko sat with his back up against what was left of the bed.

"Alive," Ise-I'let gasped, almost sobbed. "Dame Ivers, sir, is she—did she—"

"Just here," Koscuisko assured the pilot, gesturing very carefully with his right hand. His right hand had swollen to twice its normal size, his wrist as thick as she imagined his knee might be; not a good thing, for a surgeon, but at least he had been in rest dress when it had happened. Loose cuffs. "Keeping me company. Get the litter. She's been injured."

As if he hadn't been. Koscuisko was a doctor, though, and apparently the rescue team responded to his authority as well. They carried the emergency patient transport over to where she was, and began to stabilize her body to be moved. It wasn't pleasant. She was still certain that she wasn't badly hurt, or not badly injured, but that didn't have a particular relation to the amount of pain it caused to move a muscle.

"Him next," she told the senior man. "Don't let him fool you. In worse shape than I am." But Koscuisko was talking to Ise-I'let, and not listening to her.

"I'm sorry," Ise-I'let was saying. "Sir. About the knife. She's gone. No trace of her."

"What's that?" Koscuisko asked. His words were a little indistinct because he had his face turned away from her, talking to the pilot. "Knife, what knife?"

Oh. Yes. She remembered. Koscuisko had thrown a knife, and brought the blast walls down to seal the ship. It had saved their lives. It had all happened very, very fast.

"We'll get Dame Ivers another one." Koscuisko was sounding increasingly groggy. They were rescued now; they were safe. He could let go. It was a common shock stress reaction—she'd done it many times herself. "Have it inscribed, perhaps."

The pilot shook his head. "No, sir, your knife. Her. Behind your back. I saw her. You threw the knife, your Excellency, don't you remember?"

Apparently not. Jils lay very still as the rescue team prepared to move her, listening to what was going on in order to distract her as much as possible from what was about to happen to her.

"She threw the knife," Koscuisko insisted. "I haven't thrown any knives. I'd know. I've been lying against it for however long it's been, Shona, I know the feel of an empty sheath and it is not. See for yourself. Go ahead, I have to—sit up—anyway—"

"Don't move," one of the rescue team said, suddenly and firmly. "Your Excellency. You know better than that, sir. Not a twitch. Unless you don't think we know what we're doing?"

It was a well-chosen challenge, one medical professional to another, and both accustomed to absolute and immediate obedience in their own areas. Koscuisko apparently surrendered.

"It's there," Koscuisko assured Ise-I'let. "It was Ivers who threw the knife. Trust me on this. You'll see." Koscuisko was doomed to embarrassment, because Koscuisko was wrong. He'd thrown the knife. She'd seen him. She remembered. She was wearing three knives, not five, though one was at her back.

She had much bigger problems to worry about, and if she was going to live she had to start in on it immediately. "Keep this quiet," she said to the closest rescuer, a woman who wore rank. "No report to Brisinje. Must reach Brisinje as soon as possible, secured mission. See to it. No word."

The officer nodded. "Very good, Bench Specialist," the officer said. "You'll be on your way as soon as we can bring up a new courier. Medical team on stand-by."

There was nothing more that she could do for now. What had she been thinking, about Koscuisko? That all of the stress unwound on one at once when the pressure was taken off the line? It overwhelmed her in a wave. She was just tired and hurt enough to let it.

THERE WAS ONE tile on the table between Rafenkel and Vogel, and Rafenkel stared at it morosely. "Isn't there any way around this?" she asked. "Any way at all?"

Four days and then some since Vogel had arrived, since their focus had shifted from "anything but confederation" to "is there any way around confederation?" Not long enough. Rafenkel had observed the tiling debates; she had participated in the tiling debates. She could see what the future held in store as well as the next man— or better from the point of view of her birth-culture, since she wasn't a man at all but a woman with inherently greater powers of foresight and reasoning.

"Setting aside the issue of crimes that may have been committed," Vogel said gently, "even if we placed a team of Bench Specialists at Chilleau to help—we're damned good but we're not perfect, at least I'm not—how long would it take for partisanship to come between us and the rule of Law? Inequities between Bench Specialists at Chilleau running the Bench administration and other Bench Specialists, tying Bench Specialists to administrative tasks rather than what the Bench chartered us to do—we're better off with confederated Judiciaries than with Bench Specialists trying to do a First Secretary's job."

He pushed the tile toward her. His role was to represent Chilleau—he was doing so a little oddly, arguing why they didn't dare—but the situation was even more odd than it had been. What Brisinje's First Secretary was going to make of it was anybody's guess.

She already had most of the other tiles. In terms of the short-term stability of the Bench, of crucial measures of quality of life for average citizens, confederation was better than chaos. And chaos was promised under any other circumstances that she could consider. First Secretary Verlaine could rise from the dead—but that would cause as many problems as it solved, surely.

"No, not quite yet," she said with an upraised hand, declining to accept the offered tile. She spoke for Sant-Dasidar, or at least she had come here in order to speak for Sant-Dasidar. Vogel had introduced Gonebeyond as an element into their joint deliberations. "I've got one last thing for you. The Combine. One of the single most aggressive economic forces under Jurisdiction, Vogel, and that's just because the Bench took their guns away."

In a manner of speaking. The Dolgorukij Combine had been its own thriving little empire when the Bench had made first contact, and had shown a brisk and bloodthirsty eagerness to absorb the Bench rather than the other way around. That was history. The Bench had demonstrated its overwhelmingly superior firepower and suggested that conquest was simply an inefficient form of trade, which the Bench's overlordship would enable the Combine to do better.

The Combine had cut its military forces back to its Home Defense Fleet, the Bench had created Sant-Dasidar Judiciary to contain the Combine and the miscellaneous planetary systems that had been next on the shopping list of the Dolgorukij dire-wolf, and they'd sorted well enough together over the years. Until now.

Vogel was waiting for her to continue. "If we confederate, there is no curb on Sant-Dasidar's ambitions. The Judge is an honorable woman, but the Combine will be moving into Gonebeyond space,

Vogel, you know it will. The last time the Dolgorukij landed to develop a market, it was on Sarvaw."

Vogel gestured with the thumbs of his folded hands, as though they were nodding their heads—his thumbtips—in approval. "True enough," Vogel said. "But that's not to say good didn't come of it. Sarvaw forensics are among the best in known Space. All of those mass graves to practice on, and not all of that very old, as collective memories go. Ugh. Never liked those people. Present company excepted, no offense meant, Rafe."

She had to smile. "None taken. But if we lose a single prevailing voice, we lose control of the Combine—at least the Combine in Gonebeyond. These are my people, Vogel. I'm telling you this as a native daughter. It is not a good idea to unleash the dogs. It's almost certainly a bad idea for Gonebeyond itself."

What he might have said in reply was interrupted before he could get it out. The talk-alert: Zeman, in the theater, at the master communications console. With seven people, they could run two sets of tile-debates, but that meant one person left over with nothing to do, and everybody wanted to know where everybody was at all times.

"Station alert. Incoming from the surface, Specialist Delleroy, alone, confirmed. Arrival in five eighths."

Delleroy was back. Not a moment too soon. They had to announce a solution, publicly and quickly. Any idle speculations about Delleroy's potential involvement in murder were just that: speculations. First things first.

They had to proceed carefully. If Delleroy was guilty of conspiracy to commit murder, it would be a tenth level command termination, and she'd seen the tapes. Koscuisko could hold a man for eight days at the tenth level. The Bench would demand no less.

She hadn't shared the discussion she'd had with Vogel and the others with anybody who hadn't been there, three days ago; because it was just speculation, and because she had no way of knowing who his accomplices might be, if any.

"We'll collect in the theater," Capercoy—who was observing—suggested. "The discussion is tabled on Gonebeyond versus Dolgorukij economic development. Ah, involuntary market development in Gonebeyond. Something like that."

Their procedure had gotten less formal over time as they'd learnt each other's strengths and weaknesses. It wasn't for any lack of sensitivity to the importance of the subject matter—quite the contrary.

"Be with you shortly," Balkney said over the all-station. "Going through the kitchen on the way there."

Good idea. "And Capercoy away here," Capercoy said.

Delleroy would have news from the outside. He could tell them what was going on, and they could see his reaction to the news that it was his position that seemed to have the most strength.

Maybe those reactions would tell them everything they needed to know about the suspicions that had arisen as to his role in the murder.

CHAPTER NINETEEN
WARRING STATES

"IS THAT THE lot?" Vogel asked Rafenkel as she carried the ninth tile box into the theater. "Right." He shut the door. There was no particular reason to shut the door, but it was habit common to them all—Bench Specialists closed doors. "I don't know where you're going to find room on that table, though."

It was seven shallow steps down from the upper level to the floor of the theater, seven wide and spacious, carpeted steps. They'd carried Ivers out of here after the incident with the chair perhaps as long as eight days ago, and had had no difficulty getting the litter up and out into the corridor.

The table in the middle of the theater, on the lowest level of the floor, was stacked with tile boxes already—some of them sealed and others not. The lab chairs that had been Ivers' downfall had been removed; there was no sense in taking any chances. The communications console depended from the far wall, opposite the double doors into the theater, and between it and the table stacked with boxes stood Padrake Delleroy.

He looked a little stressed to Rafenkel, and that was unusual. She didn't think she'd seen him so grimly determined ever before, and that was unusual too, because Jils Ivers was his friend and had been his lover, but Rafenkel didn't think that he'd been so visibly harried even after Ivers had been forced to kill Nion to save her life.

"I spoke to the First Secretary before I came," Delleroy was saying to Balkney. "I was in a hurry, but he is the First Secretary, and he expected to be heard. We're asked to announce a decision within the day. He'll be coming down."

Rafenkel saw Delleroy's glance over his shoulder at the console board behind him. One of the schematics there would tell them when someone was coming, so that they could meet the party at the airlock. It was all part of station monitoring.

"How long have we got?" Balkney asked. "You got in what, six hours ago?"

"Yesterday," Delleroy replied, with a grimace. "It's taken me this long to brief and clear Chambers. There's so much going on. We have our work cut out for us."

She could understand that, Rafenkel thought. They all needed to get out of here and back to work. They were going to, too; maybe not as Delleroy had planned it—if he had planned anything—but they had to get back to the rule of Law and the Judicial order, while there was any of either left.

"Then Tirom's due any minute now," Vogel said. "Let's get started. Who goes first?"

Delleroy closed his eyes and spun around three times, stopping himself with one hand slapped decisively down atop a tile box. "Here," Delleroy said. "Who's this one? Oh. Rafenkel."

Rafenkel shrugged. It really didn't matter. Sitting down at the table, she opened up the box. There were the tiles she had taken, and the ones that had not been played. Plucking one out of its slot in the box, she placed it, face down, into the scanner, and rested the middle finger of her right hand atop its surface while the scanner did its work, comparing her biometric profiles against the information encoded in the chip she'd used to seal it once it had been played.

"Rafenkel," the scanner announced. "Element four, the cost of infrastructure. Chilleau four. Confederacy three."

The scanner read to the communications console, and the communications console was talking to a secured receiver under Arik Tirom's personal seal. Capercoy had brought flat-form and stylus, Rafenkel noted, and was marking a grid. She had to smile. Yes. A crosscheck was always a good thing to have. She picked up the next tile.

"Rafenkel. Element two, the availability of goods and services for sale. Chilleau five. Cintaro two."

Not all of her tiles had been played but there were still a number of them to get through. At least they wouldn't have to go through Nion's; Nion was dead, her voice stilled, her tiles inaccessible, and she hadn't been getting very far anyway.

"Rafenkel. Element six, civic involvement and ownership. Chilleau four. Fontailloe three."

Cintaro, Fontailloe, Chilleau, confederacy. It went on and on and on. "Tanifer. Element sixteen, productivity in manufacturing. Fontailloe six. Cintaro one."

When it was Capercoy's turn, Vogel took over Capercoy's recordkeeping, making little sums of tidy figures, setting running totals in tiny script off to one side. Rafenkel watched over his shoulder for a little while: Cintaro dropping rapidly in relation to everybody else, Fontailloe's position as a losing proposition more and more obvious by the tile, but Chilleau and Confederacy—too close to call, and alternating back and forth on almost every tile.

"Capercoy. Element fifteen, equitable tax burdens. Cintaro four. Chilleau three."

When Capercoy was finished and Rinpen was done, Delleroy reached out for his own tile box and pulled it toward himself, sitting down at the table with an air of confronting an anxiety-provoking task. He pulled out a tile. "Delleroy. Element twelve, effective population policing and management. Confederacy five, Chilleau two."

She thought she remembered that one. On the board behind Delleroy's back, the telltales engaged to give notice: somebody was in the lift-car, coming down. She decided against disturbing anybody. It would only be an interruption. They were all tired. They needed to get this over and done with.

"Delleroy. Element eleven, the common weal. Confederacy six. Fontailloe one."

That sounded a little extreme. Was it her imagination—Rafenkel wondered—or did Tanifer frown? Tanifer would remember, though, surely. Tanifer had been there when the tile had been judged and awarded. Who had proctored that discussion? Had it been Nion?

Balkney had noticed the comm console's message. He caught Zeman's eye, and nodded toward the doors. Someone was going to have to leave to meet the lift-car and open the airlock, or risk a breach of atmosphere. Delleroy looked up sharply as Balkney and Zeman left the room and closed the door behind them, but he didn't seem to think about the First Secretary's impending arrival. He put another tile in the reader, and held it in its place with the tip of his middle finger.

"Nion," the scanner said. "Element two. Confederacy five, Fontailloe two."

Wait, Rafenkel thought.

Delleroy had picked up the next tile, putting it into the reader with a methodical sort of precision. "Delleroy. Element seven—"

No, the scanner had said Nion. She'd heard it. Rafenkel reached for the tile that Delleroy had just put down. He brushed her hand away with an impatient gesture that sent tiles flying. There were tiles all over the floor. Which one had just said Nion?

"Delleroy. Element seven. Chilleau seven, Confederacy zero." That wasn't right either. Delleroy didn't seem to have noticed. He went right on as though he hadn't heard, reaching for the next tile in his box—his tile-set, his, uniquely his, Padrake Delleroy's, the tiles he had won in debate with his peers. He had not argued for Chilleau but against it. She must have misheard. But she remembered no such polarized result from Delleroy's debate with Ivers—that had been one of the things she'd noted from the start—almost all of the spreads were within one or two points of each other.

She was frowning, watching Delleroy. He seemed to take notice, like a man hearing a message on time-delay. "What's wrong with these tiles?" he asked, his voice light and aggrieved. "I never won that from Jils. Has someone been tampering with these?"

"Nion," the scanner said. "Element—"

Delleroy sprang to his feet, backing away from the table toward comm console on the wall. "What kind of a trick is this?"

"Well, damn, Delleroy," Vogel said. "I was hoping you could tell us."

Silence. Delleroy stared, the fingers of his right hand twitching as though feeling for the butt of an absent weapon, coming to rest on the comm console behind his back instead. The contact seemed to calm him. "Explain yourself," he suggested. "You've gone in and what, altered the tile's secures? Changed the data? Is that what you've done? We're all waiting to hear, Vogel, tell us."

Vogel shook his head. "Sorry to disappoint," Vogel said. "I don't have the expertise. Feeling my way through the secures on these tile boxes, that's about my limit. All I did was trade a few tiles between your cache and Nion's. Wanted to see what would happen when you tried to log someone else's tile into the scanner."

DELLEROY HAD STRAIGHTENED up; his expression was contained, even confident. "I'm glad I don't have to be the one to tell Jils," he said. "That it was you. Trying to shape the future to your own liking, and what does it get you, after all?"

"It's a good effort." Vogel sounded almost admiring. "My cap's off to you, for that. But the evidence is in these tiles. Or are those booby-trapped, as well? That was a sweet job, on that record. Whoever did that was a genius, on my tally board."

"Recess," Rafenkel said. "Time out. Share the story, you two. Why did the tile think Delleroy was Nion?"

"Because Delleroy told it he was Nion," Vogel said. "Or at least that'd be my guess. A genius, I tell you. But you'll come to a bad end yet, Delleroy, I'm sorry to say."

Rafenkel stood where she was, behind Capercoy—who had resumed his tallying when his tiles had been read—and listening, and trying to make sense of this. Capercoy had set his flat-form to one side and was beginning to stand up, slowly and carefully, not making any moves sudden enough to attract the attention of either Delleroy or Vogel.

Vogel had his back to them, including Tanifer. He wouldn't see Tanifer exchange an uneasy glance with Rinpen and start back up to the upper level of the theater. Delleroy could see that, though. Delleroy apparently did.

"Empty talk will get you nowhere, Vogel. This is all a diversionary tactic, isn't it? Something to distract us all from the holes in your story? Tell you what I'll do."

It was a confident, in-control, fully in command of the situation tone of voice, the sort that went with a folding of arms across the chest and a casual leaning back against the wall. Delleroy wasn't folding his arms across his chest, though. And he wasn't leaning back against the comm console, either. Comm console. Rafenkel frowned.

"Come on," she said. "The two of you. I don't know what your issues are, but I'm sure they can be more efficiently addressed than this."

Delleroy should step away from the comm console. Delleroy wasn't moving. She didn't know exactly what she didn't like about him being there, but she knew she didn't like it.

"What will you do?" Vogel challenged, seeming to ignore Rafenkel's attempted intervention. Rinpen had reached the opposite end of the room, and was opening up the doors as unobtrusively as possible.

"I wouldn't do that if I were you," Delleroy said. "I may need you to bear witness. Or do you have this pre-arranged amongst you all? Don't open that door."

Reluctantly, Rinpen turned away from the door to put his back to the wall. "Just thinking, somebody should go after Balkney and Zeman," Rafenkel said. "If there's going to be a confrontation, we should all be in on it at once, wouldn't you say? Delleroy?"

The doors to the theater opened as Rinpen spoke. Balkney and Zeman back after their errand, but who was with them?

Brisinje's First Secretary, Arik Tirom; Bench Specialist Jils Ivers. Glancing quickly at Delleroy to see how he was taking this unexpected appearance, Rafenkel noted that the quality of his surprise seemed to be of a different order than just that Tirom was here before Delleroy had expected him to arrive. Vogel took advantage of the distraction to take half a step forward, closing in on Delleroy where he stood; Delleroy stopped Vogel with a word.

"Don't. It's not worth your life, Vogel. Jils, what are you doing here? I thought you were on your way to Chilleau."

Ivers was white in the face, limping badly as she came forward. There were other people behind Ivers and Tirom in the corridor, Rafenkel saw. Security.

"I don't think I need to get to Chilleau to resolve my problem." Ivers' voice was calm and controlled, but bitterly regretful. "On behalf of the Second Judge at Chilleau Judiciary, I accuse you, Padrake Delleroy, of the murder of Sindha Verlaine, and of attempting to subvert thereby the Judicial order and the rule of Law."

Jils hadn't wanted the First Secretary to accompany her, but she knew that she was operating on fuel reserves that were running dangerously low. She couldn't spare the time it would have taken to dissuade him; perhaps it would be for the best after all, she'd decided. She had things to say to Padrake that he wasn't going to like hearing. Maybe Tirom's presence would help keep the situation under control. She was under no illusion that the simple act of bringing a squad of Security was enough to do that, where Bench Specialists were involved.

When the doors to the lift car opened at the bottom of the access shaft, she took a position squarely in front of the others in the car, determined to gain and maintain control of the situation. They would know that she was coming. They would not know about the three squads of Security who had started down the air well hours ago. The cable car was a careful mover, but it was slow. According to the calculations she had reviewed, they would be arriving soon, but there was no way to tell how close they were without compromising the secrecy of their descent.

It was Balkney waiting for her there, and Zeman. Balkney was startled to see her, and perhaps a little startled at her appearance as well. She could walk in the scaffold boot, but not quickly. The brace they'd put on her shoulder was cumbersome and annoying, even if it didn't show underneath her uniform, but it was better than having her concentration interrupted by periodic bouts of intense pain every time she breathed too deeply or turned her head the wrong way.

"Where is everybody?" Jils asked, not moving out of the doorway of the car until she knew what she was walking into. "Where's Padrake?"

"Preliminary count, in the theater," Balkney replied, not asking the questions that were obvious to both of them: *what are you doing here, what's going on, what happened to you? Why do you want Delleroy?* "Left 'em all there. Zeman and I came out when we saw your signal."

Good. Everybody in one place—better chance of keeping this as clean as possible. It wasn't going to be clean. It was going to be ugly. It was going to be painful. She needed to get it done.

"Follow me," Jils said to the Security squad, because she didn't give orders to First Secretaries or to other Bench Specialists when she could safely rely on their curiosity to motivate them to do what she wanted. "We'll just be joining the rest in the theater. I have some tiles to tally myself."

She couldn't take the chance of saying anything more. The knowledge that she held within her was so painful as to be all but intolerable. She hadn't told Tirom what Delleroy had done. She didn't know how much of it had been Tirom's idea.

Balkney and Zeman followed without comment. Was Balkney remembering what she'd told him, days ago? That Verlaine's assassin was hers? Karol had told her Balkney hadn't done it. Now she knew who had, though she did not have evidence in hand. Evidence would come.

Koscuisko's injuries were not to be permanently disabling. The medical staff's initial evaluation on his right hand was guardedly positive. He was the best there was. He would get answers and obtain evidence.

She was forgetting something; she knew she was. The doors to the theater were closed. She could hear voices inside, angry voices raised against each other. The voice nearest the door sounded more cautious than angry. They wouldn't hear her if she signaled, so she simply opened up the door. It was awkward, but one of the Security helped her, once they understood what she was trying to do.

There they all were: Rinpen and Tanifer, by the door; Capercoy and Rafenkel on the middle tier, standing to one side of the aisle; Karol closest to Padrake; Padrake with his back to the comm console. Padrake stared at her, apparently stunned. She stared back, looking for something in his face that would let her believe that she had been mistaken.

No such luck.

Karol began to move on Padrake, but he looked at Karol out of the corner of his eye. "Not worth your life," Padrake said. "Jils. I thought that you were in transit to Chilleau."

She'd just bet he did. Padrake was at bay. Something had clearly been going on; she could gather no hint about what it might be, beyond the obvious fact that Padrake and Karol seemed to be in opposition.

"I realized I didn't need to go back to Chilleau to resolve my problem." *Because you set a bomb in my data-reader, Padrake. Because you tried to kill me, and that gave me time to think about things from a whole new vector.* "It's overdue. On behalf of the Second Judge at Chilleau Judiciary, Padrake, you are guilty of the murder of Sindha Verlaine, and of attempting to subvert thereby the Judicial order and the rule of Law."

She could see the pain in his eyes as she spoke, and felt his wince like a knife in her own stomach. It had to be said now, openly. She didn't know how many of the people here were co-conspirators. Padrake would tell her, though. Koscuisko would leave Padrake no choice.

"Jils." She couldn't quite interpret the choked sound in his voice. "That's in rather poor taste, isn't it? Arik. Nice to see you again."

"Murder," Jils said. She wasn't going to let him defuse this situation. She wasn't going to let him talk his way around it, through it, over it, underneath it, out of it. "To the great despite of the common weal. Single-handedly throwing all of known Space into turmoil and confusion and civil anarchy. You. Padrake Delleroy."

She took a step down the shallow flight to the table in the middle of the room, behind which Padrake stood. Padrake laughed, but there was a little fear in it. She might be the only person here who could detect that note of deeply submerged panic, but she knew Padrake better than any of the others. Oh, she knew Padrake. She knew his laugh and his smell and the weight and warmth of his body in her bed, her body knew the comfort and security that his embrace had given her. She knew Padrake. She heard fear.

"I think the doctors need to adjust your medication, Jils," Padrake said. "You aren't making sense. What possible reason could you have for making such a wild accusation?"

The others weren't moving. Why was that? Were they waiting to hear what she had to say before they cast their lots, deciding whom to believe?

"Preponderance of circumstantial evidence." She took another step but stopped, reaching for the back of a chair to steady herself. He hadn't been entirely off target with his remark about medication. She had to be careful to focus what energy, what strength she had left, on the crucial points. "The traffic records that were destroyed to draw attention away from the ones that were only slightly altered. Your relationship with the chief medical officer on Galven, and where Noycannir got the record."

It would make little sense to the others. They'd heard the rumors about a forged record, yes, but they couldn't have guessed at its significance—unless they were all much smarter than she was, and it was possible, of course. She doubted it.

Padrake knew exactly what she meant, but more than that, it was clear from the look on his face that he knew what she was saying. So the others would know that much. She had to keep on, she had to get it all out before she lost the threads.

"You let me believe you didn't know Lazarbee. You didn't know how much the pilot had told me. You weren't sure I'd notice that the traffic data had been tampered with. That was why you tried to blow up the whole ship."

"Jils!" It was a cry of honest anguish; she could hear it echo in her heart. "Jils, why would I have done such a thing as that? Even if. Even. If I had. Why would I have killed Sindha Verlaine?"

It wasn't the question she wanted to hear. She knew that, and was ashamed. The question she wanted to hear was "Jils, how could

I ever try to harm you?" She had let herself go. She had lost her professional detachment. It was the others who answered for her; had they known all along?

"Well, you did tell us that Verlaine was the worst threat to the stability of the Bench that the Jurisdiction had ever faced," Balkney said, very gently.

"And that Bench Specialists should be running the Bench," Rafenkel added. "We had a talk about it. Remember? Verlaine would have put an end to that idea."

"So what better solution all around than to remove an enemy of the Judicial order, and take his place at Chilleau while the administration struggled to recover?" Karol's question was rhetorical. Unfortunately. They made it all too clear. Altruism and self-interest, duty and honor muddled up with the lust for power and privilege—too much sense by half.

"This is beginning to sound suspiciously like a set-up job." Padrake spoke with aggressive bravado, but he was afraid. What was he afraid of? The truth? "What's your take on all of this, Arik? Don't tell me they've gotten to you, too."

The First Secretary. Jils had forgotten that he was there. Now he came forward. "It's perfectly true about Verlaine," he said. "You and I were in complete agreement about that, Padrake. You were out of contact for some days, around that time, and you told me exactly where you'd been. You don't usually seem to feel a need to do that. A man could wonder."

But we will find out, Jils thought, and knew what Padrake was afraid of. He was right to be afraid of Andrej Koscuisko. Any sane person would be—not of the man himself, not necessarily, but of what he could do. What he would do. What he was going to do. As it stood, even in light of the gravity of the accusation, the evidence against Padrake was enough to go to the extreme levels of the Protocols—and the Bench would want to know how deep and wide the contagion had spread. Padrake. The Bench would do that to Padrake. Padrake, whom she loved.

"You've all taken leave of your rational faculties," Padrake said firmly. "Or worse. I can't believe that you'd be in on a plot against me, Jils, not even to save yourself."

Padrake whom she loved, and who'd tried to murder her. That Padrake. Putting her hand to the holster at her side, she drew her sidearm; she'd come prepared. She was in no condition to fight. "Nobody's plotting against you," she said, as calmly as she could. "It's you. Isn't it? Don't bother denying it. We'll have the truth of the matter soon enough."

Koscuisko, here. Would his sense of duty allow him to go home, with this unresolved? Could Koscuisko sacrifice the greater good of the Judicial order to his personal morality—put his wife and child above the chance that a lesser torturer would lose Padrake to death before the crucial question of co-conspirators had been answered in full?

The inquiry would just spread and keep on spreading, and the Bench needed all of its resources to concentrate on restoring order and the regulation of trade. Verlaine was dead. No number of collateral torture-killings could reverse that and set the Judiciary back to where it had been before.

If there were other Bench Specialists involved, the Bench needed them to do their jobs. The Bench couldn't afford to throw any of them away, whether they'd been traitors to their sworn duty or not. It didn't matter what anybody had done, not now. It was what they did next that would make the difference.

"And if you think I'm going quietly to be drugged into self-incrimination, you're insane, all of you." Padrake straightened up proudly, one hand at his side, but one hand touching lightly against the comm console behind him.

She knew exactly what Padrake was saying, if nobody else did. *Do I have a bomb? Maybe not, Jils. Can you take that chance, with Arik Tirom in the room? No. You have to kill me. And we both know it.*

He wouldn't. He couldn't possibly. There was no bomb. It was a bluff. He meant to escape the retributive punishment that he had earned. But there could be a bomb, and she—and Karol—were perhaps the only people here who knew that.

"Stand away," she warned, raising her sidearm. If there was a bomb, she needed to make sure that he didn't touch a toggle with one last desperate gesture as he died. She could hear a commotion in the corridor behind her. The squads of Security that she'd sent down the air well had arrived. One bomb; thirty-eight souls on station. "Hands to the front, Padrake, or I'll shoot."

He'd tried to kill her. He'd been willing to sacrifice the courier and its crew to protect himself. There was no guarantee that he might not decide to take them all with him, since he was going to die—more or less quickly. The game was up. He was discovered. There was no hope left for Padrake now.

"You couldn't hurt me, Jils," he said, but it was a challenge, calculated to make her angry. Angry enough to shoot him. His hand went out across the comm console behind him, his fingers searching for something on the board. "We love each other. I love you, Jils. Always loved. You couldn't—"

Hurt me.

She could hear Andrej Koscuisko's voice, explaining it to her. *Killed him because I loved him. Because. Not despite.*

She could see Karol moving again, so smoothly that it was almost invisible, and knew that within moments he would be on Padrake, to subdue him. The room was full of Bench Specialists. Once let Karol close with Padrake, and they would all mob Padrake at once. Padrake would be taken alive. She couldn't let that happen.

She fired the round to strike him full in the chest at his left side, so that the reflex of his body would pull him away from the comm console. Her aim was off. She hit more of his chest than she'd needed to, stenciling patterns in blood and flesh against the back wall.

It was messy, but it worked. His body spun away from the console under the force of the impact, the walls and floor and furnishings drenched in an instant with the blood from the cavity in his chest. The uncoordinated flailing of his limbs was terrible to see. She couldn't bear to look, even though his face was turned toward the wall. How many fractions of consciousness were left to a man, when blood ceased to carry oxygen to the brain?

Padrake's blood was all around him, the walls, his clothing, the floor. His body wriggled like a crushed insect's, and it was unspeakably grotesque to see him—beautiful Padrake—made over by her hand into an object of horror.

At least it did not go on for very long.

She didn't need to go down. She knew that he was dead. They didn't have the resuscitation equipment here that they would need to even try to salvage him, and when traumatic injury led to such a sudden massive loss of blood, there was very little chance of any medical intervention succeeding even in the best of circumstances.

Always loved you, Jils. And the Hell of it was that he had very possibly been telling the truth about that, even though he had tried to kill her with a bomb—and who knew what his role had been in the earlier incidents, the one with Nion, the one with the chair?

She sat down in the nearest chair very suddenly. Crossing her arms on the back of the seat in front of her—her sidearm still grasped in her right hand—Jils began to weep.

Always loved you. Killed him because she loved him. It didn't change the fact that she had killed him, or that he was dead. She wished that somebody would do the same for her, right here, right now; but nobody had ever loved her as he had. And nobody ever would.

"Down the air well?" She heard Balkney's voice as though in another room, and knew that he was speaking to the Security. "Well done. You need to get out as quickly as possible. We don't know what Delleroy may or may not have done."

Karol was beside her with a hand around her upper arm, carefully. "Let's go, Jils We're evacuating. Now. First Secretary, tell her."

"Get up and get back to the lift car, Ivers," Tirom said. "I'm not leaving without you. Come on. We need to leave. We need to leave immediately."

And abandon Padrake's body on the floor, there at the far end of the room? Let it lie there to rot without a word said over him, without a wish for a speedy passage, like vermin? Even vermin were cleaned up, cleared away, burned—how could she leave him here like an embarrassing lump of body-waste best left ignored and unacknowledged and forgotten—

She had to get the First Secretary out of here. She had to get them all out of here. Padrake knew bombs. There was no telling. He might well have been down here well before any of the others had arrived, under pretext of making necessary preparations.

Leaning heavily on Karol, she stood. She could hardly sense where her own arms and legs had gone. She moved clumsily, but she could move. Out of the theater with Padrake left behind like a soiled tissue. To the lift car with Tirom and Karol, Rafenkel and Security, to make the ascent to the surface before some fail-safe device of Padrake's could explode and kill them all anyway.

She had done her duty. It could not touch the comfort she had taken in his body, but it was all she had.

"This is your Captain speaking. There has been an announcement from Brisinje with respect to the selection of a new First Judge."

It was end-of-shift on *Scylla*, and Doctor Benal Lazarbee was on his way to quarters with a little something extra in his duty-blouse. He'd heard the announcement. Irshah Parmin had gathered all of the senior people on board to the officer's mess to hear the news— Ship's Primes, Security warrants, staff officers and all, promiscuously together. The man had no sense of propriety, but Lazarbee didn't care. Irshah Parmin was immaterial as of now, him and all the rest of his crew.

The Bench has determined that the rule of Law and the public weal is best served in the immediate future by adopting a modified confederacy model for near the term.

The message was being broadcast on all-ship three times a shift for four shifts, just to make sure that everybody had a chance to hear the news and meditate on its implications. As a senior officer, his quarters would be blessedly quiet, however; and Lazarbee had plans for his peace and quiet, plans that involved the narcotics in his pocket and something that Delleroy had brought him on his last visit.

"Doctor Lazarbee!"

Someone was running after him through the corridor. Moderately annoyed, Lazarbee turned around. One of the clinicians, one of the Old Guard, one of those tiresome people who were all too prone to tell tales of how it had been when they'd had Koscuisko as their CMO. "What is it, Galins?"

Once order has been restored and trade relations regularized, the Bench will revisit this interim governmental model. All souls under Jurisdiction are urged to cooperate with the authorities to the maximum extent in their power in order to maintain the benefits of peace and justice for all.

Galins was in a state: flushed in the face and sweating, speaking quickly, and a little out of breath. She'd been running hard. "Need you to release the secures on scheduled narcotics, your Excellency. We've got a pain management issue, and Doctor Phinny not on shift for another four eighths."

What business was it of Galins' if he'd ended his duty shift a little early today? He was responsible for validating the narcotics inventory on a periodic basis. He'd signed off on the report and locked the stores. It wouldn't do at all for him to open the stores on his own codes again before the pilferage was discovered. "Galins, I've had a very long shift, and I'm tired. I'm returning to quarters. It'll have been four eighths by the time you get back to Infirmary. Aren't you on duty? Better hurry."

No, he needed Phinny to open the stores; that way the reconciliation was Phinny's problem. All of the stores had been accounted for when Lazarbee had signed off on them, after all, and there was his chop, to prove it. And a nice little present from himself to himself in his pocket to help while away the time, as soon as he could get to quarters.

Fleet will continue to work closely with Bench officers to ensure a smooth transition and protect the rights of citizens from disorder and anarchy. Your pay and benefits will not be affected by this decision, but will continue to accrue according to the contract you have made with the Bench.

Firmly ignoring the tiresome person behind him, Lazarbee betook himself down the corridor toward quarters. Galins wasn't going to follow him. "Go take yourself off to polish my boots, or something," he said to the orderly who waited at the door to his rooms. Security. Another chapter of the Andrej Koscuisko Admirers club. "I want my privacy, for once."

We remain attached to the Ninth Judiciary, and depart Emandis Station for Brisinje shortly. This is your Captain, thanking you in advance for your flexibility, your professionalism, and your continued support of the rule of Law and the Judicial order.

Finally, he was in his sanctuary, and it was quiet. Stripping off his uniform blouse, he poured himself a drink and toasted the irony: the confederacy model after all, and Delleroy had been dead set against it from the beginning. Not as though it mattered. Delleroy would continue to deliver. A Bench Specialist knew how handy a cooperative Writ could be, and made generous and tangible gestures of appreciation.

The chastral that Delleroy had brought him was illegal because its therapeutic applications were too unreliable for practical use, and silly people were always overdosing. Reasonable people understood how to manage chastral, though, and properly handled chastral provided a wonderfully satisfying experience. That was the other reason it was so expensive. Lazarbee had counted up the profit he would make on Delleroy's gift and decided that he truly deserved a little treat for himself by way of celebration.

The trick was to mix the stuff with a narcotic, and to have a reputable supplier. The narcotic served as a natural supplement that smoothed out chastral's rough edges, and a reputable supplier could be counted on not to adulterate her product with cheap synthetic imitations. Lazarbee himself used a reasonable amount of an inert starch, but he had a quality product, and it was up to the buyer beware, after all.

Lazarbee opened up the box that Delleroy had brought him and smiled happily. His flask was half-full of drink; he dropped a beautifully formed crystalline lump of chastral into the liquor, and poured the narcotic he'd taken from stores in on top. He was Ship's Inquisitor. Under any other Command he would be free to prescribe himself whatever he liked, but Irshah Parmin was an uncooperative fellow who knew how to make himself tiresome, and Lazarbee didn't like any of his subordinate staff enough to worry about the explanations they'd have to invent to cover the discrepancies. Who cared?

He let the chastral dissolve in solution while he peeled himself out of his boots and unfastened his waistband. Taking up the glass-ful of elixir, he lay down on his back on his bed and sighed deeply and happily, taking a drink. This was going to be so good. He could feel the sensation creeping into his fingertips almost immediately—a tingling in his earlobes and his nose—and hastened to finish the glass, so as to have the full dose before the drug distracted him.

It was wonderful. The prickling in his extremities had pro-gressed to the palms of his hands and the soles of his feet, and he couldn't help but shift uncomfortably as it took his genitals. All he had to do was wait. First there was the tingling—the alcohol helped to smooth that out—then there would be a warming, and a sweet glowing sensation, and a swelling wave of rapture would take mind and body alike in its embrace and carry him away into the realm of the gods.

Delleroy had gotten his hands on some really good stuff. The prickling was more intense than he could remember ever having experienced before, and it seemed to be getting worse. Much worse. It wasn't prickling. It was burning. The pins and needles had turned to shards of glass dipped in acid, and his skin was melting, drip-ping off of subcutaneous tissue, soaking into muscle, eating away his bones—

No. It wasn't happening. It was just a stronger-than-usual reaction. There was no fire. There was no acid. All he had to do was wait. It would be worth it. He knew it would be. All he had to do was last this out, and he could smell the fragrance of resin and wet leaves perfuming the air. He breathed deeply, trying to focus, shaking with the intensity of his pain. Resin. Wet leaves.

Poison.

Delleroy was going to have a lot of explaining to do, trying to foist an inferior grade of chastral off on him as though it was worth money—this stuff was filthy with insecticide. A lot. A lot of explaining. A lot—

But the pain would not go away, and Lazarbee could not move. Security. Security would be back, the officer's orderly, with his third-meal. Eventually. He'd quit his shift early. He'd sent Security away.

The drug was not adulterated. The drug was poisoned. It wasn't a drug at all. It was just poison. Delleroy wanted to kill him. Why?

It was working, too. The narcotic paralyzed him, but did not stop the agony that was traveling up each nerve fiber in his body to his spine and up the spinal column to his brain. He couldn't move. He couldn't speak. He could not even scream. Delleroy had killed him, but Delleroy was taking his own good time, and somehow that was the worst part about dying.

"No, Jils," Karol said, sounding like a man who was tired of the argument. "There really isn't any might-have-been there. Delleroy might have gotten away with fudging the tiles if you hadn't taken Nion out, but by the time he got back from Emandis Station, it was pretty clear that the unimaginable was in fact the best solution we had for now."

The launch fields of Brisinje lay in smoldering ruins. From where Jils Ivers stood with Karol on the wide white-scrubbed terrace of guest quarters, facing the river, she could see the towering clouds on the far horizon, the turquoise-colored mountains, the work crews in the river with divers sieving the bottom clear of ash. There were work crews all over the city, washing and decontaminating as they went.

Traffic was far from normal—no heavy freight would move through the Ninth Judge's capital for some time to come—but passenger traffic could get in and out, small ships, couriers. There was one out on the improv field, waiting for Karol to fly Andrej Koscuisko to Chilleau to file his documents before the Second Judge, and then go home. Not Karol, of course. Karol was for Chilleau, since Chilleau was short a Bench Specialist. Jils wasn't going back. Brisinje needed her. Padrake had done damage in this place; she meant to right the balance.

"If you'd have told me when I got here that there'd be no Selection, I would have laughed." The announcement had been made months ago, not as though she was ever going to get used to it. It was the end of the Bench as they knew it—the confederation model after all—but if it was the uttermost failure of everything that she'd believed in and worked for all her life, still the Bench had not fallen into chaos and anarchy. Not yet.

"There are a lot of things I'd never have predicted." Karol sounded amused, in a sad sort of a way. "All we can do is keep our eye on our duty and hope for the best."

There were going to be problems with Fleet. She just knew it. Already *Scylla* had tried to poach Koscuisko out of his hospital bed and back into his old berth as its chief medical officer, Doctor Lazarbee having suffered an unforeseen accident involving excess quantities of the wrong sort of recreational drugs.

That Padrake had had other accomplices—even among surviving Bench Specialists—was almost certain, but it didn't matter now. Nobody was going to have time or energy to corrupt the Confederation and subvert the rule of Law. Everybody had far too much work to do.

"Well, come and see me from time to time, Karol." Tirom had made her feel wanted here, as well as needed. Padrake's old office had been returned to a senior administrative official and one found for her in much more congenial quarters—hidden away in the under-corridors, far away from Tirom and the Judge alike.

Maybe they felt regretfully responsible about Padrake's role in the nightmare that Verlaine's murder had been making of her life. She didn't care what their reasons were. She liked it here. And she couldn't bring herself to like the thought of working with the Second Judge again, not after those months of arctic suspicion, disapproval, frustration.

"We'll see." Karol was turning his campaign hat around and around in his hands, as though committing the precise details of its sweatband to memory. "I'll be getting out to the launch field. Wouldn't do to keep Koscuisko waiting."

No, of course not. Jils had to smile. Koscuisko had been as restless as an imprisoned animal, a predator thirsty for blood— but in a good way. He'd be wearing a cyborg brace on his right hand for some time yet to make absolutely sure of some of the reknits, but the medical facility had run out of excuses why he had to stay. The interns were all in mourning. Having a surgeon of Koscuisko's caliber captive in one's own rooms had been the chance of a lifetime for Brisinje's teaching hospital, and they had exploited their access fully.

"Better get moving," Jils agreed. She had decided, lying in the ruins of the courier's bed-cabin, that Karol hadn't killed Captain Lowden—Koscuisko had. She hadn't said anything to either man about it. It somehow did not seem all that important. "But if you ever disappear into Gonebeyond again, I'm coming after you. I promise."

He didn't seem to feel effectively threatened, which was a shame. "Later, Jils," he said, and embraced her briefly, fraternally, almost shyly.

She watched him go across the terrace back through the building, heading out to take a ground-car to the improv field where his courier waited. It wasn't an Emandis courier, this time, but something that the Combine had sent for Koscuisko's use; Karol would be piloting alone.

A Combine courier could almost fly itself. They were the best that there was to be had in Jurisdiction space. Karol was a good pilot, too, she knew that from experience.

If anybody could see Koscuisko safely to where he needed to be, it was Karol Vogel. With that reassuring thought, Jils turned away from watching the divers in the river to get back to the administration of Brisinje Judiciary.

EPILOGUE

KAROL VOGEL HAD things to do and people to see, but first he had to get Koscuisko back to Koscuisko's home ground. Koscuisko would have his hands full on Azanry, Karol was sure of it. Sant-Dasidar was doing as well as any of her sister Judiciaries and better than most; it was an artifact, perhaps, of the fact that the Dolgorukij had always understood hierarchy.

Halfway across the Anglerhaz vector to Chilleau from Brisinje, Karol eased back on his record checks and slumped against his clamshell, tired but satisfied. He'd land Koscuisko at Chilleau. The Second Judge would want him to get right on things. He'd already heard a few words on the subject but, under the circumstances, he thought he could probably insist on ferrying Koscuisko on to Azanry himself. Good public relations. Respect for high-ranking civilian persons of importance.

Hearing movement from the direction of the doorway behind him, Karol looked back over his shoulder at Koscuisko standing on the threshold with a lefrol in one hand and a somber expression on his face. People didn't usually smoke lefrols in wheelhouses; smoke carried particulate matter, which could get into the mechanisms. So could dust and dander, though, and that didn't stop people from sitting in wheelhouses shedding both like it was going out of style.

"Come on in," Karol said. "The water's fine."

Bending his head, Koscuisko stepped forward to seat himself to Karol's right, in the second seat on the boards. It was a very nice courier, but it was Koscuisko's, after all. If he wanted to smoke in his own wheelhouse, it was between him and the wheelhouse. There was a dish for the ash, built in to the console. He inhaled a deep draught of the smoke, and set the lefrol under the vapor-capture hood before he let his breath back out again.

"I have heard many interesting rumors about where you have been, Bench Specialist," Koscuisko said, left hand to right wrist as though his fingers hurt. The cyborg bracing that crept around his right hand glinted dully in the low light of the wheelhouse, and made a clicking sound when it struck a hard surface. "Talk to me about Gonebeyond space."

Why should he? Because Koscuisko was trying to make conversation, that was why. And why not? Karol had covered up Koscuisko's murder of Captain Lowden in Burkhayden; he'd declined to execute a Warrant for Koscuisko's life. He might as well talk to the man. That didn't mean he had to make things easy. "What've you heard?"

"I've heard that people go seeking Gonebeyond, but I've never quite understood what one is supposed to find there."

Koscuisko had arranged for six bond-involuntary troops to escape their Bonds for Gonebeyond space. Maybe he was anxious about it. Karol looked at the little ticket on the console that held the calculations for his vector transit from Aznir space, and shrugged his shoulders.

"Well, I've heard that it's depressing. Nobody there but refugees. No nightlife to speak of. Why do you ask?"

"I may have sent a surgical kit into Gonebeyond with no qualified user. It was irresponsible of me." It wasn't the answer Karol had expected, but if he, Karol, wasn't going to admit having been in Gonebeyond, why would Koscuisko confess to what he'd done with those Security troops? "There cannot be much by way of infrastructure in such a place."

"There isn't." Maybe, if he made the first move, he'd find out what was on Koscuisko's mind. "Doesn't matter much. People in Gonebeyond are living on borrowed time anyway." Because they were escapees, and usually from a threat or sentence of some sort. "The environment keeps the population down. Could be done on a budget, though. A hospital wouldn't need any geriatric care, and very little by way of pediatrics."

Reaching for his lefrol, Koscuisko took a hit and set it back down. Karol reminded himself that he disapproved of mood-altering drugs in principle, and that was what a lefrol was, at its base—a delivery system for a psychoactive drug, one that could be physically addicting. Finally Koscuisko spoke. "I am in a position to do you a service, Vogel. A significant savings in time and effort."

An intriguing claim. What did it mean? "I'm listening," Karol said. Naturally occurring, though, lefrols—the leaf was a native

botanical of some sort. That made it a little different from taking
pure forms of a drug, perhaps.

"I will not disguise from you. It will be significantly more awkward for me to disappear once I have returned to Azanry; and yet it
must be done, in one way or another. I have business in Gonebeyond,
Vogel, and since I expect you'll be going back, it would be just as
convenient if I went with you, wouldn't it?"

Karol had to laugh. "Business, your Excellency? What business
does the Koscuisko familial corporation have in Gonebeyond? There
are no markets. There's practically no economy. It's hard enough to
make a bare living in Gonebeyond, let alone a profit, and I should
know, I've been there."

Koscuisko nodded. "Yes, but it is not as a member of my House
that I must go. I have something to do. Apologies for some wrongs
must be made in person, or they might as well not ever have been
made at all, and I have much to say to my Chief of Security."

Chief of Security. Karol thought he remembered
Koscuisko's Chief of Security. Seven people were being chased
by the *Ragnarok* when the ship hit the Dar-Nevan vector, and
only six of them were bond-involuntaries. "You're an idiot." And
Karol didn't mind saying so. "Send a nice fruit basket. You've
got a wife, and a boy-child."

"My wife will do very well without me, Vogel, and it is better
for my son if he never knows his father. But if I should drop out
of sight on some local excursion, there must be investigations, and
there will be blame. There is no help for it. Accidents are not allowed to befall the sons of princes."

Koscuisko was serious. Karol had a hard time believing it, but
there was no mistaking the somber tone of his voice. Koscuisko
was probably capable of lying to him, but Koscuisko had no reason
to do so. "And if you and I disappear together, I'm to blame? I
don't like it. Malcontents scare me."

Not so serious as not to smile at Karol's only modestly extrava-
gant claim, but even his smile was sober and serious. "To hint that a
Bench Specialist might be at fault would be disrespectful, Vogel.
And my cousin Stanoczk has worked with you before. He will know
better. It will be an unfortunate incident, but no more than that."

Too bad. Karol didn't think he would have minded the notoriety
of being Koscuisko's killer, so long as he hadn't had to actually kill

Koscuisko to gain it. "You can't possibly know what you're getting yourself into."

Still, Koscuisko was right about infrastructure, with especial reference to hospitals. His reputation as a torturer was so loud around him that Koscuisko's reputation as a battle surgeon tended to get lost in the noise, but it was there.

"I know that I sent people ahead, and that the ship to which I remain assigned followed. Trust me on this, Vogel. I mean to go into Gonebeyond, and find my ship and crew. Consider how much better my chances are of surviving for two days on end if I throw myself on your mercy for guidance and protection."

He wasn't the least bit interested. But Koscuisko was quite right about his chances of simply dropping off a vector in Gonebeyond and hoping to live for three shifts, even assuming that Koscuisko could even find his way into Gonebeyond without getting killed on the way.

The Malcontent might possibly oblige Koscuisko, if asked. So to whom did he want Koscuisko to be obliged? The Malcontent? Or Bench Specialist Karol Aphon Vogel, who had things going in Gonebeyond, an economy to nourish, a community to build?

Karol thought about it for a moment before straightening up, and keyed a communication transmit. "Chilleau" Karol said. "Karol Vogel here. Modified travel plans, will proceed to Azanry direct, please transmit." There were people who would protect Koscuisko because he was a doctor. Maybe it would work.

Koscuisko drew his lefrol out from underneath the vapor-capture hood and drank its pungent smoke deep into his lungs, the bracing on his hand casting strange low-relief shadows across his face.

"Bench Specialist," Chilleau said. "Proceeding to Azanry direct, confirmed. We'll notify the Combine vectors. Will there be anything else, sir?"

"Thanks, Chilleau. Vogel away, here." And that was that; it was done. Well, it wasn't done yet, but it was on its way to being done, and Koscuisko knew it, too, to look at him.

"Holy Mother," Koscuisko said, softly, prayerfully. "I will never see my family again."

And still he was clearly determined on his course. Karol heard regret in Koscuisko's voice, but no second thoughts. There were so many things he could say in response. The safest was the surest, however, so Karol shrugged his shoulders and stood up to stretch.

"You're going to be too busy to notice," Karol said, and went aft to the galley for something to drink.

BIOGRAPHY

Susan R. Matthews was born into a military family. Her mother moved her entire family all over the world as her father's assignments took them from coast to coast in the United States, to Germany, and to India; she spent half of the first fourteen years of her life with no access to radio or television in the vernacular. As a result the family, thrown on its own resources, read ravenously and passed books around from sib to sib as they came in. Her first exposure to science fiction came with her older brothers' subscriptions to science fiction book clubs, which brought "I, Robot," "The Voyage of the Space Beagle," and "The World of Null-A" into the house years before "Stranger in a Strange Land" or even "Fahrenheit 451."

In a resource-constrained environment the obvious response to a desire to read a particular story was to write it oneself, because there was no other way to get to read it. That's where she started, and where she still is, writing stories that she wants to read so that she'll get to read them when she's done. The fact that other people enjoy reading them to remains a slightly confusing wonderment, but she's very grateful that people do.

She's been an accountant, a business management analyst, a janitor, and the operations officer of a combat support hospital (and she's twice the woman she was then—no hope of fitting into her uniform, so it's just as well that she's gotten too old for the game). She studied clinical psychology as an undergraduate and took a yuppie degree (an MBA) that her employer subsidized. She reads mountaineering adventure literature, polar exploration stories, anthropological studies of Haitian voodoo, books about Chinese history and culture; lately she's been researching Rajputana and points north by north-east in the 1840's for her next project.

Susan has a spousal equivalent in Maggie Nowakowska, with whom she has recently celebrated a twenty-fifth anniversary (before then they were living in sin). She has two dogs, three brothers, two sisters, five nieces, and four nephews; lives in Seattle, and works for The Boeing Company. The dogs are Pomeranians. You can see their pictures and other interesting odds and ends (including Scenes from the Cutting Room Floor) on her web-site, maintained by Maggie, at www.sff.net\people\Susan.scribens; and email her at foxndrgn@gte.net. If you email her, though, she asks that you try to be sure that your subject line doesn't look like a spam because she hates it when that happens.

Susan's novels

> *An Exchange of Hostages* (Avon 1997)
> *Prisoner of Conscience* (Avon Eos 1998)
> *Hour of Judgment* (Eos 1999)
> *Avalanche Soldier* (Eos 1999)
> *Colony Fleet* (Eos 2000)
> *Angel of Destruction* (Roc 2001)
> *The Devil and Deep Space* (Roc 2002)
> *Warring States* (Meisha Merlin 2006)

Susan's shorter works include stories in anthologies "Women Writing Science Fiction as Men," "New Voices in Science Fiction," "Stars," "I, Alien," "ReVisions," and "Murder by Magic."